Matt Serafini

Sign Up for Matt Serafini's These Dark Woods Mailing List at mattserafini.com and receive an exclusive ebook

To Mom & Dad

Who always told me to keep writing

One

It was going to end tonight. It had to.

Amanda Church had never been through New England before, and if these current surroundings were an indication of what it offered, this was going to be a one-time stop.

There was nothing to see as the navy blue Chevy pick-up barrel-assed down narrow two-lane blacktop. The night sky was dark, stretched tight over roving farmland. Darkness was everywhere beyond the yellowish glow of the headlights, strengthening the illusion that she hadn't only crossed state lines, but also traveled back through time.

Did places like this really still exist?

She cracked the window as her eyelids threatened to close. A gust of cool mountain air wafted into the cab, chasing away the eager sleep. She cranked the Sirius radio and rocked along to REM's *Pretty Persuasion*.

It was all she could do to keep driving.

The road, called Mountain Road, ran parallel to Route 90 East. Unlike that highway, which somehow ran as far as Seattle, this was as rural as rural got. Signs of life were sporadic at best, often coming in the guise of dilapidated farm land or homes that resembled a shantytown in 1930s Chicago. Occasionally, a fellow traveler would zip past, leaving only trailing taillights to disappear into the black void.

They weren't big on streetlights out here. Hadn't been one since the edge of New York. Amanda was surprised by how isolated she'd been made to feel by the Massachusetts countryside. Never mind that she'd grown accustomed to living in Los Angeles, where the lack of a traffic jam jarred her, but the absence of sufficient light in these parts made a motorist's life a living hell. It meant having to kill your speed at every twist in the bend.

Mountain Road marked the start of a mountain range and, as such, the blacktop rose and fell like a roller coaster. It was bad enough that her career brought constant skirts with death without having to worry about a wrong turn. Out here that would be enough to guarantee a twisted metal demise.

An anticlimactic end to this life, she thought while reducing her speed around the bend.

There was a lot to do tonight. She needed to do it and there was no time to die in a car wreck. With fresh air circulating in the cab and her attention pulled back from the brink of dreamland, she flexed her eyes and tapped her palms against the steering wheel.

Still five hours of darkness left in this early Tuesday morning. Enough time to get the job done if she could find this fucking place.

"The Thunderbird, is it?" That's what her contact had said. *"You'll know that place when you see it."*

Instructions were to follow Mountain Road right to its front door. Amanda assumed that to mean it would be the first motel she'd see, as there weren't many options out here. If Massachusetts had a pulse, and people claimed it did, this road was like checking your ankle to find it.

Amanda shuddered at the thought of her work. She hated thinking about it beforehand. It aroused a bevy of mixed emotions she hadn't figured out how to deal with. Anxiety, anger, fear, excitement and, strangest of all, pride. She held a certain satisfaction for what she did, even when it fucked with her head.

At last, the road wound back into a straightaway. Amanda heaved down on the pedal, determined to make up for lost time. Now she was jamming to The Smiths' *William, it was Really Nothing.* Morrissey could do no wrong and she sang along as the job's unpleasantness dangled overhead like sinister mistletoe.

The song fell into a brief instrumental bit and Amanda took the opportunity to steal a few deep breaths to steady her nerves.

Relax. How many times have you done this?

But her rationale failed to quell the apprehension chipping away at her cool demeanor. She'd done this before, many times, but that didn't make it easier. Only psychopaths truly got used to this, and she didn't think she was destined for a straight jacket.

Yet.

Sometimes she wished she was manning a teller window, or answering phones for an allegedly important CEO. What did 8 to 5 life even feel like? Structure and routine were things she craved. Normalcy had been a tricky thing to obtain ever since childhood and, as an adult, Amanda dismissed it as myth.

A bright, intrusive light wrestled her attention back to the lonely road. Ahead, a red neon glow beamed above the tree line, looking ridiculously out of place against the quiet wilderness.

Her contact's words rang true in her head: *"You'll know it when you see it."*

Amanda pulled into a small dirt patch off Mountain Road, killed the engine and waited. Her neck lolled from side to side and her heart thumped against her ribs. The hypochondriac in her worried what this was doing to her insides.

She saw a motel through the trees or, at least, the loud sign used to advertise one. It announced the Thunderbird and promised luxury accommodations in every room. Last summer's trip to Dubai had been lavish, this looked like a dive.

In that moment, she realized how much she missed the 24-hour masseuse service. After this job, a Caribbean sabbatical sounded like the only option. Days spent lounging on a white, sandy beach, surfing emerald green waters and sipping salty margaritas while enjoying an endless string of back massages. Those were her incentives to survive this.

Amanda sat in quiet observation while the next hour ticked past. The few indicators of life she'd seen on her way here had ceased. There hadn't been one vehicle in either direction since stopping.

A good sign.

It was impossible to gauge foreign surroundings with true accuracy on this kind of notice, but when a job needed doing, a power hour of observation helped. No, she wouldn't know if the old man down the street got up in the middle of the night to walk his mastiff—the kind of situational awareness she preferred to have—though she felt okay with what she had seen to make a decision.

Despite the lack of action out here, Western Massachusetts shared many traits with other sparsely populated parts of the country. Commuter traffic typically wound itself down by 7 PM and straggler traffic all but ceased by 9 or 10 during the workweek. Since there's not much in the way of nightlife in these small towns and their outlying areas, the local bars saw the most activity. They were usually found closer to town center. If there were to be any travelers on a quiet stretch of road such as this, it was likely teenagers out for a bone ride or blowjob. But even the dope smokers petered out before now. In these early morning hours, there was barely an excuse for anyone to be here at all.

Except me, she thought.

She sat for another minute or so, her mind running over

potential strategies. After settling on the best course of action, she nodded. This was the worst part. Anticipation was killer. There was no way of knowing what the 'best course of action' could be. Things didn't happen as they did in the movies: the hero never slips into the enemy lair undetected and finds the self-destruct button, and in this line of work there was no girl to get.

Not that Amanda wanted one of those.

Her heart pumped harder and faster as her responsibility loomed.

There's no better time to do this.

She tugged at the seat beside her, pulling it down and reaching into the storage section beyond. Her fingers slid around the comfortable handle of an MP5 submachine gun. Fumbling further, she retrieved some ammunition magazines before propping the seat back to its familiar position. She loaded the weapon, listened for the satisfying *click*, and jammed the spare mags into the deep pocket of her coat.

Amanda switched off her phone and placed it in the opposite pocket. Then she climbed free of the cab and headed for the neon flash of the Thunderbird's sign.

She slinked through the shadows, moving in between the rows of trees closest to the road. She wondered if two extra magazines of ammo would be enough. It wasn't too late to cram another into her blue jeans, but it felt like overkill for what she hunted. A baggy polyester top hung loose from her shoulders, wrapped inside a zipped olive green bomber jacket that hid the holstered Glock—another insurance policy.

Normally, Amanda wouldn't be caught wearing such a drab get up. Life was too short to wander society looking like a fashion victim. She did her best to abide by that credo on a regular basis, but today wasn't about her fashion sense. You had to dress accordingly while in the field. The last thing she wanted was for locals to take notice of the fashionably chic young woman seen walking away from a murder.

She'd be the sore thumb in these parts wearing a designer suit. Best to dress as unremarkably as possible. Anyone would seem suspicious sulking around the woods this time of night, but if anyone did see her, they'd have a hard time recounting someone so nondescript.

"Um, she was blonde and..."

Trees loomed on either side of the darkened path. Branches curved and drooped downward, enveloping her as she approached the motel. Amanda wasn't claustrophobic, but this feeling of isolation was so extreme that it bothered her. She was entirely alone out here.

Fitting, she thought.

The motel appeared once she stepped free of the brush. Its vacated parking lot and buzzing neon sign only compounded her feelings of isolation.

She kept to the tree line where the shadows were thickest. There was bound to be an employee on duty somewhere and there was no reason to involve them. She tightened a suppressor to the MP5's barrel as she walked. When it was fully attached Amanda pulled open her coat and stuffed the gun beneath her jacket flap with her finger on the trigger.

Casually, she strolled into the Thunderbird parking lot proper. It wasn't hard to find the car. It was the only one there. Her eyes settled on the battered Chevy Corsica parked in the darkest corner, just beyond the neon sign's reach.

Hello again, she thought, boots crunching gravel as she approached.

Amanda took one last look around to make sure she hadn't missed anyone. The parking lot was empty.

The Thunderbird itself wasn't any busier. It was two stories and looked to offer a total of twelve rooms, six on bottom and six on top. Your standard roadside accommodation, a dilapidated hole you'd find on any dying stretch of road while passing through Anywhere USA.

The first floor was dark, save for a faint emission of yellow light bordering the drawn shade over a door marked OFFICE. The manager on duty was probably asleep and Amanda did not intend to wake him.

On the second floor, a faint beam of weaker light escaped through a thin slat beneath a door marked twelve. She might've missed it if not for the neon sign buzzing the parking lot into momentary blackness.

Has to be them.

The car was dirty. She didn't have to examine it to see that. She'd known the color as dark gray from having seen it on the road so many times over the past few weeks. Another flash of neon revealed dirty windows and a mud-caked body. It might've passed for an off-roading vehicle if it had been something other than a Corsica.

Its owner, something to be stressed loosely, considering it had been stolen off a murdered teenager all the way back in Valencia, didn't care about cosmetic appearances and had been squatting out of it for as long as she'd been in pursuit.

The desolation of the Thunderbird at last worked to ease her nerves. This was, she supposed, easier when you didn't have to blend in among a crowd. Amanda tightened her grip on the MP5, heightening her sense of security. She squinted through the dirty windows into the interior, wondering what the next neon flash would reveal.

Nothing of interest: empty soda bottles, fast food wrappers and porno magazines that helped the car match its exterior grime. The upholstery was littered with strewn clothes and the floor consisted of crinkled up papers caked with mud and dirt. A dire lifestyle choice made more surprising by the fact that one of the travelers was a woman. Why *anyone* opted to exist in squalor was beyond her, but of greater interest was why *this* woman allowed it.

She turned her attention back toward the motel and crossed the gravel lot, opting to avoid the wooden staircase directly beside room twelve. It was most probably a creaky old relic, and there was no sense in altering the lodgers to her approach. The element of surprise was one she couldn't afford to forgo.

So she walked to the opposite edge of the motel and climbed the steps there. Her boots creaked during her slow but steady ascent. At the top, she continued to room twelve while stepping on the balls of her boots.

Amanda ripped the MP5 from beneath her jacket and adopted the stance of a trained soldier: legs bent at the knees, back crouched and weapon steadied at what would be the chest of any approaching hostile. From behind the red, paint-flaked door labeled with a brass twelve, Amanda heard faint moans and cries, a mixture of ecstasy and anguish.

Here it comes.

She drew a long breath, wondering and worrying if this was her swan song. No telling what waited on the other side.

How long am I going to keep getting lucky?

Because that's all it was, luck. She had no illusions of it being anything more. Dexter liked to say she was born and bred for this shit, but he was being supportive. Nobody was truly cut out for this sort of life.

Least of all me.

Her life would've been over thirteen years ago had it not been for him, and she'd found it difficult to escape the feeling of borrowed time ever since.

Adrenaline and anxiety swirled through her. Without giving it another thought, she steadied the muzzle of the weapon just above the doorknob and squeezed off two, three-round bursts. The shots were little more than muffled whelps that found their target with a sound no louder than splintering wood. The wounded lock failed as Amanda kicked it, sending the door swinging open into the smoky interior.

She was inside before the inhabitants knew what was happening, her nose wracked by a bouquet of miserable odors. Through the haze, she took aim at the mass of bodies, two by her count, strewn naked across the bed.

Her nostrils flared at the noxious scent, a mixture of bleach, excrement, and what she vaguely recognized as spoiled milk. It was almost enough to knock her off kilter.

Almost.

The man and woman were entangled and just now pulling themselves out of the throes of passion. The woman turned first, startled by Amanda's intrusion. The man got to his knees, his bare body glistening with sweat in the nearby light of the desk lamp. He was faster than his lover, leaping for the intruder in one swift motion. Then he was on the floor and moving forward. Amanda didn't let it go any further than that. She squeezed off another three bursts, sending nine bullets into his upper chest. They tore into him with a bloody puff and he tumbled, knocking the desk lamp to the floor as he crashed atop it.

His blood splattered across the nude body of his lover, who roared with rage.

Amanda already had the gun pointed at her. She fired off two more bursts, blowing her brains across the mundane decor. The corpse fell to the natty Berber carpet. Amanda rolled it over with her boot and took aim, firing again. The heart stopped beating beneath three smoking and bloody holes.

All that was left was to confirm their deaths. A check of their vitals revealed they'd be in hell for breakfast.

A quick sweep of the room yielded nothing of interest. These degenerates weren't likely to have anything on them, but it bore checking. Protocol, according to Dex.

Her boots stepped into a moist spot directly in front of the bathroom. Water seeped into the rug from beneath the closed door.

Amanda tensed, reloaded, and pulled the sleeve of her shirt until its length overextended the olive bomber coat. It covered her hand and she pulled at the door handle. It came free and opened inward. She lowered the weapon and splashed onto flooded linoleum. Water cascaded over the side of the tub, raining a mixture of clear and crimson. Submerged in the bloody bath was a girl that might've been thirteen, but probably younger. Her glazed-over expression indicated she was only faintly aware of Amanda's presence. Her neck and shoulder was mutilated hamburger: broken and jagged bones poked up through the wound while blood erupted like a geyser. It ran down her naked chest, into darkened bath water. Her mouth hung open. A faint moan came from her throat that bordered on inaudible.

She was in hell.

It was much too late. Amanda aimed the MP5 at the girl's skull.

"I'm sorry," she said and turned away.

The kid tried to speak.

Amanda's trigger finger lightened.

The girl appeared more aware of Amanda now. Heavy eyes looked up. Her voice was weak but distinct.

"I'm going to be okay," she said with a forced smile. "This is what needs to happen before it can work."

"They killed you," Amanda said. "That's what you wanted?"

"I want what's next."

You'll get it, Amanda thought and felt a swell of sadness as she wished there was more to be done. No way of telling how long they'd been using this girl, but her wounds were fresh.

"Rest," Amanda said. Her finger snaked back around the

trigger. "Close your eyes."

"Will you stay with me? They said this was going to be the scariest part. The nightmares..."

"Of course."

"You seem so nice." Her voice trailed, taking the last traces of life with it. Breathing was almost nonexistent now, and her face was as frozen as a statue's.

Amanda watched carefully and noticed the tiniest spark of life moving underneath those eyelids. They had dulled to the point of extinction before roaring back with some sense of forgotten urgency.

"Will you call my mommy?" Her voice was suddenly animated. "She might be worried and I want to tell her she shouldn't be."

This bleeding mess of a girl provoked in her measures of pity and rage. What little life she'd lived was over, severed by creatures so cruel that, to them, torturing a child was just something to do.

Amanda's past hadn't been terribly different—only Dexter had managed to reach her in time. This aroused memories of her violent teenage years and she felt no desire to relive them.

"Don't worry," Amanda said, determined to end this. "I'll take care of you."

"I just need to sleep," the girl mumbled. "That's what they told me to do. Said that I'd wake up and this would all seem like a bad dream."

They lied to you.

"Do that," Amanda said. "Go to sleep."

Turnings were ugly and witnessing them never got any easier. Once this girl slipped under, her humanity wasn't coming back.

I can't let that happen.

Amanda crouched beside the tub and aligned her eyes

with her narrow and lifeless slits. "Where did you meet them?" She had to know this was truly the end of things. That after tonight, it was over.

The girl smiled, as if in possession of nostalgic memories of *them*. Blood dribbled down her chin as her mouth curled. "Asked me if I wanted someone to belong to. Told me I would be joining a cause. That I'd finally have a family I could love. Please, just call my mom and tell her I'm okay." Her head slid back against the acrylic tub. Her eyelids were curtains that drifted down, covering foggy eyes forever.

"*Where* were they taking you?" Amanda asked. "Where's this new family?"

No answer. The room was silent, save for the dribbling faucet. Amanda remained at the girl's side hoping she might regain consciousness. After a few minutes, once it was certain she would not, she stood and raised the gun. A three-round burst tore her skull apart. Her head slammed black and then disappeared beneath the rippling crimson water.

Another search of the room, this one more thorough. Amanda found herself powered by renewed curiosity. Motivated by unease over something the girl had said.

"I would be joining a cause."

She had never known them to recruit.

She fished through a blue duffel bag that reeked of perspiration, pulling a crinkled sheet of paper from the bottom. It was a map of Massachusetts marked up with green marker. A line was drawn along Route 90 from where New York became Massachusetts, branching off onto Mountain Road and running all the way into a town called Greifsfield.

"Great," she mumbled. No idea what was there but she was going to have to check.

Four nights away from bubble bath and endless wine, and now this.

Amanda was going to need those bottles to forget about

tonight. Even though it was for the best, she had to keep telling herself there was no other way to save the girl. That in the end, she had given mercy.

She folded the map, slipped it into her pocket and finished her sweep. When nothing of interest turned up, she tucked the MP5 beneath her coat and slipped back through the busted entrance.

Amanda's steps were soft as she went downstairs, taking the closest set this time. A quick glance over her shoulder said nobody was following. In fact, there was no sign anyone had heard anything. There wasn't any reason why anyone should've. Aside from kicking in the door there hadn't been any noise, and that shouldn't have sounded any different than somebody slamming one.

Her truck was a sight to behold. A welcome sign that upon view seemed to congratulate her on survival of another job. She climbed into the cab, flicked the MP5's safety catch on, and stuffed it back into the storage space. Then she switched on her cell phone and brought the engine to life, driving into the night and leaving the obnoxious neon glow of the Thunderbird behind.

You can relax for now.

The motel vanished from the rearview as the road twisted around endless woodland. She brought her speed down to 40 after passing a sign for the posted limit. No need to get pulled over for that.

Amanda couldn't take her mind off the slain young girl. That memory stung the same as any fresh injury, only they had drugs for every kind of physical pain. Nothing she could take would reach deep enough into her psyche to make her forget about the things she'd done, necessary or not. Those emotions brought tears.

That child, mutilated and suffering, had clung to the belief that she'd get better. Those animals had preyed upon her naïveté. It was their fault she'd been forced to kill an innocent girl.

Amanda couldn't help but feel she'd let them off easy. Was there a career out there more thankless than this?

There wasn't time to ponder that, because her search of the Thunderbird begged a more troubling question: Who in Greifsfield was expecting them?

She dug the map from her pocket, switched on the cab's interior lights and glanced at the marked path. An address was scribbled in pencil in the upper most corner.

Christ.

This was ballooning into something. What did they want with a freshly turned child? Her mind calculated endless possibilities.

"Oh shit," she said. "Dexter."

She pulled up his number on the cell. She was supposed to check in with him as soon as she'd crossed state lines—ninety minutes ago. Her thoughts had gotten lost in the wide-open air of the countryside, making her temporarily forget about procedure.

Dexter answered halfway through the first ring.

"Christ, girl. I was worried about you." He didn't bother masking his annoyance, not that she could blame him. These checkpoints were an important component in their line of work. Miss one and people tended to think you were dead. She immediately felt bad for making him worry.

"I know, I'm sorry," she said. "I'm okay and we're clear."

"I thought we were all clear yesterday?"

"Supposed to be. Ran into trouble in Albany. Had to follow them to Massachusetts. I'm in the Berkshires now."

"I'll put in for clean up. Where'd you find them?"

"The Thunderbird on Mountain Road. Real nice place. They had HBO."

"How many?"

"Three."

"I'm calling it in. You won't even read about it in the papers."

"Who reads the papers anymore?"

"Your phone then, or whatever the fuck."

"Good," Amanda said. "That's how I like it."

"Making your way back?"

"Not yet."

"Trust me, you won't like Massachusetts in the summer, it's too sticky."

"I'm sticking around a day or two."

"Finally find a guy worth your time? It's Massachusetts, kid. Probably a liberal."

"*I'm* a liberal," she said. At least she had been. Life was bad enough without letting modern politics bleed into it. "Heading to a town called Greifsfield. They seemed determined to go there and I'd like to know why."

"Probably figured it's a small backwater town with lots of tourists. Nobody notices it when the occasional one goes missing."

"There's more," she said. "I've got an address to check up on. I think something's up."

"Careful," he said. "Check in twice a day. First time you don't, I'm coming out there myself."

"You? This job requires tact."

"Fuck you. And be careful."

"As can be."

She tossed the phone into the empty seat beside her and yawned. Mountain Road didn't yield another sign of life, although she might have welcomed one. The creepy isolated feeling was coming back. For some reason, the barren landscapes unnerved her. Frustrating, considering she usually felt victorious after pulling off a successful job. Not tonight, though.

Amanda did her best to combat the dread, switching the radio over to 80s hits and piping along to *Flashdance, What a Feeling*.

The bad feeling gnawed at her no matter how many times

she tried dismissing it as intuition. It told her things were going to get a lot worse in the upcoming days.

    I'm too much of a pessimist, she thought.

    She passed a sign that said: Greifsfield, 40 miles.

    Amanda read it with a sigh.

    It wasn't ending tonight.

Two

The dinner date was a sinking ship taking on water fast.

Conversation around the table had come to a grinding halt for the fourth or fifth time, and Jack Markle was ready to throw in the towel.

Some situations couldn't be helped.

Jack scanned the restaurant out of boredom. People were crammed around small tables, laughing, drinking, and enjoying mutual conversation. A row of miniature booths lined the back wall, occupied by couples enjoying intimate chatter. This place, The Cove, had managed to squeeze an impressive amount of patrons into a relatively small space. It had to be guilty of a fire code violation or two.

But The Cove wasn't a building. Not technically. Set back a ways from the resort's swimming pool, it consisted of three phony rock walls, each about twelve feet high. Discrete neon lights decorated the tops of each one, occasionally changing from green, to blue, to red, to yellow. The bar counter was backed by a cascading waterfall running behind Plexiglas.

It was a little tacky, but the outdoor environment was both novel and refreshing. Enough to make Jack wish he'd been enjoying tonight.

The early June breeze blew from the west, ruffling several hairs on his scraggly head. His eyes were desperate as they dropped to his cell phone.

It wasn't even nine yet.

Damned if it didn't feel later. Everyone should've been beyond inhibitions by now, dreading the bartender's final call. But nope. They hadn't been at this an hour yet and the discomfort percolated.

The damn heat wasn't helping, either. His shirt was sticky against his chest while beads of sweat formed at his hairline.

What was the proper edict for bailing on a double date? His room wasn't far and it wouldn't be that hard to feign ill. But the bigger question was whether or not he tried to get Lucy away from this disaster, or left her to fend for herself?

While he pondered this, all four members of the dinner party made eyes at their entrees, each of them feigning hunger to excuse their lack of sociality.

Jack stole a quick sideways glance at Lucy. She stabbed a crouton in her Caesar salad, refusing to reciprocate the look. It was difficult to gauge whether she wanted out as much as him. Considering Allen was his friend and not hers, there wasn't any reason why she'd want to stick around.

No one would go willingly through this.

He lifted the fork to his mouth and pulled the juicy slice of steak off the prongs with his teeth. Then he looked across the table at Allen Taylor. His attention was still locked onto the pulled pork sandwich; he sawed the roll in two, careful not to get barbecue sauce on his purple button-down.

Jack winced at this puzzling display of manners. He'd never seen a college guy slice a sandwich in two before eating. It was pseudo-etiquette and Allen only subscribed to it when there were ladies present.

As a counterpoint, Jack felt an urge to regale the table with stories of Allen's most unmannered moments, though he thought better of it. If Allen's date was truly impressed with table manners, she'd be in for a rude awakening soon enough. This guy couldn't be bothered to wipe excess hot sauce and bleu cheese off his chin while chowing buffalo wings. He liked to eat and to hell with etiquette. Jack had seen the ravenous appetite first hand every day of the semester in the campus dining hall. It was the Allen Taylor he knew very well.

The guy sitting across from him now, with his blown out brown hair and gold chains, might have been a *Jersey Shore* reject, but Jack wasn't sure he recognized him as a friend.

He steadied his disapproving sneer and found Allen's date, Elisabeth, staring across the table at him while sipping her second glass of wine.

Jack's eyes skittered back to his plate, uncertain why she made him so nervous. Maybe it was the inappropriate grin stretched casually across her mouth. Why the smile? Couldn't she see this was a miserable evening? Was she enjoying the endless awkward pauses and failed attempts at sustained conversation?

Jack didn't know her though, and supposed it said more about him that he always assumed people were hiding sinister motivations. He'd have to thank his parents for making him this suspicious the next time he saw them.

Maybe it was her faultless appearance that set him on edge. Jack couldn't look at her for more than a few seconds. He didn't want her thinking he was leering, and definitely didn't want to boost Allen's ego any higher.

Damn my insecurities, he thought.

Elisabeth made him feel like this was high school all over again. He might as well be hurrying past the cheerleading squad on his way to choir practice.

She took occasional bites of her dinner, stopping every now and again to glimpse her surroundings or take another sip of wine. Never to speak. Unlike the rest of them, she showed no discomfort over the table's rising disconnect.

Either that or she just didn't care—a common trait in Allen's conquests. The more vapid, the better, he seemed to think. Jack might have been okay with that if Allen hadn't sworn up and down this one was different.

"You've got to meet her," he'd said. "She's an artist! You'll hit it off!"

It was possible that Allen had spent some time attempting to build enthusiasm for his friends in Elisabeth. A horrifying thought, Jack realized, wondering what approach he might've taken to get her excited.

"He really likes Meat Loaf!"

In all fairness, Elisabeth probably didn't want to be here any more than Jack did.

Fascinating then, that Allen could meet someone so quickly while on vacation. He'd always been a fast worker, much to Jack's chagrin. He'd never seen his best friend as particularly charming, but he'd outdone himself this time. Not only did he have a gorgeous trophy sitting disinterested by his side, but he appeared smitten.

As smitten as Allen Taylor had ever been, at least.

Not hard to see why, Jack thought as he snuck a few more glances at the raven-haired ice princess, eyes dipping toward her generous display of cleavage. She wore a black dress with a v-cut that ran to the bottom of her ribs. Her firm and round breasts were bare at the edges of the fabric, revealing enough to get his blood pumping. His gaze lingered long enough for Lucy to catch him, knocking a soft knee against his thigh.

Elisabeth Luna didn't fit Allen's prior type in terms of age or looks, but that was because she didn't look like she belonged anywhere outside a fantasy.

It was difficult to guess her age, but she looked like an artist's rendition of the perfect woman. The sort of creature whose face existed only in magazines and on billboards: narrow, piercing blue eyes offset with a tiny ring of green that circled the pupil. That vivid color created a compelling contrast with her porcelain white skin. Pink lips, full and thick, almost exaggerated, with corners arched ever so slightly upward, gifting her with a constant and seductive grin. She wore her black hair straight, allowing it to drape past her shoulders and accent her impeccable complexion.

It was Allen who finally broke the silence.

"The food here's great, Luce."

"I'll tell my dad." Lucy said, relieved to be talking. "He spent like six months screening the right chefs before giving it to some guy who beat Bobby Flay on *Iron Chef.*"

"It's awesome," Allen said. "The whole place is. I never would've thought twice about visiting the Berkshires until Jack told me your father opened up a bona fide resort. I feel like I'm on spring break at the Riviera Maya."

"He doesn't believe in doing anything unless he can be the best at it. A trait he tries imbuing in his kids...and why I'm currently majoring in liberal arts. The furthest I can get from his business acumen."

"I don't know, he did something right by getting this place up and running. Why rebel? What made him think to put this place all the way out here?"

Jack chewed his food and eyed Allen with a mixture of suspicion and resentment. First came the upper-class table manners. Now this. Total civility between his two most uncivil friends.

Even Lucy seemed surprised by Allen's cordiality, stammering before speaking. "That's my father," she said, her words flanked by pronounced hesitation. "Always enterprising. We used to vacation here when I was real little. That must've put the idea in his brain. Every other hotel up here capitalized on the history of the mountains and the area's rustic charm. My father realized people would fork down big bucks to stay in a resort without hesitation. He figured people might come here for sightseeing, but would jump at an alternative. Tourists would be happy to relegate tourism to a single afternoon of their weeklong getaway."

Jack struggled to suppress a laugh. He should be grateful for the shattered silence, but the artificiality of this conversation was too much. Lucy had uncharacteristically decided to be a good sport about the whole thing, which kind of dug at him more.

Allen couldn't stand Lucy. Their relationship was, at best, complex. Her fault, mostly. Never one to tolerate the arrogance of college pretty boys, Lucy was at odds with Allen from the moment Jack had introduced them. Their acquaintanceship came from a mutual admiration for Jack. In its best moments, their passive-aggressive rivalry had produced instances of genuine hilarity, often at Allen's expense.

The three of them had gone to a party off campus last December, where Lucy had taken the liberty of telling everyone she and Allen were a thing. She'd been smooth about it, too, managing to reveal this fiction to every girl there, selling each syllable of the lie with the utmost conviction.

A strategy that crushed Allen's game early in the night, making him look like the world's most lecherous man. Here he was, trying to hook up while his 'girlfriend' sat in the next room. Each of his smiles toward the opposite sex, every suggestion to take a walk, was met with mounting derision. Until, in a show of solidarity, one of his potential targets slapped his mouth and called him a *skeeze* before storming off.

Allen's stock had plummeted.

And he'd been mystified.

Lucy hadn't done it for any real reason. She *had* spent a bit more time with Allen than usual that semester, two classes back to back on Tuesdays and Thursdays, and found herself subjected to excessive amounts of unfiltered ego as a result. More than enough to corrode the mettle of even the most patient of souls, of which

Lucy was not.

Her spiteful exhibition didn't produce a long lasting victory and Allen's ego returned with the arrival of the spring semester. Lucy was annoyed that her lesson didn't stick.

So how was he supposed to take this situation's *faux*-affability seriously?

"Does this place have a monopoly on the tourism in the area now?" Allen's interest was nearly believable. "Look at the line of people waiting to get in here to eat. Must be devastating the competition."

Lucy shrugged and offered a modest nod.

"The locals can't be too thrilled with that," Allen said.

"They're not," Elisabeth said. She wasn't looking at anyone in particular.

"Excuse me?" Lucy said. "I don't recall seeing you at the town council when my father was fighting tooth and nail to get this place built."

"Pointless," Elisabeth said. "Deep pockets are louder than protest. Many realized it was futile to argue against big business."

Lucy leaned closer, tapping her fingernails against the table. "My father never paid anyone off if that's what you're insinuating. But The Big East put 300 jobs in town. Where do you get off making an accusation like that while you're sitting here, a guest in his resort?"

Jack's eyes were anchored to his meal. He swirled mashed potatoes around with his fork hoping the budding argument would resolve itself before things worsened.

The solidifying tension didn't faze Elisabeth. "I have not lived here for very long, but I do know what Greifsfield natives tell me. They speak of Rory Eastman's monopoly on the hotel business. How it threatens the competition, generations of bed and breakfasts built long ago to accent the beauty and nature of this area. This place doesn't pay homage to that, existing instead to dominate and outshine it."

Elisabeth was expressionless as she reached for her wine. Narrow blue eyes dared Lucy to argue her father's legitimacy.

So that's what Lucy did, her temper burning redder than her hair.

"I like it here." Allen had managed to slide in during a quick lull. "Lucy's father is putting Jack and I up for the summer... in one of their best cabanas, too."

Elisabeth was unimpressed. She stabbed at her steak, soaking it in its juices before taking a bite. She said nothing after swallowing. Just sat there looking at her date. Her face impossible to read, as it had been all night.

Jack felt Lucy's eyes burrowing into his side. The idea that she would spend the rest of tonight tearing Elisabeth apart as soon as they freed themselves from the shackles of this dinner all but guaranteed.

Since this was at least partially his fault, Jack decided he would have to nod his head, smile politely, and allow her to vent. Tonight was supposed to be fun, and he was an idiot for thinking that possible with this cast of characters.

Lucy's cheeks were flushed with fire and her jaw clenched, as if resisting the urge to speak. Elisabeth made no notice of inciting this, which incited Lucy more.

Instead, Elisabeth smiled while listening to Allen wax enthusiastic about the eighteen-hole golf course he was planning to master this summer. She even chuckled, a hollow and empty sound, when asked if she'd ever played.

"I cannot say I've had the pleasure."

"Soon," Allen said.

"If you say so." She pressed the wine glass to her mouth and drained it, licking away the thick red residue staining her lips.

Jack watched the way Allen looked at his date. Puppy dog eyes and a dopey grin. A worm farmer who had just won the lottery.

It was difficult to say whether or not Elisabeth shared the affection. She politely dismissed Allen's big push for a day on the green, saying she wouldn't rule it out in the same tone a parent tells their child *maybe* they can stop off for ice cream on the way home.

"It does not seem like it would be an easy game to learn," Elisabeth said in response to Allen's continued persistence. "You must want to see me humiliate myself."

"That'd be impossible," Allen said.

Jack felt Lucy's eyes doing loop-d-loops in her skull. Hard to believe women bought lines like that. It appeared Elisabeth was capable of civility and small talk, too, meaning that her vow of silence toward him and Lucy was a conscious decision. An insult.

"There are other things to do around here," Elisabeth said. "Things more interesting than whacking a ball with a club."

"A bold statement." Allen grinned.

"Trust me."

They sat in silence making eyes at one another.

Elisabeth did at least hold some regard for Allen. It should've been enough to suppress Jack's growing disdain for her, but it wasn't. Things got worse as he tried to ignore their flirtation. It grew into a quiet, exclusive mumble that alienated Jack and Lucy once and for all.

Allen and Elisabeth had succeeded in extracting themselves from the evening's unpleasantness without leaving the table.

This wouldn't have ticked him off so much had it not been Allen's idea to begin with. Jack agreed to it out of loyalty. His real interest tonight was in catching a Depeche Mode cover band, It's No Good, playing in downtown Pittsfield. Instead of a guys' night out, increasingly rare these days, Allen had pitched a couple's night out.

"It'll be great. Lucy and Elisabeth will get along well," he'd said.

It wasn't and they didn't.

Across the table, Allen mumbled in Elisabeth's ear, prompting laughter along with a healthy jiggle in her chest.

"Allen," Jack said, determined to interrupt the private party. "They're doing a Bronson double header to close out revival week. Tomorrow night at 9."

Allen kept speaking in Elisabeth's direction. After a long minute he turned to Jack and shrugged.

"That's cool," he said.

"I know it is. Interested in checking it out?"

"I don't know."

"What's not to know? How can you turn down *Death Wish II* and *10 to Midnight*?"

"I'll play it by ear."

"C'mon, it's one night."

Allen turned to Elisabeth and whispered an interrogative tone. Was he asking for permission? Elisabeth glanced in Jack's direction, avoiding eye contact. Had she actually looked him in the eye once tonight? He didn't think so.

"I don't think I've ever seen a Charles Bronson movie," Lucy said. "Maybe I'll join you. Although...some of the crappy movies you've made me watch over the years, you'd think I'd learn my lesson."

"Bronson's not the type of thing women generally enjoy, Luce."

Lucy wasn't having it. "The narrow-minded ones, sure." She made a point of locking onto Elisabeth as she said it. "I'm one of those open-minded gals, though, and hate that *guy movie* elitism anyway."

"It's just I don't think I've ever met a woman keen on Charles Buchinski. Back me up, Allen."

"Well they're not exactly good movies," Allen said. "An acquired taste even for film geeks really."

Jack glared. It wasn't Allen's sudden change in opinion that got to him, although they had bonded over Bronson's Cannon Group collaborations many times in the past, but the dismissal of their mutual hobby. Who was this asshole sitting across the way? *Death Wish II* was more than *an acquired taste for film geeks*. Allen couldn't suddenly believe that. How many times had they championed it? It was a historical document proving that they used to make action films with balls. Not like that watered-down, special effects-driven bullshit today.

Jack wanted to argue this rhetoric, opting for a disgusted sigh instead. Allen was eager to turn his attention back to Elisabeth, anyway.

"*I'll* go with you," Lucy said. "God knows that you've got to spend time with someone this summer."

If Allen heard the insult, he didn't bother acknowledging it.

Jack reached for his beer and took a frustrated swig, glaring at the infatuated couple with equal parts disbelief and disgust. Elisabeth had subtly swiveled her seat to one side, editing Jack and Lucy from view. Her long fingers stroked the lusterless pendant that dangled against her breastbone as she listened to her date intently.

The waitress came by to check in. Lucy whispered something about the bill being thrown on her tab before anyone could get a word in. Then she adjusted her own seat to face Jack.

"What's on *our* agenda? Dessert for two tonight?"

"And tomorrow, apparently."

"And the night after that," Lucy said.

"And the night after that."

Lucy laughed. "Pittsfield isn't far, and it only feels later than it actually is. If you've really got to see some fifty year old belt out *Just Can't Get Enough*, we could make it happen."

Jack smiled. Lucy never shared his appreciation for cult

and exploitation flicks, and she preferred that electronic dance crap to anything of musical substance, but he appreciated her offer. They weren't a couple, so there was no need to accommodate him. Tonight's proposal wasn't anything more than a pity invite, but a touching gesture all the same, especially considering Allen had more important things to do.

Could he blame Allen for his sudden immersion into the world of Elisabeth Luna? She was a striking creature without argument. But did that mean he had to spend every waking minute with her? Ten days straight by his tally, and with no sign of slowing down. He hadn't even been back to the room the last two nights.

With dinner service all but finished, Jack reached for his wallet. Without the bill, it was tough to know what to tip the waitress, but he decided that a twenty should cover it.

He spotted a familiar face moving through the crowd.

Molly Perkins.

She bobbed around overcrowded tables with uncertain gait, a familiar sight to anyone who went to Fitchburg State frat parties. Her head flopped around as she approached, the margarita in her hand sloshing up over the glass rim and spilling onto the floor. Staining her white tank top. She took a shaky stance at the table's edge, smiling down at Allen.

Popular guy, Jack thought.

"Well, welllllllll." Her eyes fluttered and rolled as she attempted to make contact. "Been trying to get a hold of you...you don't wanna talk?"

"Hi, Molly." Allen appeared humbled for the first time this evening.

She continued as if he'd said nothing. "Just 'cause you dumped me doesn't mean we can't talk...*spechhhially* since we're both staying here."

"Talking isn't a great idea, Molly."

Something changed in the girl's eyes. Her glazed greens

came back into focus. "I can't fucking believe you!"

Surrounding tables looked on, which seemed to outrage Allen more than anything. He leaned in and told Molly to keep her goddamn voice down.

She didn't.

She wouldn't.

His castigation only made her more rebellious. Her attention found Elisabeth, crawling over her with scrutiny. "Allen and I used to go out. Used to *fuck*." She managed to pop that word so it was louder than even the music.

"Alrighty." Lucy bolted up out of her seat. "I'm gonna walk you back to your room."

Molly ignored her, fixated on Elisabeth who watched the drunken girl with a cocked and curious eyebrow.

"Did he tell you what he likes? Do *you* lick his ass while jerking him off?"

"How very charming," Elisabeth said.

Molly wasn't done prodding, though. "He can almost never finish. And when he does, he has to concentrate *really* hard." Her glassy stare wandered back to Allen, gagging twice as if she were going to vomit, but managed to choke it down. "She deserves to know what a disappointment you're going to be, don't you think?"

More and more people were taking note of this scene. Nearby tables looked on, fascinated by the train wreck. Some sympathetic eyes fell on Allen while Molly garnered a volley of disdainful glares.

"Okayyyyyyyyy, really." Lucy slid an arm around Molly. "You had a few too many margaritas tonight, hun, and who can blame you? They're delicious. But why don't you let me take you home, okay? We can talk there."

A tiny part of Jack had been enjoying the character assassination. He would've felt bad for his friend under normal circumstances, but having just been subjected to the most uncomfortable dinner this side of *The Texas Chain Saw Massacre*, this was par for the course.

Molly stumbled back, latching onto Lucy to prevent a fall. Then she threw her palms down on the table and leaned in to Elisabeth so close that their noses touched.

"What are you trying to do to me?" Her voice was drowned in despair.

Elisabeth didn't bat an eyelash.

"He was mine, you know. I would've won him back if not for you. We were going to get married."

"*Was*," Elisabeth said.

Molly's head dropped between slouching shoulders, defeated. She shook her head as if answering a question that hadn't been asked.

Allen, taking a page from Lucy's playbook, tried to get his date's attention, but Elisabeth wasn't interested. Molly continued to have her curiosity. The tiniest smile was visible at the corners of her mouth, completely unmoved by the girl's desperate plea.

A woman who likes to win, Jack thought.

"You should have a bit more respect for yourself, girl." Elisabeth said. "Men do not find this behavior alluring. You're going to invoke sympathy if anything at all."

Molly's volume cranked up to eleven. "Like you know me? You don't know *shit*! You think being older makes you sexier? Only makes me wonder why you're not married. Oh, the issues you must be hiding. And how old are you, anyway? Huh? Thirty-five? How long 'til that shit starts to sag?" Flakes of spittle sprayed as she spoke. "Remember that day I saw the two of you downtown..."

"This is the first time I have laid eyes on you."

"Allen saw me and tried pretending he didn't. But I sure as shit saw you. I even asked some of the people in the store about you. Come to find out that you've got yourself a little reputation. You might as well tattoo a big ol' red A to those tits on account of the number of marriages you've ruined, you fucking whore."

Lucy scooped a quick arm around Molly and yanked her away. "Well you've definitely said your piece, girl. Mine too." Her eyes flashed to Elisabeth as she spoke. "Now let Allen sit here and think about what a jerk he is, okay? Let's head back."

Molly wobbled back and forth in Lucy's arms, reluctant at first, but eventually allowing herself to be led off. Lucy glanced back over her shoulder, mouthing "call me" to Jack before disappearing into the sea of patrons.

"So that was my ex," Allen said. "You might be asking yourself how I could afford to let go of such a treasure..."

"She's pretty," Elisabeth said. "The most I can say."

"That's kind enough, believe me. I'm sure you can see why she's an ex."

"Everyone's got them," Elisabeth's tone was humorless as she continued rubbing her necklace.

"Had enough excitement for one night?" Allen asked.

"I haven't had any excitement yet," she said. "I'm expecting that to come later on."

Allen looked at Jack with that recurring dopey grin. "We're going to be getting out of here, buddy. You need any cash or anything?"

"Forget it. Get me next time."

"You got it." He and Elisabeth stood up in synchronicity. "Take it slow, buddy." Allen wrapped an arm around his date's waist and together they followed Lucy's trail to the exit.

"Nice meeting you," Jack called out, annoyed by Elisabeth's refusal to say goodbye. Neither of them turned to acknowledge him.

He sat alone, realizing this was the first time he'd felt comfortable all night. His beer had warmed to swill but he finished it anyway. Contemplated ordering another but thought better of it. Too much beer made him sleepy, which wasn't going to work if he wanted to catch It's No Good.

He waited for the waitress to return, handed her the twenty and then headed back to the cabana. The walk relaxed him. It was a little past ten and the grounds of the Big East showed no signs of slowing down. He headed away from the activities range, walking past the fenced in swimming pool area, still abuzz with children's laughter and booming splashes following the *boing* of the diving board. Most hotel pools closed at sundown, but this one sported enough halogen lighting to maintain the illusion of permanent daylight.

His cabana was tucked away in the furthest corner of the grounds, accessible from a narrow path that wound through a series of pines. The mountain breeze was faint, but felt cool on his face as he headed down the darkened trail marked by string lights.

He contemplated taking a quick right toward Molly's cabana. Lucy would be there, but he wasn't interested in crashing that party. One of two things had to be happening right now: Lucy was holding Molly's hair as regurgitated margarita got puked into the toilet, or there was full-on waterworks with a lot of 'why me' theatrics.

Either way, no thank you.

As gratifying as Molly's verbal assault on Allen and Elisabeth had been, it was also irritating. Molly Perkins wasn't in high school anymore, though her frequent actions indicated otherwise. She couldn't get over Allen, God knew why, a year and a half later.

Jack had done his best to dissuade Lucy from inviting Molly to the Big East, but Lucy and Molly had grown close, a fact that occasionally made life miserable for Allen.

Their bond seemed sincere. Molly was overdramatic, but that didn't make her a bad person, even if Jack couldn't understand why anyone would want a drama queen for a friend. Life with Molly was more of a one-way street than most friendships should be.

Jack stayed to the left and followed the trail of lights back to his room. He'd call Lucy's cell once it was safe.

●

"Whooooo-boy."

Lucy whipped her handbag down onto the couch as she entered Jack's room, slamming the door shut behind her.

Jack was stretched out in the recliner, watching TV with a can of diet soda in his hand and a bag of chips nesting on his stomach.

"Good times?"

"Incredibly," she said. "I don't know what I was thinking, I really don't. I just sort of figured they could put up with each other."

"That was your first mistake."

"Hey, I don't need criticism from the cheap seats."

Lucy went for the kitchen and grabbed the open bottle of Stoli sitting on the counter. Thankfully, there was lots of orange juice in stock to go along with it. She didn't much like straight alcohol and tolerated screwdrivers only slightly more. After tonight's debacle, she needed something to burn the edge away, and this would do.

"Wasn't that the perfect ending to a majestic evening?" Lucy took a seat on the couch.

"One way of looking at it," Jack said. "If I had your sunny disposition, I probably wouldn't mind whatever job I get next year."

"When life tosses you lemons..."

"Life tossed you oranges."

"Don't remind me."

Lucy drank, remembering why she hadn't had one in years. The acidity of the orange juice wasn't exactly a pleasure, and pulp had a disgusting texture. All of it contributed to the over-all miserable experience of the beverage.

Her brow wrinkled at the second sip and she wondered why she did this to herself. She was only twenty-two. It wasn't like today was a hard day at the office, offering a cock and bull story to unhappy investors, or whatever her father did. It didn't bode well for her future that she was already seeking the assistance of alcohol.

You're entitled, she thought. *Things have been shitty lately.*

"I hate these things. I really do." She stuck her tongue out to get the taste off it.

"Allen loves 'em," Jack said, explaining why they had a case of Stoli on hand. "I suspect he goes that route because he can't handle a real drink."

"Drink shaming," Lucy said. "I forgot how tough you are with your Wild Turkey. I'm in the presence of a man's man...I wasn't even thinking."

"Shut up."

Lucy put the glass beside the couch and stretched out, arching her back and breasts. She'd purposely worn this low-cut, tie-died number because she liked the way her boobs looked in it. The shirt conformed to her shape, rounding tight around her bosom while accenting her flat stomach.

She watched Jack to see if he'd sneak a peek as she yawned, but his attention was bolted to HBO.

That's disappointing.

With Allen running around Greifsfield like an obedient dog, Lucy hoped Jack would take more interest in her. They'd been friends for years and, for as long as she could recall, she want-ed them to be more. Jack, as far as she could tell, did not. Not ever.

He shoveled more chips into his mouth than he could fit

and washed it down with a swig of soda. Crumbs scattered onto his shirt, landing in the recliner's recesses.

Why do I want him again?

But Lucy knew why. It wasn't entirely a physical thing. It couldn't be that with Jack. Not to suggest he was a bad-looking guy, with his constant stubble and unkempt hair. He had a look that was his own and he pulled it off. Jeans and black t-shirt chic, for lack of a better label.

He had acne that pocked his face on occasion, and that ever-expanding potbelly hadn't been there last year. Still, she liked looking at Jack and decided long ago that his indifference to physical appearance was part of the attraction. And it wasn't like he had bad hygiene. His aroma had never really changed in the years she had known him: Mennen by way of Yankee Candle.

Reliable and comforting.

Plus, he somehow managed to keep a cute ass, like he did squats in secret or something.

Lucy's campus roommates couldn't understand her hopeless crush, but she never gave a damn about what they thought. Their company was serviceable throughout the school year, but she was hard-pressed to think she'd remain friends with any of them after graduation. Most chased social prestige and were content to wrap their lips around the shallowest guys for that very reason. Suffice to say their life goals weren't exactly aligned.

Lucy crossed her legs so that the bottoms of her shorts rode up, flashing a healthy amount of thigh.

Jack went for another handful of chips instead of looking.

"Didn't you want to see that band?" she asked.

"Starting just about now."

"Gotcha. That explains it..."

"Explains what?"

"Why you're pouting."

Jack was looking her way now, even noticing her bare

thighs. "I'm not pouting."

"No?"

"Maybe I am. I don't know. It's just that tonight was terrible. Allen pulls this crap all the time."

"I know. But usually the girl realizes what a flake he is in no time. To be honest, I'm shocked this one has lasted this long."

"I'm sure it won't last," Jack said. "But it's annoying. Did you notice how he tried to skate around every topic that *she* might object to?"

Lucy shrugged. "I don't know why you'd continue associating with someone who's chosen to disavow all knowledge of Dokken."

"I thought you didn't like anything but that DJ crap."

"I've got a classics playlist on Spotify. I'm not a heathen, you know."

"Up for debate," Jack said.

"Are you sure you don't want to go see pseudo-Depeche? We can make it in no time."

"Nah."

"If you're not up for that...something else?"

"I don't know, you know how *Celebrity Rehab* hooks me in..."

Lucy flung a decorative pillow at him. "Let's go, jerk."

"Where?"

Lucy picked up the rest of her drink, winced and swallowed it. She thought it'd be easy to confide in Jack. If anyone would give a friendly ear, it'd be him. Even flirting didn't help bolster her confidence. And neither did this shit screwdriver. "I don't mean to add to the day's misery, but I kind of need to talk."

"Shady," Jack said. "About what?"

Lucy hoisted him from the recliner and a smattering of chip crumbs plummeted off his shirt.

"Just...stuff," she told him. "Maybe we'll take a ride, but

for now I sort of feel like walking."

Jack disappeared into his bedroom and returned with a black fleece. "Do you want this? You're the coldest person I know."

"How can you say that after we've had the pleasure of meeting one Elisabeth Luna?"

"Different kind of cold."

"True," Lucy giggled and took the fleece. Jack was right, she could be cold in July.

They stepped outside. Jack locked up and they headed toward the Big East's main grounds, footing it in silence until Jack asked about Molly.

"Sleeping, I hope." It hadn't been a pretty sight. "After an hour of me explaining why she's better off without Allen, I think she started buying it."

"Until tomorrow."

Lucy agreed with a sigh. It wasn't Molly's fault she couldn't get over an ex, and had to keep reminding herself of that. It happened to everyone, which meant it would definitely happen to Lucy at some point. Heck, it was already starting.

Her nipples stood at attention despite the humid evening air. They poked through the tie-dye, but Jack Markle hadn't bothered to notice.

They emerged from the forest and hit the green, headed for the main lodge sprawled across the horizon like some alien mothership. El Debarge's *Rhythm of the Night* rocked The Cove as they passed, its herd beginning to thin as midnight approached.

They circled around the main lodge's back, through a door marked EMPLOYEES ONLY. Stairs brought them into the kitchen where familiar staff faces offered friendly, if forced, nods. A few stared blatantly at her best attributes.

She led him to the end of a hallway that was so white it was nearly clinical. The heavy fire door at the end led up two flights of stairs. Behind her, Jack's asthma announced itself with a string of steady wheezes.

"Almost there," she said, turning to catch his eyes on her backside.

He played it cool and ignored it. "Don't worry," he said. "I could climb thirty flights."

"Even so," she said. "We're here."

The second landing opened into a long hallway that led to the Big East's lobby. Down another corridor that ended with a single locked door signed RORY EASTMAN.

"What's with the roundabout way to your dad's office?"

"Just a surprise," she said, noticing the drawn window blind. That didn't happen unless he was out of the office, but she had to be sure. So she knocked several times before pressing an ear against the glass for a better listen. No sign of habitation on the other side.

"Bastard," she hissed. "He's not here."

"Should he be?" Jack was taking a hit of his inhaler.

Lucy didn't answer. The question of his whereabouts was bothersome. Mom said he wouldn't be home tonight, that he would be here. He sometimes worked late in order to personally tend to VIPs, although she didn't think the resort currently had any.

The Big East's lobby was a hub of activity. The lounge was jammed full of people packed like sardines, laughing, talking, and drinking. The Black Diamond, the restaurant bar and grille, brimmed. She glanced through the windows as they passed it, certain it was a fire hazard.

It was on most nights, but that didn't matter when your father had the county fire marshal on his payroll.

Elisabeth's obnoxious insinuations echoed between her ears. *"Deep pockets speak much louder than protest."*

God, Lucy thought. *What a bitch.*

The front desk clerk perked up when he saw Lucy approaching. His expression went from blank to shit-eating with the flip of a switch.

"Evening Ms. Eastman..."

"Lucy, please. Would you happen to know if my father's around?"

"Haven't seen him in a while."

"What's a while?"

"I came in at three today. He stopped by the front desk to check on a few reservations. Haven't seen him since."

"Dammit," she whispered, turning away from the desk.

"You're getting worked up, Luce. Why are you looking for your father all of a sudden?"

"I want to catch him in the act."

"What act?"

"He's cheating."

"Oh man, I'm sorry." Jack stared like there was nothing more to say.

"It's worse, too," she said.

She stepped close and dipped her head, pulling Jack's ear to her mouth, determined to keep this from earshot. With this much background noise, it shouldn't be a problem, but one could never be too careful.

"Two nights ago that son of a bitch tried to rape me."

●

Elisabeth guided the cherry red Eclipse Spyder to the tip of the gravel driveway and killed the engine. Without a word she slid out from behind the wheel and ascended the steps to the second floor deck, leaving Allen in the still of the night.

He watched her trim silhouette slink into darkness and debated his next move.

She wasn't making things comfortable for him.

Dinner had not gone well, despite Jack and Lucy's appreciated efforts. He'd have to give them a call in the morning to apologize.

The porch light came to life, jolting Allen from both his thoughts and the encompassing night. Above him, Elisabeth leaned against the railing and looked down from the raised veranda. She did not speak, aware that her plunging neckline was plenty inviting.

He didn't wait another minute. His minor grievances dissipated, replaced with endless desire for her.

"I thought you were going to make me sleep in the car tonight," he said, reaching the top of the stilted deck and taking hold of her slender waist. His hands glided along the surface of her silky dress, desperate to see her slip from it.

"For?" She parried away and her hand, smooth and soft, brushed his forearm.

His heart thumped against his ribs with just a little more force than usual.

"You know," he said. "The whole thing with Molly."

"Ah," she said as if she'd honestly forgotten about her. "It does call into question your taste in women, I suppose. It doesn't make this evening your fault, however."

"I'm relieved."

"I was somewhat relieved myself. Otherwise we'd still be there listening to that redhead's prattle."

"You really hated it that much?"

Elisabeth didn't answer. She took Allen by the hand and led him along the deck with gentle steps. Her prolonged touch spread warmth to every cranny of his body. Any guilt over tonight had eroded in the wake of his one-track desire for this woman. He thought about defending the honor of his friends, but knew it wasn't worth his breath. She didn't want to hear it, and he had other things in mind.

Like getting some, baby.

Her home was spacious. They entered through the sliding door and stood inside a large living room, complete with a vaulted ceiling and white marble tiling. The black leather furniture and contemporary décor contrasted the light color scheme. He'd been here a few times and still couldn't imagine Elisabeth living here.

"You really should lock that door," he said as she closed it behind them.

"I've lived by myself for a very long time."

I don't understand how.

Elisabeth invited him to take a seat on the couch. Her fingers pressed tenderly against his chest, guiding him onto the cushion. Her dark hair swung against his face as he allowed her direction. The sensation provoked a slight reaction in his pants.

"Relax." Her grin was mischievous. "Have a nightcap with me."

Allen bit the inside of his cheek as he watched her and her tight ass disappear into the hallway. His heart thumped faster than normal, harder than the night in eighth grade he lost his virginity to Christina Banville.

Elisabeth's vibes were different tonight. Playful and inviting. It could only mean one thing and he shifted in his seat at the conclusion.

So far every one of their dates had ended the same way: a fleeting kiss on the lips and promises of a next time. He hadn't tasted her mouth yet, let alone anything else. They'd been a couple for less than two weeks, and normally that was plenty of time to know what her morning breath smelled like. But not this time. Elisabeth was the exception to just about every rule he'd lived by in his twenty-two years.

He kind of loved that. This was a challenge.

Was she even a good kisser? She got his blood pumping without effort, but what if she couldn't kiss? Or there was some other problem? That would ruin everything. He was used to games, but this was the first time he recalled being beaten so badly at one.

In a sick way, this was exactly what he wanted. She didn't need powers of observation to know she drove him absolutely wild. Elisabeth Luna kept him wanting more and knew it. He'd left her house two nights ago throbbing so hard he couldn't think about thinking straight. Had to pull over and finish things off on the side of the road like the star of some degenerate Internet porn video.

Sealing this deal was all he could think about these days: her warm touch, exotic eyes, thick lips, great tits…

The tickle in his pants became a full-fledged throb.

And then Elisabeth returned carrying two wine glasses, each brimming with crimson liquid.

He shifted his posture to conceal the blooming blood rush, even as his eyes roved her ample cleavage while she bent to hand him the glass.

"I hope you like this, it's an old family recipe. My relatives still make it."

Allen brought the glass to his nostrils and swirled. It smelled like every other wine in the world as far as his amateur palette knew, but he didn't want her to know that. And if it wasn't wine, it sure looked like it: thick, full-bodied, and ruby red. It splashed against the fancy crystal goblets, leaving the inside stained with splotchy residue.

Elisabeth watched him, smiling.

"You didn't just poison me, did you?"

"Just curious what you're going to think. Drink it."

Even if Allen had an aversion to whatever this was, he was going to pour it down his throat. It was Elisabeth's own creation and he would love it—as far as she knew.

"Cheers," he said.

"Cheers," she repeated, smiling with bemusement.

It *was* wine. Hard to say what kind since, much like the smell, it *tasted* like every other one he'd ever had. It stained his lips, tongue and teeth, coating his throat on its way down.

Then it started to change. The familiar, fermented mixture of berries and grains faded, leaving instead a lingering, acidic taste. Maybe it *wasn't* like every other wine he'd tasted. The flavor riled his taste buds. He took another sip, then another. There were traces of bitter amidst the fruitiness and it took a minute to kick in.

He put the glass down on the freeform coffee slab and noticed Elisabeth's blue eyes studying him through the table's reflection.

"How do you like it?"

"I love it," he said, probably a bit too quickly.

Her mouth broke into a wide grin. "I'm so glad."

Her smile was more than stunning. It disarmed much of the night's anticipatory tension. More than anything, he was compelled to push his lips against hers. He wanted to taste her mouth, suck those juicy lips, and explore every inch of her curves. His eyes dipped again to his favorite site, the v-cut top and those breasts bound behind it. Her chest heaved with each breath, demanding his attention.

"I love that dress on you," he said, deciding to play the game. He wanted her to know he was looking. Ogling. "The color goes perfectly with your hair."

"Thank you."

More than that, the dress was unique. Not a generic number found on the hook of a local department mall. Something a movie star might wear to an awards show provided she wanted to be the talk of the town the next day.

"Is it silk?" he asked.

A bored nod. "Got it in Italy last time I was there."

Italy. The word conjured an image of Elisabeth charging armfuls of designer outfits without regard. Allen didn't know her situation, but suspected she was financially liberated.

He took his drink, shaking off forward desires. Why was he afraid to make a move? He didn't lack for confidence, but suddenly was eleven years old again. Standing on the playground at St. Anna's School, fixating on the perfectly round and juicy bubble belonging to Sarah Spradling.

Sometimes he walked right behind her just to get a look at it peaking out from beneath her schoolgirl skirt. He loved to look. And that was all he did. Because he'd been too timid to try anything more.

As much as he craved it, the thought of making a move on Elisabeth was enough to provoke heart palpitations and cause a tingling sensation in his fingers.

They chatted and drank. Elisabeth confessed to being a fashion addict, detailing her favorite places around the globe to shop.

"You've been to all those countries?"

"Of course," she said. "There was a time in my life when I decided I was going to see the world. All of it. Been a long time since I've been back to any of them, though."

"And you live here? In Greifsfield?"

"So?"

"I don't know. It seems so...plain? Especially when you start talking about all of the other places you've lived."

"I like Greifsfield because of its tranquility."

"But it's a tourist spot."

"And Rome is not? Besides, tourists don't bother me." A smile. "I keep to myself and spend most of my time out here with nature. It inspires me, my work. When the creative spark dims, I shall take the hint and move along once more. But for now I am content."

"You've only lived here for seven months?"

"I tend to get bored quite easily. That, and I see this place changing for the worse."

"The resort?"

"The resort among other things."

"Kind of makes you yearn for a nice little villa in the Mediterranean, huh? Malta, maybe?"

Her eyes, typically narrow and seductive, bulged with the kind of excitement he had not yet seen in her. "Malta is among my favorite places to live."

"And how can you prefer this place to Malta?"

"Have you ever traveled?"

"I've been to Canada twice."

She laughed. "You only think that way because you haven't seen the world. There are many beautiful places to see, sure. But then you see them, and you quickly realize that they, like Greifsfield, have their faults. There is no one place that equals paradise."

"Yeah, but man, I'd love to just get away from all this sometimes."

"Get away from what?" Elisabeth said. "This country?"

"Well, school. Work."

"Won't you do those things when you *get away*?"

"I suppose I'll have to. Gotta make a living."

"And after you've gone and relocated somewhere, do you not see yourself tiring of that *escape*? Pretty soon you'll find yourself craving a way out of whatever job you've taken. You'll become desperate to escape whatever debt you incur. You might even start to miss your home here."

"That is obviously experience talking." Allen sipped the special batch of wine. He decided it was as odd and exotic as she, and the taste was beginning to wear him down as much as the game. The back-ended bitter tang lingered in his mouth, on his tongue and in his throat.

Elisabeth finished her glass as if it were water. "Partly experience, yes. Another part, though, comes from seeing it happen to others. It's always the same. People tend to focus on some far off land or new opportunity. They insist it's the answer to their problems."

"I'm not necessarily saying I want to leave my country," Allen said. "I just can't help but wonder what it would be like to live elsewhere."

"Maybe you'll find out. You've got your whole life."

"I suppose."

"Do you want another glass?"

I don't think I can handle another one.

"Sure," he said.

Her warm hand slid into his. "Then come."

The kitchen resembled a sterile room from a futuristic movie. Elisabeth refilled both glasses from a large carafe and then led him down a long hallway to the opposite end of the house.

Are we going to the bedroom?

His heart fluttered and his mind danced ahead of his body, projecting images of them, sweaty and naked, entwined in each other's arms.

The last room on the right wasn't a bedroom. Elisabeth flung the billowy curtain aside and stepped through the doorway.

It was dark, save for flickering candles spread across various furnishings. The room smelt of lilac and pine and came equipped with old, handcrafted furniture—the exact opposite of every other room. In the corner stood an easel, its canvas blank save for a very rough sketch of what looked like a tree line.

"This is your sanctuary?"

"It's where I come to get away from everything else. Reminds me of home."

"You are home, I thought."

"This reminds me of when I was a girl, back in Iasi." Her tongue shifted into a foreign accent for the pronunciation of her hometown.

"Where's that?"

"Romania. I was born there."

"Why'd you leave?"

Elisabeth paused, looking uncertain. It was oddly refreshing to see her searching for an answer. "To pursue my art."

Allen examined the room's every detail with more interest now, as if something might provide a clue to the enigmatic woman before him. It was strange to think of her growing up in what might've been poverty, but it made sense that she'd want to keep some semblance of her home intact. Even if it was just a little piece tucked into one corner of her home.

Nostalgia was a very human trait.

Her paintings littered the room. They ranged from the abstract to renaissance and most failed to garner his attention, until he came to one hanging above the couch. It depicted several nude women impaled on pikes, stabbed between their legs, the pointed tips ripping through their gaped mouths or throats. Blood poured down their lengths.

Jack had shown him a movie once depicting a similar scenario, though he couldn't remember the title.

"My favorite piece," Elisabeth said, noticing his lingering fascination with the image.

"Why is that?"

"Reminds me of how brutal and unforgiving this world is."

"Grim."

"That's the world."

"Wow, Elisabeth."

"Disagree?"

"I don't dwell on it. You can bum yourself out thinking about everything that's wrong with the world."

"I choose to dwell...on occasion. Helps me keep my perspective."

Allen turned toward the picture again. "Is this part of your perspective?"

"A result of the Spanish Inquisition." Her voice abandoned its sultry resonance. "These women were accused of being...I don't know what you'd call it. Satanists, in modern speech, I guess. The method depicted shows a crusader's means of cleansing a village of the devil's brides."

"Seems like an overreaction."

"The luxury of hindsight. Many did not believe their work held any legitimacy even then. They saw it as an opportunity to make some money in plague-ridden times. The road they traveled was long and the pleasures of the flesh were too much to deny. That's what it was really about. *Men* having their fun."

"The stuff they leave out of history books," Allen said.

"They leave everything out."

"I bet."

Elisabeth sat on the fresh-made mattress tucked against the wall, folded her legs and took a sip of wine.

Allen studied the painting longer, transfixed and appalled. He felt Elisabeth's blues on him, his fascination with the picture fascinating her.

She refused to break eye contact when he turned.

Allen slid beside her. Moon glow kissed them through the skylight above, casting Elisabeth in ethereal glow.

Allen glanced up. "This house, this room especially, is perfect."

"You would not think places like this still exist in an overpopulated world. Makes me wonder how long it can last. Not hard to imagine endless apartment blocks littering this place one day."

"You pessimist." Allen smirked. She hadn't spewed this much negativity in the last two weeks combined.

"Am I so awful?" Elisabeth asked.

"Of course not! I doubt you have to worry about Greifsfield selling out."

She scoffed in his face, a sound that was bitter and cruel and soaked with experience. She looked at him as though he knew nothing, a glare that made Allen feel even dumber than that. "It is already happening," she said. "The resort you are staying at, for example. What would you assume was on that land prior to that abomination?"

"Forest?"

"Correct."

"Does that mean Greifsfield's days are numbered?"

"I would be willing to bet. Someone always wants to build a McDonald's sooner or later."

"Probably won't happen in your lifetime. And that's not much of a consolation I bet, but we're here now. No sense in worrying about it."

"If everyone thought like that, nobody would stand up against anything."

"Greifsfield's okay for now. That's all I'm saying."

Her lips parted. Something on the verge of escaping them. She reconsidered, offering a simple laugh instead. "You are kind to indulge my tirade."

"I love it. When you're passionate about nothing you're not truly alive." Allen wondered if he believed that.

"Artistic individuals are tenacious in our beliefs," she said following a long sip of wine.

"I have a cousin who moved to Greenwich Village in New York City. He works at a Barnes & Noble to pay the rent and he's virtually broke."

"He should not live in Greenwich Village, then."

"This is true," Allen laughed. "But he's an artist. And by that, I mean he's incredibly thick-headed. Real stubborn-like, ya know?"

"Of course."

"So my cousin, Donnie, he spends his weekends and most of the week playing guitar...coffeehouse gigs. But he's so determined to make it as a singer/songwriter he can't be reasoned with. Wants nothing else out of life, either. Just to keep trying until he makes it. He'd be the first to agree with your sentiments about McDonald's and Wal-Mart."

"Well then...where did you say your cousin lived, and does he look like you?"

"He's gay."

"We'll see."

They both laughed. The second time tonight he'd heard that sound and it was fantastic. Elisabeth was warming to him. That or she was drunk off her home brew.

"It is the nature of the beast," she said.

"What is?"

"Your cousin. People like him. Artistry, of any kind, is never a lucrative vocation, save for a chosen few. But I have met many in my life who are content with their existence. More outside the United States, I suppose. Things are too materialistic here. We assume the more money one has, the happier they must be. That sentiment is true in other corners of the world as well, though hardly as predominant. When I lived in Italy, I knew many artists. Material possession was the furthest thing from their desires. We didn't spend evenings cruising around the city in a sports car."

"Like an Eclipse Spyder?"

"Hypocrisy is another human characteristic."

"You have an answer for everything," Allen said.

"It wasn't about exclusive restaurants. We congregated in local pubs with pitchers of beer and bottles of wine. Enjoying each other's company. Enjoying life."

This hypocrisy was off the charts to Allen's ears. *She* was a woman who gallivanted around in a hot new car and spent her evenings in a post-modern castle. Saying she'd done okay didn't begin to cut it.

"That's how I pictured you living," he said. "When you told me you were an artist, I had you pegged for someone who lived off the land. Living in some one-story, one bedroom. But you've practically got your own street."

Elisabeth sat in silence. Her eyes narrowed. Even by candlelight, her stare intoxicated him. Ocean-blue eyes were as wild and unpredictable as waves in a raging storm.

He found his buzz at the bottom of the wine glass. Once finished, he put it on the floor beside them. Things clicked into place and this suddenly felt very right. The insecure schoolyard boy disappeared as Allen moved in for a kiss. Before closing his eyes, he saw Elisabeth moving forward to meet him.

Their lips met. He pressed against hers and she reciprocated, mouths leaving tiny pecks. Her tongue traced his bottom lip, leaving moist trails that tasted like full-bodied red wine.

Their tongues paraded around each other like curious animals. She caught his between her teeth with gentle force, backing off with a slow suck. Allen pulled away for a momentary grab of breath. Then he came back, licking and sucking with ferocity. His hand caressed her shoulders in mounting passion.

This was every bit as sensual as he'd imagined. Elisabeth's flesh was pillow soft and her sexuality, the way she moved against him, was so raw he wasn't sure he'd be able to match her once their clothes came off.

Any minute now, he thought with all the impatience of a child on Christmas morning.

Slow fingers traced the outline of her round breasts and faint moans sounded at his touch. She arched her back and pushed her full chest against his hand.

Testing the waters.

She breathed approval into his ear with a sticky hot exhale.

And his caress became a grope. Elisabeth's kisses strengthened and she leaned against his chest, trapping his explorer's hand
between their bodies.

His pants throbbed and begged for release. Her hand
brushed the top of his bulge, and Allen was disappointed that it
didn't last longer.

Through mashed teeth he whispered, "I want you."

Elisabeth broke away but stayed nose to nose. She licked
his mouth like an animal, snarling as she did it. "I want you too,
but now is not right."

"Feels right." He tried kissing her again.

She rejected his advance with a turn of her cheek. "It's
not," she said with finality.

Bitch was Allen's first thought. Bad enough she'd treated
his friends like lepers, but now he was traipsing off into the night
with the bluest balls of all time.

"So the night's over?" He said, trying not to sound aggra-
vated.

"Didn't you want to get an early start tomorrow?"

Allen suppressed a sigh. "Absolutely." Tomorrow they
were going to one of her favorite spots in the forest so he could
watch her paint. The interminable things guys did for a chance.

"Good. Take my car tonight. You can pick me up in the
morning."

"I could always stay here. Might be faster."

She brushed her fingers against his cheek and smiled.
"You're cute."

Worth a shot.

When Allen wasn't with her, he tended to obsess over her.
Borrowed Jack's car, unbeknownst to him, for a quick ride past her
place on days he hadn't heard from her. A total stalker move, but
he couldn't resist.

Allen followed his goddess back into the kitchen, hoping the throbbing would subside before she noticed it was alive and well.

He loved the way her ass looked in that dress, how it clung to her shape and teased him with every sway. He drank the image up as they walked.

Elisabeth grabbed her keys off the barren countertop and underhanded them to Allen. "7 am, right?"

"I was hoping to avoid 7 am until September."

"I prefer the nights as well. But this piece requires daylight, and I like the way the morning sun hits the lake."

"The most I can get is eight hours of sleep...if I leave now."

"Better hurry then," she said. "Unless you weren't serious about watching me." Her voice was suddenly cold.

He kissed her goodnight.

The drive back to the Big East was excruciating. Just fifteen minutes ago, he was sure this was *the* night. That body, writhing under his, and then writhing on top of his, and all the combinations in between. And now, nothing. Couldn't feel more defeated.

The Big East was lit up like an exaggerated ski lodge. It peeked out between several rows of pine trees as the road wound right to it. He pulled to the guard gate and flashed his room badge. The partition separated, allowing him through. He took a parking spot at the edge of the lot, isolated from most other cars. Didn't trust other drivers and wouldn't be responsible for denting this joy ride.

The trek back to the cabana made the night feel even longer. Elisabeth had awakened specific urges that required attention. That tight black dress flashed in his mind as he hurried his pace.

Allen was relieved to discover an empty room upon his arrival. He poured a glass of water to alleviate the inevitable dry mouth symptoms spurred by wine. He carried the glass into his bedroom, killed the lights, cranked the air conditioner, stripped off his clothes and climbed beneath the sheets.

There, he masturbated to Elisabeth before rolling over and falling asleep.

He was there in no time, lost in a fantastic dream about a blue-eyed woman.

●

Elisabeth stepped out onto the porch and into the balmy summer night. The humidity brought miserable flashes as she closed her eyes. The stagnant air whispered silent encouragement.

This was impossible.

Was this child, Allen Taylor, getting to her? He'd wanted her badly tonight. Tangible desire nearly too powerful to resist. Just thinking about him made her insides flare.

And it was already much too hot tonight.

She slid the dress off her shoulders. The straps fell across her smooth arms until gravity tugged the fabric away. She stepped from the silky puddle at her feet and felt the air against her bare body. It wasn't the sticky weather that brought gooseflesh, but thoughts of Allen.

There was something about him.

She tugged the necklace that swung against her neckline. When it swayed against her skin it brought a cold sting and a modicum of guilt.

That was a long time ago, she thought, smoothing the sharp white tooth between two fingers.

She walked down the steps and into the cool grass that welcomed her bare feet.

Tomorrow was another day. Maybe the right one to tell Allen how she felt. After tonight it was obvious he would be happy to hear it. She had stifled the urge to tell him after opening up in ways she had never planned.

What's wrong with me?

There were going to be repercussions.

"Of course there will be," she mumbled as she strolled through the yard. "There have always been."

Something else troubled her, too. Allen's ex-girlfriend. Molly, was it? No excuse for the way that fool had acted. The little bitch shamed herself in the eyes of a dozen people and yet, she did not seem to care.

As long as she got what she wanted.

Elisabeth's jaw tightened as she contemplated her options.

But there weren't any. There was only what had to be done.

The thought made her smile.

Three

Sunlight burned Lucy's eyelids, lifting her from restless sleep.

Downstairs, Mom was lecturing Nick about punctuality, threatening to somehow cancel summer vacation if he missed the bus.

"Because I am not driving you, mister. Now MOVE!"

Lucy rubbed hardened sleep from her eyes and sat up.

Mom's back?

Her cell phone said it was only a little past seven.

She climbed out of bed wearing sweats and a loose tank top, trying not to wince at the static nightmare that was her bed hair as she passed the vanity mirror. Today saw another acne outbreak she was also determined to ignore. Any other morning, this combination of frazzled hair and zits would've been an emergency. Today, her priorities lay elsewhere.

She ran a hand through her hair to calm the frizz as she ambled downstairs. The kitchen table was cluttered with plates of bacon, sausage, and eggs. A pitcher filled with pulpy orange juice sat in the middle of the action with little more than a swallow remaining.

Lucy studied the display, perplexed. She snatched a piece of cool bacon and looked through the bay window. Mom stood at the edge of the driveway with Nick at her side, together waiting for the approaching bus to Camp Wahkan.

"Son of a bitch." Lucy marched outside.

Nick noticed his big sister's approach as the bus pulled to the curb. He jumped on board, waving to Lucy with a quick look back. Then he darted for the rear.

"Call me as soon as you get there, honey, okay?" Mom tapped the side of the bus beneath Nick's window.

Lucy folded her arms and struggled to maintain her composure while they watched the bus rumble off down the road.

When it was out of sight Mom said, "What are you doing up so early, honey? I figured you hit the hay not too long ago."

"Are you fucking kidding me, Mom?"

"Watch your mouth."

"Oh, don't even start on my language. The way things have been, I thought it was you who hit the hay not too long ago. What time did you get in last night, anyway?"

Mom seemed surprised by her hostility. "You're right. The girls and I got a little carried away. Probably wasn't the smartest thing. I knew I'd be putting Nick on the bus this morning, but it's been forever since I stayed out like that. I missed your father entirely, you know. He was already gone by the time I came in."

"Yeah, well that's because he never came home."

"What?"

"You're surprised? Don't tell me you were really expecting him to be home last night. Quality time with his son? What a startling concept."

"Don't talk about him like that."

"So he told you he'd be home, never shows up, and I'm not allowed to criticize?"

"He said he would..."

"Well, he didn't. Nick was home by himself. Didn't have dinner until late, Mom. When I got home. And what girls are you suddenly spending all of this time with?"

"Girls my age who have been coming into the store since forever...are you sure your father didn't come home?"

"He keeps weird hours, has a more unnatural nightlife than you. God knows what he's out doing."

"I told you not to talk about him that way. You act like we're children, Lucy. Your father doesn't have to answer to you."

"He does when he acts like one," she said. "I think a solid case of child neglect validates my scrutiny."

Mom slapped her palms against her too-tight Levis and marched off.

The dismissal infuriated Lucy. She followed her inside and continued her verbal assault. "This is how you deal? By ignoring it? Pretend it's fine?"

"Nothing's fine, Lucy. I've got work in half an hour. I'm at that place more than I'm here, and when home I have the pleasure of listening to my daughter tell me what a terrible mother I am."

"You should've thought about that last night when you were out reliving your twenties."

"If I were reliving my twenties, I'd be changing your diapers. I wasn't as fortunate as you, Lucy. Never got to spend summers at daddy's resort sunbathing with friends. I was raising you while he was building these luxuries you take for granted."

"Don't hold back any resentment, Mom. Like I somehow prevented you from doing what you wanted with your life." Lucy's voice cracked before she could finish speaking.

Mom noticed, sighed. "I didn't mean..."

"You meant it. You're sorry you had kids so young. But guess what? You did. Knocked up right out of high school. You made that choice. And lately you've been making me, and especially Nicholas, pay for it. How is that fair?"

"It was one time. One. And I'll bring it up with your father..."

"Yeah, if we ever hear from him again."

"He's probably working, Lucy! That's what people our age do! This conversation is over. I'm angry, too. At your father. But I won't apologize because we tossed a wrench into your plans. God forbid *that* ever happen again."

Mom stormed from the kitchen. The bathroom door slammed a moment later, leaving Lucy alone with her thoughts.

"Whatever, *Rachel*." Lucy screamed as if Mom's name was an insult. She took a seat at the breakfast table and eyed the food through watery eyes. She wiped the tears with her hand, wondering why she felt so selfish all of a sudden.

Because Mom always turns things around on you, dummy.

It wasn't the easiest thing to admit, but her mother had made a point. Wasn't her fault Dad never came home. The bastard. Lucy needed to find a way to have *that* conversation, but they couldn't remain civil long enough to bring it up.

Rachel Eastman wasn't going to like hearing that her husband of twenty-three years had been shacking up with every waitress and maid who worked for him. She'd probably like hearing that he tried forcing himself on his own daughter even less. Mom didn't handle any criticism well. A life-altering bomb would push her over the edge.

How to mention it?

"Hey Mom, guess what? Dad grabbed my tits and tried sliding his tongue down my throat the other night."

It was a humiliating topic and the thought embarrassed her more than anything.

And yet, you told Jack.

Last night came flooding back. She had confessed everything to that geek. Of course she hadn't gone into last night's dinner with the intention of doing so, but the way things had ended up, it felt like the right thing to do.

You should've told Molly, she thought. *At least she wouldn't have remembered.*

Allen's date, Hester Prynne, or whatever her name was, had successfully derailed the evening with smug accusations. In any other situation, Lucy would never have defended Dad, but that bitch's tone made her feel momentarily loyal. Somehow. Allegations dangled from lips that were probably collagen-infused while Allen Taylor, that idiot, dangled off her every word.

How I want to strangle him.

Not only was the professional home wrecker content with insulting her father, she spoke as if his corruption were fact. Lucy knew there was truth to it, but she didn't like hearing it from the mouths of others.

She tussled her hair wishing it could make her thoughts fall into place.

Maybe assaulting Mom full on hadn't been the best course of action. She needed all the friends she could get, and now she had one less. Before bed, Lucy was certain she had every right to be angry with her, but things didn't seem as clear now.

Two parents with midlife crises, lucky me.

Guilt forced her to do a quick clean up of the kitchen, throwing out all the food in the off chance her father came home. A petty gesture that made her smile.

Mom re-appeared in the doorway. "Time for work." She didn't bother with eye contact. Footsteps disappeared down the hallway and into the garage. The Pathfinder started up, reversed down the driveway, and sped off in a second.

Lucy cursed beneath her breath, frustrated by how poorly things had gone. She headed for her bedroom to finish packing for an extended leave.

At least Nick was out of here for a month. Better that way. She wouldn't have to worry. Spending last night here made her feel gross, but there was no way she was leaving Nick alone with Dad, that sick asshole. She didn't know if he would try anything on his son, but why not? He sure did with his daughter.

Two small suitcases filled up faster than she liked. She stuffed a shoulder sack to the brim with necessary accessories and placed all her luggage in the hallway like she was going back to school.

College had spoiled her in so many ways. Fall and spring independence made it much tougher to come home for summers. Once again you answered for every action, from staying up too late to drinking the last can of diet soda. Leaving the trash in the garage on garbage day was an offense punishable by execution.

It was all so jarring.

Lucy took one last sweep of the room and decided it was time to go. She trudged downstairs to load up the Civic. Once packed, she felt the temptation to steal one last piping hot shower from the master bathroom.

If there was a drawback to the Big East, it was the lacking water pressure.

Feeling refreshed, she left her hair wet and changed into capris and a brown tee that hid her curves. She was in no mood for head turns or catcalls.

On her way out the door, she footed it through the kitchen for a bottle of water. Eyes popping as she glanced through the window.

Her father's jet black Audi screeched around the bend and skidded to a halt at the foot of the driveway. He sprung from the driver's seat and headed for the front door with urgency.

Lucy's eyes sprung wide and she darted for the exit, but Rory was already in the house. He moved toward the kitchen, heavy stomps pounded the thick Asian carpet along the way.

Dread jutted through her gut as she wished she'd been two minutes faster.

His large frame filled the entire doorway, blocking her exit.

All of the tough words and actions she'd practiced crumbled away as he started toward her with a stranger's smile spread across his face.

She screamed.

●

"Elisabeth bailed on me today," Allen said. "You up for something?"

Jack had to resist doing a double take when Allen stepped onto the tiny brick-topped patio behind their room, his eyes locked onto the newspaper.

"Not sure," he said. "Doing something with Lucy later."

"You mean she's not helping Molly recover?"

"She's not."

Allen dropped into the empty lounge chair and tore the paper from Jack's fingers. "Could you believe that debacle last night? I can't wait to see Lucy and give her the old *I told you so*."

"Not sure that's necessary," Jack said. "She realized the error of her ways."

"I just want to rub it in."

"Leave it alone," Jack snapped. His short fuse was two-fold: Allen wasn't getting off the hook for dinner, and Lucy's late night revelation had stayed with him after dropping her home early this morning. He pleaded with her to come back here where she was safe, but she refused. What was it like going home after something like that?

What broke inside of a father's brain when he can't keep his hands off his child?

And how was Jack supposed to continue staying here on a rapist's dime? He had been adamant about leaving, but Lucy begged him to stay.

"I kind of need you here..."

It was all she needed to say.

"What about that double feature tonight? Bronson?" Allen's dismissive words catapulted back. *"They're not good movies, really."*

Elisabeth wasn't around now, so it was safe for Allen to be himself again.

"I'll play it by ear," Jack said, glad to serve Allen a spoonful of his own medicine. Childish, sure, but he wasn't a proud man. This felt good.

"Let me know what you're doing," Allen said. "I'd hate to get stuck in this room all day. I'll tag along with you and Lucy as long as you don't go anywhere near Molly."

Jack rose and stepped inside the room without another word.

He'd accepted Lucy's invitation to spend the summer in Greifsfield, Massachusetts under the pretense of a raucous guy's vacation—lots of hijinks as a precursor to their final year of college. It was impossible to know where their career paths would take them after. How many more times would he get to see his best friend without the restriction of a full time job? Sure, the presence of women was to be expected, but Jack had assumed they would be one-night stands. This was still college, after all. Random hook ups, walks of shame, beer goggles. This was supposed to be a summer of those things.

But Allen seemed content to ignite a relationship with the town pass-me-round, rather than say goodbye to their young and stupid days.

It was leaving Jack a little sore.

There was Lucy, at least. Her company was enjoyable, same as ever. But they weren't best friends and he wouldn't have made the trip just to spend two months with her.

Especially in light of recent developments.

Jack grabbed his wallet and keys off the table and left the

room through the front door without a destination in mind.

He felt awful for thinking about Lucy's problem so selfishly, but it was there, bobbing around in the back of his head. Wasn't something he'd ever admit to anyone, but there was no sense in lying to himself. He pushed the thoughts further down and hoped they'd drown.

He was better than that.

"Hey," Allen called from behind. He came jogging down the path like a lost puppy.

Jack swore beneath his breath and Allen was too far away to hear. "I'm just taking a walk," he said, his words loaded with defensiveness.

"Okay, I'll walk with you."

"Fine."

"I get the sense you're completely pissed off by the way things went at dinner."

"Best night of my life."

"I don't know why Elisabeth acted that way. She was all for meeting you guys, so I was taken aback by the cold shoulder. It sucked and I apologize. Just wanted to get the hell out of there after a while, so if our exit was hasty, that's why."

The apology was unexpected. Was there a shred of common decency remaining beneath Allen's trendy exterior? There was a laundry list of things Jack wanted to say about last night, but they felt trite and spiteful now.

"It's fine," Jack said. "I guess we're not going to be doing it again, but it's fine."

"Next time I see Elisabeth, I plan on probing a bit deeper." Allen nudged Jack's arm. "Hopefully in more ways than one. This is starting to be a tough summer."

Jack couldn't resist grinning. "The two of you haven't?"

Allen looked defeated. "Not even close. I thought I had it locked down last night, but she went all cold fish. Something about it *not being the right time* or whatever."

"You mean she's not smitten with you yet? Stop the presses."

Allen ignored the jab. "You and Luce? Still *just friends*?" He threw air fingers as he spoke.

"We are *just friends*." Allen wanted to hear otherwise. If Jack and Lucy became a thing, he was absolved of all guilt for the remainder of the summer. Even now it was about him.

"I don't get you, Markle," Allen said. "Don't get Lucy either, but she's not here so let's focus on you. Chick pines after you for years. Wants you. You. The football team wants her. The basketball team. Theater dorks. Every semester she's got hoards of admirers for some reason. And yet, she's hung up on Jack Markle. The guy with no interest. And why might that be? Because freckles are a turn off?"

"What?" Jack said. Lucy's body was dusted with freckles, but they were anything but a turn off, enhancing her cherubic face, bright green eyes, and rock-hard figure.

Allen favored this criticism because, in his mind, it reduced Jack to his level of shallowness.

"Eh, doesn't matter," Allen said with a wave of his hand. "I just want to make sure we're cool. We cool?"

"Definitely." Jack's answer was half-hearted, but so was Allen's apology.

"Excellent. So how 'bout those Bronson flicks tonight."

"Sure."

●

Rory watched her run for the door, that tight little ass wiggling with desperation. Her resistance provoked him, and he followed close behind, licking his lips and wiping away the drool.

She got there first, faster than he'd realized, and flung it open. A startling amount of sunlight spilled into the hall. Even though he'd just driven home, he had managed to forget it was day.

Couldn't say what type of hours he was keeping lately. Everything blended together. Minutes, hours, days and weeks—what month was this?

She was at her car. He watched her retreat from the doorway. He squinted through the blinding light of Wednesday morning and wished the nights lasted longer. Perhaps the New England winter would be more to his liking now, but shorter days were a few months away. Until then there was no choice but to adjust to this fucking glare.

He needed sleep but fought against it. Didn't matter that he hadn't had any rest since forever, only that fatigue settled into his muscles. Parts of him ached for the first time ever. Bones and muscles he never felt.

This was going to take some getting used to.

Who can sleep, he thought while watching her fumble for her keys. He wanted to go after her. To grab her and take her on the spot. With force.

His fists clenched, his teeth gnashed, and his heart skidded.

Figuring that the neighbors would have something to say about that, Rory realized he required more patience.

Repulsion dripped from her like sweat. He smelled it from here. Short breaths and wracked snobs completed the stimulating assault on his senses, and an appreciative smile brushed across his face. His head bobbed as if appreciating the grand finale of a symphony. Finding her here had been the smooth and buttery icing on an already sweet cake.

At last she got the door open and dropped into the driver's seat. She was driving off before he had time to blow her a kiss.

Fucking cocktease.

Rory rejected the sun's rays with a forceful slam of the front door. The hallway was haunted by her scent. He stood savoring it and got hard again.

This was wrong. A tiny part of him protested. The same part that told him fathers did not lust after their daughters. He didn't care, though, thinking instead of all the times she'd paraded around in cluelessly revealing clothing. All the times he stole glimpses of her forbidden areas as he tried to forget about their blood ties.

It used to be he ignored those thoughts. They were unwelcome and had no part occupying the head of a decent and dedicated family man.

Hadn't I been that once?

Shit, he didn't know.

Lately the urges were too strong. He tried hiding them in the beginning, but that gave them more credence. His efforts to kill them only made them stronger.

He was beyond it now.

So far beyond that this morning was a welcome surprise. He no longer cared there was no coming back from it. They had stopped being a family long ago.

He dropped his pants and fell into his favorite chair, taking himself in his hand. Through gritted teeth, he choked her name amidst a series of grunts and growls that sounded barely human, even to his ears.

The outskirts of his nostrils detected traces of her. More than just body wash, he could smell her essence.

That wasn't enough. The fantasy was nothing now. He reached for his phone and dialed a number. It rang only once before a familiar voice picked up.

"You're early," she said.

"I want to see you."

"So soon?"

"Right now,' he grunted.

"It's not even lunch time."

"I'm coming over."

"I'm serious, don't..."

"I wasn't asking, whore."

A long pull of silence followed and then at last, "fine."

"And I want it like last time."

"Of course you do."

Was that a sigh?

He was in the car in less than a minute. Speeding toward that voice, ready to explode.

The drive was less than eight miles, but felt like a goddamn eternity. Bend after bend through the sparsest areas of Greifsfield. The late morning sun poked through the endless trees as he turned onto Adams Street and slowed.

"Which house was it?"

It should've been familiar, considering the number of times he'd been here, but everything looked the same out this way. These homes were hopped up on steroids.

His place was nothing to scoff at, but this was old money. Most New York tycoons trekked out to Connecticut or Long Island to hang their hats, but the Greifsfield hills displayed just as much wealth and luxury. It was harder to find anything out this way considering the forests around the town were so damn dense.

His eyes scanned mailboxes for number 56. It was the one dwelling on Adams Street that hadn't ever been for sale. Greifsfield's Historical Society had given it landmark status in order to preserve it—something to do with the maze of tunnels running beneath.

Rumor was Benjamin Sarandon had once used them to smuggle slaves safely into the Mount Greyrock forest en route to the New York coast. Slaves who made it to the North weren't always free and clear, and many northerners had worked to help them escape the country altogether.

In recent years, the town tried removing its association with slavery altogether, no matter how noble a cause, by asking local plumbers and engineers to sign off on the probability the passageways were actually drainage pipes designed to carry basement water to the Greyrock slope.

It worked, but it also helped Rory wrestle the home out from underneath the historical society's grip. Since there wasn't anything historical about drainage pipes, they begrudgingly agreed to sell to a very high bidder.

Anton Fane.

He paid with more than money.

Hard to believe a year had gone by that quickly.

Number 56 was after the house with the gables. Rory noticed it over a stretch of hemlocks. The Sarandon House was conveniently obscured save for the wrought iron gate at the foot of its drive.

It was open. No need to stop and deal with the hassle of guards. He sped through and found his was the only car in the driveway. A fantastic sign!

There'd be no audience this time.

Rory knocked at the door once, twice, three times. He knocked a fourth, just for good measure.

Open up, he thought, desperately.

Finally it opened.

She looked good. Perfect. Everything but that red wig, anyway. It wasn't quite right, but it'd work for now.

Besides, the rest of the package made up for it. She wore a dark mesh nightgown that dangled open. He drank it in through greedy eyes. The way the lace hung over big tits, obscuring all but tiny hints of nipples. Her athletic stomach was a sculpted work of art. The gown gave way to a perfectly bald cunt, and Rory licked his lips. Black, fuck-me pumps completed the picture, adding a few inches to her *come hither* stature.

He didn't let her speak because he didn't give a shit what she had to say. He seized her and pressed on her mouth. He licked her lips while her hands rubbed and squeezed.

"Not like this, daddy!"

The impression of his daughter was shit, but Rory Eastman wasn't going to let that stop him.

"I'm going to fuck you, Lucy. And you're not going to say anything to mommy. Not a thing. Are we clear?"

'Lucy' smiled. "Fuck me, daddy," she said without missing a beat.

"I've been waiting to hear you say that."

●

"I made myself look like a complete freakshow." Molly was only now experiencing total recall.

"Well, yeah, you did. But there's nothing you can do about it."

"Lucy, how stupid do you think I am?"

Lucy was thankful for the bug-framed sunglasses that completely obscured her eyes. Molly would've caught one hell of an eye roll, otherwise. She offered her friend the sincerest smile she could muster. "I don't think you're stupid at all, kiddo. I think you're in love. Which, now that I think about it, is probably the same as being mentally challenged."

They lounged poolside, the two of them lathered in suntan lotion. Their flesh baked in the sweltering heat, and Lucy never felt more vulnerable.

This was the last place she wanted to be, but Molly's company, no matter how vapid it could occasionally be, was better than nothing. What's to be done after your father tries raping you a second time? Sit somewhere and sulk? That was last weekend.

Police? What would that accomplish? He hadn't succeeded in doing anything. It would just make him more cautious ahead of the next time he tried his luck.

"How old do you think she is?" Molly said.

"Allen's girl? Early forties, easy."

"I love you. But seriously, how old?"

"Dunno," Lucy shrugged. "Late twenties, maybe. Jack's age."

"Do you think she's all that?"

"Oh my God, no." Lucy said. But that was a lie. She hated, *hated*, to admit it, and would never do so to Jack or Allen, but that one had her stuff together. Lucy had put her under a microscope last night hoping to find flaws, and would've settled for just one by the end of the evening. No age lines or Botox, no chicken neck or toe thumbs. Nothing. Her damn boobs even jiggled with authenticity, same as hers.

Elisabeth would make someone very miserable one day, but she was all-natural. Flawless. Molly didn't need to hear the truth, though, so she told her, "She looks like a cheap escort."

"How come every guy around this pool can't keep his eyes off me, but Allen won't look twice?"

Why can't you be happy with one of them? Lucy wanted to ask. She wasn't into girls, but could admit Molly had a nice rack herself, and nipple tape might've covered more than her bathing suit did.

"Men have stared longer at a lot less," Lucy said with a shrug. There was no need for modesty if you had the goods and you felt good about showing them. It'd been instrumental in boosting her own confidence once she realized she could turn heads.

In grade school *freckle face* insults fell by the wayside as the boys who tormented her just a year or two earlier suddenly vied for her number.

Lucy gazed down at her body, stretching across the pool

chair. It was impossible to think of anything other than her father trying to touch her.

Somebody get me a robe.

She sat on her hands in an effort to stop shuddering. Her eyes were next, welling up behind the bug frames, relieved she didn't choose glasses like bikinis. These puppies were so large she felt like she was behind a Halloween mask.

That suited the afternoon fine. No need to explain things to Molly. Bad enough she'd had a weak moment with Jack. He was in pity mode now, even concluding an earlier phone call with the obligatory, *"Let me know if there's anything I can do."* That was never going to stop. Jack was about to become her personal white knight.

The thought prompted a quiet laugh. What was Jack Markle going to do? His concern should've warmed her, but she felt like mocking it instead.

Molly continued to prattle. "I don't know why I'm freaking out, it's not as though Allen has ever been able to keep a relationship longer than a few weeks, right? He'll be done with her soon enough."

"He kept you for longer," Lucy said, unable to mask the boredom in her voice. It pissed her off that Allen had been right about inviting her up for the summer.

"Yup! So I guess that means we're going to get back together at some point. We're practically made for one another. He's never been able to make it work with anyone else."

Lucy considered appealing to Molly's last bastion of common sense, but decided against it. That skull was thicker than a phone book, and soaking up the June sun was a real drain on her motivation. Besides, Molly's *Degrassi*-ish problems couldn't have felt more trivial right now.

So she listened.

Heard a lot more about Allen Taylor than she'd ever wanted to hear. Molly drudged up some old classics, such as the time she and Allen spent the night in the back of Lucy's Civic—not a wink of sleep between them, she was sure to include.

Every pining word, every nostalgic syllable filled Lucy with equal parts disgust and disdain. This stupid bitch was unrelenting!

Back off, Lucy reminded herself. *She doesn't know. No way she'd be droning on about this if she knew what was bothering you.*

That made her feel worse. "Molly," she said. "Don't take this the wrong way, but I feel like shit. I'm gonna head back to my room and catch a nap."

"Too much sun?"

"Yes."

"I'll sit out a while longer and work on my tan. Plus, look at that forty-five year old father over there. How bad does he want us?"

Yeah, we must be hot stuff if desperate dad is looking. "I'll see you later."

"Still on for clubbing tonight?"

"Call me, okay?"

Lucy wasn't outside the pool area when her lip began quivering. She bit the inside of her cheek and quickened her pace to the lobby, feeling dirty, cheap, and ugly in the light of this morning's events.

Her eyes were wet and tears streaked down her face without control. She broke into a jog, eager to get back to her room.

Out of sight.

●

A wonderfully relaxing day on the links proved to Allen that he still knew how to swing a golf club.

Stepping back onto the fairway made him feel as though he'd never left. It had been over a year since he last set foot on the green, and he wasn't sure he could still tee off like he used to.

Golf skills weren't like riding a bike. You needed to continue working at your game in order to maintain it. This course was a par 72, and he'd come in two under for the day. The magic was still there.

He took the long way back to the cabana, walking the darkened nature trails that wove throughout the grounds. There was much less danger of running into a drunk and attention-starved Molly Perkins this way.

His phone rang.

"Elisabeth, what's up?"

"I need to see you tonight, Allen. Come to my place at nine-thirty." Her voice was a whisper, spoken with urgency.

"What happened? Shit, I've got your car don't I? Need me to come and get you?"

"I'm fine. I do not mean for you to worry."

"Too late."

"Don't. Just meet me at nine-thirty."

He kept the receiver pressed to his ear until he was certain she'd hung up.

Why the mystery?

Allen was tense as he got back to the room. Jack wasn't going to be happy that tonight's double feature was off, but there was nothing to be done.

If Jack didn't like that it was because he didn't understand, or was too selfish to care. Funny how Elisabeth made everything else seem unimportant.

Jack wasn't there. Allen considered this a stroke of luck. He grabbed his personal things like a cat burglar, taking only what was most valuable: mints, body spray, and a handful of rubbers. Then he made a clean break.

Allen held his breath while dialing Jack's cell. The call dropped him to voicemail so he muttered some nonsense about plans he'd forgotten he'd made.

My lucky night.

It wasn't yet nine-thirty, so he spent the next hour navigating Greifsfield's back roads while contemplating whatever bombshell Elisabeth was about to drop. He always figured she was too perfect and that some dashing ex-lover would reappear in her life just in time to complicate matters.

He hoped it *was* that and nothing more. A tough guy could be dealt with. He might even welcome something like that because he wanted to prove his mettle to the woman he loved.

What type of guy might Elisabeth go for?

Allen couldn't answer that. It was easy to imagine her alongside some trendy artist or designer, but he didn't think so. What about the contrarian image of a burly biker sporting head-to-toe body ink—grim reapers, zombies, demons. Maybe. He didn't want to rule out a pretentious coffee drinker, either.

He turned onto her street at twenty past nine. A little early, but waiting was torture. At the end of the quiet road he banked left and rolled up a dark and narrow driveway.

Elisabeth's place was nothing but a silhouette against a sea of trees.

The sliding door was unlocked. He slipped inside the living room and stretched across the leather couch, determined to relax.

But he couldn't.

He took up pacing, wondering again what sort of urgent topic his girlfriend wanted to speak about.

She can't be breaking up with me.

Maybe she could. She hadn't granted him access to her body yet. Two weeks was a long time to go without getting his tip wet. Was she uninterested?

That'd be a first.

He had a regular workout regimen, ate right, and removed beer from his recreational diet.

The result was a tight stomach, shapely arms, and the beginning of a taut and toned six-pack. He fucking loved when women traced his definition with their tongues. He wanted to feel Elisabeth enjoying his body as much as he would enjoy hers.

Please don't let it be a break-up.

He paced his way over to the bar and poured a half glass of Johnnie Walker Black. It didn't do a damn thing to steady his nerves. From the large bay window overlooking the driveway, the Mitsubishi was a shadow on the dark gravel.

Where in the hell was she? How did she get around without her car? The ex-boyfriend theory strengthened.

Allen felt hot. The alcohol was partly to blame, but so was the aggressive humidity. He stepped outside, closing the door behind him. The mountain air was pure and deep breaths of it helped slow his heart.

More time passed and no one came. He was going to insist on buying her a cell phone tomorrow, providing he was still in this relationship.

A sharp gasp cut through the night. A harsh intake of air suddenly severed. Allen froze and the hairs on his neck stood on end. He remained still and hoped not to hear it again.

It could've been anything. They were in the country, surrounded by a host of unfamiliar sounds.

The deck's motion light switched off. The darkness was like being draped with a heavy blanket. Another burst of anguish shot off somewhere in the forest gloom.

It can't be her, he thought and trotted down the steps. *Why would it be?*

His advance to the tree line was cautious. More so reluctant. The motion light cut the dark and gave full view of the impenetrable forest. He stepped between two hemlocks and squinted into the haze.

The porch light clicked back off. Allen sidestepped some fallen branches as his eyes adjusted to pitch blackness.

What the hell am I doing out here?

Allen was a rational man and knew full well this was stupid. He could live his whole life without knowing what freakish woodland creature could expel that alien a sound.

You hope that's what it is.

Still, the idea of Elisabeth being in trouble propelled him without delay.

Trees closed in, forming a constrictive pine canopy. Not an ounce of moon glow could be seen beneath it.

Alone in the dark.

Not alone.

There *was* someone out here. His hands acted like feelers as he moved, the only way to prevent a headlong collision with a tree trunk.

A moonbeam broke through a slat in the piney overhang, throwing a spotlight on a clearing further ahead.

A human whimper brought him to another halt and the forest seemed to go mute because of his curiosity. Even the insects were silent, daring him to make the next move.

He cursed and kept moving. It might've been a terrible idea, but he didn't care. Someone was out here and needed help. If it wasn't Elisabeth he couldn't simply forget what he'd heard.

The noise sounded again. A throaty moan slithered from the shadows. He wanted to call out, but courage had long fled. There was something sinister about the hiss and, the closer it got, the more he realized how foolish he had been.

Repeated stomps, fists pounding dirt, grew louder.

Allen was too terrified to move, too reluctant to go further. The pounding grew louder.

Fast approaching.

A gallop.

Something charged for him. He spun around and caught sight of a flailing shadow growing larger with each trot. It had no discernible shape, but was coming fast.

Allen ran, his shoulder slamming against a tree as soon as he got speed. The side of his body fell numb and his legs bucked with a few frivolous staggers. He wasn't outrunning this. It was just behind him. Hot breath spraying down the small of his back. He kept moving, or tried to. His head throbbed and he knew at once he had smashed more than just his arm.

The side of his face was soaked, humidity dripping from his hair. Dizzy, injured, he dropped to the dirt and rolled onto his back to face whatever animal wanted him, fists clenched and ready to lash. If he could strike the beast's nose or mouth, he might still have a chance.

It was a wolf. Far bigger than anything he'd ever seen on TV. It got onto its hind legs and towered over him, snarling and swiping his fist away with talons like daggers.

Allen pulled his bloody hand back with a whelp. Crimson shards reached back and splattered hot against his skin. He kicked up dirt as he scurried back, but the wolf narrowed its eyes and plowed through it. It wasn't about to let him escape.

It lashed at him with those claws. He whelped again as his clothes and flesh turned to shredded ribbons. He collapsed onto his good side and the animal lashed again, ripping his left arm, blood drenching the wolf's pelt.

The predator sunk its front paws down, piercing his shoulders. Then it dropped back to all fours, its weight knocking the wind from him.

Allen tried to scream but all he managed was a sputter. The wolf brought its snout to the tip of his nose, a growl constantly rumbling at the back of its throat.

White-hot pain ignited from every wound. The wolf sniffed him with curiosity, cocking a head to study him.

Beneath Allen's terror remained enough rationale to be incredulous about life's end. He thought back to the kickball games on the St. Anna's School playground in fifth grade. Racing to a friend's house after school for *Resident Evil* on PlayStation. Not a care in sight.

Life seemed so open. So possible. If he had known at ten years old that he was halfway through his menial existence, he wouldn't have taken anything so seriously.

His vision blurred. The last thing he saw was a pair of bulbous blue eyes looking down at him.

His last thought before oblivion was of Elisabeth. At the end, he had been in love. He was thankful to have experienced it.

If only he could see that face one last time.

Allen hoped his parents' faith hadn't been misplaced. They taught him to believe in God. In the afterlife. And he did. Most days. That meant he'd see her again one day.

Allen was thinking about how much he couldn't wait for that when the snarling beast sunk its jaws through his torn shoulder.

He screamed out, spit blood that plopped back into his face, shook in violent spasms as the wolf ate, and then was gone.

●

Arlo Losey heard the knock at the front door.

"Is it Derek?"

"Nothin' you gotta be fussin' about," he said and slid his feet out from beneath the sheet.

Goddamn it, when did it get so hard to climb out of bed? His knees cracked and popped as he swung his legs down off the mattress. The bamboo floor felt cold on his feet but there was no time to fumble around for slippers, there was that knocking again.

Didn't they have the good sense to realize decent people

were asleep at this hour?

He shuffled toward the front door when Bessie stirred back in the bedroom. "Arlo, is Derek finally here?"

"Don't you move a muscle, dammit. I'll be comin' right back."

When Bessie didn't protest, he headed toward the knocking again.

Poor bird, he thought. You read about confusion, dementia, Alzheimer's—whichever one she had. It had a pretty good hold on Bessie. Started on her months ago, right after the cancer did. That's when she started looking for Derek.

Arlo didn't have the heart to tell her their son had been dead for five years. Killed in the desert while hunting towelheads. The United States government told him their boy made the ultimate sacrifice, but he didn't see it that way. Shit, Bessie was lucky she couldn't remember.

Was getting ready to join him anyway.

Arlo pulled open the door and stared up at the wide shoulders of a powerful shadow.

He didn't recognize this man but knew the reason for his visit.

"Sheeit," he said, ushering the gigantic son of a bitch through. "Here I was thinking you weren't gonna show yer face 'round here."

The visitor's face came to the light by way of the old wall lantern, offering Arlo his first real look at the man all of Greifsfield wanted to meet.

He was a big bastard, real bruiser. Shoulders broad enough to land on with arms the size of tree stumps. His jawline was jagged and his eyes were steel and cold. He looked like any one of those Kraut bastards he'd unloaded on in WWII. His appearance startled Arlo, who had been expecting a slippery, evangelical type.

The visitor smiled and extended a hand. "Of course, Mr.

Losey. I completely understand your frustration. I had every intention of meeting you and your lovely wife this afternoon, but there were unexpected tribulations that prevented me from making your acquaintance. I only make myself available to you now because I fear I will not be able to do so for the next several days. From what I understand, your wife is in a lot of pain."

Arlo found his smile uncharacteristically warm. It lessened the severity of his other features, every last one of them harsh.

"Doctor ain't sure how much time she's got," Arlo said. "Cancer is spreading inside her faster than socialism in this country."

His laugh was polite but dismissive. "Of course, Mr. Losey."

"Arlo."

"I am Anton Fane."

Arlo made damn sure his smile was polite, but it couldn't mask his skepticism.

Fane must've noted his hopelessness. "I realize this seems impossible, Arlo. I understand some of your trusted friends, people you've known for a very long time, have vouched for my services. I only wish to offer people such as your wife an escape from the terminal illness that defines them."

"People have talked, yessir."

"Good. Please take me to her."

They walked side-by-side to the bedroom, Fane's physique filling the hallway as they went.

"This is as far as you go, Arlo."

Fane stopped him with a hard press against his frail, old man's chest. "You're not going to like what you hear, at least not at first. Please understand it is a byproduct of this service. It will happen to you, too, but not yet. You appear to be in both good health and mind."

"When you're eighty years old, son, you're thankful you

can still wipe your own ass. But I want to watch. I got a right to see what you're doing to my wife."

Fane shook his head with a soft turn, and then patted Arlo's shoulder. "I'm afraid you wouldn't be able to process the remedy. It's quite radical and it may come as a shock. For that reason alone, I never allow an audience to witness the rebirth."

"How the hell do I know this is going to work? I ain't never seen you before, and now you're telling me to leave you alone with my wife?"

"In a few short days you will recognize this as the gift it is. Not only will she be cancer-free, but will have no more trouble remembering things. You'll have her back the way she was before the sickness. The woman you loved."

"I still love Bessie."

"Of course. Of course. You're skeptical Mr. Losey and rightfully so, but if you don't trust me, have faith in your acquaintances who've told you about how I have improved their quality of life."

Ain't so sure about that, Arlo thought.

Wasn't like old Bill to lie, let alone Maddie, but this miracle seemed like science fiction, and he never liked that horseshit.

"She's dead either way, I suppose," Arlo said.

"Not either way," Fane said. "This will grant the two of you more time together. Much more time."

Arlo didn't need much time to think it over. It was this or watch the old gal whither and, after six more months of suffering, die.

"Do it, Mr. Fane. Please."

That warm smile again. "It is my pleasure. Now please, my associate, Mestipen, is outside the front door. Go to him. He will elucidate so you are not completely closed off to what I am doing. I will warn you though, do not come in here after me. If you do, I am not responsible for what happens. Leave it to me and everything will be fine."

"You don't have to say that again, sir."

"Good." Fane placed his hands on Arlo's shoulders and looked him square in the eye. "You are making the right decision. Not only for her. Not just for you. But for this town. And the only thing I ask in return is that you remember this. What I did for you."

Arlo forced his skepticism aside as best he could while Fane pushed in on the bedroom door. Bessie's startled cries were immediate. Beyond that came a tear, followed by a howl punctuated by harsh gurgles and crunches.

This had to be a mistake. His hands stiffened on the doorknob while his wife called out in conscious panic. Fane's words crawled his thoughts and encouraged him to overlook the struggle.

But how could he?

That was his wife.

For how much longer? Doesn't even recognize you some days.

He turned and headed for the front of the house, thinking that Anton Fane's associate best have a good explanation for whatever the hell was happening in there.

●

Molly was glad to be back in her room.

A thrust of her hips slammed the cabana door. She leaned against it, rocking her head from side to side. Everything in here was spinning.

She'd mixed it up with a group of local kids tonight, chugging tequila and Jager like it wouldn't be there tomorrow. There had been temptation to keep going, to boost her self-esteem. Each guy had expressed interest in bedding her, but she got what she needed out of the festivities.

Attention.

That was enough. No need to compound her errors by making a drunken ass out of herself two nights in a row.

Steps toward the bedroom were slow and careful, and she was determined not to fall victim to the spiraling room.

The comfort of the king size bed promised a satisfying end to the evening. She dropped onto it and kicked her Prada sandals into the shadows. They thudded against something she couldn't see.

Right, lights are off.

Maybe it was a good idea to at least flick the bathroom switch. A little background glare never hurt anyone, and there was a good chance she'd wake up in the middle of the night in a hurry to get there. Her head was already worse than it had been a second ago and she dropped back onto the box spring, rubbing her temple with an exasperated moan.

"I'm never drinking again," she slurred.

Molly knew full well, even beneath a booze-soaked haze, that Allen was the real reason for calling it a night. Their confrontation continued to nag her. She hadn't given him a single reason to want to spend any time together, a fact she had trouble reconciling.

He was winning the game so far.

Molly's lips were dry and her throat scratchy. As drunk as she was, she had upset herself with that realization and spent a few minutes tossing and turning before abandoning the endeavor. She made it to the kitchen on wobbly knees, determined to purge the threat of a consecutive hangover.

Once her thirst was quenched, she toggled the living room dimmer to its lowest setting and stripped naked, leaving her clothes strewn about as she headed for the bathroom. A nice bath would clear her head once and for all.

She emptied half the bubble bath bottle into the tub, watching it fill to the brim with foam. A faint coconut scent lifted into the air and made the cabana smell like suntan lotion and tropical drinks. Molly eased herself into the steamy water, dipping beneath the lather and nestling into the corner. She moistened a facecloth and twisted it free of excess water, placing it atop her forehead hoping to steam the headache into submission.

So she waited, letting the piping hot bath soothe her whole body. Muscular tension and mental weight came away as she stretched out beneath coconut bubbles, amazed by how quickly things fell into perspective.

Of course.

The challenge wasn't to win Allen back, but get on good terms with him. Starting with an apology he wouldn't be expecting. Over the course of their turbulent relationship there had never really been an instance where she'd expressed regret, even when she'd been at fault. This would make him think she'd changed.

Then, as he was out with his forty-year-old whore, Molly's apology would grow from the back of his mind. It wouldn't be enough, of course, but it would make the gears turn. He'd realize she had changed.

From there, it would be important for Allen to catch glimpses of her around the Big East, preferably with other men. Make him think the apology had been sincere and for peace of mind only. Make him think she'd moved on. That was going to be the fun part.

Phase two.

She knew Allen well. The last time he broke it off it had only taken her lips around a few of his friends to reignite the flame. This time she'd prove to him she could have any man she wanted.

He'd come calling because he liked challenges.

Molly didn't plan to give in right away. Allen was going to have to fight for her affection. And then, when he proved how much he needed her, she'd watch him crawl back on hands and knees—just in time for senior year. In time for them to start planning the rest of their lives.

A knock at the cabana door jostled her out of a sudsy day-dream where she and Allen were moving into a three-car garage home at the end of a cul de sac.

Molly pulled the facecloth from her eyes and winced at the bathroom light. She lifted from the tub and stepped onto the fluffy, pink throw rug as suds and water dripped off. Shuttering in the chilly cabana air she reached for a towel.

Through the peephole Elisabeth leaned against the lamppost, arms folded across her chest.

Molly opened the door before she even knew why.

Elisabeth's smile was cool and her eyes fell to the towel pulled tight against Molly. She wore a dark dress that was cinched at the waist and cut low enough to display her firm assets.

It must've been the liquor, but Molly had to admit this bitch had game. A challenge she might not be able to conquer.

Elisabeth spoke once it became clear Molly wasn't about to.

"Hello." Her voice was calm, devoid of emotion. "I thought we might be able to speak for a few moments."

"Uh, I guess so." Molly's heart pounded as the prospect of getting punched in the mouth became a concern.

"Shall I come inside, or would you prefer to do it out here? I know it's summer, but the night air does bring a bit of a chill, and it seems you may be underdressed."

"Right." Molly stepped aside and gestured for her rival to enter. She considered running into the other room for a change of clothes, but decided against it. No sense in being intimidated. She'd worked hard to hone her body over the last year, and tonight's adventure was proof of her success. So she stood her ground in a small white towel, facing the woman currently in possession of the man she intended to win back.

This was war and there was no time for weakness.

"Let me reintroduce myself, please. I am Elisabeth Luna."

"That your real name?" It took all of Molly's efforts not to scoff.

"It is. My parents were from a small village in Romania."

"You're foreign?"

"I grew up there, though I remember very little about that life now."

"Anyway," Molly said, believing this hag to be even older than suspected. "I'm Molly Perkins."

Elisabeth circled the room, stepping around discarded clothing. Her stare never breaking from Molly's.

"Of course I know you, Molly Perkins. Allen practically begged me not to come here, you know. He thought you would do something crazy like try and attack me. I find his opinion of you... amusing."

Molly hated passive-aggressive people.

"I do not mean you any insult," Elisabeth said. She walked into the kitchenette and peered out the window at the forest's dark underbrush. Her dress, a deep shade of blue, clung tight and illustrated a figure Molly envied.

Elisabeth turned in time to catch her looking. "Allen thinks you're crazy," she said and took a step toward her. "I do not." Her face was stoic. Almost threatening.

"Look," Molly said with rising impatience.

"I mean to say the two of us are very much alike. I understand why you grew so incensed at the sight of Allen and I. You've got a fiery side, same as me. I want you to know I respect that."

Molly laughed loud and hard. This woman, probably five years from menopause, *gloated* in the middle of her room.

"You know what, uh, Elisabeth? I'm not super comfortable with this."

Elisabeth smirked, studying the outline of Molly's body beneath the towel. "With what? Our discussion?"

"It's not much of a discussion from where I'm standing."

"Well then we must sit." Elisabeth went into the bedroom and sat on the edge of the bed.

Molly only stared. "Are you fucking nuts? Get out of my bedroom!"

Elisabeth was unfazed by her temper. She stayed where she was, narrow and shifty eyes daring Molly to make the next move.

Refusing to be outdone, Molly strode in with confidence. She would not be the one who yielded. She sat close enough to notice Elisabeth's eyes weren't actually blue, but an exotic amalgamation of blue, green, and hazel. Transfixing wild fire. Their gazes locked.

Neither woman willing to back down from whatever this was.

Elisabeth leaned back on her arms and watched Molly with marginal interest behind a sleek grin that felt condescending.

Molly's first instinct was to grab the bitch by her jet-black mane and drag her kicking and screaming to the door. She suppressed the impulse just long enough for Elisabeth to get another sentence out.

"I did not come here looking to fight."

"Oh really?"

"That is that last thing I want. I'm here to talk, nothing more."

As angry as Molly was, and as much as she wanted Elisabeth wiped from the picture, her civility was impressive. Almost likable in a weird way.

Or maybe I'm just too chickenshit to put an end to this with a solid fuck you.

There was a comfortable gap between them, despite Molly being close enough to smell Elisabeth's lilac scented skin. She crossed her legs and inadvertently flashed a generous display of thigh.

Elisabeth glanced at Molly's exposed flesh. Her eyes lingered, making no motion to hide it.

"What's on your mind?" Molly asked, suddenly uncomfortable.

"Last night you said some things about me which I might have been offended by had I not been able to understand so well."

"Okay."

"You're still in love with Allen. He might not realize that, but I only needed to look in your eyes to see it."

Was this what it sounded like? Was she conceding? Maybe Elisabeth was intimidated by true love and decided not to stand between it.

Maybe I could like her, after all.

Elisabeth angled herself toward Molly. "You're a passionate person. The things you said, to someone you'd never met, were abrasive. I did not take offense, though. It came from the heart."

"Thanks?"

Elisabeth put a hand on Molly's exposed knee and watched her face for a sign of rejection. When none came, she kept it there.

Molly's emotions were a mess. They threatened to tear and spill. She was too numb to feel Elisabeth's hand, thinking instead about how she could not afford to be intimidated by this forwardness. Hoping her gut was right and that her enemy was here to surrender. It felt that way. Or maybe it was those fingers she felt, working her leg with a technique like a massage on knotted muscles.

It might've been the remnants of the Jager shots, but Molly found herself entranced by the kaleidoscopic nature of Elisabeth's eyes. Their color was both relaxing and sensuous, maybe a little trusting. The room around them fell away, and Molly could look nowhere else.

Am I fucking crazy, she thought.

Full and luscious lips were dabbed with mischief in the form of a grin. When she spoke, her voice was soft and throaty—devoid of the malice that had been there earlier. Molly submitted, carried willingly to a place she'd never been.

She sat with her mouth agape, listening to Elisabeth's words, but staring at her mouth. At those lips.

"I'm not going to come between that kind of emotion. That kind of love." Elisabeth spoke tenderly and her hand skirted the length of Molly's thigh. A finger reached the smooth curve of her buttock and traced it back and forth while their eyes remained locked.

The touch was electrifying. Unlike anything she'd ever felt. Her head fell back with a sigh. A muffled cry of ecstasy lazed out.

This is exactly what I need right now.

Elisabeth leaned in, bringing the lilac aroma with her. Molly let it fill her nostrils, awakening even more unanticipated urges. She moistened even before the dark-haired beauty pressed her mouth to hers. Molly's mouth parted to receive her lips. She couldn't believe they were natural. Pillow soft, with each pat offering sensuous comfort. Molly moaned with delight each time they pushed on her.

"I want someone capable of that passion," Elisabeth whispered between kisses.

If Molly's emotions had been confused before, they were jangled beyond reprieve now. She couldn't lie to herself about this, every one of these feelings and desires felt right. She allowed Elisabeth's kisses wherever she planted them, and kissed back with frenzied eagerness. She wanted to feel her everywhere.

In some ways, this was like her fist time all over again.

The confidence she lacked was abundant in Elisabeth, who worked a hand over Molly's toweled body, stroking her guarded breasts while slipping her palm beneath her leg, caressing with firm grips.

Molly bit her lower lip and whimpered. Elisabeth's hand trailed to her inner thighs, growling with approval over Molly's readiness.

"I want to see you," she said and tore the towel from her body.

Molly covered herself in reflex, embarrassed by her body in that moment. There was no good reason to be ashamed, but self-consciousness couldn't be reasoned with.

Elisabeth looked at her with an expression of raw lust. She was the perfect combination of angel and devil, and when she waved a finger back and forth to protest Molly's bashfulness, it was all that was needed in order to exorcise her hang-ups.

"I want to see everything," Elisabeth said.

"So do I." Molly tried matching that level of confidence, but her trembling tone betrayed her words.

Elisabeth didn't seem to mind. She stood and unfastened the fabric belt on her dress, conceding her curves until the straps glided off her arms and fell, revealing the most incredible nude body Molly had ever seen.

Before she could finish admiring, Elisabeth dropped atop her, soft breasts and hard nipples sweeping against her own. Molly grabbed Elisabeth's head through the rain of black hair, pulling her close. Her tongue went exploring first, pushing inward without resistance, desperate to convey newfound affection for her former enemy.

Elisabeth ventured down her neck, marking her descent with wet kisses.

Molly's body was primed to explode. When Elisabeth's mouth moved to the crevice between her breasts, she arched her back and screamed out. Elisabeth responded by pinching her nipples, biting and sucking.

This was unbelievable. Beyond a few superficial party kisses, she had never been much for the same sex. This combination of physical pleasure and emotional connectivity brought companionship greater than any man in her life had been capable of.

It felt amazing to be desired.

Elisabeth's mouth left trails of saliva on her stomach, on her outer and inner thighs, and all the way down to her feet. She took time to work Molly's toes, licking and sucking them—somehow of the knowledge that Molly loved having it done. A current surged all the way to her head, and the only thing she could do was squeeze her eyes shut and beg for more. It was unlike anything. It couldn't stop. Not yet.

She glanced down and begged Elisabeth to keep going.

But Elisabeth did not. She let Molly's feet drop and angled her head in such a way that her pronounced cheekbones and jutting tongue gave a sinister appearance. She lashed out and took Molly's hips, lifting her onto her side and pressing her mouth to the small of her back and buttocks.

Molly was in tears, eyes wetter than anything else. She slid a hand between her legs to stimulate herself while Elisabeth worshipped her curves.

"No." The whisper was short and harsh. An order that Molly would not dare violate. "Do not hurry this."

"Taste me, then." Molly's confidence continued to stun her in the moment.

Her thighs pressed on Elisabeth's head, and her hand tussled her lover's hair. Cries of "yes" and "don't stop" became the songs of the session. Bodies thrashed and sweat slicked their flesh with increased abundance, despite the frosty central air hum. Every now and again, she caught a glimpse of Elisabeth's determined eyes, the look only making her crazier.

So crazy that Molly came twice at the mercy of Elisabeth's tongue. When the lilac beauty crawled up between her legs for a kiss, Molly realized how much she missed her mouth. The thought of tasting herself was arousing in strange and nasty ways that had never been stimulating before. With a pounding heart and coursing blood, all she could think about was how dirty she wanted to get.

It was Elisabeth who was going to benefit.

Molly shifted her weight and rolled on top, exploring the voluptuous body with an open mouth. Elisabeth spread eagle, pushing Molly's head into her.

Her thighs were muscular and smooth and she loved the way they felt against her cheeks. No disgusting, steely body hair to contend with here, just a figure so soft and perfect.

Elisabeth rocked her hips to meet Molly's mouth. Her juices were sweet on her tongue. A far cry from the veiny, hairy obstructions she was used to. Men were not capable of passion like this. Tonight, Molly had never felt sexier. There was no pressure here, just mutual adoration.

No worrying about using too much teeth to get him there, and if she never had to hear *"did you cum yet?"* again, she might never go back to playing for the other team.

But that was getting ahead of things. Right now, Molly's world was the size of a sweaty bed, inhabited by only two.

Once spent, they straightened out and Molly reached for the cabana's central air dial, cranking it. Nestling into Elisabeth's sweaty arms was the perfect conclusion to an unexpected evening.

"I've never felt anything like that before."

Elisabeth said nothing in response and instead kissed her head and cheek.

Molly hugged her tight, pressing against her body as they reclaimed their breaths. Central air spilled from the vents in steady gusts that cooled their body temperatures. Molly pulled the bed sheet up and got under it to hide her goose bumps. Elisabeth remained atop, staring at the ceiling in silence.

Does she regret this?

Molly sidled up to her hoping she did not. Another kiss atop her head said she was probably safe. She was comfortable at last and, as great as the sex was, it was no match for cuddling. It was a chance to lay and reflect on the sweaty exchange. Embracing the woman she had been certain she despised brought strange waves of comfort.

Life was funny like that.

Tonight's pleasant surprise started her thinking about Allen all over again. Only now he didn't seem so integral to her happiness. In fact, he seemed kind of repulsive. She wanted to ask Elisabeth how she felt, but thought it could wait until morning.

Would she be willing to kick Allen to the curb?

Hell, I think I might be.

After one bout of lovemaking, Elisabeth had succeeded in making Molly feel necessary—an emotion she was already addicted to.

Maybe this was the beginning of something truly special.

She drifted to sleep, consumed by thoughts of Elisabeth and what she hoped would be the beginning of an incredible relationship.

●

She awoke shivering and the bed was empty.

The air was so cold now she thought she saw her breath against the dresser clock's digital glow. It was a little after four. She'd been asleep for two hours.

"Elisabeth?"

She curled up and pulled the sheet tight, hoping to settle the chill. She waited with her eyes closed for several more minutes, only able to think about why Elisabeth was no longer here.

Please, no. She wouldn't leave me.

Her mind raced to all the worst conclusions as she got up

without bothering to dress.

The living area light should've been on, but the room was dark. Off of it, the bathroom door was ajar and equally black.

"Molly."

The familiar voice comforted her pessimism. From beyond the bathroom's slivered door, Elisabeth said, "Come here."

"You okay?" Molly did as she was told.

Elisabeth was shrouded in blackness, standing against the rear wall. Molly's eyes adjusted in time to make out her naked silhouette. She reached for the light switch.

"No," Elisabeth hissed, her voice dirty gravel. "Do not do that."

Startled by this urgency, Molly yanked her hand away as if reeling from electric shock. What in God's name was wrong with Elisabeth's voice?

"Come, Mollyyyyyy." Her name trailed off in an agonized snarl. "Come heeeeeere." Was there a hint of laughter there?

"I'll call someone, okay? You sound sick."

"Not sick."

Right. Molly stepped away.

Time to call for help. If tonight's tryst had been the result of some drug-fueled instinct, Molly didn't think she could handle the disappointment. It had felt so pure. There wasn't time to think about that anyway. Elisabeth needed help and she was going to call for it.

"Just come here, Molly." Elisabeth cleared her throat. It sounded like a wad of phlegm was wedged in there. "Let me touch you again."

Conflicting feelings arouse in Molly. A reluctant step forward, progress halted by the appearance of two bluish-yellow orbs hanging suspended in the darkness, appearing over Elisabeth's silhouette—right where her eyes would be. They grew into perfect circles as she stepped forward.

"Don't be scared."

Molly was a deer in headlights.

Elisabeth's eyes were no longer. They'd grown into hideous blue globes. Her face looked artificial and her skin, once impeccable, was rough and pulsing. Scraggly hair appeared on her forearms and shoulders, and that was nothing compared to her mouth. Jagged teeth so large they forced her lips into a permanent grin. She stood smiling like an insane jack o' lantern. Her breasts heaved and convulsed before disappearing beneath a tuft of fur, while her head tilted back to deliver a horrible laugh that was heavy and inhuman.

Molly screamed and ran.

But animal limbs wrapped around her naked body as she reached the sliding door. The struggle only provoked Elisabeth to hold tighter. Her strong forearms grew around Molly's torso with the constant crack of breaking bones. In desperation, Molly jammed her nails deep into throbbing arms. Her attacker let loose an animal's roar and then hurled her to the tile.

Molly's skull collided with the kitchenette's marble finish and her vision whitened. She wasn't yet recovered when the creature raked its talons across her back, stripping away flesh in perfect ribbons. Pain was hot and flaring. She scurried to her feet only to find herself face-to-face with a hulking animal.

A wolf.

Elisabeth snarled and flashed her teeth. Saliva pooled at the top of her gums, spilling onto a heaving, pink tongue. Blue eyes found Molly and followed her like the prey she was as she attempted to escape.

Elisabeth was faster and stronger and would stop her before she reached any exit. But even if Molly got outside, what then?

The only option was the bedroom. Molly darted for it, slamming the door behind her. The wolf roared and grunted, suggesting Molly would pay for that insubordination.

The inhuman sounds terrified her, every howl provoking an equal scream Molly couldn't control. How to process this? What happened to Elisabeth? She was sure she'd seen her turn into that thing, but that couldn't be right.

Could it?

Molly kept her weight against the door, fearing the wolf would pummel the low-density wood at any second. Where had she placed her damn cell phone?

It's always in my purse.

Which is where?

She hoped to see it on the end table or lying on the floor, but no dice. It had to be in the other room. The massive wolf snarled, reminding her that it might as well be on Mars.

There had to be another way out.

The door exploded into splinters. A hairy arm fired through and snatched hold of her throat with incredible speed. So fast she hadn't seen it happen.

Screams were severed by the animal's strengthened grip as her larynx buckled.

The wolf lifted her, leaving Molly kicking the air in helpless flails.

Suffocating, she clawed the creature's long fingers to pry one or two of them free. Her vision was a blur and gnarled black fingers tipped with pointed claws squeezed tighter still, drawing blood. Her breath was bottlenecked, escaping from her mouth in asthmatic wheezes.

The wolf shouldered through the door. A sliver of wood caught Molly's eyeball dead center. She reached for the stabbing pain while the creature dropped her once more. Instinctively, she pulled the splinter before her mind realized the severity of the wound. Vision sputtered out of the injured eye, leaving her periphery impaired.

The wolf hoisted her, this time in both arms. Its rancid

snout sniffed her naked flesh with curiosity. Behind those sickening eyes was a hint of the women she'd been with hours ago.

If she could reason with her.

But Elisabeth wasn't interested. She pushed Molly through the air, her bloodied back slamming against the wall. The decorative frames shook and then went crashing to the floor atop her.

Elisabeth grabbed her like a limp rag doll and hurled her onto the bed. Molly landed on rumpled sheets, spraying them with drippy, yellow-ish crimson that poured from her damaged eye. The black wolf climbed on top and yanked her upright with an ironclad grip on her scalp.

They were eye-to-eye once more.

Molly was horrified, despite sitting on the verge of unconsciousness. Her runny wounds triggered the wolf's hunger. Elisabeth shifted her weight, perching atop Molly on all fours. Her nostrils puffed, savoring the aroma. Her eyes wide with anticipation.

Molly realized with a sick, defeated feeling that everything earlier had been a warm up. An hors d'oeuvre for this monster.

Elisabeth's killing teeth flashed. Hot spittle smacked her chin. Her snout brushed against her neck. She bit Molly, tearing through her flesh with a savage grunt.

Molly's vocal chords stressed. What little voice she had left heightened into a shrill cry that might've cracked the bedside windows. Her chords stretched and snapped apart between the wolf's jaws.

Cries of protest were replaced by a spastic gargle. She wiggled and kicked the monster, anything to get rid of it.

Elisabeth continued her feast, undaunted, biting mouthfuls of flesh. A hunk from her love handles, a piece of thigh, and then a growling bite that clamped down and tore off one of her breasts.

Molly's eyes rolled back. The pain too great. Her body numb.

Elisabeth devoured her in thick, bloody pieces, chomping through bone without pause. Molly was only vaguely aware of it at this point, her eyelids heavy and muscles relaxed. There weren't more than a few seconds left. Just enough to feel one final devastating chomp into her belly.

And then there was nothing.

Four

Allen thought he was dead.

Knew he should've been.

The last thing he remembered were those hungry jaws coming down on him.

He was in the woods. Still. The familiarity of Elisabeth's back yard was lost, however. This was someplace worse. Surrounding foliage looked sickly. Wilted bark, broken branches, browned leaves. Apocalyptic fall. Gypsy moth webs blotted the overhanging canopy and resembled rotten clouds. Coiled weeds the color of ash matted his steps, and his legs were like Jell-O as he moved. The pain in his head was precise, like the tips of two rusty nails scraping the back of his eyes. Waves of acid reflux broke in his stomach.

Up ahead, torches danced. Crackling fire hissed and popped. Allen used his faltering sight and marginally better hearing to follow it from the gloom. The decaying forest led straight to an old graveyard where he felt like digging a hole and crawling in.

Most of the tombstones wore faded etchings. The worst of them had been traced over in hasty paint, a last-ditch effort to remember those long passed.

Torchbearers stood at the top of the hill beyond the stones, bound in a loose circle.

He might have been glad to see people after a long night,

but something about this congregation suggested they weren't looking for company.

Allen headed for them anyway, and it took every effort. His chest was tight, breathing labored. He shambled up the incline in a zombie's stagger.

The woman nearest the top took notice, watching his efforts with interest. She wore no clothing and her face suggested she felt no shame in that. Her torch threw scurrying shadows up and down her chunky figure, and the firelight revealed jagged glyphs carved into her skin, bordered by patches of moist blood.

But her face was somehow pleasant and he might have believed the lie if not for the contradictory circumstances surrounding them.

Every torch holder was nude. Erect men held fiery staffs overhead, staring with eagerness at the women posed in similar fashion. Each body was marked with fresh-carved wounds, though nobody seemed too concerned about the running blood.

Allen took an uneasy spot beside the inviting woman. She licked her lips and ran her free hand over a saggy breast. Her head turned and he followed her line of sight. The rest of the heads moved with them, settling on a small path at the hill's far side. Bodies began taking unified steps, marching toward it.

They descended in pairs, each moving to either side to form a fleshy corridor of human sconces that enabled Allen to find his way down.

When he got there, flailing, naked figures were entwined on the dirty graveyard floor. He recognized some of the fleeting faces as they passed through the sparking firelight. Some were resort guests while others he'd seen around town. Anxious bodies attacked one another with angry lust. Man on man, woman on woman, mixed company—it didn't matter. This was about gratification. He'd heard about these types of parties, just never in the forest around a family vacation spot.

This was pretty far from his scene—well beyond taking a few girls to bed at once. He'd always wanted two or three girls vying for his attention in the bedroom. It was a dream he had yet to forge. But there were too many men out here for his taste. It couldn't be arousing this way.

Allen didn't like watching guys finish their business in porn movies, let alone hearing their moans and seeing their o-faces up close and personal.

He nearly stepped on an elderly woman. Her mud-slapped thighs were apart, and an eager head hovered between them. He might've passed the awkward sight without thinking twice until he noticed the head was disembodied. The lady gripped its remaining hair wisps and dangled it in front of her sex. A rotted tongue lapped and she buckled in ecstasy.

This should've shocked him. He wasn't so dazed to accept it as normal, but Allen was only revolted because a part of him felt that he should be. It was an easy thing to accept because his brain suddenly held knowledge that shouldn't be there.

The hungry head was all that remained of the old woman's husband. And she was glad to feel him on her body after so many years away. She was new here. Newer than Allen. There was no reason to question it further. It wasn't his place to judge.

A better man would have been revolted to the core. He roved the crowd and saw mothers fucking sons while daughters watched. Married adults carried on affairs, willingly reduced to sniveling sex objects, forced to endure the bloody and brutal whims of demanding partners as cuckolded husbands looked on, cheering and masturbating to violent dehumanization.

"Well, well, well…"

Amidst the sea of writhing bodies a woman ascended from a slithering pile of men. Her eyes glinted with recognition as desperate hands reached for her belly, legs, and what was between them.

"We've been waiting for you," she said. He shouldn't have been able to hear from so far away, but her voice was between his ears and louder than everything else.

Lithe steps carried her through the orgy, stepping over thrusting bodies, swatting away gropes like a house cat. Her hips swayed in the kind of hypnotic rhythm Allen found tempting, capable only of staring. It wasn't Elisabeth, though these movements were almost as timed.

"Have some fun," she said, reaching him at last. It was impolite to stare, though Allen found it hard to resist. Up close she was speckled with runny streaks of soapy body fluid. It coated her face, lips, and chest—the spend of every man here. What had he done to arouse such interest? Or was it simply because he was the last one to get some.

"You're with us now, sweetie."

Familiarity struck him like a ton of bricks.

Only one person had ever called him that. Not Elisabeth, or any former lover. It was so much worse. His body and mind refused to react accordingly, working instead to rationalize his attraction, reminding him that it was the result of body chemicals and, really, perfectly normal.

But fuck that. There was nothing normal about this. He tried making that point, but the stubborn side of Allen Taylor was in control now and would listen no longer.

Sweetie had been the last thing his mother had said to him as he'd gone out the door to Greifsfield.

"Don't be a stranger, sweetie."

He remembered this while staring into the matronly eyes of Jane Taylor.

Only it wasn't Mom as he knew her. Her hair wasn't silver and highlighted by fading streaks of brown. It was *entirely* brown and braided, flowing past her shoulders—a style he'd seen her wear in photographs. Her brown eyes held more vigor than ever, and her skin, especially around the eyes, was smooth and wrinkle-free. She cupped her breasts together in her hands and grinned ear-to-ear.

"Have anyone you want, sweetie. We're all yours, now. *All* of us, you know."

Jane's eyes reached back through the crowd to where his father's corpse was sprawled beneath a sexy young girl named Missy. She worked customer affairs at The Big East, and had sat around the pool with he and Jack the first night they had arrived in town.

"Get that shit hard," she said, kicking his father's purple, unresponsive face.

"Stop it," Allen called out, his voice lost beneath the music of sated moans. He was a helpless voyeur to this barbarism.

"This one's fucking dead," Missy said with a chuckle. Her announcement brought vultures from the crowd to converge on him.

The taste of vomit rose to the back of Allen's throat. He choked it down, somewhat grateful that something was at last bothering him.

His mother took his hand and placed it over her belly, forcing him to caress the globular bulge that hadn't been there a second earlier.

Something kicked inside her stomach.

"You know why you belong here?" Her voice was cruel. "Because I never wanted you. Right now you're rotting my insides. Sucking away my life as you come into yours. You didn't really think your birth would make a respectable woman out of this whore, did you?"

She swung the rusted kitchen knife suddenly tucked in her hand. Her clenched teeth and narrow eyes determined, unswayed by his protests drowning in a whirl of orgasms.

"I want you out of me, boy!" The blade plummeted. Her

ripened belly tore. The knife burrowed through her bump with an echoing *phlock*. She smiled and pulled it out in slow increments, giggles growing in volume with every inch of blade revealed.

Allen's instincts failed him as he stood witness to his own abortion.

Jane cackled and the knife sliced in and out, cutting her stomach until a flap of ragged skin dangled like an unhooked overall.

"Get *out!* Out of me!"

Her eyes shriveled into tiny, ambivalent beads. Her insane smile became a snarl. She threw the blade into the puddle of blood that swallowed her feet to her ankles, taking the desiccated fetus in between her thumb and forefinger and pulling it from incubation.

The preemie human, Allen, twenty-two years earlier, managed to raise his underdeveloped head. The strident newborn whine became a high-pitched hiss. It was all he could hear.

She threw the twitching fetus into the dirt where it flopped. Having dissected herself, she collapsed onto her hands, vomiting the same clear white liquid that splattered her skin. Her opened body cavity expelled every ounce of blood she carried. Her skin color drained until her flesh was nearly translucent.

Allen was ready to run when a hand seized him from behind. He tripped over the twisting bodies and landed against the corner of a gravestone. His head hurt far too much to bring any new pain sensations. A man dressed in military fatigues hovered above and a pointed boot crunched his neck, pinning him there.

Beside them, Jane continued gagging as she hoisted her ass into the air in a supplicating gesture, mumbling something that sounded like inspiration but came out an incoherent mumble.

Uncle Jett strengthened his heel on Allen's neck while grumbling.

"I should press down until I hear a snap. Put you out of your fuckin' misery, pussy boy."

Allen's windpipe buckled. He lapsed into a coughing fit.

"You are your father's son," Jett said. His voice sounded like he'd been up all night gargling razor blades. With Allen's incapacitation satisfying him, he turned his attention to Jane and lifted his boot heel.

"Watch this," he said, unbuckling his belt.

Jane moved into position while Jett slapped his palms against her jiggling behind.

It was time for Allen to stand. He had no desire to see this and needed to get far away. His legs were near useless, refusing to lift at the knee, willing only to shuffle.

That didn't matter because the orgy and its audience of torchbearers were gone. Behind him, so were Jett and Jane. The dying forest vanished next.

He stood on cement steps that led into a church. Its heavy mahogany doors were open and inviting, but he felt compelled to resist entrance. Past endless rows of pews, a blonde woman sat nude on a pillared stack of dirty bones. Her finger wagged in a hypnotic and beckoned call.

The blasphemous allure motivated him. It was inviting in ways it shouldn't have been. Something about the mockery of familiar iconography stirred urges he thought were held exclusively for Elisabeth.

Her fingers raked the stacked human remains, and her large breasts glistened in the blades of moon glow that stabbed through the altar's stained glass. Her long legs crossed and her foot slid across tanned shin.

He crossed the threshold, approaching the altar with reluctance and desire. There was something majestic about this woman that compelled him to pledge fealty. Magnetism that was impossible to resist, even if he wanted to.

He didn't.

His innards flashed hot white and he took hold of the

nearest pew to steady his lumbering weight. His back joined the brigade of other useless body parts ailing him. It cracked and sent him doubling over. He looked at the throne of skulls for answers. The satanic queen was slow to rise.

A trembling hand reached for her.

Why was it covered in thick brown hair?

Another flash.

The church was gone.

The wooded path was narrow and ever thinning as he walked it. A healthier forest than the one bordering the graveyard, his stuttering heart took the opportunity to slow. Nothing here to be scared of. His body relaxed. The pain rescinded.

He hastened his stride, legs eager to carry him someplace he didn't know.

The trail opened into a clearing centered by a glossy lake that was silent and undisturbed. On the far end, a human outline dipped a foot beneath the surface. An echo of concentric circles rippled outward.

The outline slipped from its clothing, revealing a woman's figure. Lenient steps brought her into the lagoon. With a splash, she was fully submerged.

Allen waited for several minutes but the swimmer never reappeared. The lake's surface quieted and fell solemn. Dead silence afforded him a moment to think back on the night. Only now was he beginning to understand how wrong all of this had been.

The swimmer darted up through the blue at Allen's feet. She propped herself on the embankment and her elbows rested in dirt.

Molly Perkins smiled.

"I think you should join me for a dip."

"I don't think so."

"C'mon, sexy. It'll relax you."

"I am relaxed."

She laughed, but the sound taunted him.

"That's funny?"

"*You're* funny. Are you afraid we're going to get back together because we occupy the same body of water for a few minutes?"

"No, it's just...I, uh..."

"You're stuttering. That means you're tense."

Molly's invitation brought much needed comfort. The impassiveness with which he'd witnessed the evening's events melted. Bottled panic spilled from him, leaving him affected by all he had seen.

"You're shaking. Allen, come on, I swear I'll behave."

Her familiarity promised security. It was just a swim with someone he knew (who happened to be naked). It would get his mind back into sorts (and get his rocks off).

Allen tugged his shirt collar and pulled it off. He unbuckled his belt and got rid of his jeans. Molly treaded water in silence. She drifted into the corner, avoiding pockets of moonlight, favoring shadows.

He stripped down to his boxers and asked if it was cold.

She shook her head.

"Why don't you come into the light so I can see you?" He stepped ankle deep into the icy lake. Goose bumps pocked his arms and legs.

She hoisted herself over the water to show the rigorous outline of her breasts.

"You want to see me, Allen, you're going to have to get a lot closer than that."

He waded in and swam for Molly's silhouette, surprised by how badly he wanted her.

She dipped beneath the black-blue for a moment. Then she held her corner perch, kicking her feet in a playful gesture that splashed him.

He felt her eyes watching with excitement.

Allen wouldn't need convincing tonight. His desire throbbed. He wasn't thinking about Elisabeth. She was nowhere to be found, and it was Molly who offered comfort. It was Molly who could take away his pain. It was Molly who would vanquish the horrifying images of his pregnant mother, the decadent mass, and the demon queen.

When he neared, she launched from the inlet and slapped against his chest, closing her arms around his neck. Her wet body slipped but he was determined to keep her near. His hands dove and squeezed her shapely ass. Her ample chest pushed in against his hardened abs and instigated his lust.

He went in with his tongue but her head snapped away to avoid it. Undeterred, he went for her tits, grabbing and squeezing with greed. She moaned and giggled. Without any effort at all, she again had everything she had wanted. He supposed that made him weak. That it put her in control. He didn't care. He needed Molly in this moment. Anything to take his mind off that severed head, his father's desecrated body, and Uncle Jett.

His neck hurt just thinking about that.

They were adrift and floating. Their bodies thrashed without aim. The splashing water enhancing the shared experience. Allen tore his attention away from her body, desperate to feel her mouth against his. That was the relief he craved.

Her lips were missing.

As was her nose. There was a crooked and triangular recess in the center of her face. One of her eyes had been drained of its color and was nothing more than a milky white blur, clear liquid spilling from its corners. Three jagged slashes ran the length of her face, destroying all the beauty that had once been present.

Allen screamed and kicked away. He spun and cut through the water with a desperate paddle. Molly giggled again and her voice was infantile.

An unflappable weight piled on his back and pushed him beneath the surface. He twisted until he was on his side and facing his attacker. Watery eyes showed Molly's mangled visage. Her shredded lips revealed the exposed gum line above and below her mouth. An awful grin and perverse mockery of her once infectious smile.

He screamed again, several gulps of water filling his lungs as two hands slid around his neck.

"Stay down here with me, Allen," she said. Her voice was crystal clear despite being under water. "With *us*."

Allen flailed but Molly was more powerful in death.

Then he realized what she'd meant by *us*.

Groans erupted off the lagoon floor. Cries of misery that grew louder and more constant as his struggle against the living corpse aided their descent.

Molly was determined to deliver him to those voices. Her expression intensified in what remained of her face as she positioned herself on top of him. Her thighs were clamps, locking and riding him to the nautical floor.

His back bowed against the pond's cold, jagged base. The surface was a glimmer of hope several feet beyond.

Calloused and blistered hands burst from the ground, wrapping his shoulders and fastening him there. Rotten arms broke through the rocky floor and clamped his feet. A third pair broke out, followed by a fourth and a fifth. They took his ankles, thighs, and stomach until he was locked.

Molly released her grip and hovered overhead like a perverse angel.

"We're keeping you, Allen."

He screamed, trying to appeal to her mercy. His mistake was assuming she had any left.

In his periphery, the pond floor exploded. Debris clouds

puffed. Bodies vaulted from gaping craters. They'd been people once, but were disarrayed corpses now. Flesh tones were gray, others rotted to the bone. Several of the bodies ambled toward him, wearing tattered clothing that flowed behind them like sails.

Two drifted near, their eyes hollow sockets, bowls of bone that cast judgment.

His deranged angel pumped an excited fist.

"Take him," she cried. "He did this to us."

Allen didn't know what that meant and couldn't ask.

He threw his mouth open, determined to drown before these things could have their way. Gallons of water filled his throat, but his consciousness remained firm.

Shimmering bodies took residence all around him. They dropped to their knees in unison, pulling him.

He screamed, his mouth a continued vacuum for pond water. Their grips were like Molly's, firm and impossible. He squirmed, but their constricting hands hadn't allowed their grips to waver.

Fingers closed around Allen's shoulder, piercing his skin and tearing his arm off. There was a loud POP as the limb broke, accompanied by an eruption of red water. At his heel, one of the zombies took his foot and bit through his big toe. Another explosion of crimson six feet away.

His attackers mumbled audible glee as the dismemberment continued.

Every bite and pop hurt worse than the last. He rocked his head, screaming in agony until his angel drifted back down, hovering horizontally so that their lengths matched. The mob of undead backed off to become a circle of horny onlookers.

"You're mine forever," she said and pressed her mutilated face to his. Her tongue glided out and plunged into his mouth, finally giving him what he wanted.

Only the muscle was coarse. Somehow dry, despite this

soggy grave. A reminder of the decaying body it belonged to. His nose poked into the rivets where her own had been.

Her fingers crawled like a spider along his wounded chest, slipping under his boxers and grabbing his shriveled penis. It fit entirely in the palm of her hand as her tongue continued to probe his protesting mouth.

"I love you baby," she said, squeezing until it popped.

He tried to swim but his waist had gone numb. Molly pushed on his chest, and he fell back against the lagoon floor while watching her dangle his severed member. Bloody contrails dissipated and she opened her palm and let his battered cock drop.

It sunk onto Allen's chest where the cut side faced him. Ligaments flailed against the current. The mob of creatures resumed their assault, pulling and tearing at his remaining appendages.

The last thing he saw was the dark outline of his unholy angel, ascending to the surface while grinning manically.

•

Lucy tried to enjoy the resort's complimentary breakfast of eggs, bacon, and toast while sitting on her room's small terrace overlooking the golf course.

Behind aviators she watched a foursome of elderly men struggle to carry their golf bags off hole three. Gold retirement jewelry hung from their necks and glinted off their wrists. They had the bread to stay here, but were apparently too cheap to pay for caddy service.

The sun inched over the Greifsfield forest tree line, but the rays hadn't yet cranked up the temperature to where swamp ass was a concern. Maybe today would bring the rain these mountains sorely needed.

There was still time to enjoy the slightly cool mountain

morning, and being out of the house was a huge plus.

Even though you're still on your father's dime.

Not for very much longer.

Maybe if Mom had been more sympathetic, or actually listened to reason, Lucy would've put more of an effort into making her understand. It was hard to escape the feeling of wasted effort. For some, the only way to make it through life was to deny reality.

For now, Lucy was content to communicate by text. Phone calls to the department store only when necessary. Until school came back around the fourth floor of the Big East would have to be home. She was tempted to leave town, but the endless bustle of this place offered more safety than hiding out in a Springfield apartment.

She thought about taking a cabana, but after booking Jack and Molly in two of them, it was impossible to justify taking more money away from the resort by sequestering a third. It wasn't her father she'd be hurting, but the maids and servers who depended on this place as a source of income.

The golfers spent the next fifteen minutes trying to tee off. After a series of frail and humiliating slices they succeeded in slapping their balls down the fairway. Slowly the plaid shirts moseyed off behind an embankment. Lucy dallied through an issue of Cosmo, amazed that staff writers were still capable of unearthing *99 Secret Sex Facts* after all these years.

She texted Molly after deciding it was too early for a phone call, curious as to whether or not she'd survived last night alone. She waited for the READ confirmation to appear. It didn't. Phone must've been off.

Just as well. There was another call to make.

Her fingers moved through her contact list like molasses. Mom answered before the phone had a chance to ring.

"Lucy, the store is incredibly busy this morning."

"Top o' the morning to you too."

"For real, I don't have time right now."

"I'm sure Carla can hold the fort for a few."

"She could, if she hadn't called out today."

Big surprise. Carla, the store's only other full time employee, called out every other week. She forfeited vacation time in order to have more sick days. She needed all of it, too on account of the perpetual black cloud that hung over her. If it wasn't her health it was her cat's health, or her son and his impressive collection of DUIs. Even her car got sick on the fly. It was also ancient parents, both over 100, who practically lived in hospital rooms.

"Did you see Dad today?" Lucy said.

"Your father's out of town. I tried getting up with him to make breakfast, but he was in a rush. A last-minute meeting with some VIPs."

"He sure has a lot of those."

"Your father's a businessman. What do you think he's off doing?"

I could guess, she thought.

It was all so typical. Mom could rant about his shortcomings all she wanted, but joining in to rake Dad across the coals was always over the line. Probably because it was a reminder that her judgment was so impaired it was nearly broken.

She had to know it, deep down, even if she couldn't stand to hear her daughter say it.

As for Dad, she pictured him already checked into a swanky New York City suite, prowling for the next twenty-something gold digger willing to give it up.

"Do you know where he went?"

"No. He said it was another big opportunity for Greifsfield and left."

Elisabeth's words echoed back again, inciting more anger than ever. *There are many of us who realized it was futile to argue with big business*.

"Do you need anything, Luce? We *are* very busy today."

"I want to talk about Dad."

The line was silent, frustration simmered.

"I want you to know that I haven't been looking forward to this," Lucy said. "It's going to be hard to hear."

Lucy didn't know how to say it. It should've been as simple as stating what happened, but those words were absent from her vocabulary. It was tactless to tell a woman over the phone that her husband had tried molesting her daughter. It wasn't about Lucy's convenience, but doing the right thing.

At the danger of losing her mother's ear, she blurted out, "Dad's cheating on you, Mom." That was also true, and, unfortunately for Rachel Eastman, the lesser of two evils.

"Lucy!"

"Mom, I've seen it. He does it here. He thinks he can get away with it."

"What the hell am I supposed to say?" Mom's voice was hushed in an effort to keep customers from earshot. "Do you want me to get a divorce? Take you and Nick and live off child support?"

"You know you'll get everything."

More silence on the other line.

"Mom, I've been debating whether or not to tell you for a while."

"I wish to hell you hadn't. You don't have any proof. Your word against his, right?"

"I told you so you can do something."

"Do what?"

"Something. Anything? Am I supposed to have the answer for you?"

"I can't right now. Why would you even...I have to go."

"I'm going to come by the store."

"Don't," she pleaded. "I can't do this here. And Kassie

and Sara don't have to hear about this."

"If Dad's gone, I'll come by the house tonight."

"I won't be there...I'm going out with the girls."

"What is this, Mom? College again?"

"Fuck you!" The line clicked dead.

Lucy sat stunned.

Does she even believe me?

That was difficult to answer.

Mom's immaturity had been compounded. It couldn't be an easy thing to hear your husband chased pussy like a dog chases his tail. But Rachel hadn't even taken it with a grain of salt.

Because she knows. And has always known.

The next decision was difficult.

Lucy pushed the cooling breakfast away. Why in the hell was she up at this hour, let alone wide awake and contemplating these options? Because seeing the bastard she called Dad in her dreams didn't make sleeping that much fun.

She thought about calling Jack, but they'd had a late night driving back from the world's worst movies that nobody should remember. Calling so soon, and this early, risked coming on too strong.

"Oh, hey, I know we parted ways five and a half hours ago but I thought I'd call to see how you were doing, and if you wanted to spend the day listening to me rant and rave about my asshole father."

Lucy was stunned to discover she could still think about Jack at a time like this.

She texted him and assigned him the tragic responsibility of looking in on Molly later. He wouldn't be happy, but he remained in *Über support mode* and would do whatever she needed. It wasn't like Lucy to manipulate people, but this needed to be done and the stubborn jerk was too sweet to not do it.

That would give her time to figure things out. Her options weren't impressive. She could drive to the store and force Mom to hear her out. How would that go over? Mom was all about denial. She needed time to collect herself. Maybe that explained the ridiculous, mid-life crisis behavior.

Lucy wanted to help it sink in.

Which meant there was only one thing to do. She'd been to New York with her father several times. Back before he tried having her. She was familiar with his hotels of choice. If Mom didn't want to listen, or needed an extra push to acknowledge things were wrong, she'd force the issue.

Lucy dialed information and asked for the number to the Mandarin Oriental. She scribbled the address down on resort stationary and jammed it into her pocket.

She was out the door two minutes later, hoping a plan would come together before she got there.

●

When Jack saw the text, he rolled over and buried his face in the pillow. Molly wasn't worth waking up for. He hoped instead for another hour or two of sleep. After a year of eight AM classes, sleeping in was life's greatest luxury. No set schedule and no obligations.

Except for checking in on Molly Perkins.

Gah.

No going back to sleep now.

Why do I have to check in on that mess?

The prospect of having to spend a single moment with her incensed him. Once a girl stopped being your friend's beau, you deserved a clean break.

Just when I thought I was out...

He threw on last night's clothes and stepped outside without bothering to comb his morning shag. The sooner he checked in, the faster he could get out.

The things I do for Lucy.

Where was she on this wonderfully sunny late morning, anyway? Her text had been sent before eight. Completely out of character for the girl who'd politicked to keep every class out of the morning block for three years straight. Then again, her current situation was unenviable, to say the least. He wanted to be there for her, but didn't want to keep asking how he could help.

This text was his answer.

He was in high spirits as he traveled the cabana trails. Last night had worked out pretty well despite Allen's cancellation. Lucy turned out to be a more than sufficient partner at the movies. She laughed and cheered at all the right moments, and asked a lot of questions on the drive home. It had been music to his ears. Jack had taken the long way back, through the scariest back roads Western Mass offered. Her interest felt genuine, even as she derided him for championing films that *"no one in their right mind should possibly like."*

They talked about plans after college, both idealistic and realistic, and figured their tracts were more or less aligned. No children, not for a while, at least, and a future rife with travel. He'd felt a connection beyond their collegiate friendship for the first time, and those possibilities were exciting. He drummed up plans for tonight, thinking dinner somewhere would help get her mind off Greifsfield for a while—romantic without being *too* romantic.

Lucy would never let him live it down if he came at this too strong.

He knocked on Molly's door only to have it swing open. "Hello?"

Two men dressed in Big East official digs, hiding beneath full-faced sunglasses emerged from the bathroom. "Help you?" The accent was thick. Unmistakably European.

"My friend's staying here," he said, embarrassed to have referred to Molly as a friend.

"Not anymore."

"Wait, what?"

"Checked out in the middle of the night. Went home."

Jack's first instinct was relief. She wouldn't be around to make Allen's life a living hell, nor would she be the third wheel on nights out with Lucy.

His next thought was that it seemed too easy, and that was never Molly's style. Not when there was attention to be stolen. Why would she leave in the middle of the night without at least saying goodbye to Lucy?

Then again, if this disappearing act would net her any attention in Allen's eyes, then it was a stunt worth pulling.

Yeah, that was the likely story.

"Okay, thanks." He offered a wave and turned to go.

"No problem, friend."

That was all the convincing Jack needed. No matter where the girl was, she wasn't here and it wasn't his job to worry about finding her. Lucy might buy into this ruse, though, meaning to-night's pseudo-romantic evening was falling by the wayside before it had a chance to take shape.

Hope you're ready for a night of finding, then consoling, Molly Perkins.

Exactly what she wanted.

As Jack left he glimpsed the splintered bedroom door, cracked and busted. It rested off its hinges against the far wall. The tall, silent guy disappeared back into the bedroom while the shorter one noticed his curious gaze.

"Installing new door. Your friend had an accident last night. Too much to drink, stumbled in and broke it down."

"She okay?"

"Yes."

"Her friend's father owns this place, she'll want to know if something's happened."

"Everything fine, buddy." Gruff demeanor and broken English didn't make the situation any less suspicious.

"Thanks."

It wasn't hard to imagine Molly had stumbled in here and either collapsed through the door in a display of trademarked negligence, or threw a hissy fit in the form of her patented outbursts.

She'd wreaked worse havoc on campus.

Jack walked cabana trails without aim, thinking that Lucy should hear about Molly's departure. Didn't want to appear too eager to speak with her so soon, though, despite having a good excuse. Last night had gone too well to risk coming off like a schmuck.

He decided to call Allen. News that Jack had succumbed to his emotions for Lucy would be insufferably placating to him. Their friendship felt like a sweltering sack of fruit in the summer sun. It was stagnating. Dialing his cell phone felt like a herculean effort, performed more out of duty than any real desire to touch base.

Allen's voicemail picked up.

"Hey, call me back." He hoped he didn't sound too relieved to have missed him.

Maintaining positive thoughts about Allen was a challenge and yet, there was no hesitation in considering him his best friend. If only the stupid son of a bitch could compartmentalize his relationships and strike the ever crucial balance between the social and romantic.

Maybe that was asking too much of some people.

He took a stroll around the resort, thinking about ways to kill time. There was supposedly a very cool flea market over in Clarksburg, but he couldn't remember where he'd heard about it, or if they were open during the week. Besides, not knowing the destination meant more of an excuse to get Lucy to accompany him.

The lobby supposedly had a game room, but he couldn't

find it. Lucy had used it as a selling point when luring him here. He was slightly ashamed that The Big East boasted a pristine copy of the *Indiana Jones and the Temple of Doom* arcade game, and that he hadn't gotten around to playing it yet.

As a kid it had sucked endless quarters out of his pockets for two summers straight. Now that hand-eye coordination was a little better, Jack wondered if he could finally escape the sinister Pankot Palace.

The clerk at information, a nice girl named Missy, pointed back the way he'd come, telling him to bang a quick right just before the entrance.

The arcade sat at the end of a long hall just past the handicapped bathrooms. He went on his way, fiddling through his wallet for some single bills to change into quarters. Something caught his eye beyond the glass doors leading into the side parking lot. Molly's familiar blue Audi, a hand-me-down from her father, was only now pulling away.

Jack ran outside in time to see the car pass through the opened gates and disappear around the bend. He stood on the sidewalk, confused. It was definitely Molly's car, the dent in the back bumper, caused by Lucy herself, was unmistakable.

So who was the bald-headed man driving it away?

He reached for his phone and dialed the police.

●

Elisabeth sensed his anguish from all the way down the hall. Occasional whimpers made his deep-rooted agony even more obvious. Occasionally, he'd wake up screaming for help. The Turning was never easy, and Allen's fight against it was determined.

She could not recall a time when any of her fledglings had put forth this much resistance. The way humans clung to their humanity as though it were a gift worth fighting for was infuriating. Their lives were banal and materialistic—hardly worth such a desperate battle.

Even if the Turning could be reversed, why would anyone want to?

Once Allen pulled through, she would lay the question at his feet, genuinely curious to hear what someone so young had to say. Would he understand that she'd given him a gift? He'd better. Surely he'd agree that humanity was disgraceful, that it was a species of hypocrites, complete with *faux* sincerity valid only in times of shared misery. Otherwise, it was sink or swim. Man was not concerned with helping one another, only with surrounding himself with like-minded echoes.

She'd witnessed it too many times.

Did they honestly believe that life was about making good money to afford things they didn't need? Or was it a way for them to instill their lives with pointless short-term goals so to validate their meaningless existences?

Either way, it IS meaningless.

The living room interior was dim, exactly the way she preferred it. The blinds were drawn on this late morning. The ceiling fan spun, blowing an amiable breeze down over her. The coffee table held a glass of home brewed iced tea that was slick with condensation. Central air hadn't been working properly, which angered her. It was one of *their* most inspired innovations. Hardly a substitute for an evening's breeze, but life in this guise was more comfortable because of it.

She stretched out on the leather couch, trailing fingers across her nude form, admiring her figure with curiosity, as she often did whenever the wolf questioned this shape's appeal. Aesthetically, she considered herself to be a perfect specimen. The wolf could not understand this penchant for two legs, but had grown to accept it.

Many peers had not the patience to find peace with their daytime conduits, and that was a pity. Elisabeth never felt more relaxed and attuned than in this skin.

She wondered how Allen would take to it and thought of him now: slathered in beads of terrified sweat, a newborn consciousness flooding him with fresh principles and urges. His helplessness kept her gut in perpetual knots that prevented her from accomplishing anything more with the day. Too worried to relax. He'd gone into shock during the bite, and she brought him back and cleaned him up before making a rendezvous with that insolent girl.

Elisabeth wondered if she hadn't gone too hard on Allen. Were her emotions so conflicted that she had been willing to leave his life to the fates? The wolf had been uncertain even as she offered her bite.

Allen was a bloody and pathetic mess when she left the house. She wondered how she could love someone so weak, but that thought, and others like it, were defensive tricks of the mind. The way her heart lurched at the sight of his mangled body told her everything.

The worst part of the Turning was that she couldn't help it along. The longer someone survived the bite, the more likely it was they would pull through. But they had to do so on their own.

Elisabeth sat up in an effort to shake free the frustration. How long had it been since she'd last felt this? Was she even ready to go through it again?

He must be so scared and uncertain.

She hadn't relocated to Greifsfield for this. Their first meeting, bumping into each other while both reaching for a bottle of wine at the general store, pegged him as a meal and nothing more. His cocky swagger would've normally incensed her, though she'd liked his eyes, sky blue and lighter than her own. They held more optimism than she ever remembered having.

She had accepted his offer of a night out, and pictured its inevitable conclusion to be a feast of his spent and toned corpse. But their conversation awakened something she hadn't felt in ages. He became more than a pretty face and a tight, gorgeous body. They exchanged ideas, discussed the art of poetry, music and painting with shared enthusiasm that reached beyond a university boy's textbook.

She also wondered if his stomach was as chiseled as she suspected.

Her initial plan was quickly abandoned and she allowed him to ask her out once more. He wasn't the first romantic pursuit to suppress her instinct while arousing her passion, but every now and again someone came along and tempted her to reconsider exile.

It's just that life was easier when lived alone.

For some reason, though, Allen Taylor warranted reconsideration.

A high-pitched scream came from down the hall. The question of the moment was whether or not his mind would successfully fuse with his new existence. She wanted to think the worst was over and that Allen was on the mend, but there was no way of knowing until he was standing on the other side of this.

If he dies now it's because of my indecision.

This concern propelled her desire to check in on him. So what if it hadn't been thirty minutes since she'd last looked?

Allen's belongings were piled against the couch, and she went rummaging for something to wear, slipping an extra large Camp Crystal Lake t-shirt over her form.

He looked the same when she got there. Naked, save for the thin white sheet that blanketed his lower half. His forehead, chest, and arms were drenched in sweat. The bed sheet soaked through and plastered to his skin.

"Stop fighting," she said and patted his forehead with

gentle strokes. His heart thumped brutally in his chest. His body couldn't take much more of this.

Turning a human was a delicate act and she scolded herself for taking him in such a careless fashion.

"Come back to me." She kissed his wet scalp. "The sooner you do, the sooner we will be together. I desperately need to hear how much you love me." It was true. She felt his desire even now. It was as potent as his will to live, and made his anguish-laden face an easier sight to take.

Even now, Allen's bandaged shoulder was stained by a perimeter of crusted puss and dried blood. But was it less severe than earlier? It was hard to say.

You couldn't know how long a Turning would last. It depended on how strong the body was before the bite, and even then, the spirit had a lot to do with it. Typically, the bite prompted an infection as wolf's saliva and bacteria invaded the body. Once the wolf takes over, the body heals itself much quicker, staving off the infection in the process. The accompanying fever regresses within a day or two. And once the brain accepts metamorphosis, the body is recharged.

She wondered why Allen fought. Love for an old flame? She thought of his previous romance, Molly. It could not have been her that kept him going—could it?

That possibility incensed her. Her fists balled with rage, wishing she had not been so quick to snatch final breath from that whore's body. For a moment, she allowed this disdain to spill over onto Allen as she watched him through narrow slits of resentment.

Do not make me regret changing you.

It was easy to imagine tearing him limb from limb, though her rage subsided as she remembered there was no possible future with Molly Perkins.

Last night had been fun. The girl had been a capable lover. A smile tugged on Elisabeth's mouth while remembering the different ways in which she had amused herself. Most victims were taken out of necessity, but not Molly. That had been personal, and all the memories were fond.

Allen tossed and turned, shaking with enough violence to rattle the bed. His arms thrashed and his head flogged the pillow as he screamed himself awake.

"Oh my God," he said with thick gasps. His eyes were disoriented, but they pulled into focus when he recognized Elisabeth. Relief and contentment followed. "I can't think of a sight I'd rather wake to."

Elisabeth fought against a stupid smile. Allen's sincerity moved her, though he did not have to know that.

"How do you feel?"

Allen ran a hand through his short, untidy hair and shook the dampness out of his palm with disgust.

"I'll tell you this," he said and collapsed onto the moistened bed with a plop. "I'm never sleeping again. Not with the kind of things I've been dreaming about."

"Oh?" She guessed there was wolves involved, but kept her ignorance on display. "Then it is safe to assume I was not there?"

"God, I wish. It was an unending freak show. It'll take some real effort to get it the hell out of my head."

"How are you feeling? That is the important part."

"Chills. A backache. Now that I'm awake, I feel like a pile of cold hard cash. I seriously don't ever want to go back to sleep."

"It's okay," she said. "They're just dreams. You've been here the whole time."

"Maybe they were dreams, but I've never felt anything more real."

"Is that so?"

"That is so. When I was thirteen, I dreamt my cousin Trish and I decided to go for a roll in the hay. It was so vivid that

I couldn't look her in the eye without feeling like an incestuous mountain man. But these dreams...I'd rather fuck my cousin for real than think about them ever again."

"Thankfully, life does not require those kinds of hypotheticals."

"Where does that stuff even come from?"

"That bad?"

"I'll tell you about it some other time. Once my brain is convinced that it never really happened."

He felt feverish and his skin was soaked. There was a long road of recovery before him, though he seemed alert. A good sign, even if his flesh was pasty white.

"I'll get you something to drink. You must be dehydrated."

She got a large stein of iced tea from the kitchen. The cubes clanked as she set it down on the nearby hutch.

"This will cool you down some."

Allen gulped it and licked his lips before handing the cup of cubes back.

"That could be the most refreshing thing I've ever had."

He took his time with the next glass, asking about his injury in between sips.

Elisabeth did not have a problem with stretching the truth. She said he had been the victim of an animal attack (*"probably a coyote"*) and set his mind at ease by lying through her teeth about how he had staggered back here before passing out cold.

"I don't remember that at all."

"I do not wish to think about what would've happened had you not been able to make it back. I would still be wondering what had become of you. Thinking you had left me."

He reached for her but she pushed his hand back down onto his chest.

"Conserve your strength."

"I'm sorry I scared you. You must've gone out of your mind when you found me all messed up."

She shook away his apology, wishing she could remove pangs of guilt as easily. She maintained the charade by telling him the town doctor had already been out here twice to check on him.

"Twice? Shit, is it September already? I may need you to buy my school books for me."

She laughed and his eyes softened following the sound. "It's not even been twenty-four hours, but I am not taking chances. We worried about your heart but it appears to be steadying itself out."

"I should call Jack."

"Already done. I spoke to him this morning when I stopped by the resort to collect your things. I even invited him to stop by. He said it could wait until you were feeling better. Your friends all know where you are. Safe and sound with me."

"What would I do without you?"

You would be knee deep in banality.

"Just get better." She stroked his wet cheek with soft fingers, lost in his summer sky eyes.

"I am feeling better."

"Not by a long shot. You look better, true, but only because you looked dead before. You are in the eye of the storm now, just as the doctor predicted. Finish your drink and go back to sleep."

"I really feel okay. Here, I'll prove it." Allen tried to stand, wincing as his mangled shoulder moved. He fell back onto the mattress and swore.

"Believe me now?" She took his cup and scraped a hand across his face, ignoring the sweaty scruff. "I just want you to feel better. So that we can pick up where we left off the other night."

"Maybe that's what I need to feel better."

"Do you really want our first time to be rife with the possibility of disappointment?"

"Good point."

"See." Elisabeth kissed him. She was gentle to start but applied more force when she saw he could stand a little of it. "I want you back in top shape. Get some sleep for me."

Allen's smile was meek. "I'm not through with you."

"I would be disappointed if you were. I shall be in the next room if you need anything."

Hopefully he would not. Not until he was through the Turning. This was just the start and she was not excited about the questions that would follow.

How would he respond to her answers? What if he blamed her? Resented her? Not everyone was happy to receive this gift. Still, he had been wrapped around her finger long before last night, and she was willing to bet he would continue to be.

Really, he had no choice.

Worrying about the future was tiresome. With Allen improving for the better, she figured it best to be productive with the rest of the day.

One of the many challenges of adapting to domestic life was home upkeep. This place was furnished with all the trappings, right down to a sophisticated washer and dryer. They were tucked into an alcove off the main hallway, and she kept her dirty laundry piled there with every intention of using them.

But she could not.

When it came time to do a wash, she hoisted the basket of clothes and headed outside. Adapting to needless advances was the quickest way to lose one's roots, even as she lamented broken air conditioning.

A brook ran through the back yard, splitting the land with a zigzag of babbling water. She dipped loose sundresses into the stream one piece at a time. The water was cool as she forced the fabric against assembled stones, careful not to stretch the material. Her mother had shown her this technique that separated the dirt from the material by slapping clothes against flat-faced stones. Something about this manual labor was preferable. A properly executed stone wash preserved the integrity of fabric in a way chemically dependent machine washes could not match. She never went out in public reeking of bleach, and the luster of her outfit didn't die a little with every wash. Keeping the art of stone washing alive was important to her because it was one of the last memories she had of her mother that wasn't a distant haze.

Smacking damp fabric against the submerged rock was all she could do to remember her face. Her warm smile and sunny eyes—it might have been nostalgia that made her features irreversibly affectionate, though she did not intend to question it. That final image before the *holy men* came to Iasi.

Before they came, Elisabeth would watch her mother drape garments over two massive rocks that poked from the river bend just outside the village. She used to sit on the bank, a little girl no older than nine, wondering about her future.

Things did not shape up the way she'd imagined.

They came when she was a woman in her twenties, torn between caring for her then-ailing mother and leaving in search of a better life.

History has been rewritten so many times that those religious barbarians are now heroes. There had been nothing heroic about their massacre of her homeland, about their door-to-door exterminations. They had taken her far away, same as every woman her age and much, much younger. Young and clueless, they were prisoners to be prepared for a life of servitude in the sisterhood of Christ.

After they tended to lonely killers and their more immediate needs.

"You know it's not the Dark Ages anymore, gorgeous."

Elisabeth felt her neck hairs stiffen.

"We've got people to do that for you, don't gotta use the stream, either. Life can be grand."

Mestipen was behind her. How had he been able to sneak up unnoticed? As deep as her thoughts ran, her senses remained attuned to her surroundings no matter which form she took.

She turned toward the gypsy's voice. He strutted across the grass wearing loose-fitting jeans and an open chest moccasin vest, an outfit intended to showcase his admittedly impressive physique.

Indelible anger returned at the sight of him. He was not intimidating, with his gelled-up hair and spiked wristbands, rather his mere presence was an insult, and intended as such.

It would be nothing to take his life now, even in this form. The thought of sinking her teeth into his jugular made her heart flutter.

It would be so easy.

So final.

But not without a price.

"You and I are not on a formal basis, Mestipen."

"I'm here to talk, babe. And trust me, you want to hear what I have to say, okay?" His English was better than last time, with only a hint of European intonation outlined in his vowels.

She got to her feet and glared at the unwelcome visitor. At his back, discomforted cries carried through an open window. She kept her poker face and pretended they weren't there. Mestipen didn't appear to notice.

"I'll take your silence as my cue to continue, yeh?"

She said nothing.

"Well, it's like this, then. Our mutual acquaintance wants a word. I'm here to ask when you feel like having it."

"Never."

"He told me you'd say that. Told me to extend the most gracious of invites. He would be honored to host you tomorrow night. If that doesn't work, he is happy to come here."

"Tell him he'd better not do that."

"Said you'd say that too. Said I shouldn't let you say that."

She laughed, and it was more than just an act of defiance. It was because Mestipen thought he was untouchable. Even though his threats carried no weight, and he could inflict no pain, he acted above her station. It incensed her so much it was funny.

"Tell Fane to forget about me. I did not come here for his sake and he knows it."

"Why would anyone believe that? Don't think Fane didn't realize when you showed up. It might've been the very night you arrived when he took me aside and whispered, 'the Huntress is close by.' He told me all about you. And Fane says if he can feel your presence, then you, Huntress, can surely feel his. That's why he does not believe that your arrival in Greifsfield was coincidence. Know what? I don't believe it, either."

"I don't care what you believe. Just because Fane and I have history together does not mean I owe him an audience."

Mestipen glared at her thighs. The shirt stopped after her hips, covering her modesty but not her legs. He lacked the perspective to understand the only reason he lived was out of courtesy for Anton Fane.

"I would have you tell Fane to send a real diplomat next time, but I do not want there to be a next time."

The gypsy smiled. His grin was as sleazy as his hairdo. "Will you really be so quick to refuse?"

"Look around. Things are different, just as they have been for a very long time. Does Fane believe I came here for him? I've chosen to avoid the interference of outsiders."

"Why the isolation?" The gypsy continued to undress her with long, obvious looks.

"With filth like you in these woods, I realize I am not isolated enough." Elisabeth would not allow a peasant trespasser to ogle her like a pinup girl.

Allen screamed. His agony morphed mid-protest into a howl.

The gypsy snapped his head toward the house, and then looked at Elisabeth as if she'd been caught red-handed.

He was off and running for the house.

Elisabeth was faster. A fistful of hair closed around flexed fingers. The gypsy snapped back and choked. She threw him to the ground with an animal's snarl, tossing the torn clump and bloody scalp roots atop him.

Her bestial side pounced. Muscles tense, bones shifted. Instinct raged to the forefront. Her lower jaw writhed in tiny, concentric circles while her lips wound back to reveal a snarl.

There was no longer a cowering gypsy beneath her, just prey. The panic on his face incited the inner beast—taunting her to unleash it. Between wolf and woman, she leaned in like they were old lovers and bared her teeth.

"If you kill me he'll find you, and him!" Mestipen's voice was choppy.

She licked her lips with anticipation, eager for a feast that would satisfy the animal's hunger. She needed a small distraction from Allen and this would do.

Allen.

The gypsy was right about one thing: if she killed him, Allen would suffer the consequences.

Mestipen was lucky. One more moment and her instincts would've been in complete control. She wanted to tear him to pieces and worry about the repercussions later.

She lifted her head from the nape of his neck and took her weight off him. Mestipen did not stick around, scampering down the gravel driveway in tears. Elisabeth watched until she could see him no longer. The roar of a motorcycle started up, and sped back to town at life-threatening speed.

Crash and die.

Coming down off of a partial transformation was about as uncomfortable and unsatisfying as fucking all night without orgasm—an unfulfilling experience in every regard. She stretched her arms and legs as her muscles tightened. The wolf did not wish for excuses, but she made them anyway, promising a Greifsfield buffet in the near future.

She walked back to the house, to the living room confines where she felt as caged as the creature inside her. Part of Mt. Greyrock's base was visible through the large bay windows, the sun blotted by an onslaught of drab clouds casting gloom overhead.

Her ears flinched, wondering if Fane had more underlings nearby. It was unlike him to be this foolish, but she didn't know him anymore. No telling how time had changed him. Nor did she wish to find out. It was bad enough that he had been living in town for a few months before her arrival, now he wanted to relive their past.

How unappealing.

I should have devoured that gypsy and his innards.

The truce with Fane was forfeit if she moved against him, but there never should have been a truce to begin with. Their kind wasn't intended for bureaucracy. She wouldn't have known the meaning of that word if not for Fane and his ridiculous treaties. Why Queen Alina tolerated his impositions was another mystery.

Unease dissipated as her thoughts returned to Allen. Warmth filled her as she curled up on the uncomfortable leather sofa and imagined life with her soon-to-be cub.

Outside, thunder tore through the sky, teasing the quiet valley with raindrops. She imagined rain splashing the windows as the final semblances of sunlight gave way to stormy darkness. But no such luck. This summer was dry and there would be no relief.

She remembered the unfinished basket of laundry left abandoned by the stream and shrugged. No sense in trotting out there now. What mattered more than anything was getting Allen though the next few hours. There was temptation to sleep them away, but that would be foolish. If anything happened, if he needed her for something, she would never forgive herself.

Her stomach rumbled, aware now that she hadn't eaten anything since the girl. The refrigerator was loaded with slabs of beef from the town butcher, but it was never as satisfying as a living meal.

The easiest solution was a return trip to that abysmal tourist trap resort. Any vacationer would do, but there was one in particular she wanted. A delicacy. No better time to separate Allen from his friend. If not, he was bound to show up asking questions and demanding answers.

He would have to die, and it was easier if Allen did not know. At least not until his humanity had waned. Hopefully, he would leave it behind easier than she did.

Allen's friend would be this evening's main course. The way he had looked at her two nights ago, with repressed desire, it wouldn't be difficult getting him to drop his guard. The poor soul wasn't comfortable around women—that much was clear. He had been unable to meet her eyes, despite wanting her badly.

This could be fun.

But how much fun was *too* much? She had to think about Allen now. A meal could only be a meal if she was going to take a lover. Monogamy was of no interest—not when sights, feelings, and tastes of the flesh offered countless pleasures—but Allen deserved a say.

Relationship obligations. It felt like hundreds of years since she last worried about them, realizing that was about to change.

She stripped off the Crystal Lake shirt in anticipation, stalking through the house in restless motion. A caged animal waiting to escape. The thought of taking another person from Allen's life put her in a good mood. Before last night, it had been years since she had last planned her victims. Molly had been so pleasurable, the build-up, the meeting, and the prolonged feast, that this felt necessary.

It was a part of her old life coming back.

She looked in on Allen. He had rolled onto his good shoulder. His breathing was shallow, but steady, and his heart was calm.

She sighed with relief.

A trail of darkened hair ran from the base of his neck to the small of his back. Thick clumps that hadn't been there earlier. His beautiful complexion was gone, replaced by patchy tufts of hair. His ears were slightly pointed, but had a long way to go.

He was a beautiful sight.

"That's right," she whispered, unable to contain her excitement. "You're mine now."

●

"I already told you, the police were here for two hours." The assistant manager acknowledged Jack's inquiry with a patient smile that revealed two rows of absurdly white teeth. His high forehead housed a perfectly kempt head of hair. Every strand was brushed into place and showed no signs of graying, despite his age. His face was dark and leathery, a man who spent his nights sleeping in a tanning bed. He was big, with a large frame heightened by the extended shoulder pads atop the white sport coat. Pinned to it was a bronze, sparkling nametag that read: ASSISTANT MANAGER BALTHAZAR DAVIES.

"I never saw them," Jack said.

"I'm sorry they didn't stop to say hi."

"You look broken up about it."

"It was more than enough time for our guests to wonder what in the blazes is happening. We pushed the panic button today, forced all our people in for a mandatory shift to get our ducks in a row. Damage control, Mr. Markle, because one of *your* friends would rather play adolescent games."

"Not one of my friends," Jack said. "One of Lucy Eastman's friends."

The namedrop didn't faze him. He straightened his New Wave tie and pulled the linen sport coat over his bulging stomach.

"People tend to assume the worst when they see the police. Our staff has been tasked with convincing our guests that they shouldn't worry."

"Shouldn't they?" Jack said.

The plaque-free grin fell away as Davies folded his hands across his desk. "I told you, Mr. Markle, your friend checked out late last night. Of her own accord. If you saw somebody driving off in a car similar to her own."

"Her car."

"She had been gone hours before you saw that car leaving our grounds. Please be reasonable."

Jack sighed and glanced around Davies' office. It sat in the lobby's rear, opposite a utility closet. It wasn't overly furnished and said very little about the man who operated out of it. Save for a beached sailboat painting on the wall, the room was devoid of personal touches. No family photos, no trinkets, or indication of hobby.

He got the impression that either Davies hadn't had this job very long, or that people were shuffled in and out of here so often they never bothered unpacking.

"Let me ask you this, Assistant Manager Balthazar Davies."

If Davies noticed the sarcasm, he wore a hell of a shit-eating poker face.

"What in the hell was happening in Molly's cabana when I went by? Two guys fixing a door that was shattered to pieces.

Everyone tells me she checked out and then I see someone driving off in an Audi that just so happened to have the same bumper damage. Damage that happened while I was with her."

"Regrettable coincidence." The answer dropped so quickly Jack could tell Davies had been waiting to say it.

"I guess there isn't much left for us to talk about. Have a good night."

Jack shook Davies' leathery hand, his grip surprisingly firm, and thanked him for his time. The assistant manager said nothing more and watched him leave without expression.

The elements didn't gel: the broken door, the bald driver and the apathetic police. Jack was wholly stumped over what to do next.

He walked around the fenced-in tennis courts, abandoned most nights after dark, on the way back to his cabana. A string of low-wattage lights lined the path alongside the patio, but they failed to do much except illuminate his next few steps.

Beyond the last court fence was the cavernous woodland of Greifsfield Forest. A canopy of trees dimmed the walkway further. Soon he was moving through blackness, the only confirmation he was still on the path was the scraping gravel beneath his feet.

To his relief, the trail spilled into the light soon enough. He followed it, choosing the shortest distance to his room. Suddenly, he didn't feel like thinking out here.

Though he didn't think the cabana would help, either. Its contemporary over-design was a reminder that he was staying in a glorified hotel. The one his friend had disappeared from.

He opted to continue his walk, keeping to the resort's most public confines. The Big East's grounds pulsed with sporadic activity. A young couple hurried past, pushing through the gate and into the pool area. They were laughing and whispering in one another's ear.

Jack made his way back to the main building, eager to speak with another of the Big East's employees. The lobby was nearly vacant, save for the middle-aged woman sitting behind the reception desk, eyes planted firmly in a romance novel. She didn't even look as Jack passed.

The Black Diamond restaurant was closing for the night. Only the furthest corner table occupied. Beyond that, employees mopped the floor and stacked chairs on top of tables.

He ducked down the corridor leading to Rory Eastman's office, unsure of why he was even checking. Rory wouldn't be here and, if he was, what was there to say?

The door to his office was locked and a shade blocked the window. He couldn't see inside but it appeared clear.

Jack's mind danced in circles. Each time he worried about Molly, his rationale introduced the possibility that she had engineered this whole thing as the ultimate ploy for attention.

Allen had always said she was crazy and if she really had to run away to prove a point, the resort probably wouldn't lose too much sleep over it.

And if that's the case, screw her for making me worry.

He started back down the hallway, stopping in front of the door marked EMPLOYEES ONLY. Jack twisted the knob without knowing why. It was the stairwell Lucy had led him up a few days ago. He didn't know what he was looking for, but it couldn't hurt to poke around.

Get caught and he had an excuse: *"Oh, I'm just looking for Lucy. She told me to meet her here. You know her, right? Lucy Eastman."*

They'd give him a slap on the wrist, but nothing he couldn't handle. And if word got back to Lucy, she'd cover for him.

He stood on the landing and looked down. The lower levels seemed most interesting. Above them were several floors of hotel rooms, meaning this stairwell likely doubled as a fire escape.

Going down.

He followed the stairs with curiosity, descending as far as they allowed. He passed three landings only to reach the bottom, an unmarked security door. It was metal and lacked any sort of depression or knob.

Impossible access deepened his curiosity. What was behind there that warranted tight-knit security? The resort's power-source? Something about this was sinister. If it did lead to the power, shouldn't there be signs warning of electricity?

He ran his hands over the smooth metallic surface. His fingers worked the edges, attempting to pry it away from the jamb. A frivolous effort.

He explored the landing behind him, finding only a mop bucket and a broken broom handle.

Figuring that Lucy should know what was down here, Jack dug his cell phone out of his pants.

No signal.

"Son of a bitch."

This was the natural culmination of the day's events. The anonymous nature of the door was another confirmation that the Big East was hiding something. He had to get past this and see what was inside. And there was only one way to do that.

He knocked. Repeatedly.

It looked to be the only way. There wasn't a keyhole or doorbell that he could see and guessed anyone coming had to get in with a knock.

So he did it again, then again.

So much for that.

Defeated, he started the return climb, cell phone in hand. Lucy was going to have to tell him everything she knew about this. If she didn't know, they were going to find out.

He reached the first landing, his footsteps echoing throughout the empty stairwell, and hooked around to the next set of steps. He was halfway up when the sound of grinding metal froze him solid. Hushed and urgent chatter followed, and then came rapid footsteps, running that hit the stairs and refused to slow.

The urgency startled Jack and he was running too, skipping steps as he climbed. He leapt onto the next landing and pulled the doorknob. Locked. He was climbing again, the next flight. Behind him, pounding footsteps approached too quickly for his liking.

He wouldn't turn around. Didn't want to find out what the hurry was, because he felt like he knew. Someone was pissed that he was poking around. Someone fixing to take care of the problem Jack was beginning to pose.

He grabbed the landing banister and flung around to the next flight of stairs, pushing his legs as fast as they went. His periphery focused on an approaching figure on the lower landing, gaining ground fast.

Jack grabbed the next door.

Locked.

He pushed off it, taking the boost of momentum it offered. The stalking footsteps were almost to him.

The next landing had been his starting point. He stumbled across the way and lunged for the knob. It was sedentary and his fingers slipped off it.

The footsteps were right behind him.

Jack couldn't look. He pounded on the door, panicked. He might've cried "fire," but he was too scared to recall the hysteria coming out of his mouth. His opened palms slapped the door while the fast approaching steps slowed.

Was that laughter?

Unbelievably, it swung inward. Jack dodged it with a quick sidestep, and then pushed past the custodian who looked at him with a wrinkled brow silently accusing him of being an asshole.

He didn't try explaining. He patted the guy's arm and

then hurried off down the corridor. His fingers were pins-and-needles numb and he was sure his pulse was seconds away from bursting through his neck. The lobby was nearly empty, but with just enough activity for him to find comfort.

An obese woman complained to guest services that the complimentary drinks in her room were not being adequately stocked.

"There were four Cokes in there the first two nights. And now they're only putting two."

Jack took a seat on the sofa near her, finding coziness in her trivial complaints. His legs stuttered as he looked for his composure, watching the hallway's entrance to make sure there was no further pursuit.

The woman's complaint shifted to a whirring noise coming from the room's ceiling, keeping her and her husband awake at night.

"Why do you think I'm here complaining at this hour?" she said.

Jack's shaky fingers navigated to Lucy's contact info. He tried calling on his hurried trek back to the cabana. It rang several times before dumping into voicemail. He left a polite message asking her to call back, but offered no definitive reason. He didn't want to freak her out.

The cabana was empty when he got back.

He pulled the closest chair beneath the doorknob and went to the sliding door, ensuring it was locked tight. He pulled the blinds shut and slid the kitchenette table in front of it. Then he poured a glass of Wild Turkey on ice, not because he wanted it, but because it was the only thing that might tame his erratic nerves.

With a few swallows, Austin Nichols 101 set fire to his throat. He closed his eyes and hoped to hear the Lucy-specific ringtone, *LoveGame* by Lady Gaga, any minute.

That minute turned to unconscious hours. He awoke with sandpaper tongue so coarse he thought the roof of his mouth was bleeding. The room was dark, still night since there was no light bordering the drawn curtains.

Jack fumbled for his cell phone.

4:34.

Groggy, he made his way into the kitchen for a glass of water. Moisture returned to his throat, cleansing the dry mouth. He leaned against the kitchen counter and downed the entire glass in a few gulps.

There was movement in the cabana's solid darkness.

Jack stared at the affected area to make sure he hadn't imagined it. Moments passed in complete silence and Jack felt no additional presence.

Regardless, it was the last straw. His hand touched his back pocket, making sure he still had his wallet. His keys and phone sat atop the table beside him. He was done with this place.

He was nearly gone when the darkness in the doorway of Allen's room shifted. Whoever was there made no sound.

In a swift motion, Jack brushed aside the barricading chair and flung the door wide. The uninvited guest simply raised its arm and pointed.

Jack was already outside and on the run.

He didn't stop until his feet hit the concrete of the Big East's parking lot, his hands fumbling through his key ring as he ran toward the Cavalier.

He pulled out of the parking space and navigated to the gatehouse where they waved him through. Things had gone from sketchy to downright bad in a matter of hours and if he hadn't suspected something severely wrong then, he was positive now.

Disappearing people, psychotics, and burglars. What the hell was happening in this supposed vacation town?

His gut was in knots as he sped away from the Big East,

imagining his options. With Lucy and Allen missing in action, he decided there was only one alternative remaining.

The sheriff's office wasn't far from here.

●

Trever Ingram swatted the green spider that crawled across his desk. Beneath his balled-up fist he ground the arachnid into paste. Then he brushed the massacred contents aside and returned his attention to the computer monitor, to where he was embroiled in a less-than rousing round of solitaire.

He didn't much like the game, and it certainly didn't have the suspense or payoff of, say, poker, but it was a shitload better than being out on arbitrary patrol.

Some of Greifsfield's citizens had been vocal regarding his lack of lawman presence over the last couple months, but those ingrates were easy enough to ignore. It only troubled him when he thought about it, preferring to do his rounds in the midnight hour. That was the easiest way to minimize the disappointed glances of town regulars.

The thing was, even those glances were less and less these days. That's what scared him. Over the last two months, Trever Ingram hadn't felt like heading into the dark mountain nights. Things were happening here. Things he couldn't control.

There was plenty he couldn't control these days. Massachusetts' Bureau of Forest Fire Control, for starters. Sons of bitches were doing a stellar job of drumming up panic all over the western part of the state on the count of this heat wave. Their last rainfall was back in April, and the forest was a might susceptible because of that. They warned that one smoldering campfire was all it was going to take to create an inferno, as if his men didn't know how to take precautions.

Trouble was, he didn't have many men left.

His eyes fell to a pile of folders against the edge of his desk—a collection of missing persons cases that had been opened within the last few months. He sifted through them every so often, when the guilt wasn't too much to bear. When it was, well, that was when the bottle of Southern Comfort came out of the bottom drawer.

He was going through that stuff must faster than usual these days.

"Not like I can help the poor sons of bitches," he said aloud. He was going to need more convincing than that.

He glanced up and, through the opened office door, frowned at the sight of the empty station. It was just about five, an hour or so 'till sunrise, and about two hours left in his shift. Time to go home and sleep off another miserable day.

Once he saw the coast was clear, he rifled a crumpled soft pack of unfiltered Pall Malls from his breast pocket and pressed a cigarette to his lips, immediately filling his mouth with potent tobacco.

One of the few things left to enjoy.

The men wouldn't start filtering in here until seven. The family guys appreciated having their nights free and since he'd been a bachelor for all of his fifty-six years, he sure didn't see the fuss in working nights. As sheriff, there was a responsibility to keep the morale of his men as high as it could go. Allowing them nights off to be with their wives and children meant the world to them. At least, it had. Before something wicked this way came.

But the men seemed happy still. If anything, it kept him safe, even if this job felt more like a prison camp these days. The irony was not lost on him.

A pair of headlights sliced through the night. A car pulled into the spot in front of the door.

Trever, Pall Mall pursed between his lips, shot upright, and looked down the length of the station, into the parking lot.

His hand fell to his holster, curling around his Glock.

The engine went silent and a slamming door followed. Someone trotted up the stairs and pulled the doors apart, storming through.

"Hello?" The voice was decidedly shaken. Trever felt bad because the poor son of bitch had come here looking for help, and would find none.

"What can I do for ya, boy?"

"Are you the officer on duty?"

"Sheriff Trever Ingram." He took a lengthy puff on his Pall Mall and approached the visitor with trepidation. This son of a bitch wasn't here because he needed help changing a tire.

They usually don't get as far as the police station.

"Okay, the sheriff," the guy said with a gust of relief. "Good. Sheriff…Ingram is it? I'm staying at the Big East. My friend, Lucy Eastman, had a few of us up for the summer. I called the police earlier today when one of our friends disappeared."

Trever listened to this guy, Jack Markle, weave a yarn featuring missing friends and sinister pursuits. He thought back to the folders on his desk, but didn't exactly have the heart to tell him his missing friends were gone for good.

The new law of the land.

The guy was concerned for his friend, a younger twenty-something named Allen Taylor who'd been screwing around with that Luna nympho. The same broad who turned every husband in town into a willing adulterer, although the rumor was she wasn't much for giving up her goods.

Markle had other questions, too. Asked about that Perkins girl. The boys had responded to a call up at the Big East earlier today, but they weren't planning on doing much investigating. The mop flopped that way most days.

Trever waited until he was finished speaking and then lit another Pall Mall, offering one to the drowning man before him.

He waved it away.

"Suit yourself."

This was a bad situation, one that needed glossing over. The boys had been more than clear about looking the other way—a condition of the deal.

It left Ingram with an impending sense of dread that continued to mount. What would they do with him once he outlived his usefulness? It wasn't the only worry that gnawed his innards like goddamn dysentery. What happens if Markle does the smart thing and leaves town? Sooner or later, someone would, but his boys didn't seem too concerned about that. If Markle made a scene about missing friends, it was over. All the news needed was one word about missing tourists in Greifsfield, Massachusetts and they'd swarm like buzzards, asking questions and uncovering missing persons cases by the ton.

That'd be a prelude to about a thousand other fucking headaches he didn't feel like considering. There were guaranteed to be lots of questions and he, as sheriff, would be responsible for answering many of them.

Something's gotta give.

His eyes crawled to the clock directly over Markle's head. It was half past five now. He thought of the loaded Glock and wondered if cleaning up splattered brains and blasted skull was within the realm of possibility before the town came to life.

The thought of cold-blooded murder buoyed his mind with shame. Too many blind eyes had already been turned, including his own. Trever Ingram wasn't a monster, though.

Just a coward.

So he lied. Told Jack Markle that he was going to drive on up to the Big East and check into this missing girl, Molly Perkins, and her disappearance. Assured him that he would also find out the deal with the unmarked room in the basement. Promised that he wouldn't stop kicking ass until he'd taken every name.

Markle seemed satisfied with this approach. "Thank you, sheriff. It's to the point where I'm too messed up to even go back there. Maybe I'm overreacting, but I felt like my life was in danger."

"Just leave it to me," Trever said. "I want you to prepare for the possibility that this is just one colossal fuck up on the part of you, but if anything did happen to your girl, I'm getting to the bottom of it. As for your friend, I'm not going to consider him missing just yet. You said yourself that he'll sell his one-year-old sister out for a piece of pussy. If he's shacking up with the town cooze, I see no reason to assume he's in danger."

"Whatever you can do, sheriff. Anything."

Ingram walked him to the door and patted his back while offering undeliverable assurances. The kid looked nervous, saying he wasn't sure where he was going for the night, though it wasn't likely to be anywhere in Greifsfield.

Good for you, boy.

Ingram recommended a little roadside motel off Route 80, heading into Pittsfield.

"That's where I'll go."

"Tell Gillian that Trever sent you. Might not net you anything more than a spoon for the continental breakfast, but it's worth a shot."

"Thanks."

"Go on, now. I'll be sure to give you a call a later on. After I've checked things out and talked with a few of my boys."

Markle finally left after repeated *thank yous.*

Ingram headed back to his office and went straight for the Southern Comfort. After a few sips and another Pall Mall, he felt okay about things.

He fumbled for the radio. Dan Fogelberg's *Leader of the Band* was playing, its somber melody fit his mood like a glove. He slumped in his chair and swiveled to face the wall. Cracking black sky gave way to dim light while songbirds ushered in the arrival of another beautiful mountain day.

They'd be here within the hour.

He unholstered the Glock, clutching it tight with a blank stare. How could he have allowed this to continue for so long? Re-election in this county was impossible after his laissez-faire approach to local law enforcement. Berkshire County had already been taken from him anyway. Soon there wouldn't be a law to uphold.

He thought through his options and didn't like a single one. It was all shit, no matter what he did.

With a final swig of SoCo and another puff on his Pall Mall, his thirty-third today, he stubbed the cigarette out and pressed the Glock to his temple.

"Fuck it," he said and pulled the trigger.

Five

"I feel fantastic," Allen said to no one in particular as he watched breaking morning from the lawn chair on Elisabeth's deck.

There was plenty to feel good about. The fever was a memory, the tranquil glow of nature calmed him, and heightened awareness of his surroundings made him feel like a new man.

An adorable family of deer scavenged breakfast just beyond the tree line, hooves stomping the forest floor with compacted echoes.

The woman of his dreams was currently asleep in bed, relieved he was finally awake. He closed his eyes and listened to her soft breaths, thinking he had never heard anything more wonderful.

To say he felt fantastic was an understatement, but only because Allen lacked the words to convey it any more succinctly.

Senses fired on all cylinders. Crisp mountain air gave him more energy than ever. His ears flexed, picking up on a sparrow's treetop song. He stifled the urge to get up and do something, because Elisabeth had made him swear he wouldn't.

"Do not get into trouble while I am asleep."

There was no better way to recharge his batteries than bathing in all this serenity. Finally he found the value in a good country vacation.

The lazy morning gave way to an eventual rumble in his stomach and Allen trekked back into the house. The impish wildlife dropped a few decibels in his ears as he closed the sliding door. Elisabeth didn't keep a stocked fridge and what contents there were made him indecisive. He wondered if a quick trip to the grocery store would better sate the hunger.

He reached for an apple but reconsidered when the thought of eating it did little to entice him. Everything in the fridge, from clean-cut steaks, cold cuts sliced too thin, and without enough substance in the bites, to a box of pastries, failed to satisfy his craving.

He decided on pasta, ignoring the fact that the thought of boiled macaroni and tomato sauce suddenly churned his stomach. This had always been his go-to dinner whenever indecision struck.

He emptied the boxed spaghetti into a pot of boiling water and stirred it, catching the sound of an approaching car. A slamming door smashed his eardrums like a hammer. A moment later someone was ascending the porch steps, carrying an unmistakably feminine scent—a floral aroma that tantalized him. Bath and Body Works danced around him as he hurried to greet it.

A young brunette woman stood beyond the sliding door. From her expression, she was surprised to see him.

"Who the hell are you?" She took a step back.

Her hostility was startling. She was stained with fear that spread through her like aggressive cancer.

"I said, who are you? What the fuck are you doing here?" Her head bobbed to see over his shoulder. She was looking for someone else.

"Elisabeth's asleep," Allen said.

"Who's Elisabeth? Who are you people?"

"I'm staying with her."

She stared in incredulous silence. Blood flooded through

her veins and her heart was a jackhammer. Constant drumming brought violent, painful knocks to Allen's ears.

The woman flashed her cell phone. "I'm on the phone to the state police right now."

Police? This was escalating beyond his control. Allen felt threatened by her tone, aggravating him to where his own heart began thumping in competition with hers. He wasn't a confrontational person, but confusion made him feel flustered. And that made him angry.

No time to diffuse the situation. He sprung onto the deck and the slightly older woman jumped back, startled.

"Listen," Allen said. "I don't know what you're upset about, but..."

"You're living in my parents' house," she said with tears in her eyes.

Allen felt derailed. No response would get him on track.

"I haven't been able to get in touch with them in months. Local police have been no help, and you don't know why I'm upset."

"There must be a mistake here."

"Mistake? I grew up in this house. There's no mistake."

"I'm not sure what's happening, but..."

"Fine." She turned to leave but Allen, much to his surprise, lashed out and squeezed her arm. She yanked away and gave a violent push that sent him colliding with the deck rail.

"Get the fuck away from me." She started down the steps in a hurry.

Whirling emotions attacked, and he couldn't sort them. Anger brewed, persistent confusion stoked it, and he suddenly realized he hated this woman.

Allen jumped over the rail, landing on bent knees. His feet continued without slowing. Again he reached for her. Again she evaded, this time retaliating with an open hand slap across his eyes.

"Fucker!" She pulled the car door open and dove inside. Her beating heart pumped out streams of thick blood he suddenly craved. Her body trembled, fear transforming into something palpable. It teased him to see and feel her like this. Forbidden fruit.

Allen realized what he wanted to eat. It wasn't boiling pasta.

This would be more fulfilling.

He snatched her ankle and tore her from the car, her nails cracking and breaking along the upholstery as she smashed head-first into gravel. Tried kicking his advances away, but he brushed aside her resistance with minor annoyance.

His strength surged and he was able to lift her in a single motion, taking her in bursting arms. Her petrified breath gusted.

Allen inhaled it, drunk on this terror.

"You want to treat me like this?" He growled, angrier than he'd ever been.

Her wiggles weren't enough to escape. Between his legs, he throbbed against his jeans. An unconditioned response he was beyond fighting.

She felt it too, eyes bursting wide with terrified possibilities.

Allen's muscles stretched and expanded like helium balloons floating beneath his skin. He screamed out in pain, but also horror. What was happening to him? He flung her to the dirt with a harsh growl, and she skidded across the pavement as his vision stretched and blurred. Pressure squeezed his eyes. Hissing bones popped in unison, then re-formed immediately.

He blamed her for this, and dropped his weight on top of hers. She kicked and punched blindly, every blow strengthening his determination to kill her.

She might have whimpered "please," but his thoughts were no longer human. They too had been transformed.

Allen stared at the nape of her neck, at the pale and scraped gooseflesh. His now-elongated nose pushed against it with a curious sniff, offering an ecstatic sigh while inhaling the delicious scent.

Then he bit in and felt the backwash of squirting blood mixed with chunks of raw meat.

Beneath him, the hysterical and pathetic face wept for life. His newborn consciousness wasn't phased. Wolves favored instinct over emotion, and right now Allen's hunger demanded satisfaction.

The wolf pushed his mouth against the wet and runny wound and continued eating.

●

Elisabeth sat in the painting room, perched atop a wooden stool, balancing while she stared at the empty canvas.

The first image that came to mind was a tiny male pup curled at the foot of a larger black wolf. Protective claws draped over the fledgling, the beasts yellow eyes staring outward, daring the world to separate them.

Too motherly.

She did not want this to end up on a Wal-Mart t-shirt.

Next, she considered naked human bodies, groping one another in lust while spirit wolves haunted the sky overhead. She liked this idea and thought about sketching an outline before worrying it was perhaps too hackneyed.

Too on-the-nose.

Elisabeth knew better than to rush creativity. The urges were flowing. She had sprung out of bed compelled by the urge to create *something*.

She put a finger in her mouth and nibbled it while thinking it over. Things were looking up. Now was the time to enjoy life.

If your pup can accept his new existence.

When she heard the growl she hopped off the perch and tossed the paintbrush into the water bucket at her feet. She popped the window and listened.

Her pup wasn't far. Elisabeth fought the urge to go to him, deciding it was best for him to discover the wolf on his own.

She closed her eyes and listened to his ferocity, hoping it was being used against one of his silly friends.

Her next vision was of a man and woman strolling through a field of mangled bodies. Their faces turned toward each other, concerned with nothing but each other.

This was an idea she liked. Simple, clean, and of the moment.

Elisabeth smiled and went back to work, fueled further by the sounds of dying cries and tearing flesh.

●

Allen awoke when he tried turning his head and found it plastered to a mutilated corpse. His clothes were ragged strips, and his mouth was filled with blood. His teeth ached from the shredded meat wedged between them.

He needed floss as much as he needed aspirin.

This woman had come looking for her parents. He remembered it, and everything he'd done to her. Worse had been the things he'd wanted to do.

He wondered for a second if he was going crazy.

No.

Lunatics didn't question their sanity, did they? Everyone else had a problem as far as they were concerned. Try as he might, Allen couldn't hang the blame for this anywhere but at his own feet.

His throat heaved while realizing he was covered with

stranger's blood. Crusts of it hardened at the corners of his mouth and covered his hands and chest. The lump of disgust in his gullet plummeted into his stomach. A dry heave exploded in a disgusting burp. Then his stomach buckled again. A vicious circle.

Getting vertical calmed his stomach. The dry heaves went into submission, leaving a lingering taste worse than stale cigarettes. Every swallow recalled the sensation of ingesting a stranger's plasma. Every swallow made him want to buckle and vomit.

That vicious circle again.

Greyrock's mountain air was cold on his nearly naked flesh, and his manhood was tiny and shriveled, adding unshakable embarrassment to his list of traumas. He couldn't believe he cared about that in the wake of what he'd done, but vanity knew no bounds.

Allen stumbled back toward the house, steadying himself against vinyl siding as he went. The shower was inviting and he stayed beneath the soothing stream longer than intended. When he dried off, he took twenty minutes to floss his teeth, which was awkward thanks to his pruned hands.

Elisabeth was in the living room. She wore an earth-toned sundress and sat stroking the necklace that always dangled above her breasts—animal's teeth that stabbed straight down toward her cleavage. Any other day, he might have taken the time to inquire about it.

She whipped a small bundle of clothes at him.

"Figured you'd need a change." There was plenty of curiosity in her eyes, though she refused to say anything more.

Allen knew she was waiting for him to lose his mind. He felt her tension from here and was surprised she cared this much. He might've gone to her for comfort had it not been for the figurative bloodstains on his hands.

"I've got to go back to the resort," he said, eager to get the hell away.

"You shouldn't go back there, Allen. Let me go and get whatever you need."

"I need to talk to Jack. Tell him..."

"Tell him what? Do you think there is anything you can say to your old friends that would make them understand what's happened to you?"

"What *has* happened to me?" He wanted her to say it so he knew it was real.

Elisabeth was unreadable. She got up and kissed him as soon as he got the shirt over his head.

He was angry and confused, but kissed back anyway. Her mouth was sweeter than usual.

"You probably have a lot of questions."

"Give me some time to myself," Allen said.

He threw the rest of his clothes on in a hurry, eager to be alone. Elisabeth's comfort wasn't needed, because it wasn't comforting. It was a reminder of her culpability. She had done this, and because she had, somebody's life had been taken.

The need to vomit returned.

She agreed to lend him her car. He headed for the driveway a second later, stopping in front of the small white vehicle belonging to this morning's victim.

The corpse was already gone.

He looked up and saw Elisabeth glaring from the living room window. She offered a forced smile, but he didn't feel like returning the gesture. Yes, there was an urge to go running back into her arms, but he fought it. Let her know he was angry.

Curiosity got the better of him and he pulled on the car's door handle. It creaked and gave way to dueling odors: a fruity air freshener and trendy skin moisturizer.

These scents wouldn't have been overbearing for human senses, but the monster was part of him now. Sitting in here was like suffering from a sinister allergy. He took the Gucci bag sprawled on the passenger's seat and hopped out.

A hairbrush, a compact mirror, lip-gloss, breath mints, and whitening gum—none of this interested him. The pink wallet packing a fifty-dollar bill and several credit cards, however, did. He pulled a driver's license from behind its plastic shield and studied the picture.

Definitely her.

Sondra Gleason. Two years older than him. She really had come here looking for her parents.

He remembered grabbing her. Her self-defense had only heightened his ferocity. He'd wanted her to fight harder because it was more sporting.

I did all those things. Somehow.

Ever since his fever broke he didn't recognize himself or the disgusting urges propelling him.

I wanted to fuck her, he thought with particular repulsion. *And the more she struggled, the more I wanted her.*

Allen couldn't handle this. He was a monster now.

The Eclipse Spyder revved to life with the flick of a key and he was on his way. The roads offered little comfort, instead prolonging memories of this morning's jaunt through the woods with a dying woman in his jaws.

He sped toward town and was at the Big East before he knew why he'd driven here.

He wanted to speak with Jack. There was nothing partic- ular to say and he certainly didn't intend to tell him the truth. He only needed some normalcy.

But Jack wasn't here.

Allen followed the familiar twinge of body spray back to the parking lot and hopped behind the wheel of the Spyder. With his window down, he hit the road again, honing in on that musky odor as if he'd been equipped with radar.

The Tavern on the Hill wasn't a hard place to find, and

Jack's musk was unmistakable. It was a hole in the wall that, quite inexplicably, looked to be booked solid. An elderly man in overalls painted the signpost, replacing the faded and flaking red with a yellow so bright it made Allen's eyes wobble.

"No vacancy here, boy."

"I'll manage. Got a friend staying here."

"Make it quick. I got paying customers. You're taking a parking space from one of them."

Allen smiled and nodded. His nose took him to an upstairs room where he knocked and waited. Jack cracked the door before pulling it open. The poor bastard looked worse than Allen felt.

"You go on a bender?" Allen said.

Jack rubbed his five o' clock shadow. "What are you doing here?"

"I want to leave town, I guess."

"How did you know I was here?"

"Went by the resort this morning and you weren't there. Was joyriding around and happened to see what I thought was your car. Turns out I was right."

"You want to leave town? I'm guessing it wasn't true love after all?"

"Don't sound so happy. Anyway, why are you staying here? You look like you're hiding out."

"Something's happening at Lucy's place. I pretty much got chased out of there last night. And Molly's disappeared."

Allen remembered his nightmare for the first time since the fever broke. Molly's face at the bottom of the lake, tormenting him first with her body and then with her death. What else had he done and couldn't remember?

"She disappeared?"

"Off the face of the earth," Jack said.

Allen listened to the story, overwhelmed by sinking feelings. Molly's disappearance, strangers in her bungalow, a lunatic's early morning visit to their cabana—hiding in *his* room of all places—none of it was good. Allen couldn't explain it, though it reaffirmed the notion that it was time to get the hell out of Greifsfield.

There was more wrong here than just him. The good news was that it shouldn't take any convincing to get Jack to pack up and go. The bad news was that Allen couldn't run away from himself.

"Let's head out," Allen said. "You'll dial the cops on our way out of town and tell them what you know. You're not doing anyone any good running up a motel bill here. A poor college student shouldn't be maxing out his credit cards, at least not on some shitty place like this."

"Not until I find Lucy," Jack said. "The police are involved already. Waiting to hear from the sheriff. Once we can get Lucy out, we'll all go together."

Jack's always so selfless.

"I'm not staying here," Allen said. "Not for another night."

"What's got you so spooked?"

"Some girl got killed in the woods behind Elisabeth's house."

Jack's brow wrinkled. His glare was suspicious, or maybe that was Allen's paranoia creeping in. He already didn't trust himself anymore, might as well give everyone the same treatment.

"Elisabeth thinks an animal is the culprit."

"You think different?"

"I saw the body while taking a walk. I practically tripped over it."

"You're willing to leave Elisabeth because a girl got killed in the woods?"

"By someone or something."

"What aren't you telling me?"

"I'm thinking my stuff and your stuff are the same stuff,"

Allen said.

"Did you report it? Because I'm not sure why you think that these things are connected."

What if Elisabeth was the stranger you saw in my room? Instead of that he said, "What are you going to think if they fish Molly's corpse out of some lake at some point? You'd believe me tenfold, wouldn't you?"

If the argument got through Jack's thick skull, he made no indication. "Hang out here for a while. When the sheriff calls, I'll tell him about the dead girl and we'll figure something out."

"I reported it, Jack." He lied. "It's not the point. The point is that I can't stay here, in this town, any longer."

Jack, whatever mess he'd gotten himself into, was no help. If the cops went to Elisabeth's house, they'd find Sondra Gleason's car and, most likely, her corpse. Elisabeth would never forgive him and, as much as he currently hated her, he couldn't let that happen. There was a binding sense of loyalty to her he only now realized.

"Call Lucy right now and figure out what she's doing so we can all get lost?"

"I tried her."

"Try her again."

Jack did.

Allen waited as it rang, and then watched Jack toss the phone onto one of the twin beds.

"Nothing."

With Jack staying put until Lucy reached out, he was on his own. He lied and told Jack he was going back to Elisabeth's place.

"Where is it, in case I need to reach you?"

He was reluctant to divulge this, but it wouldn't hurt to jot her address down on the motel stationary. It would make Jack more suspicious if he refused to tell. This way it looked like had nothing to hide.

He handed Jack the paper and said, "Call before you come, okay? Make sure I'm there. She doesn't like visitors."

"Big surprise," Jack said.

Allen left with little more than a fleeting goodbye. He went back to the Spyder and drove to downtown Pittsfield, eyes peeled for a bus station. It was a tiny building on the downtown strip, nestled in between a real estate agency and a PC repair shop. He parked Elisabeth's car and loaded the parking meter with all of the change he'd been able to fish out of the seat cushions. No reason to draw suspicion to himself until Western Massachusetts was a distant memory.

Had he told Elisabeth where in Central Mass he lived? Considering that he'd been able to follow Jack's trail like a bloodhound, he supposed it wouldn't matter. He felt defeated knowing he couldn't run from her. If she wanted him back, she'd find him.

And she was going to want him back. She had bitten him, made him into something like her. He was an investment.

A ticket to Boston cost thirty-five bucks. He took a seat on a bench beside the door, watching the street-level window for any signs of trouble. The clock ticked its way toward two-thirty and he tapped his foot on the coffee-stained tile while the time neared.

He sat thinking about the best course of action for a guy with the deaths of two women on his conscience. It was hard to say with accuracy whether he'd played a part in Molly's untimely fate, but deep down he had already holstered himself with the blame.

Why else dream about her?

Three men appeared in full view of the window, eyes tuned directly to him. They wore tattered blue jeans and various vested attire, their bare forearms littered with tattoos that heightened their uniformity. Hair was long and matted, slicked with a possible mixture of gel and grease, each spouting their own distinct facial hair. As out of place as they looked in this part of the world, they were *rough*. Guys you didn't cross.

Allen tensed as they entered, springing from the chair as one approached the ticket kiosk on the far end, striking up conversation with the booth woman. They should've been out of earshot, but he heard every word spoken in a thick European accent. His was a bogus story about accidentally buying tickets to New York City.

It was an interference play, nothing more.

The other two men approached Allen fast, stealing the seats on either side of him.

"Please." Another thick accent. "Take your seat again, Allen."

It didn't matter how they knew his name. They weren't telling him, even if he asked.

"Here is how this is going to work. You are going to get up when we do, as soon as our friend over there has concluded his business. When we stand, you will follow. We are going back to Greifsfield."

Allen's escape had been thwarted by some of the same guys he guessed Jack had been ducking.

Why did I leave him there?

They'd go for him next.

"Where are we going?" Allen asked, his tough guy façade was obvious and ineffective.

"Once you're born, you do not come and go as you please, asshole. Your cunt girlfriend might've done you a favor and made that real clear. Good thing our boss cares. Don't question another word unless you want bullets in your heart."

He didn't open his mouth again.

●

A walk into town was a relaxing way to pass some time. The sparse country roads made it easy to buy into the illusion of solitude. All you had to do was overlook the thin spread of driveways leading to homes that couldn't be glimpsed from the road.

Elisabeth might've been able to sense these habitations, but she ignored her prowess whenever she had no need for it. Just as people who lived near train tracks eventually grew immune to the constant rattling of locomotives, Elisabeth had to be listening, looking, or sniffing for someone in order to know they were coming.

This was preferable to the wolf's way of life.

With Allen out sorting through his convoluted thoughts, she hadn't felt like lounging. He wasn't supposed to have tasted blood yet, but that foolish girl's intrusion on what was now Elisabeth's property had given him little choice. That his gut instinct had been to rip her naked and feast on her organs was a sight for sore eyes. If anything she'd gotten off a bit easy, but Allen's ferocity was a positive sign. He would adjust nicely to this life. The way he'd savaged her made her stomach tingle.

This pup was worthy.

But that did not make his insistence on being alone today sit any better. That ridiculous human conscience was riddling him with more guilt. It wouldn't be hard to ease him beyond that side effect, but he had to *want* to get past it.

Perhaps that meant letting him take her. He'd wanted it more than anything, which was why she delighted in making him wait.

The pavement vibrated beneath her and her ears wiggled, signaling a repugnant arrival. Long-forgotten memories she had hoped never to recall were right around the corner, coming in time with the approaching vehicle.

She would not run, stepping off the road and pushing her shoulders against the nearest hemlock. She folded her arms as standoffishly as she could manage as a shiny dark sedan glided around the corner, its waxy coat gleaming in the sunny sky.

Its windows were blotted and its tires were outfitted with garish golden rims that continued spinning even as the car idled beside her.

I should've expected this.

The rear door opened, inflating the frame with Anton Fane's massive shoulders. His concrete eyes stared while he flashed an untouchable grin.

"Remind me again, Huntress, what it is that you see in that boy." He rubbed an open palm across her shoulder with the same brash entitlement.

"I will remind you of nothing." She slipped out from under his hand and resumed her walk.

"How perfunctory." Fane jogged alongside her while the car crawled along in silence like a secret service detail. "There is no reason for attitude, Huntress. I was merely injecting our reunion with some levity. I thought it might help smooth the somewhat awkward nature of our meeting."

"We have not reunited, Fane. *I* am walking to town. *You* are following like a stray animal begging for scraps."

"Is that where we're going? Town? I've had my fill of those...*yokels* for a while. You wouldn't believe how needy this community has proven."

She hoped her glance would register as disdainful. Everything about him was irritating. The bland and characterless get-up, a dark suit fit over a mocha button-down and capped off with a wide, brown and orange tie. His dark hair, peppered with sprinkles of gray, and brushed into a perfect, unnatural existence.

"Where's your briefcase?" she said. It came out more playful than intended.

Fane's eyes roved her back, choosing to ignore the insult. Instead, he dangled a familiar necklace between her eyes.

Elisabeth snapped it away with haste that made him flinch.

"So you still are capable of giving a damn," he laughed. "We stopped by your home first. You weren't there."

"So you stole this?"

"Never. Just wanted to see if you remembered where you came from."

The violation brought her anger to a boil. She placed the band around her neck and locked the clasp, sliding her thumb and index fingers along the pointed teeth. "Do not talk about *him*. Not ever."

"Of course not. I don't want to insult your latest boy toy." Fane smiled.

They walked in silence for a while and Fane showed no interest in breaking it. He kept in step, looking her over on occasion, but kept his thoughts vaulted.

The road dipped down, sloped up, and wound to the left, then the right. It would've been a peaceful walk if not for the unwelcome company. She hated herself for allowing him to get a rise out of her, if only for a second. She supposed it didn't matter. They went way back and, the sad truth of it was, nobody knew her better than Anton Fane. Their lives had taken them far apart, and in directions that conflicted, but fate was a comedian, deciding to reconnect them in the westernmost corner of Massachusetts.

They passed Ben Marshall's Placid Pines campground, a place that made nightly feeding an all too easy pastime, and moved onto scenic Main Street. Downtown Greifsfield was an old New England-style village, complete with a sweeping view of Mount Greyrock that solidified this place as a major player in the tourist industry.

Elisabeth crossed the street to Sheila's General Store when Fane took her by the arm and hustled her to the rear of the building.

"You were once a valuable asset to us." There was venom

in his voice as he spat the words. Licentious eyes ogled her breasts, but he didn't touch. "You might be under the impression that I'm here to catch up, and I understand that. I'm proud of the way I conduct myself in this dreadful body. But do not mistake civility for weakness. I'll gladly bruise your pretty face if you'd like to test me."

Elisabeth put distance between them.

"Your arrogance is no longer amusing," she said. "I have never doubted you. *Ever.* After all this time, you choose to treat me as one of your devotees?" Elisabeth fingered her necklace, straightening the fangs as she spoke.

"I should've done more than send an envoy to remind you I am in control of this pack."

"Pack? I did not come here to join any pack, least of all yours, Anton. I'm certainly not part of any following you may have somehow amassed."

"Relax, Huntress."

"I have not been a huntress for a very long time."

"Once a whore..."

"Finish that thought and I'll make you a fucking eunuch."

Fane stopped to compose himself.

"You say you are no longer a Huntress, fine. Yet here you are, close to me and mine. What am I supposed to think?"

"You're not."

"More curious still, you slink through the night turning clueless tourists into fledglings."

"I came here to be left alone," she said. "To be near our kind, yes, but for no ulterior motive. Greifsfield would have fallen off my list of real estate had I known that Anton Fane was already here. I sought the seclusion of the woods to be alone, not to admire you from afar."

"How fiercely independent. You've become quite the modern woman, haven't you?"

Elisabeth did not respond.

"Very well," he said with softening features. "Something important is happening in town, whether you choose to ignore it is up to you. But I cannot have you running around turning these horrendous *fleshbags*."

"I will say this, Anton. I did things for you that no one else would have. The south of France?" She waited until she saw acknowledgment turn over in his eyes. "That night should've been enough to stain my dreams forever and yet I followed through without question." She tugged the necklace again. "And when the inquisition hunted us, I did as you instructed. Every time."

"You hunted them for revenge."

"Eventually, yes. But for how long did they hunt us? Before we even knew there was an order, how many assassins did we send to the grave?"

"Simpler times," Fane said. He looked at her with a hint of nostalgia.

"Why can't you leave it at that?"

"I'm not trying to make you feel like an exponent but, just as it was back then, you will do what I say without question."

"You are not relevant anymore. Until today, you seemed to have no trouble remembering that."

"Choosing to disregard our little covenant, then?"

"It's you who perverts our customs to suit your convenience. I don't know how many other fools you have at your disposal, but you are wasting your time if you think me one."

Elisabeth studied the terrain behind Sheila's should he try another advance. With a dumpster to their right they were obscured from all passersby, and the wooded veil to their left offered futile escape. She would never run from him. Decades had passed without fear, but that didn't mean she'd forgotten what a monster he was. No need for a clash. Not that Fane would let that happen, anyway. He could have others attempt to do the job for him. Apparently everything was beneath him now.

Everything except speechifying.

She stood her ground, unflinchingly and with reflexes queued, ready to break away.

"I have come here today with a considerable lack of respect, I admit." Fane's shifted tactics were hollow, always a soldier and never the politician. "The Huntress deserves more than that. I am here on business and without the time needed to reunite old friends and lovers."

Elisabeth shuddered.

"Let me start again, Hunt-*er*, Elisabeth. Let me explain why I had one of mine come to visit you yesterday." He advanced, anticipating her flightiness.

After a cautious moment, she relaxed.

Then he lashed out, seizing her between powerful arms. She leapt back but Fane had been faster. Her dress was caught in the ball of his fist and, with a grunt, he yanked her forward into an unwavering grip.

"See that," he said, his eyes darting up and down the length of her face before lowering to enjoy his view of her assets. "You *are* a complacent little whore when it comes to me." His hand clamped around the small of her back, then dropped lower, caressing her ass over the thin layer of chambray. He forced his lips to her own, licking her clenched mouth. His tongue crawled through the barriers and lashed her pearly whites.

She whipped her neck away, refusing to validate the intrusion.

Elisabeth squeezed her eyes, racing to escape this as Fane's interest in her mouth waned. He nibbled on her neck with playful laughter, little beads of unwanted saliva leaving stains she couldn't wait to wipe.

"Stop," she said.

Her objection fell on Fane's apathy. He pressed close, rustling her hair. Slapping her cheeks. Squeezing her neck. Violently, he yanked the fabric of her dress, tearing it, and squeezing her breast tight in his hand.

"What did I just say to you?" It was time to vacate this despicable rendezvous.

He laughed at her retreat. This wasn't an old friend. He was an immoral king making an unsolicited advance on a chambermaid. All of it too predictable. He lunged forward again, just as she knew he would.

"I know you too well," he said, closing the gap between their bodies. "You only think you're in love with that boy."

Shit, he knew.

It was no surprise, she reminded herself. Mestipen had told him everything. Too much. That gypsy peasant would die as soon as the moment was right.

He was upon her again, licking his lips. Small steps inched closer to the dumpster, moving toward the empty liquor bottle that rested atop a pile of stretched trash bags.

"You are still probably the most gorgeous creature to have walked this earth," he smiled. "How's that for being nice?"

"You," she snarled, "are not *half* as charming as you've been led to believe."

"You have recruited more of our kind in any given decade than some huntresses accomplish in a century. I would think that the mystery of love would be dead to you by now."

"I did not think you this foolish."

"Don't tell me you still believe love is possible." He flicked her necklace. "You more than anyone else."

Her rage popped like a cork as she seized the empty bottle by the neck. Fane lunged but she was too fast, evading him completely. She swung the bottle and broke it across his head with a smash that sent shards of glass raining. He roared in pain, rubbing his eyes free of Jack Daniels as she dashed for the front of Sheila's.

Curbside, Fane's sedan continued its clueless idle.

This isn't going to end well.

She slowed her step once inside the general store. The elderly clerk behind the counter, Maddie, squinted from behind her tiny wireframe glasses.

"Elisabeth, you look radiant in that gown."

"Thank you, Maddie." She ducked into an aisle and followed shelves of cereal, pastries, and juices all the way to the rear of the store. To where she'd been known to grab the most basic art supplies on occasion. Somewhere behind her, Fane stomped in pursuit.

Music to her ears. She was delighted to have sparked such ire.

He appeared in the back aisle, shoulders rising and falling in cold, mechanical fashion.

Her hand closed around the shelved scissors as he thundered forward. She spun on the balls of her feet, meeting his stride.

Stopping it dead.

Elisabeth pushed the blade against his throat, applying only a hint of pressure. Enough for the sharpened tip to indent into stubbly skin. He froze, his eyes swinging down to assess the threat.

She poked the blade into his flesh with just a tad more force, threatening to draw blood at any wrong move.

"You're going to bury *that* in my throat? For what gain?"

"It will make you squirm, and it will hurt. At the very least, it will make you look very silly in front of your men when you go back home, tail between your legs."

Through clenched teeth he said, "The Huntress will sit at my side when I need her to."

Elisabeth cocked an eyebrow and popped her lips into the shape of an o to feign surprise. "You think so, huh? Is it your newfound wealth that fuels your ego?"

"You will witness the largest Turning in our history. It will be unlike anything you have ever seen." Fane's teeth mashed, sprinkling little beads of spittle across her skin.

"I. Don't. Care."

"I'll kill him before this is over."

Elisabeth swiped the scissors across his neck in fury, leaving behind a scrape of wet crimson. "If you show up at my home again, or if you so much as speak to Allen, I will make sure you spend the next few days explaining to your kin that certain appendages do take some time to grow back."

Fane seethed, pressing fingers to his wound.

"I came here to tell you that I wanted your pup at the Turning with you. I wanted him to be programmed the right way. He should also have the opportunity to witness his Huntress in all her glory, fulfilling a function for a higher purpose. You are a part of something larger, Elisabeth, and you do not turn it off whenever you feel like it. What sickens me is that you pretend not to realize this. You have a history with me. In many ways *you* are history. Those full moons on the moors where we'd vie for the most vicious kill, just you and I. We are responsible for so many of the stories passed down. And now you tell me you don't care about any of it?"

Elisabeth felt like slashing his jugular a second time, but held her ground hoping he would leave.

"I will call on you again," he said. "And you'd be wise to be ready. I have your pup. What happens next, his new life or sudden death, depends on you."

Fane backed away, walking off with the wound dribbling down his neck.

Just like that, he'd defeated her.

He would kill Allen without hesitation, if he hadn't already. Anton Fane was an adversary who left nothing to chance. Threats on Allen were not idle. If he said he had him, he was not bluffing.

Elisabeth listened as Fane's vehicle trailed off. She was going to have to find Allen quickly. And if it was too late, Anton Fane and his entire pack of followers would burn.

She'd come to this sleepy little tourist town for inspiration and here she was considering war.

She swallowed hard, knowing full well it had to be done.

And there was no turning back.

●

Allen's captors moved without regard for the speed limit or traffic laws. He bounced between his backseat captors, hoping for a direction. His curiosity was rewarded with a fist to the gut whenever he did anything other than look at his shoes.

"Told you not to look, yeh?"

"Do it again." The one riding shotgun turned and jammed the gun barrel in his face. "If you even sneeze, I'll assume you're turning into a fuckin' animal and splatter your shit all over my friends. It'd get messy real quick, but they'd understand."

It wasn't hard to avoid looking down from then on. They knew exactly who and what he was.

"I don't care if he does turn." The guy beside him said. "Let him try. A lot of good it will do." He pushed a slab of cold metal against Allen's temple. "I'll blow his brains all over Loiza before his fangs come out."

To his left, Loiza laughed. "I don't think yer doin' that." His voice was soft but authoritative. "Less you want to join this mutt in a world of hurt."

Shotgun offered a playful slap against his cheek and his hand climbed into Allen's disheveled hair, stroking it. "I do not see what she sees in you."

"You should probably know it's her fault you are going to

die," Loiza added. "Bitch could've easily saved your life you know, but pride is a tricky thing."

"I love her," Allen said, throwing as much defiance as he could muster. He should've been on his knees begging for his life, although it wasn't death that scared him. It was never seeing Elisabeth again.

Shotgun laughed and said something in his foreign tongue. Then, in English, "You cannot stop a whore. Not even with a hundred horses. An old gypsy saying. When you are gone, she will move on."

"Do I stop here?" the driver asked.

"Yes," Shotgun said.

The car slowed beside a ticket booth. A posted sign read TO MT. GREYROCK SUMMIT AREA. A clerk worked the gate and while the driver handed him a twenty, the thug on Allen's right jammed his pistol into his ribcage to prohibit any ideas. "I will fucking splatter you," he whispered.

Allen believed it. What help would a lanky college-age kid be, anyway?

"No visitors to the summit after dark," the booth jockey said, rejecting the money. Shotgun reached over with a hundred dollar bill. "But who am I to deny anyone the majesty of the Berkshire skyline?"

Shotgun laughed and waved to the jockey as the gate rose. They were on the move again.

"Why didn't you kill him?" Loiza asked.

"This mountain employs more than Greifsfield. I kill some kid from Pittsfield, people start asking questions. You want to explain to the boss why people are suddenly asking questions?"

Loiza said nothing.

Allen's nose wrinkled. The men on either side of him reeked of cigarette smoke, alcohol, and more. His nose studied the menagerie of smells until he discovered the anomaly. Loiza wore the scent of Mr. Thick European Accent and vice versa. They were awash in each other's musk.

He supposed he could add sense to his list of superior strength and speed.

"Pull off up here," Shotgun gestured to a dark turnoff.

The driver swung the car onto an inclined path that brought them to a cul de sac marked SCENIC AREA I.

Shotgun got out and fumbled to retrieve the weapon he must've stashed beneath his seat while passing through the gate.

Loiza stepped from the backseat and tugged at Allen's shirt, tearing through the seam. He fumbled into the dirt and suffered a kick to the stomach, then the balls, then his head. More feet joined in, winding and pouncing as his vision went white beneath bursts of stabbing pain.

"Blow his fucking brains out and toss him over the rail. Let the bears have him."

Two hammers cocked, a mini-firing squad ready to go. His body tensed.

Next came a stomp, deep and severe, followed by an explosion of glass. Allen spun in time to catch the sedan windows burst into shards.

His would-be killers were startled, speaking in terrified native tongues. They fanned out, guns drawn on the gigantic mass perched atop the sedan's caved-in roof. It squatted on hind legs, glaring at its targets while offering a persistent growl. Beneath it, from the driver's seat, a bloodied arm dangled out of the crushed and collapsed window. Thick black gore trickled down the swaying limb.

Shotgun was furthest from the car, legs spread apart like open scissors. His weapon gripped tight in both hands. To either of Allen's sides, the lovers took trembling aim at the wolf.

As if sensing the ballet of oncoming gunfire, the monster launched, leaping over the bullet rain. It hit the ground on all fours, the top of its ruffled shape visible over the sunken roof. It banked around the sedan's rear, trotting for Allen.

The gunmen shouted and struggled to keep aim. The beast was too quick, lingering in a patch of moonlight long enough to reveal a mane of midnight fur. The thick-accented killer screamed out as he fired two shots that went too wide. The animal snarled and took a swipe at the bad shot, breaking his leg off below the knee, the severed limb flying into the woods like a golf ball.

Loiza only had time to cry the very beginning of a pained protest. The wolf's sights were set. It bounded over Allen and landed on its hinds, towering three solid feet over the gunman. Loiza didn't go out fighting. He dropped his pistol and propped his forearms over his face to shield himself from impending carnage. The wolf batted them away with an annoyed snarl, carving bloody rivets in both his arms with a single swipe. Now the killer's terrified face was wide open for something worse.

And it came.

Massive jaws stretched, spraying ropes of saliva before they closed on Loiza's face. Talons dug into his chest with wet *thunks* that seemed to echo forever.

Shotgun's frantic gunfire caught the wolf by surprise.

Loiza's face tore from his bones like slow roasted chicken. Broken flaps of stubborn skin snapped back against his faceless skeleton.

The wolf came back for another bite, this time chomping into neck meat. Loiza's head spun into the air, rocketing into the night and spraying the car with a stream of gore. The head plopped and bounced off the hood, crashing into the dirt at Shotgun's feet.

To Allen's right, the legless killer whimpered as he reached out and grabbed the discarded weapon. He'd never fired a gun in his life and thought maybe he wouldn't need to, watching the wolf disappear, this time around the front of the car.

Shotgun called out for mercy, but received none. A sickening yelp and a wet gargle signaled his end. Allen was still, his injuries screaming.

The wolf sauntered back around toward him once it was finished eating. Its gigantic body brushed against his side, then dropped into the dirt and placed its nose against his to show its blue-yellow eyes. Only now did he realize how familiar they were. The animal's gentle eyes watched him struggle to his feet, despite throngs of pain that tried keeping him down.

Allen's anger was washed away by a stronger wave of relief.

Using her snout, Elisabeth motioned to the one-legged killer who sniveled beside them. Her eyes did not leave Allen's, and the inaudible growl, the tiniest noise ringing in his ears, was easy enough to understand.

He understood because, what she wanted, he wanted, too.

The air around him was fetid, but hunger outweighed the stench. An unquenched thirst, the same that had propelled him to take Sondra Gleason, drew the animal out.

He would regret this once it was over, like the worst one night stand. There'd be nothing but shame tomorrow. Tonight, though, the spilt blood was a succulent marinade, and no more convincing was necessary.

Allen fell to his knees beside the mutilated man.

"Please."

Elisabeth's cavernous blues swirled with perverse delight. The moment was about pleasing her as much as it was about feeding. Her yawning gaze said, "Do it."

He didn't need an invitation. This day would end as it had begun. He picked up the gypsy's wrist and sunk his teeth straight in, canines only now growing into points. His lips flushed with delicious crimson sprays, every drop exciting his tongue.

The wolf came running out of him. Once the gypsy's

forearm was nothing but a mess of broken bone and sinew he moved onto the man's chest, batting the open vest away with a furry palm. He dug in, gnashing against the meat and pulsing organs. He'd always liked bloody steaks, but this was even better. As fresh as fresh could be.

He changed as he ate, glancing at his lover in between bites. He was like her now, tearing the human body apart out of necessity for preservation.

The animal took over, save for a lingering spot at the bottom wrung of his consciousness. It knew enough to recognize his woman—the radiant bitch across the way. He observed her nodding snout and proud orbs that continued to encourage his every bite.

"I have you now," they seemed to say.

But Allen didn't care.

He wouldn't have it any other way.

Six

Lucy had started feeling out of her element about twelve hours ago.

She'd been lucky enough to secure a parking spot across the street from the Manhattan Mandarin Oriental. The only downside to this vantage point was that you had to crane your neck all the way around in order to keep an eye on the hotel's awning. Its patrons came and went at all hours.

The coffee shop three steps from her car offered a steady stream of caffeine and a few flirtatious exchanges with the middle-aged owner bought her anytime bathroom access. Wouldn't have gotten this far without a constant triple cappuccino espresso in her hand, but a busted bladder would've stopped this Nancy Drew stakeout long ago.

The last thirty-six hours hadn't provided the desired result, but Rory, he wasn't Dad anymore, was up to something. She hadn't found out for certain until the following morning when a limousine picked him up out front.

Trailing one of those through a sea of impatient Manhattan traffic wasn't easy. New York drivers were attuned to aggression. Slow down at a yellow light and it's a front bumper jammed up your ass. Hope you've got collision insurance! If the limo had recognized a tail, it made no indication, crawling in and around the impatient slew of honking vehicles until traffic thinned and they hit the Port Authority warehouse district. The limo slipped through an opening that led to a dilapidated waterfront three story, and then two security guards tugged closed the giant gate, leaving things to her imagination.

She had jotted the address down on her phone's notepad and waited for Rory to resurface. Three hours crawled by before he did. She followed him back into Manhattan and, by then, the streets were abuzz with lunch hour traffic. The limo dropped him off in front of what looked like a ritzy, five-course restaurant with small portions and massive prices.

Two middle-aged men dressed to the hilt in nicely tailored suits had accompanied him inside, their demeanor was forced casual and felt a bit too *upper class* for the type of company he usually kept. They put her on edge without knowing exactly why.

Whatever Rory Eastman was up to, it concerned more than just Greifsfield real estate. If he was trying to break into the NYC game by way of some ramshackle waterfront property, it remained to be seen.

What else could it be?

One ninety-minute lunch (and several drinks, based on his sloppy gait) later, Rory was driven back to the hotel, where he had stayed until late evening. As soon as he disappeared through the revolving door, she'd jogged down the sidewalk to a hotdog stand and grabbed an Italian sausage and Dr. Pepper.

The entire day passed before the trio had reappeared, and this time they hailed a cab that swung up onto the curb as if it had been waiting. Rory's two acquaintances weren't the same ones he'd eaten lunch with. One was incredibly young and pretty cute, not much older than her, with long, blond shoulder-length hair that blew in the humid evening wind. His dress was classy casual, a pink button down fastened halfway to reveal a well kempt, hairy chest. He had moved with the confidence of a celebrity, fully aware that any woman in her right mind would at least do a double take.

Beside him had been an older man, slightly overweight and dressed in baggy, unflattering clothes. His appearance was in sharp contrast to his better half—greasy, sleazy and off-putting.

Hard to imagine a life where those three had any commonalities.

They'd climbed into the taxi and Lucy was on its tail, weaving in and out of traffic with experience. Hadn't been so lucky, though, losing them somewhere over the Tappan Zee Bridge.

He had to return to the Mandarin Oriental at some point, but it was taking a while.

While she waited there, she'd considered telling Mom everything before realizing she still had nothing. It was still just her mind throwing sinister implications on what could be a legitimate business trip. She'd come here for proof.

And to think, this summer had gotten off to such a promising start: a few good friends, plus Allen, in town for a string of lazy days and sloppy nights. Summer lovin' was going to be a blast with Jack, even if the dummy was too stubborn to read her glaring signals.

Then Rory happened, causing the possibility of a carefree summer to vanish before her eyes. She needed to get even for that. Sure, Jack would help but she wasn't about to bring him into this. If they were to get caught spying, Rory wouldn't hesitate to make an example out of him.

You're alone.

And now was the time. Lucy glanced at the digital camera in the passenger seat. Sooner or later, it would be put to good use and then Rachel would have to believe her.

She wondered how Mom would react when presented with evidence. Vindication wasn't typically important, but when her mind stretched back to that groping, she wanted to hurt them both. Him for being a son of a bitch and her for turning a blind eye and leaving her children in harm's way.

Her stomach was queasy with the thought of everything.

Lucy pulled a gray Puma sweatshirt over her fiery red hair as she got out of the car. She stuffed her hands into her pockets and pushed through the revolving gateway into the lobby.

A young black woman was one of four people working the front desk and the only one available.

"Can I help you, ma'am?"

"You sure can. My name is Lucy Eastman." She plunked her driver's license down on the counter. "My father, Rory, is staying here for a few nights, and my mother asked me to stop by and give him this." She pulled a rolled-up paper from beneath her hoodie.

"Am I supposed to know what that is?" She looked at the line forming behind Lucy.

"Medical test results. Sensitive stuff."

"Leave it here and I'll see that he gets it."

"Like I said, sensitive stuff."

"Ma'am, there's a line..."

"And I'm at the front of it. And my father is staying here. Now I'm supposed to give him this."

"Then have a seat over there and wait."

Lucy looked at the girl's nameplate. RHONDA. She wasn't giving up the goods. The hotel ought to give her a raise.

"I could do that," Lucy said, "but that wouldn't be discrete. See, my father is with business compatriots. The kind of folks who'd get suspicious if they see his daughter hand off a roll of documents. Go on and look my father up. Rory. Eastman. He's practically here more than he's at home. Might be you even have my name on file. So, please, let me bring this to my father's room without incident."

Lucy pushed her license to the counter's edge, remembering the time she'd visited the city with Rory. She'd asked for her own room so that she could stay up late and watch *Rome* without worrying about Mom censoring her view of all the hot naked men. To her surprise, Rory went for it. In hindsight, probably so he could fuck an escort without discretion.

The clerk keyed in some information, then dropped a keycard down, pushing it and the license back.

"Enjoy your stay, Ms. Eastman," Rhonda said and then summoned the next in line.

"Thank you."

She made her way up to the 11th floor and found room 1108 in the furthest corner. Uncertain as to what she was looking for, she swiped the card.

The room didn't appear as though it'd been inhabited at all. Its smell was fresh, linen unlined. There wasn't so much as a crumpled piece of paper in the wastebasket. Fear and frustration gripped her stomach. Had all of this been a waste of time?

She drilled down, unwilling to accept defeat, taking another pass through the suite checking closets, drawers, and glancing beneath the bed. Not only was her father a son of a bitch, he was careful. One didn't get this far without bona fide paranoia.

A laptop satchel was tucked underneath the coffee table in the living room. The black leather blended against the wood finish, making it easy to miss on the initial sweep.

She went right for it, flipping it open and leafing through its contents. Beside the laptop, she found a handful of gritty photographs of a location she recognized.

The Big East.

They were shot through what must've been closed-circuit security cameras. The angles were all the same, looking down from ceiling level. Still photos taken of the living area in a number of rooms. It was easy to discern which had been snapped inside the hotel, and the ones taken in cabana rooms. People had been captured in varying degrees of undress while lounging on the couch

or twisted into compromising positions. Several of them were circled in red sharpie, room numbers scribbled into the corners of
each photo, along with a date that likely signified their checkout
time.

Her stomach danced, knowing there were hidden cameras in every room.

Or was this something new?

Her first instinct was to fold some of them into her sweatshirt and escape. Hightail it back home and let the police make
sense of things. But Rory wouldn't be here five minutes before
realizing some were missing. Then he'd check with the front desk
and find out that his daughter had stopped in for a visit and that
would be the end of it.

Instead, she put the digital Nikon to good use. A few quick
snaps of grainy photos captured them with enough legibility.
Then she rearranged everything just as she'd found it.

A quick sweep followed and she took cautious steps to
make sure she hadn't messed with anything else.

She was about to get away with this. One step closer to
getting Rory out of her life forever. Didn't matter if his prison sentence and legal bills would claim the family money, the Eastmans
would survive. Mom wouldn't feel the same way, but Lucy couldn't
bring herself to care that much about what she thought.

You're getting ahead of yourself.

The hotel room was free and clear. She started for the
door when a short knock froze her solid.

"Ms. Eastman, please open the door. This is hotel security."

Lucy said nothing. Her eyes swept the room, searching
for a way out. This was the 11th floor and escape was unlikely,
more unlikely than finding a dependable hiding spot. Duck into
any closet, slink beneath any bed, it didn't matter. It was only prolonging the inevitable.

"Ms. Eastman, please open. I will be forced to open up if you do not."

Lucy's trembling hand depressed the handle and the guard pushed in. He towered over her like Goliath. His uniform, a pair of black slacks and a burgundy jacket would've looked silly on anyone else, but his no-nonsense demeanor offset the monkey suit.

"You are here without your father's consent, we checked. His request is to keep you here until he arrives."

Lucy thrust her hands into her pockets to hide the jitters, and held her eyes on the good-looking Latino security officer. She took a quick round of breaths, inhaling slowly, and then breathing out her nose in powerful bursts. It helped slow her rapid heartbeat, if only a tiny bit.

"You can't keep me here because I want to see my father," she said, furious that her voice was sounded so uncertain.

"You *are* trespassing," the guard said, mustering a sympathetic look. "To the hotel, that is a crime. Just have a seat and wait for your father, who is coming directly."

He extended a gloved hand and motioned to the living area. *Be reasonable*, he seemed to say.

Lucy thought on this. When she was thirteen, she'd been caught shoplifting a Spice Girls CD, and had gotten as far as the parking lot when one of the employees came bursting out of the door. Turned out, he was willing to take the CD back if she gave over her phone number.

Dawn had never forgiven Lucy for giving *her* number, but what were high school friends for?

Any port in a storm.

The same logic applied here.

Maybe a trip downtown was best. The story could be that this was all a simple misunderstanding. That she'd come by to give her father documents (that she didn't have). And if the police checked her camera, which was a pretty solid guarantee, they'd have more than a few questions.

Ones she wouldn't be able to answer. So they'd ask Rory. He couldn't know his daughter was planning on sabotaging his life, and that would be the obvious tip off.

So, no, downtown didn't work.

Self-preservation won out. She allowed herself to be marched to the center of the room where she slid into one of the oversized chairs. It was hard on her back and stiff on her ass. Good. No sense in being comfortable. Rory didn't have to know she'd found anything. He'd check and see that the papers were still in place and that would satisfy him.

He wouldn't be expecting espionage from his daughter, and therefore, wouldn't check her camera.

You hope.

"I'll give you some privacy," the guard said. "But I'll be outside in the hall until your father gets here." He offered a consolatory frown before closing the door.

How could I have been so stupid?

Of course the hotel was going to check her story. Why hadn't she stopped to consider that? The anticipation of getting back at Rory had overwhelmed her common sense.

Now she was a venerable prisoner until Rory came back. Her mind projected all the ways in which their confrontation would go. At first, she saw herself as a self-righteous crusader. She'd get up, ball a fist against his chest and angrily demand answers.

For everything.

But guys like Rory didn't respond to hostility. They weren't used to it. More finesse would be needed here. And what lie was he going to have in place for the pile of surveillance photos? He'd been caught spying on resort guests. Maybe there's a good reason for it? Who was she going to show it to? Really, what did it prove?

The door clicked and swung open, snapping her back to reality.

A familiar face lurched forward.

She tried to smile, then swallowed.

●

Nothing like finding out your daughter was against you.

"Please, take my friends anywhere they want to go." Rory threw two new hundred-dollar bills through the partition. The cab driver gave an eager nod.

"I hope that your daughter is well." Darkho extended his hand for a quick shake. "A pity we did not reach our destination this evening, but I believe this has been a fruitful trip, regardless."

"Indeed," Rory said and forced a grin. "I trust you will be informing Mr. Fane that expectations have been met."

"*Exceeded.*" Darkho's mouth was a straight line and his eyes were just as listless. There was no trace of warmth in his face.

"Good evening then," Rory said and slammed the cab door as tactfully as possible. He marched through the lobby thinking about the deceitful little cunt he'd raised, imagining her looting through his possessions enraged him.

At the same time, it heightened his excitement.

His newest acquaintances had assured him that tonight's debauchery was merely a promise of better things to come, but what he'd received could barely be considered a tease.

It didn't matter in hindsight, however. Not if Lucy was waiting in his suite. The hotel had prepared her like the best fillet mignon.

Lucy's presence intensified with his ascent to the 11th floor. Jamming a wad of bills into the open-palmed hand of the guard, he pushed him aside without a second thought and swiped his card.

The long-legged redhead looked nervous, with fear so thick he tasted it at the back of his throat. It made him as hard as could be, and he stepped toward her with bulge that demanded freedom.

I want her to see it.

"What are you doing here?" His voice was quiet but harsh, respectful of surrounding guests, but enraged. She was snooping, and he knew that. One look in her eyes and he knew she'd seen the pictures. She couldn't know what they were in reference to, but it tipped her off to the surveillance system Anton Fane had insisted they install.

He even had his own men monitoring the thing day and night.

Lucy couldn't have known about them, either. And she couldn't know they were using the cameras to farm the most unsuspecting vacationers out to Fane—those who weren't likely to be missed.

No, she couldn't know these things. And yet, she knew enough.

The resort dug into its guests' personal lives with such ferocity it might have been the NSA. Fane's men determined who could be taken without notice, but Rory didn't know what they were being used for.

It couldn't have been good.

Lucy offered a brazen lie. "I wanted to see you."

"Don't lie, Lucy. Not now."

"You lost the right to be an authoritative figure when you tried to fuck me."

She stood up, a laughable attempt to display independence, and marched. Her tits jiggled with purpose, one final tease. All Rory could stand.

His conscience had eroded each day over the past year and now it was only an echo. That ping reminded him this was unthinkable and immoral, just like it had each time the urge stirred. But he'd tamped it down to the point where it was nothing.

Broadening lust drowned out every rational thought. He didn't give the bitch a chance to mouth off, yanking her like a ragdoll. She winced, an expression so helpless it made him laugh.

"I don't know what made you stop by, darling, but I'm glad you did."

"So you can try your luck again? Diddling your baby girl? Get used to the fact you've lost your family."

Rachel was no threat. He controlled her through a variety of means and she wasn't going anywhere. She'd come to rely on him for security, money, and her miserable management career.

But Lucy, she was on the verge of independence. Another year and she'd be completely free. The time for her flesh was now or never.

He smacked her across the eyes, knocking her head to one side with a snap.

"Come with me," he snarled, dragging her by a dangling arm into the bedroom.

"My arm's going to pop, you bastard. Let me go!"

He kicked the door and tossed her onto the bed.

She screamed for help but a quick punch to the gut doubled her over.

All the times he wanted to smack her face for stumbling home drunk past curfew, all times she'd mouthed off, the stolen twenties out of his wallet in junior high. The bitch had it coming.

All of it.

"Know how long I've needed this?"

A flurry of elbows flailed, and he brushed them aside like brambles in the backyard. Her struggle made this all the more sporting, and while she never had a chance, it would make her flesh taste all the sweeter.

Then she dug a finger into his eye.

●

Lucy was a mess of emotions and her sides hurt like hell. It didn't stop her from scrambling to her feet and leaving a crippled Rory Eastman howling in pain.

Wobbly legs carried her through the living room as fast as she could force them. The door was a few short strides away and he couldn't get her once she passed through. There were guests, staff, and cameras to contend with.

Her mouth tasted of blood and she was certain she had the physical injuries to prove he'd assaulted her.

He's finished.

She grabbed for the door hoping her camera hadn't been damaged in her tumble. The wall beside her exploded in a puff of sheetrock and insulation, shards striking her face.

Talons raked across her nose, severing her vision beneath eager streams of blood. She tried to yell but something sprung through the languishing haze and knocked her to the ground.

Her head smashed against hard floor and her eyesight exploded into a fuzzy veil.

Rory's mouth barked down through the fog, and he changed into an animal before her very confused eyes. Her face burned, but it was nothing compared to what followed. Pain was a lit fuse, eating her shoulder and rocketing all the way to her head.

She drifted toward unnatural sleep and her attacker dipped its snout forward and sniffed. She glanced at it before the void came.

The wolf snarled, looking back at her with one good eye.

●

Sondra Gleason, what remained of her, leaned over Allen. Her damaged eye looked runny, but managed a scrutinizing glare, regardless.

Up close, Allen realized just how much destruction he'd done. Most of her face had been ripped clear, and the patches of skin that remained were the color of rot.

"You're living in my parents' house," she said. The voice wasn't feminine, human, or alive. In looking at this *thing*, it was hard to tell what sex it had ever been in life.

"You're a killer, Allen. Did you get my parents, too?"

When he couldn't respond, Sondra moved in closer, and rotten vapor wafted across his face. With an arthritic groan, she hefted up and clamped her bloody thighs and gnawed ankles against his hips.

Her limber body collapsed onto him.

"You're lost to everyone now, everyone except us."

Skeletal fingers raked her shredded chest, skipping up and down her rib cage like a string instrument. "Your soul is down here with us already. It's waiting for your disgusting body to catch up to it, and it will. God died in you the moment you killed me."

Allen's body twitched, a spasm that would've sent the undead girl bucking free had she really been there. He flung upright and a sweaty, tattered sweatshirt fell off his bare chest. His breathing was heavy and stilted. That terrible taste on this tongue once again, complete with food wedged between his teeth.

He was going to need to teach the wolf to start carrying floss.

The cozy clearing beside the babbling creek was a sight for sore eyes. The way the trees hung ensconced him in a private hideaway. He felt safe here, secure.

Rippling water splashed against him and he turned in time to see Elisabeth rising from the pond. Her wet skin shimmered beneath errant moonbeams. Her eyes looked momentarily green when reflected in the dark, then turned to blue as she neared, staring down with a mixture of affection and mischief.

"You were dreaming," she said softly, standing over him

like an inverted V. Drops of water rained off her thighs, sprinkling his face and mouth. "What was it about?"

No better view to help melt away the tension of his most recent nightmare.

"Her."

"The one you killed?"

"I didn't kill anyone," he said. That wasn't true, and he couldn't sell that lie to anyone, let alone himself. He didn't bother back pedaling the statement.

Elisabeth's breasts rose and fell with frustration. "You've killed two people, Allen. You're going to kill a lot more. You don't answer to the world now."

"Do I answer to you?"

"To no one."

His mouth tasted like spoiled hamburger. Worse than cigar mouth.

"You're not used to that taste," she said as he licked the roof of his mouth, smacking his tongue in misery. "That will come in time."

"Stop saying shit like that."

"What? That you're no longer human? You are not. Why should I waste time trying to paint you a romantic portrait? You are a changed man and it is for the better."

"Better? Waking up feeling like every bone in my body has been broken and healed? Chunks of flesh caught in my teeth. Dried blood plastered to me like snot. And what about those guys who came after me? They were going to kill me. I'm supposed to feel awesome because you say so? I might get used to scabies too, but that doesn't mean I want them. You're not making a very good case for the fucking favor you did me."

Elisabeth stood and watched. Her eyes narrowed, then bugged as she chewed her lower lip and raised her eyebrows. A bunch of false starts to a reply she couldn't quite find.

"Those men were acquaintances of an old friend. It is regrettable that they tried something like that, and I'm glad they're dead. He undoubtedly knows this, though. And shall try further retaliation."

"More danger? This really is a gift, Ms. Luna."

"No. That was the last time you will ever have to worry, about anything."

"I'm worried right now, Elisabeth. I've got weight on my conscience for the people I've killed."

"One of whom was planning to kill you."

"I wish it mattered. I'm something I don't even believe exists, and all you keep saying is that it will get better. I don't feel like a part of reality. Too scared to sleep for fear I'll be visited by talking corpses of women I knew. And you did this to me."

"Tell me about your dreams."

"They're weird, but vivid. A few nights ago, I saw Molly. Remember the girl from dinner?"

"I remember."

"She was mangled. Then there was my mom, and I'll die before I ever think about that again. There was this other woman, a blonde I didn't know."

Elisabeth had dipped her feet into the brook, rinsing off the pines glued to her soles. Her body stiffened at mention of her.

"What woman?"

"Blonde, like I said, sitting on top of a pile of skulls."

"Impossible." Elisabeth's features hardened, an awful job of masking her concern. "Describe it in more detail. Where was she? What did she say?"

"Didn't say anything. She was inside a church, and she was motioning for me to come to her."

"She beckoned to you?" Her brow creased. "I do not recall the last time this has happened."

"Who is she?"

"Our...*queen,* for lack of a better word. Her name is Alina, and she has marked you from the beyond for reasons that are unknown to me."

"The beyond? Like the grave?"

"No. Alina's alive. The first wolf. She uses the beyond to commune with the living and the dead from every corner of the world, and the realms outside it."

"Why has she marked me? What does she want? How does she know who I am?" His torrent of questions was unrelenting until she raised a finger and touched his lips.

This, the slightest touch, juiced him.

"Do not worry. Alina forms a connection to those with the utmost potential. It is what brought her to me all those years ago. If she has marked you, Allen, it is not because you've been chosen or prophesied about, nothing so grandiose." Her eyes went narrow once more, and she couldn't refrain from grinning. "But she recognizes darkness in you. She wants you to embrace who you are, as do I."

"You said you didn't know why she marked me."

"It has not happened to anyone in some time."

"None of this makes me feel any better, this is a nightmare you've thrown me into."

"Do not think like that. Alina only wants you to give in to the wolf."

"Why am I seeing all this? Victims, relatives, and now you tell me there's a *queen*? Just saying it out loud sounds..."

"I know," Elisabeth said. "It is our curse, the mark of the varcolac. Until you give yourself over to the wolf, your conscience will be *haunted* by the animal's victims."

"I'm going to see these people forever? Tonight I can expect a visit from the gypsy I killed?"

"It fades. The sooner you come to terms with yourself, the sooner it happens. Your soul trails your body. While you are already a wolf, your spirit struggles to catch up. These nightmares are echoes of your past. The world to which you belonged will shun and fear you. Some will even hunt and try to kill you."

"I don't want people to fear me."

Her laughter was February cold. "Humor me, then. What will you miss most about your old life? University? Working toward obtaining a worthless piece of paper?"

Allen didn't answer.

Elisabeth continued. "The 40 hour work week? It's getting longer every year. Morning commutes, miserable faces. So many people slaving away at jobs they can't stand so they can afford little patches of land. That's living? What kind of life is that?"

"It's not all like that."

"No. Of course not. I forgot about the miserable spouse you'll tire of fucking. The bratty children you'll fool yourself into wanting because you can't stand empty nights alone. Sure you might love them, but a part of you, the honest part, will resent them. Because maybe you'd have been happier had you not bothered, looking instead for whatever you really want out of life. It goes on and on, the misery. And it does not end. I did not curse you, as you're so passive-aggressively implying. I rescued you."

"Quite the sales pitch."

"It is not a sales pitch. I have been alive a lot longer than you. I have seen this happen time after time, and I do not want it for you."

This was getting messy.

Allen contemplated the ways in which he could escape—a variation on the whole *'I'm going out for milk or cigarettes'* thing. He bounced some ideas around, though none would stick.

He already tried leaving once and it brought him right back. *Groundhog Day* with werewolves.

Werewolves.

No, they don't exist. This is something else. It had to be.

Elisabeth's back was to him, her neck craned. She smiled, but it was impossible to return the gesture. What was worth smiling about?

His resistance was melting, replaced by the urge to go to her. Taste her lips, then everything else. Try as he might, there was no way he wanted to be anywhere but beside her even as Sondra Gleason crept back into his thoughts.

There was no remorse for the gypsy steak, but the innocent girl, whose only crime had been looking for her parents, haunted him. And it was going to take more than pussy to make him forget.

What about Molly?

That churned his guts. He'd spent a lot of time wishing Molly would go away. Forever. That night in the dorm when she'd pulled her signature attention grab, storming out of Reilly's party in tears because Allen had claimed to a roomful of peers she gave terrible head. It was their third breakup.

After every girl there had finished berating him, he might've been quoted as saying, "I hope she dies in a car accident on her ride home."

But he hadn't meant it. It had been late in the evening and his stomach was full of cheap college beer.

Now that her fate had aligned itself with that earlier wish, at least the end result of it, it was impossible to feel any lower.

And while his stomach twisted and wrapped itself in regrettable knots over these murders, there was shameful relief in the knowledge she'd never make his life uncomfortable again.

He wouldn't confess this to another soul, not even Elisabeth. Not because she wouldn't understand, he was sure that she would, but because it would be acknowledging his turning.

"It gets easier, lover. That's all I wish to say. Believe me."

He wanted to believe, but every thought brought discomfort.

She lured him up and they walked in the nude back to her home. The throbbing pain subsided, becoming an inconvenient ache.

He tried getting into the bathroom alone, but Elisabeth wouldn't have it. She fed him a line about "buckling at the knees" in his weakened condition before insisting on being in the room with him. She leaned nude against the pedestal sink, watching him shower off his naked, bruised body.

He glanced at her, cross-legged, covering her curves with a deliberate pose that might've been natural if not for the woman in question. Her slender arms obscured what would be a satisfying view of perfect breasts. The tease was enough to get the blood flowing again. No sense in hiding it, either. She should see how badly he needed it.

And Elisabeth was looking, too. A sideways glance explored his sudsy body. She smirked, enjoying the private show he provided.

The forceful way that Elisabeth got what she wanted aroused him. Never before had he met a woman worthy of such worship. Blood swirled down the drain with soapy grime, leaving him newly cleansed of the day's dreadful acts. He stepped onto the cold tiled floor, staring straight into Elisabeth's calculating eyes.

What was behind them? It was that aura of mystery that made her so exciting, so alluring. Mystique was a huge part of this attraction and while he needed to know everything about Elisabeth Luna, it could wait. He wanted to be a willing subservient.

"You...are...amazing," Allen said.

"Show me."

He dropped to his knees and she uncrossed her legs. He leaned inward toward her hips, brushing against her inner thigh while planting small kisses on an upward trail.

Elisabeth yanked a handful of his wet hair, tugging it with savagery. His eyes darted over her breasts to find her gaze.

"Not yet," she said.

"Yes," he said, finding confidence in steady breathing. "I've waited long enough for this."

"Then let me hear you say it."

"I want you," he said and attempted to shake free of her grip.

She only solidified it, yanking his head harder to keep it angled. A twinge of amused cruelty crossed her face. Was this nothing more than a game?

"What do you want, my love?"

"I want *you*."

"No. I said...what do you want?"

"I want to kiss you. Taste you everywhere. I need it, Elisabeth."

She released her grip like a satisfied master. He went straight between her legs, massaging her with his tongue. Her body stiffened, trembling with her own anticipation as he danced around the pink, teasing her.

He loved feeling her body shake. Maybe Elisabeth only pretended to wield all the power. Maybe there was a way to tip the scales and seize a little control.

That was the alpha wolf talking.

He continued his taunt, adamant that she wouldn't get what she needed so soon. She'd made him wait all this time, and he wasn't finished savoring it. All of the sights and smells of being this close, he wanted to experience them all. Slowly.

Elisabeth exhaled a frustrated sigh of ecstasy while his tongue brushed against her sex.

She pulled another tuft of hair and guided him to where he needed to go. Allen obliged, tasting her sweetness on his tongue.

Her moans grew into far climbing cries, and her muscular thighs locked against his ears. Her hips gyrated in rhythm with his jaw thrusts.

She slid down off the sink and pulled him up toward her face, slow enough for him to leave kisses across the rest of her body as he climbed to greet her.

He drank in the rest of the sights and then saw her face, vulnerable for the first time. It only made him want her more. Not in lust, there was something more stirring in the center of his chest.

"Do you love me?" she begged between kisses.

"I love you," he said, panting.

Tears fell from her eyes, slicking her cheeks and cascading to her lips. Her quivering mouth found composure long enough to ask, "Do you understand why I did this to you? *For* you?"

"Yes."

"And are you angry with me for doing so?" Her hands tugged the back of his neck. Elisabeth's mouth dangled open and her heart raged. She hung on his every word, instilling him with more power than he'd ever had over anyone.

He couldn't bear to see her like this.

"I'm not angry," he said. "I don't think I could ever feel that way about you."

"You're mine now, lover. Say it."

"I'm yours."

"Again."

"I'm yours, Elisabeth."

It had to be this way. He would give anything to be with her and if she had no problem doing the things their kind did to survive, there was no reason he couldn't learn to do the same.

This kind of happiness was worth fighting for.

They fucked face-to-face on the bathroom floor, their hands gripping every part of each other with avarice. Beads of sweat formed on their heaving chests, eyes locked in a dead stare as their bodies came together and broke apart in a succinct rhythm scored to inaudible music.

"I love you," Elisabeth whispered. Their eyes stayed locked. "You feel how wet I am, that's for you. All for you."

Allen knew from then on that he was never going to leave her.

●

Anton Fane watched Julianna stand before the head-to-ceiling vanity mirror, frantically trying to look pretty for the fast-approaching visitors.

He balled his hands into iron-locked fists for how much he resented this charade.

"Do not bother," he said, taking a place beside her.

But she paid him no mind. "Yeah, I'm going to hustle downstairs to greet them looking like a bloody poser."

Fane ignored the insubordination. "Whatever you do to yourself, it doesn't matter. You're a mongrel and everybody knows it."

"Toss off, then," she said. "I've got to look me best. Anything less says more about you."

The bitch had a point. Julianna had to look unattainable for the business partners, not to mention the small group of fledglings that were due to be released into the wilderness.

She had to look the part of a huntress, which meant every single guest had better ogle her at least once. Turning heads wasn't a problem for her. Even in her human getup, she was desirable. Her stark, shoulder length white hair contrasted nicely with golden brown, perpetually tanned skin. Her breasts were large, but not excessive, and fit nicely in the palms of his hands. Her bum was smoother than a pear, toned and as firm as her ample chest. Those long legs were nicely shaped, infused with just the right amount of muscular definition.

Fane loathed the gangly form of these fleshbags, but Julianna was undeniably the pinnacle of their kind.

Besides, she was his own personal doll and he found much enjoyment in watching her build herself up for any such occasion. Having amassed an impressive collection of attire from every corner of the world, her attention to wardrobe was meticulous. So much that he'd commissioned several of the top clothiers around the world to create exclusive outfits tailored to her flawless shape.

A worthy investment, he thought, watching her slide a crimson red thong into place around her shapely ass.

There was a knock at their chamber door, but Fane didn't open. The scent belonged to Konstantin.

"A car just passed the gatehouse. It's Eastman."

Fane placed a powerful hand on Julianna's bottom, caressing it with appreciation.

"You're right, you know. I want you to look your best. You will be the envy of everyone at tonight's ceremony."

"Right, then," she said, brushing dark eyeliner under her carefully tweezed brow. Her hands worked with a surgeon's precision.

Fane threw a robe around his physique and stepped into the hallway, looking down at Konstantin.

"Eyes open, sentry. After what happened to your brother and the others, I don't want any mistakes. These next few days are going to be very important."

The sentry nodded and led Fane down the dimly lit corridor, through an ornate pair of double doors leading to an opulent balcony overlooking the grand hallway.

Rory Eastman stood against the door in a threadbare button-down shirt, but his disheveled appearance didn't stop there. A stream of gauze wrapped around his head, masking his right eye, which was stained with an expansive circle of crimson. His receding hairline was ruffled and his breathing hadn't yet returned to normal.

It was worth seeing him in such disarray.

"Please, Anton. I need your help."

"You're supposed to be in the city with our partners, Eastman. Do not tell me you can't handle the simple task for which I've enlisted you."

Eastman looked exhausted and he waved the comment away. "Nothing like that, we accomplished what you wanted."

"So you found me somewhere that will work?"

"Your friends took me all over the city scouting locations, and I've got the perfect one, a private place down by the docks. I'll be signing the preliminary paperwork with my loan officer in the morning. We even have someone to set up as a manager. He won't ask a single question, and we'll be in business."

"Good," Fane said, no longer able to mask his contempt. "But I think we will use my own people for this."

Eastman's eye was glazed, staring up at the chandelier as though it were a rocket from the future. Fane wanted to refrain from asking what happened, as he didn't much care, but Rory Eastman was instrumental in purchasing the property in question. If they needed to hire someone for the front office charade, so be it. There was no rule stating he wouldn't meet an unfortunate end once the deal was done.

"Tell me what happened," Fane said.

"My daughter," he said with all the petulance of a schoolboy. "I fed on her." His face was anguished and Fane couldn't tell if it was because of tortured remorse or physical pain. Knowing what he knew of Rory Eastman, he guessed the latter.

"And when you did, she fought back, is that it?"

A shameful nod.

The truth was that Rory wasn't fit to run with any pack, let alone his. He was a lecherous man, and that wouldn't have been a detriment if he weren't also spineless and stupid. A father's lust for his daughter was nothing new, but it became a problem when it called unneeded attention to Greifsfield.

Fane patted him with contempt. "You're in pain, Eastman. I thought I explained that all of this will pass in no time?"

"But my eye," his voice was dominated by sobs. "She destroyed it."

"It too will return. You're varcolac and therefore do not suffer the indignity of human frailty. Why don't we do this, go upstairs, get cleaned up. I'm having a gathering in the early morning hours. The last round of resort guests that my people identified have been here for a few days, enjoying their stay in my, *ahem*, wine cellar. I want them to give the newest among us the thrill of the hunt without sending them into the wild. All they have to do is go downstairs to pick a will-be victim. I find it breeds confidence if their first kill goes off without a hitch. So what do you say to having a little fun later?"

Eastman grinned like a kid in a candy store. "No problem. I had a big night planned with the daughter, but maybe she should cool off in my trunk for a while."

Seven

Jack felt like an Agatha Christie character. All around him, people were disappearing without a trace. Not just friends, either. According to Officer Sean West, Sheriff Trever Ingram was on sick leave as of Friday morning.

"He said he was going to check in with me. This was two nights ago." The Greifsfield Sheriff's Office was considerably less depressing in daylight hours. It pulsed with regular workplace sounds: a humming printer, ringing phones, idle chitchat.

The door leading to Sheriff Ingram's office was closed, the shade drawn.

The officer behind the front desk was more interested in an issue of *Outdoor Hunting Magazine*. He dropped his head into the palm of his hand and swiveled his eyes, stopping just short of an eye roll.

"What was this regarding?" He said.

"The Big East. I was staying there until two nights ago. Someone broke into my room and..."

"Oh yeah," Officer West's attention fell back to the article listing the best ways to preserve venison. "Sheriff Ingram took that up with resort management on Friday. His Deputy, Collins, wrote the report last night."

"Was he going to alert me?"

"Sheriff's sick."

"So you're saying he's out sick?"

Officer West didn't appear to register the sarcasm. "Here's what happened. Your follow-up call must've slipped through the cracks."

"That clears everything up."

"Here's what else we know. The town drunk over in Cheshire tried sneaking onto resort grounds thinking he'd break into some of the more secluded cottages and rob them blind. That's about all I can say, but go ahead back to your vacation now. Nothing to worry about."

"Missing friends?"

"Who's missing? No reports have been filed. Says right here your buddy's shacked up with one Elisabeth Luna. And if Mr. Eastman thinks his daughter's missing, he'll put a call in directly."

"You're right, I can rest easy."

"Look, Deputy Collins spoke to Assistant Manager Davies yesterday. The resort agreed that the best thing to do would be to pile on some extra security. You folks won't be able to take a shit without passing through a checkpoint up there."

"Case closed, huh?"

"As far as you know. Got something else I can do for you?"

Under other circumstances, Jack would've pressed harder on Lucy's disappearance. It wouldn't do any good to put them on Molly's trail since Balthazar Davies had most likely covered it up. At this point, the best option was to sit down with Rory Eastman and have him get people looking for his daughter. Lucy wouldn't want it, but the guy had the resources to get things done. What other choice was there?

Jack gave Officer West the emptiest *thank you* he had and exited the station, burdened with dread. Roughly ninety minutes of daylight remained in the day and he planned to be behind locked doors long before sunset.

He jogged across the street to his car and slid behind the wheel. Checking his side mirror for traffic, he caught a glimpse of Officer West standing beneath the station's entryway watching him. Jack was certain the cop had forgotten to tell him something. When West made no further motion, Jack pulled away with a sinking feeling.

Something else for the growing checklist of weird.

Greifsfield's downtown hub was eerily quiet for a Saturday in June. Even the local eateries, typically brimming with visiting couples and families, looked desperate for patronage. Odd, as these were peak dining hours. Jack had seen some of these places busier during offseason trips to visit Lucy.

He drifted through Greifsfield center, trying to get his head around everything that was wrong. People were out and about, but their movements and mannerisms were all the same. Hurried. Like they wanted off the streets before nightfall as much as he did.

He didn't want to consider that. Most of these people were locals going through their daily motions. They lived here year round and were fully adjusted to any small town idiosyncrasies.

That's what he told himself, at least.

He banked a right at the intersection and swung onto Old Walker Road, heading into suburban Greifsfield. He drove to Lucy's house for the third time today, hoping to find her car in the driveway. It wasn't and so he kept driving, dialing each mutual college acquaintance on his phone, asking whether or not anyone had seen her.

"Not since finals."

"I talked to her once, but haven't seen her since we moved out of the dorms."

"Haven't heard from the bitch once all summer."

On his way back to town, he skipped past the turn for the Big East, deciding that he wouldn't be spending another night there, despite the disingenuous assurances of Officer West.

Heading back to Pittsfield was a possibility, but he'd checked out of the Tavern on the Hill this morning and didn't want to drop two hundred and fifty bucks on another night. Which meant the only remaining option was heading home to Leominster.

The road was dark and without streetlights. At ten past eight, daylight was ready to pack it in. And so was he. Time to get the hell out of Dodge. He slowed his speed, looking for the nearest driveway to turn around.

Flashing red and blues ignited in his rearview, accompanied by a police siren. Startled, Jack pulled over and hoped the cruiser would speed by. Instead, it slowed on his bumper.

He hadn't been speeding and, as far as he knew, his brake lights were intact. Jack steadied his hands on the steering wheel and took deep breaths, hoping to smooth his nerves by the time the cop arrived.

Two knuckles rapped his window in startling succession. When his heart didn't explode, Jack threw a hand against his chest and sighed with relief.

"Holy shit," he mumbled and rolled down the window.

The stone cold face of Officer Sean West ducked into the open frame. He said nothing and just stared.

Jack's previous thought must've been right. Officer West must've been trying to motion from the sidewalk. He had something else to say. Why go through all the effort otherwise?

"Step out of the car please, sir."

"Hi, Officer West. Did I..."

"Out."

There weren't any options here. Jack was at the mercy of the law. Drive away and risk taking a bullet to the back of the head. Refuse to step outside and risk being pulled, screaming and kicking through the window.

He swung the door open and eased his way out.

"I'm not trying to make trouble for you guys," Jack said, unconsciously raising his hands. "I'm just worried about my missing friend, and I think it might have something to do with that resort."

"There's nothing happening at the resort I didn't already tell you about. As for this friend of yours, it better not be that girl you think disappeared from there on Friday morning."

"Not her," Jack said.

"You're telling me people close to you have a funny way of going missing, is that right?"

The tension in the cop's voice escalated. He was intent on provoking Jack, or trying to run him out of town, at least.

"Have I committed a crime?" Jack said.

The cop's hands shot forward, taking Jack's throat in a compactor squeeze. They tumbled back and Jack's spine slammed hard against the car door. West's grip was a clamp. "Don't try and pretend you don't know what's happening. They should've killed you long ago."

More headlights slowed on approach, pulling in behind the flashing cruiser and disappearing behind the booming red and blue glow.

It wasn't backup, not from the way West's head cranked. Keeping his hands clamped, he dragged Jack around the car headed toward the cover of forest. Jack's sneakers carved wobbly trails in the dirt. He tried to scream for help, but his voice was a wheeze. If they got to the tree line, West was going to put a bullet in his brain.

"Believe me," West said, throwing Jack to the ground. "You're better off this way, brother. Some of those others might enjoy this. I'm going to make it quick."

West unholstered his Glock in slow motion.

"Close your eyes. I don't want you watching while I put

you down."

Jack squeezed his sight to black and braced for a blast to the head. It never came. There was a thud followed by the immediate shock of two hundred pounds crashing down onto him. The wide-eyed body of Officer West had a chunk of his head missing.

Jack slid out from beneath the dead cop, wiping blood from his eyes.

"Take his gun." A female voice cut the darkness. "You're going to need it."

Jack spun in a circle, panicked. His car was maybe ten feet away. If he was fast, he should be able to make it. Then make Greifsfield a memory. Forever.

"Don't run," the voice said. She emerged from the thick foliage with a smoking silenced pistol in hand. "Try and run, they're going to hunt and kill you. That cop most likely called in your plate before pulling you over. That means his buddies are en route. If they find you, I won't be able to protect you."

"I'm leaving town."

"You won't get far." She studied the dead body with suspicion. "You hurt? He bite you? Anyone bite you?"

"Bite? I haven't been bitten."

The shadows loved her. Beyond her outline there was very little to see, save for lighter hair bunched up at the top of her head, and a gun extending in Jack's direction.

"This one must've been new, didn't quite master the art of killing and eating his prey."

On top of being violent, she was crazy. Savior or not, Jack wasn't going to argue with a vigilante. He realized he was nodding along, and would continue to do so as long as she was armed and willing to kill.

She stepped into the light wearing a blonde ponytail, clad in military getup, complete with all sorts of combat utilities. She looked *capable*, and at just a few inches taller than him, probably

5'9", her broad shoulders hinted at more strength than he'd ever have.

He wondered how she moved around town looking like she should be occupying a foreign country.

The blonde dropped to one knee and examined the body. Then she holstered her weapon and grabbed the service pistol Jack had neglected to take. She unsheathed a massive blade and stepped on her victim's neck with a thick boot, swinging it through the air. It hacked through bone with a textured crack. Two more swings until the head broke away from its neck, completely severed from the lower jaw.

"You're coming with me," she said, sheathing the bloody knife. "You have no choice. Don't give me any shit and we'll get along...ok?"

"I...sure."

"That's more shit than I'm willing to take from you. Shut up and follow me."

Jack stood in stunned silence.

"Listen, I know this type of thing demands more finesse than I'm giving. Like I said, the cops will be here any minute. You don't want them to see their friend here because, believe me, they're not going to take you into custody. I need you to come with me so you can tell me all you know. We can't do that here."

There was zero emotion in her voice and hardly any behind her eyes.

"Who are you?" Jack asked as they walked to her vehicle.

"Shut it," she said. "I have to listen."

"For?"

"Those things." She shushed him as they climbed into the cab of her pickup.

"Your car's no good. They'll be looking for it."

"If they have my plates they know where I live. They'll find my parents."

"And that's why they need to find your car. They can't think you've left town. You might not like it, but I'm the safest place for you right now. And if there's anything you need out of there, I suggest you grab it in the next fifteen seconds because you'll never see it again. Try to run from me and I'll gun you down."

"I thought you needed to pick my brain." Jack slammed the door. His belongings were clothes that could be replaced.

"I need to ask you a lot of questions," she said. "But if you try to run, those things out there will find you. And they'll either kill you or make you one of them."

"I feel safer already," Jack said, staring at the headless corpse in the brush as the truck pulled away.

●

Elisabeth heard the howling in the hours just before dawn. A chorus of cries lit the Greifsfield sky, ushering in the new day.

Being among her own kind should make her feel welcome. That howling had once been a beacon, a lure to Greifsfield, letting other varcolac know it was safe to come.

She'd never felt more foolish. Though she rarely gave a damn about what others thought, Anton Fane had interpreted her arrival as a way to reconnect. That kept her awake at night.

Seething.

Whatever Fane was doing was outside their kind's best interest, but that had always been his self-serving way.

Allen's sweaty, muscular arm draped over her, pulling her against him with possession. She traced the pleasing contours of his form while her insides glowed. He was coming along nicely. His intense passion for her made it easy, for it was always the key to corruption.

Any decent person could be tarnished for the right price. As a huntress she'd gotten better at doing it than anyone and it was still among her talents. Her only trepidation came when the pup was left to his own thoughts for too long, but her touch was all that was needed to help him forget.

To be fair, she wanted him as badly as he needed her.

Her fingers stroked the longest fang on her necklace. With Allen caressing her stomach in his sleep, she felt a stitch of guilt, but could not say for whom. Aetius was so long ago, and almost entirely a memory. Without this trinket, she might've questioned whether or not their love had happened at all.

Memories and dreams were indistinguishable after the right length of time. He would want her to be happy and would've demanded it long before now.

Remember when those men came for us?

It was a thought that hadn't recurred in full for some time. But she had lost him that night and would not allow the same thing to happen again.

Elisabeth slid out from Allen's grasp and got up off the floor. The stone tile was ice cold on the soles of her feet as she crept upstairs and stepped inside the shower. The hot steam soothed angry muscles while facilitating her panic.

Yesterday's visit from Fane gnawed at her. Why so insistent on her presence? In wartime, there had been ceremonies where pups were taken into their ranks through ritual induction. Fane, and in rare instances, the queen, explained varcolac evolution as being one step closer to the gods. In these services it fell to the huntress, Elisabeth, in most cases, to encourage pups to submit to their instincts.

And they did.

Even the most steadfast of souls resorted to debauchery once the consequences were removed and fantasy became a possibility. Priests unleashed sadism on underage virgins, brother raped sister, delighted to unleash eternally suppressed desire, and loving mothers were invaded by fully turned wolves, exhilarated by the brutal contrast of pain and pleasure.

Local villagers of all ages were harvested for these festivities, intended as playthings for the pups. They could be feasted or fucked, sometimes at once. It gave fledglings their first taste of power.

Anton Fane wouldn't dare bring that back.

Would he not? Remembering the Turning now, after so much time had passed, Elisabeth was repulsed by the sights and sounds that colored her recollections. Watching fledglings succumb to corrosive desires brought her no joy, only misery and depression.

Fane had mentioned a Turning, but it was hard to imagine even he would be bold enough to transform an entire town.

For what gain?

After showering, Elisabeth picked out the right wardrobe for her audience. A tight-fitting leather skirt that conservatively masked her curves while offering just a glimpse of flesh. She straightened her necklace in the mirror, making sure it was plainly visible as both personal encouragement and a reminder to Fane.

She considered packing her blade but decided against it. This was not about waging war. It was about making things safe for Allen. She had no desire to go, but it was preferable to losing another lover.

We will not run away.

She had never bared her neck to an adversary, not willingly, and Fane would not be the first to see that weakness.

She found Allen awake when she came downstairs, hunched over on the couch, holding his head in the palm of his hand, grunting with misery as she ogled him. Even in disheveled pain, his naked, cut body was alluring.

"Did you drink too much? So much for that *I know my limits* line you kept feeding me last night."

"We were celebrating, weren't we? I mean, I don't know

what the hell was in that stuff, but I'm pretty sure it's responsible for fueling our *around the world* game. I didn't think we'd ever make it back to the bathroom floor."

"You credit the wine?"

"I credit *you.*"

"I would not have imagined you had so much *enthusiasm.*"

"I'd like to see Sting do what I did."

"Who?"

"You were alive in the 80s, right?"

"Yes, but I spent much of it in Nepal."

"Forget it. I'm just wondering why I feel so awful. Sore, like I've been breaking rocks. And the dreams..."

She laughed. "I hope you are not telling me you regret it." Elisabeth had convinced him to get a little kinky as they spilled into her bedroom last night, dabbing his anus with hash oil and adding a drop between her legs to heighten certain sensations. Her muscles were enflamed now, but the countless string of orgasms made dealing with the discomfort easier.

"I regret nothing," he said and got to his feet.

"Get some rest."

"Had enough of that," he said. "Those dreams." He took her in his arms. "I want some more of you."

Elisabeth wanted to drop to her knees, but the temptation would have to wait. Dealing with Fane was first. "Rest, regain that strength. You will need it when I get back."

"Where are you going?"

"Someone I must to speak to."

"You're going to him."

"Yes."

"No. Not alone."

"He is an old friend. If I go alone, it will not take long." She tried to kiss him, but Allen turned an abrupt cheek.

"I've got a good case of morning breath."

"I take the good with the bad. Kiss me."

Allen offered a reluctant peck. She wanted more, but he had done as she said, and without hesitation. They were off to a great start.

She convinced him to spend a few hours recouping energy, leaving him in the kitchen, frowning over a full skillet of bacon. He was not terribly cute when he pouted.

To her surprise, she was willing to overlook his attitude. It was, after all, born from concern over what she was about to do.

"Just give it a little bit of color," she said. "You do not want to cook it too much, or it will never satisfy you."

It would not be long before a pound of raw bacon would cease to satisfy him at all.

The dead girl's car remained in the driveway, parked beside her father's Mitsubishi. The red sports car was, admittedly, a bit garish, but she'd grown accustomed to the way it handled. It would be in her best interest to get rid of the other car at some point, but the girl's fate was of absolutely no concern.

An insignificant end to an insignificant life.

She drove to Fane's home, swinging the Eclipse Spyder into the driveway and pressing past the guardhouse without stopping.

Elisabeth parked behind an assortment of cars and made her way to the front door as the overhead sky cracked an early shade of dark blue. She wasn't yet on the steps when she smelled blood and heard laughter.

Sweat mixed with other fluids combined into something pungent that, oddly, relaxed her nerves.

Because this wasn't a Turning. It was an orgy.

The door creaked and the manor lord himself stood with a loose robe draped over his shoulders.

"Huntress," he said through a knowing grin. "I sensed your arrival." He stood erect and without an ounce of shame.

Elisabeth walked inside and her nostrils flared. The smell was worse in here. To her right, a lengthy room was littered with writhing bodies of all ages and sexes. Angry passion, nauseating ecstasy.

Whatever company Fane kept, she had no desire to be a part of it.

"Giving a glimpse into your opaque lifestyle?" she said.

Fane stood behind her, powerful hands holding her hips.

"My top shelf clients," he said. "A thank you for investing large sums of money in a project of mine."

"You wanted me for this? To play bitch for these gluttons?"

"They want the full experience. You are history."

"I remember our history," she said. "I was in your service for what felt like an eternity."

"Oh it was hardly a decade, Huntress. You accused me of obstructing the one thing you could never have. Vengeance. And you decided that I was not good enough for you."

"You took my departure personally," she turned to face him. "You gave me a gift I grew to be grateful of. A chance to start over. That's what I did."

"You left because Aetius won your heart."

"What better reason?"

"Look where that got the two of you."

"You really are a bastard, Scythe."

"Never refer to me that way again."

"A Scythe for a Huntress, then."

"Huntress is who you are. Scythe is a name given by my enemies."

Exactly, she thought. "Let me ask you this, Anton, do you hate that you started life as a soldier? An automaton who took orders?"

"I proved myself," he said. "When have you proved anything?"

"I have nothing to prove to you. That's the beauty of life."

"When did the mighty Huntress become such a pithy creature? Your life has become one of seducing young girls and turning lap-dog college boys into personal toys. No story in our history is more depressing than yours."

Fane pressed against her, turning her toward the squirming orgy. It would be easy to castrate his pride. Might not kill him, though he would suffer a great enough indignity before these subordinates.

Allen was the reason she held her tongue. And hand. Hurting Fane would spark retaliation that would be done through him. Not her.

"This is not about me," she said. "You violate the one rule we're expected to follow. I hear the howling at night and I know our numbers swell. I know you are looking for more than a new cache of drinking buddies."

Fane laughed. "I expected your arrival to signal a return to your senses. Once more I am mistaken."

"I came in person to tell you we are not allies or enemies. I only wish to continue my life as before."

"Begging for mercy?"

"Should you choose to interpret this as begging, then fine. It is out of respect for our past that I am here. That is all there is to say."

"If you're not with me, Huntress, you are against me."

An oval-shaped man waddled toward them from the pile of thrusting and sweaty partygoers. He approached with excitement, wearing a chubby erection that looked like a pinkie tip.

"Anton, you have been holding out on me." He looked Elisabeth over as though she were evening dinner.

"She is not staying, Rory."

"Rory Eastman." Elisabeth could not be bothered to

mask the laughter in her voice. "Your daughter is a beautiful girl."

Rory ignored her, attempting to grab her wrist. "Spend some time with me."

"Get back to the party and forget about this," Fane snapped. "She is not a common whore."

"This is how you treat your money man?" He looked to Elisabeth. "Him and me, we own this town." When his last-ditch attempt to impress went over like a lead balloon, he gave a shrug of defeat and turned back to the party.

"How, pray tell, am I against you?" Elisabeth said, relieved to watch Rory disappear into the blob of shifting bodies. "What makes you think I would want anything to do with *this*?"

Fane was done talking. He swiveled and headed for the hall, leaving her to wonder what had been so offensive about her stance. They hadn't spoken in a century and her time as huntress was longer past. None of this should've surprised him.

He was halfway up the staircase when he turned and said, "If you're not gone in two minutes I will tell my sentries to open fire on you. Then they'll drive out to your place and execute your pup before he knows what's happening."

Elisabeth watched him disappear, never more vulnerable. With Allen in her life there was so much to lose.

She climbed back into her car and headed home, enraged by Fane's overconfidence, powerless to react accordingly. Wanting her *by his side* didn't sit well, either.

It had been the queen's mantra in times of crisis. Back then Elisabeth had been recruited to be her *huntress*, roaming the lands collecting unsuspecting and able-bodied candidates. As such, she understood Fane's tactics and knew what to expect.

Why didn't I sense him here?

Because she had tried forgetting him over the last hundred years, realizing she had managed to do exactly that. Now it was like he never left.

The wretch was creating an army of followers, meaning that Greifsfield wasn't going to be a quiet tourist trap in Western Massachusetts for very much longer.

●

Turned out Jack Markle didn't know much. Missing friends and weird behavior at the resort.

He was no help.

Amanda could've let him die and been better off. At the very least she wouldn't have to worry about what to do with him. Or how much to tell him. His questions were understandable, but no less annoying.

They'd driven back to her motel, The Mountain View, in Williamstown—a larger town west of Greifsfield. It was a believable base of operations thanks to its dense college population, even in the summer. Her temporary identity was an out of town grad student working on her master's thesis. Thanks to an error on her financial aid form, she was unable to secure campus residency and the motel offered a more reasonable rate than local apartments.

The motel's name was prettier than its accommodations. It was a roadside pit that turned a profit by catching spillover from Greifsfield and Adams. With the exception of a few check-ins over the last three weeks, there had been very little activity here, which made it perfect.

She had listened to Jack's story, beginning with their arrival in Greifsfield nearly one month ago and culminating with last night's run in. In between, one girl disappeared and there was the likely disappearance of another. His best friend had met a woman and had scarcely been seen since, surfacing only to say he was terrified and leaving town. The smart money was that he'd done just that.

Or he was dead.

She dodged most of Jack's questions. If the poor sap didn't realize what was happening behind closed doors, she wasn't going to be the one to break it to him.

Doling out the whole story in one large chunk got him nervous. Every friend had vanished without a trace, leaving him the jittery witness to a police officer's execution.

It had taken a few hours to calm him, finally arriving at a point of uncomfortable, yet calm, conversation. As far as he knew, she was a private detective looking for a missing person. That wasn't *so* far from the truth. The one that had led her to Greifsfield, at least.

"They dropped like flies," Jack said of his friends. "If you're good at finding people, then find them."

"Kind of why we're talking."

"First Molly, then Lucy. But Allen?" His frustration culminated in a plea to head back into town. "I should warn him if he's still shacked up."

"It's not a good idea. The police are looking to execute you, or did you forget?"

But he'd been persistent and pathetic. And now she was driving back to Greifsfield on Route 8, allowing him along out of fear he'd flee and do something dumb if left alone. This line of work didn't afford loose ends, and Jack was nothing if not one of those.

They hit Greifsfield's back roads, using an address that Jack had supplied. He swore it came right from his missing friend.

"What do we do once we get there?" Jack asked.

Amanda weighed her response with precision.

"You want to check up on your friend," she said. "I'm taking you to do that. I could use a few answers myself."

"I doubt Allen has the answers you're looking for."

She wasn't so sure.

"Here it is," Jack said as they rolled past an over-sized,

white mailbox. "That's the driveway."

Amanda slowed, but kept moving. Through the trees, a red sports car grabbed her attention.

Jack noticed it, too.

"I recognize that car."

She did a three-point turn, swinging around and pulling off the road. Her hand slipped through the slit in her coat and wrapped around the silenced Glock, flicking the safety off with her thumb, a casual maneuver not lost on Jack.

"Allen isn't mixed up in whatever brought you here. He's a dumb, horny guy who hooked up with the wrong girl. You'd be surprised how often it happens to him."

This friend sounded like an ideal mark for these things. Jack might've been confused as to why he had showed up on his doorstep looking to get out of town. Without context, it *was* baffling. Sure, Allen might've realized what type of trouble he was in and wanted to run, but it was just as possible that he and his new girlfriend were trying to lure Jack out of hiding to kill him.

These things always shat where they ate and Amanda was certain Jack's friend was friendly no longer.

"Relax," she said. "We're going up there to talk."

"You seem determined to dislike whatever he has to say."

"This." She tapped the gun from over the top of her coat. "It's a necessity. After last night, I thought you'd understand one can't be too careful."

"I realize that. You didn't get to where you are by flying blind. That's why I'm asking for your word. Promise nothing happens to Allen."

His sincerity stirred sympathy, but she refused to acknowledge it. This dedication to friendship was hopelessly misguided. The things in this house were likely plotting their deaths as they approached.

No, it wasn't the best decision to bring Jack here, but she

had to trust she could protect him if things went bad.

Things always go bad.

They walked down the driveway, her Doc Martens crunching compacted gravel spread, moving toward the trees to mitigate noise. These things were prone to super-sensitive hearing and she didn't intend to give them any advantage.

They already know we're here.

If Allen was inside she may be able to extract him at gunpoint. A kid that age would break at the sight of a gun in his face, and she'd know everything he did before lunch.

If Allen's bitch decided they were trespassing and came out to greet them, Amanda had a full magazine of silver to greet her.

●

For Allen, the guilt wouldn't leave.

Some of yesterday's moments already counted among the best in his life. But those times were fleeting and, once the euphoria drained, mountains of guilt remained.

Elisabeth knew this, asking him if a bear felt guilty for sinking its teeth into an innocent doe, or if a cat drowned in remorse after slaughtering a blue jay. She was freshly returned from her rendezvous, looking at him with a cocked eyebrow and roving eyes.

"You're at the top of the food chain now," she said. "Enjoy it."

Coping with guilt had never been easy for Allen. He'd spent an entire summer afflicted by it after handing in an English paper his cousin had written. Allen's professor loved it so much he made the class analyze it over two sessions. Six months after, the guilt clung like mildew to a shower curtain. He'd been a fraud and it had taken the better part of a year to get over that. So what hope was there now that he was a murderer?

"It gets easier, my love. You probably think I've been a monster for so long that I no longer understand your struggle."

"I don't think you're a monster."

"Don't you? If only you could see the wrought expression on your face. You want to be forgiven for the things you've done, but that won't take away the reality. You did them."

She touched his elbow. Fingertips glided along his arm, prompting him to close his eyes and focus on the soothing properties of her voice.

"I was like you once. Understand that varcolac live a long time, and without the burden of decay. My life started as a peasant at the time of the Spanish Inquisition. Yes, I am that old."

"Can't be," he said.

She ignored him. "I was taken from my mother by men who carried out atrocities in the name of God. I was near death when a varcolac found and *rescued* me. He wasn't doing it to protect me, rather he wanted another instrument of death. Someone to bring chaos and hatred to the world. By that point, I wanted the same."

Allen listened to the revelations. Elisabeth rarely spoke of her past and he wanted to know all there was to know.

Her eyes welled amidst recollections of her first year as a wolf. Dreams that threatened her sanity, the searing pain of each new transformation, so great she came to be terrified of every change.

"I understand your conflicts, Allen. I endured them all."

Allen moved closer and slid an arm around her. Elisabeth rested her head against his shoulder.

"Keep talking," he whispered. "You've had this bottled up for so long and I need to hear it."

"I did not bring it up to win your sympathy. I want you to understand. My bloodlust was provoked. I wanted to hurt people.

Admittedly, that made the beginning easier, but you will one day feel as I do now."

"Good." He believed her.

"I need to know that you are with me."

"I am," Allen said. That was the truth, more or less. He didn't trust her when it came to Jack and Lucy. Something about the way she glossed over their names in conversation. He knew she would try and eliminate them one day. Her outlook on humanity wasn't outwardly generous and he guessed killing them would be Elisabeth's way of unshackling him from their world.

There had to be a way he could protect them.

He pulled her closer. The touch of her skin relaxed him. He relished her vulnerability. At last she was human. This made him feel necessary. Elisabeth Luna needed him as much as he needed her. Their relationship was at last symbiotic.

He kissed her hard, tasting salt from her tears.

She recoiled.

"We have to go someplace," she said.

"Where?"

"I haven't decided yet."

"This is because of your old friend?"

She nodded and looked ashamed. "It is. We should not be around him. He taunts me with memories of a life I have no desire to relive."

"We don't have to run. We can straighten everything out."

"How optimistic," she said. "It doesn't work that way. It is better you get away from this place."

Allen swabbed her tears with his index finger. She closed her eyes and allowed him to clean them away.

"I want to know everything about your past."

"Once we are away from Greifsfield, you will know all. What matters now is that you are with me. Speaking with Fane helped me realize something, I am in love with you, Allen."

Not one of his romances had ever resulted in that phrase. Molly said it from time to time and, after a while, he'd said it back. It was meaningless on both their parts. She'd used it as a Band Aid once their relationship had passed the point of no return, a transparent move, even by her standards. He said it to keep up appearances.

To hear it pass through Elisabeth's mouth was music to his newly heightened ears. Butterflies flapped through his guts while his knees were weak and gummy. Finally, he understood why so many people pursued this myth.

He had found love. It was tangible. No way was he going to let it go.

And that's when the screen door exploded.

●

The house was a large contemporary number built for someone with too much money and not enough time to enjoy it.

Amanda kept her distance, six feet behind Jack, hand tucked beneath her coat.

If she hadn't saved him, Jack would be wearier. As it was there was no real reason to trust her. She'd been vague in detailing her career beyond claiming to be a PI. She acted the part about as much as she looked it, with yellow hair worn tight against her head, pulled into a small ponytail. Eyebrows were dark, angled in constant mistrust. It wouldn't take more than a little touch up, some make-up here, a change of wardrobe there, to turn heads, but being bland meant blending in.

Jack went for deck steps, wobbling while considering the path to the front door. Amanda gestured to the stairs with her chin.

At the top, she tapped his shoulder and signaled him to halt. She lifted her head to the closest window and peered in, taking point and slipping the handgun from her coat.

Jack didn't have time to question her actions before she opened fire.

The entryway burst into shards, littering the deck with glass. Jack shielded his face from the shrapnel but Amanda didn't hesitate, stepping through the jagged jamb, weapon raised.

Jack dashed across crunchy splinters without a plan and crossed the threshold in time to see Elisabeth straddling Allen on the couch at the center of the room. Their faces wore stunned surprise.

Amanda didn't hesitate. She squeezed off two rounds. They gave a double *pft* and pegged the black-haired woman square in the head. Bloody mist exploded in a cloud as her body dropped limp against Allen before collapsing headfirst to the floor.

Allen sprung to his feet. He didn't speak but his eyes found their way to Jack, flashing with betrayal.

Amanda lined him in her sights.

Allen didn't appear to care. He fell to his knees and cradled Elisabeth's lifeless corpse, defeated.

Jack took action before he had time to consider the consequences. He dove for Amanda's legs, tugging them together and knocking her off kilter. She tumbled with a surprised grunt, dropping onto the carpet behind the couch. Jack fell on top of her, shifting his weight to keep her pinned. He started to open his mouth to tell Allen to run, that he'd fucked up by bringing this psycho killer here, but the butt of her gun smacked him between the eyes, his vision going nuclear white.

Amanda pounded him in the same spot again and again. Jack fell aside, nose leaking blood. He saw jagged movement through dazed eyes.

Amanda struggled to her feet and Jack threw himself forward. She danced around his flails, succeeding in keeping one leg free of his grip.

He twisted her boot with a snarl, throwing his shoulder into the assault. She toppled over the couch and the Glock dropped with her.

"That's Allen." Jack shouted, but his mouth was mush. "Don't do it."

Amanda sprung to the floor and recovered the weapon. Using the couch for cover, she steadied herself against it, drawing down on Allen.

Jack went on the attack again, desperate to get this madwoman to stop.

But she was ready. Amanda pivoted, stepping back while hacking the gun down onto his forehead.

Jack fell flat on his face, the carpet an amiable pillow where to embrace unconsciousness. But he pushed through the remaining fog, reaching for Amanda with desperation.

She was having none of it, stomping his head from somewhere above, forcing him to eat a mouthful of Berber. He refused to stay put, clawing at her belt through the open slat in her coat. She reached for something, but there was no time to worry about that, as he used her belt to get vertical, grabbing hold of her trigger hand. Wobbly fingers curled around the slide, tugging the gun from her grip. It slipped from her fist again, but he saw now what she had in her free hand: a thick, gleaming blade that sliced his forearm, drawing a stream of blood.

He recoiled, her Glock now sitting in his hand.

Amanda grunted, her fist slamming straight into his jaw. Jack spiraled over the couch, toppling onto the corpse of Elisabeth. The gun cluttered to the rug, out of view.

Allen screamed in horror.

Once Jack saw Allen's face, he screamed too.

His friend's mouth hung open far wider than possible. Veins in his neck pushed against skin, bubbles rose up and down his arms.

"He's one of them," Amanda said, recovering the pistol. She clung to the machete in her left hand, watching Allen seizure.

Allen's throat growled like a rudder.

Jack leapt to his feet and positioned himself between the assassin and his friend.

"Out of my way," Amanda said, fixing the gun on him.

"You saved me last night. For what? To shoot me now?"

Amanda sidestepped him, locking onto Allen.

Jack hoped she would. He balled his fist and punched beneath her extended arm, the only vulnerable patch under her flak vest.

Amanda lurched and Jack pushed forward again, her balance askew. His weight was enough to send her toppling back, this time against the frame beside the shredded porch glass, their living room ballet bringing them full circle. Both weapons dropped from her fists.

Allen's growls grew more severe as he fell to all fours, throes of pain prompting him to wince. His back snapped as a serrated spinal column grew out of his furry mane.

"You're not going to kill him," Jack said with his best tough guy bluff.

Amanda looked between the two men and eyed the weapons at her feet.

Jack held her against the pane of glass she hadn't broken. "Stop it, damn you," he said.

Her attention wasn't on Jack, but on the monster behind him.

"You'd better be fast," she said, batting his arms away and slipping through the broken pane, cutting her losses.

Jack took one last glance and caught Allen's jaw shattering into pieces, an animal's snout stretching from the center of his face. His eyes reshaped into swollen spheres of reinforced savagery.

Jack ran.

His head pounded and his throat wheezed as he bounded down the stairs and broke into a full-on sprint. Amanda was already at the edge of the driveway. The way this had gone, if he couldn't catch her, she wasn't going to hesitate to leave him behind.

Jack staggered into the road as she hopped behind the wheel. He shuffled toward the truck, reaching for the passenger door as the engine revved.

It was locked.

"Please." He tried to say it, but could muster only a wheeze. Her eyes had no sympathy as she weighed his fate. At last came the satisfying click of the automatic lock.

The truck roared to life as he climbed into the cab and pulled the door shut. His head dropped against the upholstery, sighing a tremendous breath of relief.

I made it.

Something hit the truck. Hard. The impact on Jack's side was like the swing of an aluminum bat. The blow provoked a spidering crack up the length of his window and the truck rose up, tilting onto two wheels before smacking down onto the tarmac.

Jack screamed and slid away from the door as a massive, furry arm crashed the weakened glass. Pointed talons slashed the air an inch from his eyes.

Amanda crushed the pedal, heaving Jack and the beastly attacker forward. Its arm retracted, raking back through the broken glass as the truck peeled out.

She wasn't fast enough. The creature came down onto the hood on its hind legs, a big brown wolf glaring with familiar eyes.

Jack stared with disbelief.

Its attention was on Amanda, but her reflexes were good. She slammed the brakes as Jack buckled up. Gravity threw the creature back just as it tried lunging forward. Only its claws cleaved through the windshield.

Amanda threw her face against the seat cushions to avoid pointed death. Without missing a beat she shifted into reverse and gunned it. The wolf skittered and slipped, its hind talons scraping the hood like nails on a chalkboard.

Then she pounded forward again, aiming at the wolf. "Die you son of a bitch!" she screamed.

It sprinted off the road, disappearing into a thicket of trees.

Amanda roared off. Her breaths were like anvils as she craned around corners. Jack drifted in and out of consciousness beside her, thoughts rattling like his brain had come loose.

They were quiet until they rolled into the Mountain View's parking lot. Williamstown was a welcome sight.

"Jesus, you guys have an accident?" A guy in a tie-dyed shirt and a knitted cap bounced a hacky sack off his bare ankle, staring. He made an additional remark about breaking for unicorns, but it fell on unappreciative ears.

"Fucking burnout," Amanda said.

Jack followed her to the room, eager to crash. Vivid morning flashbacks were impossible to comprehend. He was nauseous for his part in it. The image of Elisabeth's legs pointing straight up against the couch refused to leave him. It was amazing that he could consider sleep after everything his eyes had failed to fathom, but the pain was great and getting worse. He felt sluggish. Punch drunk.

One foot already in dreamland.

Amanda slammed the door and hauled off with a fist to his face, then another to his stomach.

Jack toppled face-first to the bed, nearly numb to her knuckles. The mattress offered comfort, making him only vaguely aware of the hostility roaring down overhead.

"Stupid BASTARD," she screamed. "You wanna dick around with your friend and throw yourself at his feet, fine. But you fucked with my life today. You even think about doing that again, I'll blow a hole through the back of your mouth."

Jack's thoughts were as swollen as his skull. He saw Allen transform into a wolf, then watched a unicorn horn push through the center of his head, bleeding in every color of the rainbow.

"You and I are parting ways," Amanda said. Her shouts sounded distant.

Only half listening, Jack suppressed the need to vomit. Making it to the bathroom was impossible. He found the energy to at least roll onto his side so not to drown in puke. He was down and almost out. While Amanda dealt a righteous beating, she had missed the part where this mess was hers. She'd agreed to let him warn his friend to leave town, not go in guns blazing.

In less than twenty-four hours, Jack witnessed the execution of two people. It would've been three if he hadn't put everything he had into stopping her. And what of Allen? He was the animal that had attacked them on the road, but how was that possible?

Amanda must've known the whole time, or at least suspected.

Two fingers dangled in front of him, snapping his attention back to the hotel room.

"You've got a concussion," Amanda said. "Shit."

Imagine that.

She dipped her head close and strands of her shoulder-length hair brushed his cheek in a soothing tickle.

"You said we were going there to help Allen. You used me to find him."

"Nothing you can do for your friend, Jack. Sit up."

He didn't want to.

"Your eyes are glazed. I've got to keep you awake for a while."

He mumbled something about the hospital.

"I can't take you there. No one can know I'm here, okay? Once you can walk that's where I'll drop you. Now get up."

She slid him up against the headboard and gave him a couple of slaps until their eyes met.

"Wait here for a second."

She grabbed something off the nearby table and left the room, returning a minute later with a bucket of ice. She dumped a pile of cubes onto a towel and wrapped a compress.

"Keep that against your head where you're bleeding. And don't go to sleep."

Jack's wobbly hands took the makeshift icepack and pushed it against his hairline. The pain was worse than a thousand bee stings.

"Sit for a second while I run a bath. You've gotta get cleaned up."

"We have to find Lucy," Jack said, his order ignored. His head was clear enough to know now how Allen had found him at the Tavern on the Hill. He understood what had spooked him then and felt a swell of pity for him now.

He wanted my help and I turned my back on him.

Jack had no idea what he could've done, but his negligence would haunt him all the same.

"I've made a lot of mistakes," Amanda said once she returned bedside. "Saving your ass was just the dumbest. When I saw you walking around Greifsfield like a man on a mission, I figured that you were mixed up in this. Then I saw that cop get on your trail and I knew I was right."

The ice helped cool the excessive buildup of heat around his head. It was already easier to think and focus.

"You were following me last night?"

"I was. The people in Greifsfield won't talk, and the few leads I had brought me down some severely dead end streets."

"What leads?"

"Just get some rest."

"You can help me find Lucy, she has to be alive."

"Idealism's for millennials."

Jack thought maybe they both qualified as such. "Come on," he said.

"I followed a few of those things to a roadside motel not far from here. They had a map with a Greifsfield address scribbled on it, fuckers too low tech for GPS. Anyway, that led me to a small house in the 'burbs. Staked it out for three nights and got nothing. Looked abandoned. On the fourth night I went inside. Found a family of four, a father, a mother and two daughters, chained in the basement, one per wall. They became wolves before my eyes, tugging their chains, provoked by my presence. At sunrise they shriveled, turned back, and passed out."

This frightened Jack to his core. The monsters were all around them. He was almost afraid to hear the rest of it.

"In the morning," Amanda said. "An older daughter, I think, dropped by with the key for the shackles. I was waiting. Forced her into the basement and prodded them for information."

She seemed reluctant to continue.

Jack guessed why, urging her to finish. Whenever she talked, he had something to focus on aside from splitting pain.

"Yeah," she said. "I killed them. Shot the mother first, thinking it'd get them talking. They flew into frenzy, and the free daughter changed next. Put her down and asked my questions again. *'New huntresses'* is all I got."

The skin between Amanda's eyebrows wrinkled into the shape of an eleven as she swallowed.

"They had to die," she said.

"What are they?"

"You know what they are. Congratulations, man, now you're in on the secret. You'll spend the rest of your life wishing you could un-ring this bell."

"They can't be."

"You wanna cling to that argument? After what you saw today?"

"They can't..."

"They do. Enlightened times, right? It's easy to doubt God, miracles, and all that because there's science and technology to worship instead. Know what I wish? I wish I were a comfortable skeptic, the kind of asshole who can shrug everything off with smug certainty because she doesn't have to see the things we've seen. Because once you've seen a person's eyes become a window into hell, it's hard. It keeps you up at night."

"How many of them are there?"

"No idea." Amanda peeked through the curtained windows, the Glock in her fist. "If you've heard their cries at night then you know there's more than a few. I followed some trails around town but everything took me in circles. There's a big house on the outskirts of town that catches a lot of flow. Gotta be a hub for their activity, but I can't get near it. And nothing else made sense to me. Until you."

"How did you know Elisabeth was a werewolf?"

Amanda reached into a duffle bag at the foot of the bed and threw a photograph onto the comforter. It was a grainy surveillance photo taken from a bank parking lot. The woman in the picture had long dark hair and large glasses masked part of her face. Her low-cut attire revealed one identifying shred of evidence: the creepy tooth necklace hanging off her neck.

"My employer has been looking for her for a long time. When you told me about your friend, your description of her fit the bill. I picked up her trail in rural California a couple of years back. She was working as an artist in some unincorporated village, selling paintings and sketches. A rash of animal attacks cropped up outside her village."

"Jesus, she's the source?"

"She's a killer. And she knew I was coming, because her place was cleaned out before I got there. She fled across the state and I followed, catching faint hints of a trail here and there. A mangled body, a shred of her clothing, whatever. Lost her for good at a nightclub in Seattle, of all places. At the same time, a couple of punks, wannabe New Wavers complete with streaked make-up, skinny ties, and glowing shoulder pads, were leaving with two very underage boys. One thing about their kind. Back them into a corner, show them you've got the means to kill them, they run. I killed one before they could hurt their prey, but the other got away. Followed him and an acquaintance all the way here. One coast to the other. C'mon, Jack, get up."

Amanda helped him to his feet.

"Walk to the bathroom. I need to make sure your motor skills are functioning."

Jack felt unseen weight pushing beneath his skull.

"Get in the tub, I'll clean you up."

"I'm not getting naked in front of you."

"No time for modesty, idiot. I'm doing this to keep you mobile."

Jack stripped off his sticky clothes and dropped them onto the dirty linoleum.

"I don't have anywhere to go," he said, easing a foot into the cool tub of water.

Amanda didn't respond. Her attention was fixed on wetting a face cloth in the sink.

He knew full well he'd blown it this afternoon. Leading her to Allen had been done in a moment of weakened confusion, but with the purest of intentions. She had executed Elisabeth without a second thought, leaving Jack to witness the murder of a woman whom he'd been out to dinner with a few days earlier. He knew something had been wrong with her and this whole town, but he didn't believe in monsters. Even after today, he felt that he shouldn't. Twenty-seven years of conditioning against things like werewolves and vampires couldn't be undone with the flick of a wrist.

"Give me one more chance." Jack shivered beneath the icy water.

"Absolutely not. Even if you knew how to take care of yourself it would still be out of the question."

"I know I messed up. It was a shock for me. I mean, you killed that woman. You were going to execute my friend. You told me we were there to talk."

"I fucked up too. It's not lost on me." Amanda patted the rivet of crusted blood between his eyes. "I did what I needed to do, and you almost got me killed today."

"I need to find Lucy." He was going to keep saying it.

"You want me to help you? So what happens when we find her and she's turned? You'll go round two with me?"

"I get it now. That thing back there wasn't my friend. Allen's...a werewolf."

The word rang strange in the air. As weightless as a pothead saying *unicorn*. He figured he'd better get used to it.

"If you understood that earlier he'd be dead by now."

"I won't get in your way. If I can't go with you, I'm as good as dead. You know it. You saved me and I'm grateful, but I'm not leaving here without finding Lucy."

"I think there's more happening in this town than anyone knows." After much silence she added, "Are you prepared to deal with that?"

"As much as you are," he said.

She laughed. "That's what scares me."

Eight

Rory didn't like going home. Hated it, in fact.

Everything in life had been amplified. New sensations. Heightened awareness. Forbidden pleasures. Things had never been this exciting, and that made a quiet night with the wife such a waste.

Rachel's name vibrated on his cell phone. He opted to ignore the call, lost in the vision of his daughter's nude and glistening body. Temptation was fevered, but he decided the wait would heighten the experience—like letting Thanksgiving turkey stir in its juices for a little while longer.

Once the animal took her completely, she'd surrender.

He was hard just thinking about that day.

The old bag called again and he begrudgingly answered, slipping inside the bathroom and closing the door.

"Lucy isn't home yet and I can't get in touch with her. One of her friends came by the store looking for her last night, do you know where she is, Rory?"

"Running a few errands for me," he said. "Then she's going out with friends. Those kids up from Leominster."

"Jack said he hasn't heard from her in a few days."

"I'm not her leash."

"Are you coming home? We haven't seen each other in a

while."

"Give me forty minutes."

It might be worth tiding Rachel over. Everything was going too well to risk raising suspicion there, and Lucy wouldn't finish baking for another day or two.

She'd be okay in this Big East hotel room. He dialed down to Davies and told him to send someone up to watch over her. "If they touch her, I'll know."

"Absolutely not, Mr. Eastman. I will send Missy right up."

Rory didn't want to go. Things were tense at home and had been that way for months. No desire to look his wife in the eye, let alone sleep in the same bed. Their marriage had always been a façade, but it wasn't even that now.

His favorite child was chained up here in the honeymoon suite while the littlest bastard was off at camp somewhere. Rory didn't care if he ever saw that one again.

Navigating a romantic afternoon with Rachel was going to require a thespian's performance.

He took the long way home and found her cooking when he came in the door. "Is that tenderloin I smell?"

"That's what it is. You always get this when we go out. I thought I'd bring it to you for a change."

"You don't like it, though."

She approached with a wiggle in her hips. Slender arms wrapped around his pudgy neck and her tongue slithered around the inside of his mouth. He sucked it back, admiring the unexpected surprise. More passion than the last few years of this blessed union.

It was nothing now. Wasted effort in the 11th hour. He could have this kind of fun anywhere. And it was always more exciting with strangers. Younger girls he wouldn't have dared to look at before the gift was his. He'd made an unsuccessful play for Fane's whore, that white-haired British cunt, and she'd rejected him with a blunt chuckle that eviscerated his confidence. Then there was the Huntress who barely gave him the time of day.

He hoped he could find a way to pay them back one day without Fane knowing.

"Should I break a bottle of wine?" Rory said. "I've got a few nice reds."

Rachel pulled her mouth away from his neck. "I was thinking the same thing, honey. If you get it I'll set the table."

He trotted down cellar to the sparse wine rack tucked away in the furthest corner. He couldn't remember the last time he'd stocked it. It used to be for quiet little evenings with Rachel, but as those became less and less frequent, the wine collection dwindled.

He was faced with a much smaller choice than he'd hoped.

The 1986 Bollinger would do.

When he returned to the dining room, Rachel had set the table and was plating the beef.

"Sit down," she said. "I'll get the rice and roasted peppers and we'll be in business."

Rachel could cook. The meat was tender, broiled just north of rare and retaining more flavor than expected. The juices flooded his tongue as he chewed, reminding him he needed his meat on the rawest side these days.

"How'd it come out?"

"Perfect," he said. "Better than what I had in the city the other day. Really."

She grinned and continued eating.

There was something new about her, a confidence he'd never seen before. Chewing, he eyed her with suspicion, searching for what bothered him.

They ate and drank. Idle chitchat came and went. Even when their talk turned to possible vacation plans in August, neither could muster up enough excitement to sell it. The reality was the marriage had fizzled and neither cared.

Once his plate was clean he sat back and patted his rotund belly.

"Compliments to the chef." He winked.

She came to collect his plate and he smelled it when she neared.

He took her arm with a gentle press and guided her back toward him.

"Where are you going so quickly? I want to thank you for one of the best meals I've had in some time." He led her hands back down to the table and she let go of the dishes. He pulled her into his lap and caressed her leg.

"You're sweet," she said. "When you want to be."

"I want to be."

Now that she was close the scent was more pronounced. The smell of passion, of sweaty, hot lovemaking. It lingered between her legs. Another man's musk stained her mouth, her breasts, her stomach—everywhere.

An unexpected and maddening betrayal.

Rachel rose and collected the dishes.

He watched her retreat as the reality of infidelity settled in his stomach like a bag of cement. Who was he? A younger man? She'd always been a whore so this wasn't surprising.

She returned to clean off the table. Normally he'd be compelled to help, but it was best to let her do the heavy lifting.

He sat in a puree of venom and disgust, wondering how much she enjoyed her sordid nights out. What was the rendezvous like? Casual? Secretive? Did they go to his place? A hotel, perhaps?

He pictured her on all fours, tight ass poised upward, begging for violation. He thought about her lover, a faceless young stud, pounding away, her body heaving with every thrust.

I bet she loves it.

All the moaning and screaming.

Rory followed her into the kitchen, motivated by his bulging denim. Rachel was running dishes under hot water when he snatched her from behind, pressing hard against her.

She turned with a startled moan as he threw himself on her.

Even if she'd been tuckered out from an earlier session, she knew how to give one hell of a performance.

She wrapped an arm around his neck and slid her body up against his own.

He was disgusted, but aroused by her promiscuity all the same. There'd be plenty of time to deal with her. Right now he wanted to taste his wife, fantasizing about how she acted with other men.

Her kisses were wet and sloppy, exactly how he liked them.

He closed his eyes and allowed her tongue to run rampant. The way she kissed and felt reminded him of Lucy, whose tasty body he'd been licking not ninety minutes ago.

His hands grabbed her breasts and squeezed.

"I love you," she whispered.

He said nothing. Rory's mind was nowhere near his body.

He thought long and hard about the ways in which he would punish his wife. And once his mind settled on the most gratifying of ways, he smiled and said, "I love you, too."

●

She bolted up like a springboard, a startling scream so violent that Allen's heart nearly exploded in fright.

"Elisabeth."

He scampered across the floor to her side, wiping the moisture from her eyes while attempting to subdue her seizure. She slipped from his arms, her head smacking up and down as she contracted.

It was horrifying to watch. Thrashing limbs kept him at bay while he tried desperately to understand what was happening. He hadn't yet comprehended his own metamorphosis, let alone Elisabeth's resurrection.

She moved on the palms of her hands, scurrying against the wall, hands slapping her forehead until her finger closed in on the serrated puncture above her temple, just beneath the hairline.

Allen crawled to her side, arms outstretched in a literal display of uncertainty.

She fingered the bullet hole as her face wrung with discomfort. Her beautiful blue eyes were in hiding, rolled back beneath her brain and replaced by empty white orbs. Her screams cut into his head.

Allen dug through his pockets, wondering where the hell he'd last seen his cell phone.

Her hand swooped down and locked around his wrist.

"It's okay," he said. "I'm calling an ambulance. Just hang on."

Her head snapped in the direction of his voice and mouthed *no*.

"You're not dying like this." He fought to maintain his composure but the shock of losing her nearly shut him down. He hadn't a moment to consider life without Elisabeth, but knew it wasn't something he wanted. He'd had twenty-two years to know what that was like and he'd trade them all for more of this.

Her teeth gnashed and spittle pelted him as she struggled to speak. Between agonized spasms, she motioned to the bullet wound.

"You're going to live," he said. "Just let me call for help and..."

"No." Her voice was a pointed whisper.

She took a few chapped breaths as she worked up the energy to speak. "You must do it, Allen. Nobody else can help me."

"Do what?"

"The bullet." A gasp of breath. "Take it out. Dig it out."

"With what?"

"Anything." Another breathless exclamation. "Just get it out. Now."

Allen sprinted for the kitchen. Her screams were like a cracking whip. He rummaged through the drawers but there was nothing among the utensils and salad tongs that would help. He bolted to the bathroom next and found tweezers and a scalpel among some bandages. Elisabeth's screams snapped him back to the task at hand.

She was curled in the fetal position when he returned.

"This is going to hurt," he said, pulling the Jim Beam bottle from the corner bar. "But it's all we have. It'll have to do." He dropped to his knees.

"Hurry." Her eyes had never been more vulnerable.

Allen popped the whiskey cap and splashed a gulp onto her forehead. She rocked like it'd been a surge of high voltage.

He contemplated a few swigs to start feeling better about the looming amateur operation, deciding he needed his remaining wits to be sharp.

Here goes nothing, he thought, pinching the tweezers together and dropping them into the tiny bullet hole. The prongs expanded slightly, raking across the inside of her head with a scrape.

He pushed further into the wound, ignoring Elisabeth's inhuman cries. He stopped pressing at the first sign of resistance, attempting to pry the tweezers open by forcing his index finger between them. They wouldn't budge. The hole wasn't wide enough.

Damn.

He took the scalpel in his shaky hand. He grimaced while hacking at the jagged hole, chipping away an inch of fractured skull. Thick gulps of blood pulsed from the perforated slash, streaming down her face. Her body fought his slapdash procedure, aggressive limbs scratching and squeezing.

Through the mess of bone, blood, hair, and probably brain, the wound finally looked wide enough to get the tweezers around the bullet. He dipped them back into the hole and felt the cold prongs clasp around it.

"Hang in there for another second," Allen said with encouragement meant for him. Her body tensed under a few gentle heaves, the slug's stained silver coming into view scored by a disgusting slurp.

Her head fell onto its unaffected side, eyes underwater, quietly sucking air.

Allen dropped beside her, pushing a bandage to the wound.

"Are you going to live?"

She answered with a brief smile.

"She shot you," he said. "I can't believe I'm looking into your eyes again."

"I'll explain it soon." Her voice was nearly silent.

"Rest," he said, unable to resist kissing her thick and bloody lips. Didn't bother wiping his face, either. The plasma was hers. He wanted it as he wanted every bit of her.

"Let me carry you to your bed," he said.

"No. We have to leave."

"You can't travel, though. Not like this."

"We must go someplace safe, my love. I need rest, but it is impossible to get that here. You've done the hard part, digging that out of me, but I still need time to recover from what your friends have done."

Allen nodded. With Jack and his new acquaintance running around town, it wasn't a good idea to leave things to chance.

"Let me grab a few things and we'll get the hell going. No one is getting near you again, Elisabeth. I thought I'd lost you forever."

"You didn't lose me and you never will. I need you to pack a few things special for me."

"Whatever you need. Anything. Just tell me."

Another smile, deeper and more pronounced.

"That is music to my ears, my sweet."

●

During one fleeting moment of awareness, Lucy realized she was cold. Her limbs vibrated and her back leapt off the cool surface that housed her.

The dreams and images were so vivid they felt like reality.

Horrible things a mind shouldn't conceive.

She wanted to stand. To stretch. To get someplace warm. She could only think. There was no energy in her to use.

Her stomach rumbled, bringing strange and impetuous thoughts. She'd eat anything right now. Her mind settled on a plate of raw and bloody meat, something she never before craved. But now she'd rip it off an animal's back if necessary. Even the traditional comforts of fast food cheeseburgers and fries felt unsatisfactory now.

She licked her teeth, two of the top ones extended over the bottom row, ending in sharp points that pricked her tongue. Trickling crimson wept into the recesses of her throat, piquing her taste buds with a sticky sweet flavor.

"Wake up, sweetheart." A familiar voice crawled into her thoughts from somewhere above. "I'm going to take my daughter home now, okay?"

She was lulled back to sleep by growling that emanated at the back of her throat. A perverse lullaby that paved the way for endless dreams about a beautiful, red-maned wolf prowling the deepest green of Greifsfield forest, feasting on the flesh of whatever crossed her path.

●

What's wrong with me?

Amanda pondered this as the truck crossed the town line back into Greifsfield. The Glock was holstered beneath her right arm, loaded with a full magazine of silver. Two remaining mags were stuffed into her jean pockets. It was broad daylight, but after what had happened with Jack's friend, she wasn't taking chances. These wolves weren't shy and that confidence was troubling.

It meant there were more of them than expected.

Behind the seat, the MP5 was also loaded with silver shots, one reserve magazine resting beside it.

The question persisted: Why she was letting Jack call the shots for the second time in as many days?

"How's your head?"

She watched Jack from the corner of her eye while navigating Greifsfield's desolate streets. He was quiet, staring out the window, consumed by worry for his other missing friend. This guy collected them like debt.

His distress was an admirable, if naïve, quality.

Amanda wasn't sure she was any less stupid, though. She'd been goaded into one last visit to the Big East. It was risky, but if they relegated themselves to public areas while the sun shined, there shouldn't be any danger.

She also had enough silver to shoot her way out.

Jack thought Lucy would have answers, or could help Amanda get them. That meant squeezing daddy dearest to find her. As a bonus, if Amanda could get someone else free from this mess before it was too late, she supposed the extra effort was worthwhile.

Someone had done that for her once.

She turned onto the resort road and drove to the main

gate. Jack offered the guard his room number. Having never officially checked out, it was good enough for him. The uniformed employee flipped a switch and waved them through as the gates separated.

"We keep this shorter than short," she said, scanning the low-key parking lot for potential threats. "It might be daylight but that doesn't mean they won't try something."

"We'll beokayif we stick to the main building."

"Unless everyone here's turned."

"Shit, don't even."

"Worth considering. Plus, you're the idiot who came waltzing back. They might not want to miss the opportunity to take you out."

Amanda drove up to the front entrance and waved off valet service.

"If Lucy's father is in the office, I gotta look into his eyes and see if he's lying when I ask what happened to her."

She swung the truck into the closest parking spot, patting the holstered pistol beneath her jacket as they walked into the lobby. She followed Jack past the welcome/check-in desk, dodging the globular camera bubbles that decorated the ceiling. At the end of a long corridor, an office door sat slightly ajar.

"See." Jack gestured. "He's here."

"Make it good." She tapped the fabric of her jacket once more and felt the reassuring outline of her weapon.

Jack didn't bother knocking. He kicked the door with his foot, opening it the rest of the way. Mr. Eastman, Rory, by the nameplate on his desk, looked up from a handful of papers.

"Jack." He offered a shit-eating smile Amanda was tempted to shoot. His eyes took to her as the smile thinned into a sleazy grin, making her feel naked and vulnerable. Another reason to kill him.

"Your friend is?" He hadn't taken his eyes off her.

258   *Matt Serafini*

Amanda wanted a shower.

"She's a travel writer. Corinne Clary. I met her in the lounge a few days ago. She's doing a story on the Big East."

Rory threw an inquisitive look around the room, baffled by their understandably thin association.

"Miss...Clary? What publication did you say you worked for?"

"I'm freelance," she said. "Works better for me. No boss, so I don't have to worry about kissing ass when it's not deserved."

Rory gave a rich man's chuckle and turned his attention to Jack.

"What brings you here with her? Go take advantage of our amenities. Play a round of golf, or maybe get Ms. Clary into a bikini and sit poolside."

He looked at Amanda and winked.

Amanda was never more aware of the pistol holstered against her ribs.

"I am," Jack said. "Enjoying everything this place has to offer."

"Glad to hear it, son."

"Wondering if you could tell me if Lucy's around?"

"Just missed her, actually. Left an hour ago to visit her brother at summer camp. Older sibling day. They're aiming to be potato sack race champions three years in a row."

The well-prepared excuse rolled off his tongue like he'd practiced it in the lengthwise mirror behind him.

When you knew how to wade through it, you found good liars mixed healthy doses of truth in with their bullshit.

Rory continued, "She's been under the weather lately, probably why you haven't seen her around."

Her trained eyes had no problem identifying Rory Eastman as a werewolf. The bottoms of his palms were exceptionally hairy. She'd seen that before on some of them. Lycanthropy amplified the host human's physical characteristics, so if a man had been excessively hairy in life, he was an overgrown forest after turning.

Beyond that, Rory had been expecting them. A quick survey of the room revealed no visible cameras or monitors, so unless the gatehouse had called to let him know they were coming, Rory had sensed their approach.

Amanda was aware of her gun once more, placing her fingers against her chest so they could slip under her coat and grip the handle if necessary.

It was impossible to say how many wolves nested here. Killing Rory would risk enraging them, and she didn't have enough ammunition to fight her way out. Jack, Mr. Dashing-Do, world's greatest friend, couldn't be depended upon to do anything other than die, and she'd probably follow his lead.

Why am I letting him corrupt my judgment?

This gig was easier when it wasn't about helping others. Because of him there was a human component now. She wasn't keeping this job at arm's length—her preferred distance for all things.

They thanked Rory for his time and apologized for the intrusion. Jack explained he was incredibly worried for Lucy and that he'd helped to ease his mind a great deal.

"Indulge me a moment," Rory said. "You come here looking for your good friend, right? A concern I do appreciate. And you bring a travel writer with you? No offense, miss, but I don't know you, nor do I understand why this is a shared conversation."

"Jack was going to introduce me to Lucy. I thought putting a young girl at the center of the story, kind of a *life when you're a millionaire mogul's daughter* angle, would give it social traction if I sold it to new media. This conversation here, though? Off the record, naturally."

"Naturally," Rory said. "She's lucky to have a terrific

friend in you, Jack."

He forced an insincere grin.

"And you," he said. "Please, if you want to do a story about this resort, let me know. I will grant you access to every nook and cranny. That is how confident I am in the Big East."

"I will be back," Amanda said.

She led Jack into the hall. He opened his mouth to speak but Amanda shushed him with a wave of her hand. They walked in silence back to the truck.

"That man is a werewolf," she said once they were safely through the gate.

"How do you know?"

She explained her hunch and suggested he might be hiding more than just the fate of his daughter.

"I don't believe he killed Lucy, but he's lying about something."

"I wouldn't call off the search party," Amanda said.

"Where the hell is she?" He tossed his phone into the seat after leaving yet another voicemail.

Amanda knew the answer, as did Jack. Deep down, he knew. She kept quiet, wondering what it must be like having someone so concerned for your well being.

Dexter's oft-voiced worries were nice, though rooted in responsibility. He hadn't wanted her in this field, but her ruthlessness and detachment made her an efficient operative. He worried like a dad.

Her phone rang next. Speak of the devil.

"Yes, Dex?"

"Church, where are you?"

"Greifsfield."

"Don't get cute."

"I'm not. Doing a little reconnaissance. Just on my way out."

"Good. Stay out until help arrives."

"I can do that."

"I got another man headed your way."

"Really?" She guessed this was supposed to ease her mind, though her interpretation was more along the lines of *"Hey, I know you can't cut this by yourself so I'm sending another guy to lighten the load."*

That couldn't have been his intent, as Dexter never undermined her. Reinforcement most likely meant the situation was bad. A protocol rarity. She hated being the one who needed help.

"I know what you're thinking, kid. But you're just not right."

"Oh, so it's not that bad?" Amanda said.

"It is. But you've seen worse. We all have."

"You're not exactly filling me with confidence here."

"Kid, I'd be there myself if I could. But I've got my own thing going on back this way."

"Who are you sending?"

"Fontaine. Working a job in Philly that's winding down fast. He expects to be en route tomorrow. He'll be in Berlin, New York for rendezvous. I don't want you heading back to Greifsfield until that happens, Church."

"Believe me, I won't."

"Good. I won't lie, you're trudging through a pool of piss. The good thing is you know what you're dealing with. And that means you know how to put the rabid dogs down. Fontaine is helping you carry out your task, but you're in charge. Plus, I got the padre checking into a few things. Expect a call once he finds whatever it is he's looking for."

"Yay."

"Put this to rest and get back here, ASAP. Just know that I'm putting you on mandatory vacation once you've been debriefed. You've got about six months stacked up, time to collect, Church."

"We'll see..."

He hung up without so much as a *bye*. Part of his charm.

The cab went silent as they drove from Greifsfield with one question hanging over her.

Have I already passed the point of no return?

●

For Rory, the surprise visit had been unwelcome. He sat in silence listening to their footsteps fade.

This bothered him.

Freelance reporter my ass.

They disappeared from earshot, leaving their scent behind. Once they were gone he dialed Anton Fane.

"What now?" Fane was derisive. Rory knew he didn't like him much and didn't care. If Fane wanted a foothold in Greifsfield, Rory was who he had to know.

Bringing Anton Fane to town, to the Sarandon House, had been the start of their partnership. Now it was Rory's job to make his money legal. Couldn't go buying property all over town with that wealth. Not even Fane would say where it came from. It had to pass through Rory's businesses so it could be cleaned. Fane was free to hate him all he wanted, though it didn't change the fact they were partners.

"You have to hear about the visitors that dropped by my office asking questions."

"If I have to hear about it, tell me."

"A woman I've never seen before. Claimed to be a freelance writer, but she's no guest here. Looking for Lucy."

Fane was quieter than death.

"My guy at the front gate has the make, model, and license plate of her truck."

"Give it to me."

He did.

"I'll look into it," Fane said. "Drop by tomorrow for you-know-what. We'll discuss everything then."

Then he was gone.

For Rory, the beauty of living in Greifsfield had been the lack of real estate competition. When Fane showed up with a desire to dabble in that arena, he thought it best to make him an ally and partner rather than go head-to-head.

Fane was content to acquire the Sarandon place in exchange for other services. Rory allowed him to use the Big East, along with several other Greifsfield locales, for recruiting purposes.

He didn't know what that had meant at the time and didn't care. Because Fane had expressed his gratitude by sending that white-haired number, Julianna, sauntering into his office in nothing but a pair of crystal stilettos. He'd been eyeing her since their first meeting, overjoyed that his time had finally come.

But it hadn't.

Instead she grew into a white wolf and took half his shoulder off, opening his eyes to a new world. Women, money, and the prestige of sitting inside Anton Fane's inner circle.

Best of all, no consequences.

Fane had transformed some of county sheriff's office as an insurance policy. People disappeared from this trendy tourist trap and the investigations needed to be contained. They had always been careful, taking drifters, single people, and newlyweds. None of it mattered as long as they disappeared without a trace.

When there was a little blowback, it was all hearsay. Without guest logs the local police didn't have a leg to stand on. And they were on his payroll now anyway.

All so very smart of Anton Fane.

They recruited outward from there, snatching up some of the more important townsfolk who were content to join their ranks. Some people tried to run, but Fane never allowed that to happen. They were shown no mercy and their fates were quickly forgotten. Greifsfield, like Rory, had changed. It was pointless to fight.

Nine

In a rare display of humanity Amanda looked at Jack and laughed. It was a light, infectious sound, and the first time he felt like he was speaking to a human being. Up until now, he'd been fairly certain she was some sort of hard-boiled cinematic cliché.

"Something funny?" Jack said.

"You," she said, still grinning. "You *almost* look like a hardass."

Jack looked at the pistol in his hand and hoped he wouldn't have to use it. He sat in the 70s décor chair positioned between the motel door and the large window with drawn blinds.

"Excuse me for being a good guy and letting you nod off for an hour or two."

Amanda stretched out on the hotel bed, wearing a loose t-shirt and a pair of sweat shorts that showed off toned and tanned legs. Her gun rest beside her, six inches away, but always within reach.

"This feels good," she said, barely comprehensible behind a long yawn.

"Bet you're glad you didn't send me away. Never stopped to think I might be able to do some good."

"Don't push it. I still don't think I'm making the right decision."

"Of course you are, otherwise you'd be narcoleptic."

"I worry about lack of sleep like I worry about my cholesterol. There are bigger problems. It comes with the job and I've learned to deal with it. It's like being a customer service rep and experiencing the worst of humanity day in, day out."

"What customer service did you ever work? Hard to imagine you lasting anyplace more than a day, considering your *go fuck yourself* attitude."

"Go fuck yourself. I never worked that shit, my friends did."

"Do you guys swap work stories often? Bet yours are more interesting."

Her face dropped. She wasn't normally this easy to read, but everything was pinned to her sleeve tonight. She didn't volunteer any further information and he decided against asking.

"I should get some sleep," she said to spite the leaching silence.

"Sorry," Jack offered. "I didn't mean to..."

"You didn't know. It's okay...long time ago and all that. I just don't normally open up to strangers."

"Strangers? You mean partners."

She laughed. It lightened her features and brought a hint of rose to otherwise pallid cheeks.

"We are not partners."

"See this gun, I'm keeping watch so *you* can grab a few winks. If that doesn't make me your partner, nothing will."

She swung her legs onto the nappy carpet. "I don't know what I was thinking, letting you keep watch. You're no shooter."

"Hey, hey, hey, I wasn't insinuating that. Lay back down. Sleep. Seriously. If things are as bad as you say, you have to grab some sleep before it gets too dark. You don't want me on watch once the sun sets."

Amanda sat for a minute, wrinkling her mouth and staring at the floor. She looked up as if to say *what the hell* and got back into bed. She folded her arms across her chest and rubbed her feet together.

Jack's eyes fell to bronzed ankles and then to her feet, somewhat large for a woman of her size. Dark nail polish stained her toes, bringing out the baked tan color of her skin. Her feet stroked one another with teasing rhythm while the muscles in her legs flexed with each motion.

Jack looked up to find her staring, smiling.

"Got some kind of foot fetish?" A giggle escaped her lips but she caught herself and wiped the grin gone before she could finish. Nevertheless, it was an odd and attractive sound coming from her.

Jack's cheeks reddened, feeling like a red-handed pervert. Like a bad partner. "I wasn't being weird or anything—"

How do I claw myself out of this hole?

"—I guess it's strange seeing you like this, that's all."

"I'm making you uncomfortable?"

"No." Jack was quick to respond. He liked this view of Amanda Church. It wasn't her intention, considering her baggy attire and frizzy hair, but the casual way she sprawled out, with impeccable legs and feet, got to him in just the right way. She hadn't been anything but a soldier since their first meeting, but now her figurative and literal hairs were relaxed, forcing him to see her in a different light.

A feminine light. Or something.

"You've been a total badass since we met. Now, I'm looking at your painted toenails. It's sort of a reminder that you're still a woman."

"You're flattering, let me tell you."

"Truth," he said.

"*You've been a total badass,*" she laughed while mocking his voice.

Matt Serafini

"Okay, forgive my phrasing. How should I describe you, then?"

"I don't know. You shouldn't. Definitely not as a badass. Badasses are for comic books."

"This is improbable enough to be one," he said. "I question everything now, but what bothers me more is how quickly I can accept the impossible. It's like learning $2 + 2 = 4$. After a while, werewolves just...exist."

"Tomorrow when my partner gets here I want you to head home."

"Not until I find Lucy."

"Jack..."

"Go ahead. Waste your breath. We agreed, I wouldn't get in your way again and you wouldn't stop me from finding Lucy."

"You realize how bad things are going to get in that town?"

"Sure. But you've handled things like this."

"Not like this."

"So why are you bothering to stay and fight if the odds are impossible?"

"I don't have a choice. I have to do this. You still have a life. You can run."

"What kind of life can I have knowing I left her to die? Allen? He's a lost cause and I know that now, but Lucy? I have to be sure."

Amanda studied him with a cocked head, blinking with admiration. "And she's not your girlfriend?"

"An old friend."

"She's lucky to have you."

"We're both lucky."

"Tonight, right now, is the point of no return. I will barely be able to protect myself, Jack."

"But you know how to handle yourself...I've seen you."

"Against one or two. You can get the drop on them by

sneaking up, catching them in daylight, or sending a hail of silver spraying into them. What you can't do is sneak up on an entire town."

"Then don't. How can you be expected to do this your-self?"

"That's the job. There isn't an army that handles these things. A congregation of wolves this size is unprecedented."

"Your luck sucks."

"Worse than you know."

"Help me find Lucy so we can hit the bricks together."

"Lucy's lived here her whole life," Amanda said. "How could she not know?"

"I've been wondering that myself."

"We'd have known about Greifsfield if this nest was old news. Sooner or later, enough people go missing and the right eyebrows get raised."

"Good time for a vacation on my part."

"Yeah, well, your luck sucks too."

"I'll drink to that," Jack said.

"Are you sure there's no way to change your mind?"

"No," Jack said.

"Okay then. Think you can do some damage if you get in the mix?"

"Maybe." Jack pushed the edge of the curtain aside and peered into the parking lot. It was as deserted as it had been this morning. And the day before. He spied one dark figure stepping out of the lobby and disappearing into the nearest room, nothing suspicious or intimidating about it.

When he glanced back, Amanda's eyes were closed.

He said nothing more and neither did she. She slept and he listened. Her breathing was minimal and her drawn eyes gave a peaceful impression. Her face was softer, faint breath seeping from the small pucker of her lips. A far cry from the blunt instrument he'd seen in action the past few days. His head still hurt, his forearm bandaged tight.

It was astonishing to recall the way in which she'd killed Elisabeth without hesitation.

Then there was Allen.

Was there any way to make amends for that? He took another quick glance outside before dialing Allen's cell. Voicemail. Again. He sent another text that was sure to go unanswered, same as his messages to Lucy.

He paced the room and prayed the next few hours would pass quickly. Allen was a changed man, sure, but he couldn't allow Amanda to put him down. Elisabeth's death was already on his shoulders and Allen would never forgive it. He was not going to be responsible for the murder of his best friend, werewolf or not.

All that was left to do was find Lucy and get out of this town with their lives.

The best way to do that was by ensuring nothing came through that door tonight.

He reached into the mini fridge and pulled out a Red Bull before resuming watch.

●

"Dinner!"

Rory heard Rachel's shrill bitch of a voice all the way upstairs. He paid no attention, poking his head into Lucy's room. The heaving mass of blankets rose and fell, timed with hurried breath.

It wouldn't be long now.

He'd brought her from the isolated suite of the Big East, hoping the familiar environment would help the fever break. Feeling her limp, sweaty figure in his arms produced the greatest of all temptations, blotting out the few internal protests that still managed to reach him.

Rory never considered himself a man of discipline.

Just a peek.

He slipped into her room, soft steps across the thick pink carpet she'd had since childhood. Wheezing buzzed his ears, something to do with the mucus pooling in her lungs. A result of the wolf bite. If there was an infection, it would soon pass.

His tiptoes carried him without noise. Lucy's fiery red hair sprawled across the sweaty pillow, flowing every way possible. The thick blanket was pulled over the length of her face, leaving only a slightest bit of her forehead vulnerable to the tepid room temperature.

You'd better not be sick when you come out of this, goddammit.

Her health might prevent them from having a little fun on the eve of her turning. A thought that was enough to get Rory all worked up. He supposed he'd wanted her for years, never allowing the fantasies to settle. Always chasing them off like pesky yard squirrels.

Ever since he caught her in bed with that son of a bitch Latham kid from down the block, he couldn't think of her as anything but a slut. If she wanted to behave like that, he'd have no problem indulging her. No amount of fever was going to stop him after waiting all this time.

No, it had to be now.

"Get well, sweetie." He pulled the blanket down to expose her cheek and mashed his lips up against her sweaty flesh, holding his tongue against her jaw.

Salty perspiration was a delicacy and he licked her with excitement. There was an urge to take her here but Rachel, that bitch, might have a thing or two to say about that.

He closed her door behind him and went to the edge of the staircase.

"Honey, come up here, please?"

"Dinner's ready, didn't you hear me calling?"

"Come here."

He went to the end of the hall, to their bedroom, and stripped. While he waited for Rachel, he stared at Lucy's prom picture atop their dresser. She wore a low-cut black number that accented her D-cups, cleavage nearly bursting over. Her red hair was styled with curly bangs that matted her forehead.

Before realizing it, he was stroking his throbbing inches to the sight, degrading her as he soothed himself.

Soon.

Soon enough.

He was a free man now, untouchable and powerful. One step behind Anton Fane.

Rachel pushed through the door and Rory leapt at her, hurling his startled wife face down on the king sized bed. He tore her shorts free, revealing a blue thong that split her cheeks. Rachel moaned like the filth she was, her head buried in the mattress. Rory spanked her again and again, until the thong was a blue T that divided splotchy shades of red. Then he ripped it free and dropped to his knees to taste her.

He instantly picked up on the scent of his competition. His wife's lover. What sort of things did he do that Rory could not?

With a grunt he pushed deep inside, falling across her back as his hips thrust, slowly at first but soon much harder.

He started to change.

His bones popped and restructured. His nose broke as his face reached out toward her back, his snout sniffing her flesh an inch away from it.

Rachel didn't seem to notice at first. If her moans were any indication, she loved it and pushed to meet him.

Rory brought his mouth down, filling it with raw scoops of bloody flesh. She screamed, disengaged and grabbed the spraying wound.

Rory tumbled as his legs changed shape, arms covered in gray hair. His fingernails broke into pieces, giving way to six-inch talons.

She didn't stick around, staggering to her feet and going for the door.

His shock paused the transformation. He watched Rachel's retreat as if in suspended animation. An eternity in one second. His endo-makeover degenerated, leaving an awkward mix of wolf and man standing in the doorway, watching Rachel flee for her life.

The aroma of blood was a great motivator, arousing his senses like the perfume counter at his department store.

With a roar somewhere between howl and war cry, he charged.

●

Lucy tore the sheets away and hopped out of bed before realizing she was awake.

Her sweaty toes settled on stuffy carpet, succulence luring her into the hallway. She licked her lips, wandering in a trance, puppeted by instinct.

Dad was there, scruffy, naked, erect. He noticed her, froze, and smiled.

His hairy palm was closed around the head of an auburn-haired woman, pinning her runny red face against the wall, beyond the frame of the family portrait where broken shards dug through her cheeks.

Lucy snarled, a roar pushed up from the depths of her stomach while a matching swirl ignited her loins. Through grated teeth, she pushed toward the action in repulsion, hunger, and desire.

Hesitation tugged, begging her conscience to deny the

driving instinct. It was wrong in every way and, despite her tunnel vision, she knew it. The voice of reason annoyed her as her slicked body fell against the battered woman, ready for a bite.

Clouded eyes recognized Rachel Eastman. There should've been more objection, Lucy realized, but Mom's terrified screams provoked the wolf's predatory instinct just as the gashed face and wounded neck cemented her hunger.

Rory pulled his hand back, letting Mom fall to the ground. She crawled on elbows, a pathetic grovel falling on deaf ears.

The new wolf had no nostalgia for this woman. The memories were there, somewhere, but they were recollections of another for as much as she cared.

Lucy's innards shuffled, sliding around her expanding body like boiled spaghetti. Strands of fiery red hair burst from unseen follicles and her mouth pushed outward, away from her face. Her knees buckled and broke. Her toes sharpened. She turned her hands inward, staring at thick, red palms.

Rory fell on top of Mom, gnawing at her mangled shoulder. Lucy watched the fresh spill of blood with a watering mouth. Drool pelted the rug and the appetizing smell of raw meat brought her to her knees in immediate surrender to this ravenous appetite.

Rory lifted his snout from the notched cavity, tendrils dangling from his mouth.

With a driving snarl, Lucy licked the trim of blood around the other wolf's mouth. He reciprocated by lashing his tongue outward, catching hers with a playful yap. Her wince was reflexive, but the tease of sustenance reinforced the unbearable need to feed.

She dove for Rachel, her jaw locking around the soft meat of her throat. Her taste buds danced as blood spilled across her tongue, oozing from chewed hunks.

The other wolf inched closer.

He wasn't interested in the dead body, but in Lucy, yanking her close. He licked meaty gore off her face while working an anxious mouth down the fiery red mane of her chest and stomach.

The playful nicks of Rory's mouth offset the jarring experience of her still-altering and pained body. She encouraged his greed with a contended growl as recently developed killing teeth gnawed a lump of juicy sinew.

Both creatures picked at the meaty carcass sprawled before them. They ate for several minutes, scraping the flesh from its bones. As Lucy's hunger pains were sated she realized what it all meant.

She was no longer human.

But she remembered things. Rushing down this very hall at twelve, horrified by blood-spattered thighs. Desperate for Mom's comfort. The word *menstruation* as foreign as another language. That was ten years ago, and another lifetime.

As soon as they finished feeding, Rory bent his back and prowled toward Lucy on all fours, moving with caution so not to startle her. His tongue dangled from the corner of his canyon-wide jaws, driblets of red saliva plopped onto the mangled mass of bones below.

His eyes were loaded with anticipatory glee.

The disgusting look triggered a reaction in her, and the red-maned wolf remembered those hands when they'd been human. The way they'd rubbed her breasts one summer night not too long ago. Her wolf's mind couldn't process this, but her consciousness remained, however buried. It was vivid enough to put her on the run.

She turned and trotted down the winding staircase. The red wolf stumbling her way over tiny steps, struggling to keep her paws straight on the thin treads as she went. Lucy waddled to the ground floor and leapt through the bay window overlooking the backyard.

Shards of glass ate her flesh with tiny inconsequential slices but she wasn't stopping. Her paws hit the grass and she trotted harder. The wind cooled her face, emboldening her senses. A familiar smell danced through her nostrils but she couldn't catch it, and soon it was lost in a potpourri of other mountain scents. Behind her, Rory pounded the ground as he picked up pursuit.

New legs carried her faster than she'd ever moved on foot, and she was deeper in the forest than she'd ever gone. More surprising still was how her nose detected some of the most distinct and dominating odors all the way downtown: the bitter smell of Maddie's Bakery, or the bloody meat from Zito's Butcher Shop that tempted her with a trip to Greifsfield Center.

Lucy didn't stop moving until Rory's hunt dissolved. She skidded around a cluster of pines and nestled between them. The tree needles were overbearing on her now-sensitive nose, but she recognized the perfect cover they provided should her father come stalking. He'd be more apt to miss her here, with the powerful waft helping to camouflage her scent.

She hoped.

It was her best bet. Pine prompted fleeting memories of Christmases past. Life with the family, holidays with Jack. The familiar smell she'd sprinted past in her backyard suddenly clicked.

Body spray.

Tangy antiperspirant—a Jack Markle trademark.

The smell had been so vivid back there she might as well have been standing in his dorm room. Her heart thundered once she realized what that meant.

He's been in my house recently. Or around it.

The hunger rescinded and, with it, returned a string of Lucy's humanity. Everything since New York had been a blur, but she was awake now.

Rory might've recognized the odor as well, abandoning pursuit in favor of eliminating the intrusive friend.

She'd have to find him before. But not like this. Not after what she'd done to her mother. The wolf couldn't be trusted.

The recollection of what she now was became a shock to her system.

Oh God...it happened.

The wolf licked the roof of her mouth, satisfied now that its belly was full. The back of her tongue was stained with familiar lifeblood.

Lucy dipped her head onto muscular, red legs, nuzzling between jagged paws. A powerful breath gusted from her snout.

Taking Mom's life had been easy and Rory's advances hadn't been all that repulsive. It was enough to retch. Morality had only been an afterthought of hunger.

What chance then would Jack stand if the hunger returned while trying to rescue him?

Lucy drifted into a troubled sleep, hidden away beneath the gloom of Greifsfield forest. Its sounds soothed her angst-ridden psyche, lulling her into a false sense of security.

Howls from like-minded creatures lit the calm mountain air, asserting territorial dominance and continuing like a chain reaction across the clear mountain sky.

It was impossible to say when it happened, or even what exactly *it* was, but Lucy was suddenly hyperaware that creatures like Jack were the minority in Greifsfield.

In the distance, two human screams erupted in joint cries of pain before being abruptly severed.

The wolf fell asleep to this, a hellish lullaby for a demonic existence.

●

"Jesus," Amanda said. "How long was I out?"

She awoke to find Jack peering through the drapes overlooking the parking lot.

"Almost five hours."

"Shit."

"Yeah. That happens when you don't sleep for a few days."

"It shouldn't."

"You gonna tell your body to go fuck itself?"

Amanda took a spot beside Jack, yawning as her eyes adjusted to the darkened lot. From this angle, it was clear.

"Your turn to get some sleep," she said.

"I'm awake."

Amanda eyed the reservoir of crumpled Red Bull cans at his feet. "Try to get a little."

"Wouldn't be able to sleep even if I wanted to."

"You'd be surprised."

Amanda grabbed her folded pants off the edge of the bed and slid them over her pajama shorts. She put the flak jacket over her chest and pulled a thick sweater down over it, angry she had to do this in the middle of summer.

She pulled her blonde hair back into a tight bun, swinging a band between her two fingers to capture the length in a ponytail. She took the MP5 in her hand and slid the magazine out, examining it with a frown.

"Fuck," she grumbled.

"Are you always such a doomsdayer?" Jack said.

"Kept me alive this long."

"Cynicism doesn't keep you alive."

"You learn that in college?"

"You act like the only reason you're good at your job is because you keep yourself closed off."

Why was everyone such an expert on lives that weren't theirs? Jack's tirade hadn't been the first time someone had preached life's merits, love and happiness. Whatever. People had strong opinions on things they knew nothing about. That's what makes social media so fucking popular.

"A few days ago, you tackled me to the ground because I

trained a gun on something that used to be your friend."

"He's still my friend."

"No, you idiot. That thing is not your friend. You took *me* down over him. You risked my life and yours so that your *friend* would be spared. Why did you do that? Because your emotions got the better of you. If I wasn't there, your BFF would've torn your throat out. That's what emotion gets you."

Jack couldn't look at her. He kept his eyes low to the ground, ashamed.

"It's easier to keep moving forward when emotions don't concern you," she said.

"You think friendship is trivial?"

"Look at where it's got you. In a hotel with a stranger."

"Partner."

"*Stranger*. For what? Some girl who's maybe alive?"

Jack winced.

From the heavy look in his eyes, she'd shaken him.

"You've got a fucked up way of looking at things," he said. "You would leave a friend to fate if our roles were reversed?"

"If our roles were reversed we would've been dead a long time ago."

"No one's tougher than you, right? Whatever road you traveled to get to where you are must've been long and brutal. Because you're dead inside."

He wasn't wrong. Amanda had at least that much self-awareness. No point in refuting him, there was so little time left.

The slat of light beneath the door went dark, blotting the parking lot glow. Amanda was at the window in time to see every outside streetlamp explode in unison. Glass clouds puffed and brought down a wave of darkness.

"Drop!" Amanda screamed and charged the floor, tugging Jack's shirt as she went.

The window cracked and popped as bullets pelted the interior. The glass rain was inside now, crashing down onto them.

She crawled on her elbows into the four-foot gap between the beds and pushed the nearest mattress forward with her feet. It slid off the box spring as silent gunfire continued breaking through. She slithered onto the bed frame while bullets whizzed overhead. With another push, the mattress was diagonal against the bed and floor. One last grunt and she had it up against the blasted-out window frame.

It wasn't ideal cover, but it would lessen the impact of the shots.

She grabbed the MP5, now on the floor, and aimed at the connecting door. A puff of bullets splintered the wood around the knob and popped it ajar.

If they could slip into the next room, there might be a way to surprise the attackers with counter fire.

Amanda was on her stomach again, crawling across the smoke-stained floor between the mattress barrier and stripped bed.

Jack cried out somewhere behind her. She turned to see him staring at the bathroom. An attacker was wedged through the small window above the toilet.

Jack steadied his arms on the floor and pointed a quivering pistol at him.

"One shot kill," Amanda called. They couldn't spare more than that.

Not a second could be sacrificed to procrastination. Amanda reached for the adjoining door and gave it a swing. Another wooden door, the connecting one for the next room, blocked her escape. She repositioned onto her back and kicked it with both feet. It broke from the jamb, swinging into a darkened room. With the MP5 trained on the unknown, Amanda braced.

Jack squeezed off a single thunderous shot. No time to

check whether it had been successful. This was a tactical night-mare.

The minimal light offered a dim view of the neighboring space, a bed occupied by two naked bodies. No way were they sleeping after that gunfire. She inched closer, finding their throats gouged, and the sheets stained with sanguineous crimson.

Beyond them, a shadow moved through the thick black-ness. Amanda drew a bead on it and squeezed the trigger just as the shotgun pump went *click*. Buck exploded against her ankle as she dove free of the blast, her own shots unsuccessful. The gunman pushed through the darkness, towering above her. A uniformed of-ficer, Greifsfield PD, mashed the barrel against her cheek.

"Too bad," he said with a thick accent. "I'd love to have some fun with your mouth before I blow it off you."

Amanda rolled to her left, kicking his shin. He stumbled off balance, allowing her to fire three blind shots.

His limp body passed her as she got up, smoking bullet holes through his cheek and forehead.

Sounds of a struggle raged from the next room. Amanda turned and steadied the gun barrel.

The front door blew open in splinters, catching Amanda as she left through the adjacent one. Two uniformed men filled the doorway, guns blazing. Bullets pegged her back. Her flak jacket repelled the penetration, but not the pain. She held her ground with only a slight stagger, spinning and firing back. The muzzle lit the dark, and six shots found their targets, killing one instantly and slowing the other. He continued forward as Amanda squeezed the trigger again.

The gun clicked empty. Without hesitation she flung it into the approaching face, cracking him square in the nose.

It was all the time she needed.

She lunged, shifting off her wounded ankle. The police officer crashed to the floor with Amanda on top of him, trading blows and blood.

He was powerful, an example of why she avoided physical confrontation. Her measly body mass was no competition for this hulking muscle head and his sledgehammer fists. He reached out and locked his hands around her arms. With a spin, he pinned her without effort, despite three bullets buried deep inside him. His head reached up and snapped back down, slamming her skull at full force.

The collision gave a loud, echoing *thock* that crashed Amanda's head against the floor. With a desperate writhe, her arm slipped free and clawed his face. He laughed her limb away, pinning her again, this time with a knee.

A billy-clubbed hand smashed down, followed by another. Her vision cut to white. A third blow was coming and she tried bracing herself for it.

A gunshot boomed, freeing her from an excess of two hundred plus pounds.

Jack hoisted her up.

Amanda stuck her face in her elbow, wiping mixed blood from her eyes and nose. She stretched her eyes, hoping to pull her vision back into focus.

"There's more coming," Jack said.

"How many shots you have left?"

"A few, I think. Here."

He eased the shotgun into her hands and she pumped it while the grungy hotel surroundings filled her eyesight once more.

"We have to go," she said.

"Where are the keys?"

"Bedside table. In there."

"Shit."

"I'll cover you," she said, deciding he didn't have to know about her faulty eyesight.

Jack didn't argue. He stayed low and slipped back into

their room. Amanda followed as far as the doorway, leaning against the jamb and facing both entrances. Her eyesight was far too muddy to see past the doors, but it was a safe assumption that this siege hadn't yet concluded.

In a career of nearly eleven years, the enemy never let go this easy.

"Let's go," Jack said, scooping the keys off the table and hurrying back. "Can you run?"

She tested her weight on her wounded ankle and thought, *maybe*. "I can shoot," she said. There was no way of knowing without careful examination, but it didn't seem the shotgun blast had been a direct hit. More than likely a few of the bucks had burrowed in. Digging them out and cleaning the wound should make her good as new.

They eyed both exits with caution, wondering which would yield better odds.

Jack motioned to the spare room. "Your truck is closer if we go through there."

"They could be trying to lure us out."

"What then?"

Jack was right. Their backs were against the wall. She wouldn't normally engage the enemy on their terms, though these goons weren't a professional hit squad. There were other cars in the parking lot. How would they know which was hers?

They have you on camera after your jaunt to the Big East. That's how.

Behind them the makeshift barrier burst into a cloud of stuffing and springs. Buckshot got her in the stomach and she found herself tipping toward the floor, doubling over and sucking at air that refused to come.

Jack returned panic fire. Amanda was dazed, but she counted each shot like their lives depended on it.

Two, three, four, five, six, seven shots. *Eight.*

Click.

"Let's go." He was at the doorway now.

Amanda was sure they were sprinting to their deaths, but gave reluctant pursuit. She saw the gunman as soon as they were outside, face-up in the parking lot, head dismantled by gunfire.

Nice shot, Jack.

They reached the truck without incident and Jack climbed behind the wheel, unlocking the cab.

She pulled herself into the passenger's seat, bracing for a shot to the back that didn't come.

He threw the transmission into reverse and pulled out, then went speeding for the road. Both their heads were low to the dashboard, weary of hidden gunmen. At the road, he slammed the brakes, bringing the truck to a smoking halt. In yellow head-lights a wolf blocked their path, standing against dissipating rubber smoke. It was sickly thin with patchy, brown fur, towering on its hind legs with a salivating glare.

"Hit it," Amanda said.

And Jack did, gunning it.

The wolf parried the vehicle, sliding from its path just barely. Its hostile breath stained the passenger window as they slipped by.

"Just go," Amanda shouted. In the rearview the wolf dropped to all fours to begin its charge. A smaller wolf appeared alongside its stride, throwing itself beneath the creature's gallop, tripping its legs and knocking it to the pavement. Jack kept a steady foot on the gas, putting some good distance between them and the quarreling monstrosities.

The smaller wolf dropped onto the other, mauling it with a flurry of furious talons.

Two animals fighting over a meal.

Amanda's immediate worry was the size of Rory East-man's network. If he could get the Greifsfield County PD to launch an all-out assault on a neighboring town's motel, he wasn't concerned with reprisal.

"That's why we shouldn't have gone to that resort. They know who they're looking for now. Our scent's all over that room."

Jack was quiet for a long time. When he spoke, he said, "Those were cops."

"I don't think many cops in Western Massachusetts speak with heavy European accents. They're wringers."

Jack lapsed into silence, focusing on delivering them from evil.

You're in, she thought while looking him over. His hands trembled, though his attention was on the road. His expression fought against fear, but his eyes betrayed the struggle. And yet here he was. In one piece. He could handle himself if need be.

That made him an asset.

Good thing.

To clean up this mess, she was going to need all the help she could get.

●

The red-maned wolf stood deep in gore, watching the truck's taillights shrink in the distance.

Any later getting here and their escape might not have happened.

She'd been forced out of an uneasy sleep by thoughts of her newly murdered mother. Imagery more real than any dream she'd ever had. She would do anything to refrain from seeing her that way again.

Lucy was not going to remember Mom that way.

Urgency had burned in the pit of her stomach, telling her to find Jack, saying the howling was after him. She had wanted to get closer to him, but not like this.

Not when resisting the temptation to kill him herself had been so great.

Her muzzle dipped toward the fallen creature, its eyes now extinguishing the final signs of life.

Lucy licked the roof of her mouth with excitement, eager to taste her spoils, curious to know what wolf tasted like.

Ten

Elisabeth wandered through the backyard, feeble limbs brushing listless against assorted bushes and shrubs.

Allen wanted to help, but only watched. This had been her daily routine, one he expected to continue through the foreseeable future.

He sat at the rustic kitchen table, tapping impatient fingers against the thick oak. Despite being away less than a month, Mom's kitchen felt smaller now. As if no longer home.

Their enemies wouldn't find them here. At least he didn't think Jack would bother checking. Why would he? They couldn't know Elisabeth lived.

Through years of friendship with Jack, Allen had never once taken him to his parents' place. It wasn't exactly near anything. Fifty minutes to Boston, but only if you traversed a lot of country roads to get out this way. If they'd had plans he went to Jack's place in Leominster.

Here, they were safe.

Thank God for small favors.

Wasn't much point in thanking *Him* anymore. God, in all likelihood, wanted nothing to do with them. He was no longer a man made in God's image, but an unholy perversion of it. The guy who spent the first thirteen years of life in Catholic school, and who never really doubted the existence of the Lord, was suddenly public enemy number one in the eyes of every God-fearing Christian.

The oversized cuckoo clock spit a tiny pewter rooster out of micro-sized barn doors, clucking the arrival of nine o' clock. He jumped at the noise, and then swore about it.

Every time.

How happy he'd been to leave this disruption behind once college had started. It took him years of living here to get used to it, and Elisabeth absolutely could not. She tossed and turned over the fake bird and its hourly announcements. When her head was not cradled against his chest, it was hard for him to sleep as well.

Then she'd go wandering, leaving him to sit and wish he could do more to help.

At least the folks weren't here. They were in Las Vegas, blowing through their Social Security money at a conservative pace, gambling on nickel slots. Dad was convinced this was the best way to stretch a dollar, although he couldn't seem to grasp that he was severely limiting his winnings.

Didn't matter though, they'd made it a tradition over the last few years, speaking about it like there was no greater excitement in life. Who was he to tell them how to spend their retirement? Especially when their absence was a blessing for Elisabeth. She didn't need to answer Mom's twenty questions while recovering from a gunshot to the brain. He was also happy he didn't have to worry about her eating his family.

From the yard Elisabeth gave him a fleeting glance before turning her back.

Allen sighed. She had promised to tell him everything, but conversation had been decidedly minimal since leaving Greifsfield. It wasn't his lack of trying, either. She responded with one-word answers, refusing any offered services. No breakfast in bed, no hot tea from the kettle, and certainly no backrubs or massages of any kind. Resisting her was never easy, but more difficult now that she was off limits. Displays of affection, a kiss on the cheek or a gentle touch on the back, were met with utter hostility. And her glances were always sideways or secondary, no lingering contact. Allen wasn't much for insecurity, life was too short for it, but he'd felt an onset over the last twenty-four hours.

It seemed all too clear she regretted *changing* him. Even now she distanced herself so it would be easier to do the relationship fade. Nothing else made sense and his rapping on the oak table intensified while he convinced himself he was on the verge of being dumped.

Outside, Elisabeth was statuesque at yard's edge, staring through a line of trees, her mind lost in a veiled cache of memories she refused to share. Maybe her current resentment wasn't entirely unfounded. It wasn't everyday someone asked you to kill for them.

"Ridiculous," she'd said upon his refusal. "You've taken lives already, what makes this any different?"

It was a good point, but those lives haunted him nightly. Elisabeth didn't know Sondra Gleason did more than visit at night. She was on a mission to get him to splatter his brains all over Greyrock Mountain.

Last night the specter of Sondra Gleason was considerate enough to bring a silver pike into the dream, offering to help sever the curse. Allen wondered how long he could resist that proposition, and knew he should probably cave sooner. The hunger was alive inside him, mounting with the dawn of each new day. Even the much-coveted steak dinner did precious little to satisfy him now, with the juiciest, bloodiest cuts leaving him with hunger blue balls.

Only time it wasn't a problem was when the wolf came out to eat. But no matter how hungry he got, the motivation to stalk and kill an innocent human remained elusive, excluding that blonde trigger bitch. And Jack too, for putting her on their doorstep. That idiot looked like he hadn't intended the gunfire, and his battle with the psycho might've saved his life, but that wasn't the point.

There was no forgiving that.

Their friendship felt like decades ago. He hadn't been walking this new world for a week, but yesterday's life was a distant fading memory.

Elisabeth came in and stood at the opposite end of the table. Her lips were a straight line, eyes dead. A snapshot of utter misery.

"Hey," he said, probably sounding too eager and desperate. "You finished walking?"

Her eyes refused to settle on him. "It's gotten me as far as it can."

Allen rose and started for it, ignoring the grim implication. There had to be another way. She stepped back and turned toward the window.

"I do not want you this close to me," she said with a twinge of hatred.

"Elisabeth." He went in for her cheek and wound up kissing a tuft of her hair. "You're alive. You're healing. I saw you dead, and I don't know that I've fully been able to process it. Don't push me away, please. Let me help."

She turned. Raven-black hair obscured her grim features and plague white complexion. Eyes peeked out from beneath vagrant stands, looking almost colorless. Skin around them puffy. Little wet tracks ran vertical beneath them, staining her chiseled cheekbones.

Her vulnerability was too much. He stepped toward and she backed off, but he was faster this time. He landed awkward against her mouth and his tongue tingled with salt. Her thin and bony arms slid around him, the brush of her skin incited a spark.

"I want you," he whispered, mouths blowing hot air on each other.

"Not while I'm like this."

She allowed herself to fall against him. Her body, soft and firm, burned away his worries.

He'd almost lost her.

"What of the things I need?" She said, breaking off and heading for staircase. "I am weak and hideous. Hardly worthy of your libidinous urges."

He started after her, but she motioned for him to stay. He yielded like a trained wolf. "You're the most perfect thing I've ever seen. And goddamn you if you don't believe me."

"Allen."

"Shut up," he said. "Haven't I given my life to be with you? I'm okay with that because you make me feel like we're the only two people in the world. So please stop distancing yourself from me."

She pulled her hair aside to reveal the bullet wound that hadn't yet healed. It was smaller now, but an angry infection remained, ripe with rotted colors, green and purple, while the quarter-sized area extending outward was beat red.

But it *was* healing, that's what mattered.

"You're hurt," he said. "But you heal. That's what we do, right?"

"We do."

"So why are you being like this?" He grew indignant and didn't care. After the torture she put him through, she could listen to what had been festering in his mind. "You're acting like this has somehow changed us."

Her eyes were lost on the cherry hardwoods.

"Just tell me what's bothering you? It's more than the bullet. It has to be."

She walked into the living room and sat on the wicker

rocking chair. He followed, taking a seat on the edge of the tan couch where he watched expectantly. She was motionless, save for the chair's slow creak. She looked out on the desolate country road and her eyes were a little less distant.

When she finally turned to him, it was with a quivering lip.

"There was somebody in my life...a long time ago."

Allen stayed his urges. He thought about wiping her eyes and taking her close, but this was the most they'd spoken in days. Hearing her out was the better move.

"He was varcolac too. I loved him more than anything else." Her fingers rubbed that white tooth necklace. "We traveled the world, a pack of two, preying on anyone we wanted. The more fear we felt, the better we became. And there was a lot of fear back then. A lot more superstition. Villagers holed up in their homes thinking snarling beasts could not get in. Aetius' lit fire to them, smoking them out. There was a time when tortured cries and smoldering bones drove me wild. I would wait for the wretched souls to burst from their homes, skin half boiled, snatching them as they ran for the lake. Disgusted with me yet?"

Yes.

Not because of this confession. He focused on Aetius, almost positive he was about to be cast aside for the rekindled affections of an old flame.

Elisabeth leaned forward as if sensing his broken ego. "It was a long time ago, Allen." Her fingers stroked the back of his hand, closing around his fingers and sending a shiver to his soul. "I am yours. That is why I feel the need to tell you this. Nothing more. Okay?"

He nodded, aware that his face was marked with skepticism.

"Our reign of terror continued for years and we did not worry about consequences. Why would we? The world was larger then. People in one province were barely aware of bordering neighbors, let alone countries across the sea. Fear of the dark was widespread, while fear of the devil was rampant. We exploited this. Made whole villages disappear, corrupted some, murdered others. Chaos and bloodshed were our only motivations and we could not be bothered to think about the future. Know what happens when you overindulge? It loses its luster. My thirst for vengeance was quelled, and Aetius and I spoke of settling as best as monsters can. We had no illusions as to what we were and did not intend to abandon our hungers. We simply wanted the lives we might have had before our curses. I was an artist then just as now. I sought isolated space for a studio where the creative process would not be disturbed. What we did not know, however, was that a secret order had been sent after us. They caught up just as we were about to settle into new lives. Aetius was killed in an ambush. I was wounded. Would have died if not for my gift."

"What gift?"

She pulled back her hair once more to showcase the wound. "Figure it out."

It was on the tip of his tongue, but sounded so improbable he withheld it. She must've noticed his conclusion, for she squeezed his hand and offered a faint smile of encouragement.

"Go on."

"You can't die," he said. "At all?"

He sounded like a stuttering idiot to his own ear, but could not articulate the revelation that his girlfriend was, apparently, invulnerable.

Elisabeth nodded. "A gift from Alina, our queen. Conventional weapons cannot kill me."

"You're invincible?"

"Not completely, no. Only a few know how to do it. It is not, as you might expect, something I want known."

Allen sat stunned.

"It has advantages, but a silver bullet to the brain is like dying a thousand times. You endure the moment of impact, that singular second between life and death, until it is removed. In this case, until you fished it from my skull. I was crippled, unconscious for what felt like an eternity."

"This has happened before?"

"Once. Nowhere near as painful. When Aetius and I were ambushed I was stabbed through with a silver pike. Tracked my would-be killers for days, all the way to the Black Sea. I did not kill them as a wolf, either. I wanted them to be absolutely certain who was sending them to hell."

"You killed them? Elisabeth the human?"

"I took my revenge," she said. "But lost my desire to wage war. Aetius was too great a loss."

She pulled the teeth outward and looked at them.

"It was decades before I considered anything beyond meaningless trysts. Not a day passed where I did not obsess over Aetius, his death etched in my brain like intaglio. I was angry and unbalanced, and the things I did...I lost the urge to kill, but sometimes I lashed out worse."

She collected her thoughts and centered herself with a deep breath.

"Part of me believed my curse was to never find love again. Fear controlled me. Loneliness defined me. Until you."

"What an ego trip," Allen said. "First real love in what? A few hundred years? I feel pretty good now."

A fleeting smile.

"When I resigned to falling for you, I realized how much happier I was. When we were attacked I thought for certain I had lost you. While lying there, dying over and over, I could not stop wondering whether you were alive. I thought I lost you no sooner than I found you. That it was, in fact, the curse once more."

Allen gave a lopsided smirk. His cheeks were hot and rosy

while he felt a familiar flutter of butterflies in his gut once more. Elisabeth was an expert at sending them scattering.

She slid from the creaking chair and moaned in his ear. "I love *you*, Allen. Which is why I need your help." She bit the side of his cheek and sat back wearing a wicked smile.

"What?" He stammered in the wake of her vivacious assault.

"You heard me," she said, cupping her open palm against the sudden bulge in his pants. "Help me feed. The sooner you do, the sooner we can start our life together. Truly together."

Elisabeth tugged his zipper down and slipped a hand inside, sliding below his boxers without effort. She fished it free and looked at it with admiration.

The approval on her face aroused him more.

"Will you help me?" she asked, gliding onto her knees. Color flooded back into her lustful glare. "I throw myself on my knees for you, begging you."

Her mouth slipped over him.

His breaths were heavy, his moans soft.

That wicked smile again. "You will do as I ask?"

"Anything you want. Anything." He guided her back down with a vicious tug of her hair. She growled and closed her mouth over him.

It didn't take long to finish and he did so in her mouth. She swallowed him without a wince.

They lay on the couch after, wrapped in each other's arms. Allen had never wanted to experience this before. An orgasm typically brought him back to his senses. To the point where he realized he couldn't stand whoever had just gifted him. Normally, he couldn't get out the door quick enough.

With Elisabeth he wanted nothing more than to feel her impossibly soft flesh, drifting asleep to the sound of her cadenced heart.

The clock cuckooed six times the next time Allen paid any attention. They were still entwined, Elisabeth's head resting comfortably against his chest. He stretched indolent muscles while suppressing a yawn, but it was enough commotion to wake her.

"Can you believe we slept all damn day?"

"I hate that clock," she said.

"It was bad when I was living here. Now that my hearing's *better*, it's even worse."

"Can I break it?"

"Please don't. Better we leave here with as little controversy as possible. Smashing a beloved family artifact will mean one more useless conversation with my parents. No thanks."

"Since you said *please*."

"Is that all I have to do with you? Say *please*."

"Actually, that does not often work."

"I didn't think so."

She tweezed his nipple and laughed as he winced. "I have an idea for tonight."

Allen braced himself for the pitch. She wasn't going to simply forget what he agreed to hours earlier. He'd been somewhat surprised she'd allowed so much sleep. Maybe it was best to get this inevitability out of the way so they could get on with their lives.

"Go out and bring somebody back here. A nice romantic dinner."

"That's not what romantic means."

"It is what I mean. And you agreed."

No getting out of this. "If it's what you want."

She stood and stripped her dress away, offering a fleeting glimpse of that tight, round apple bottom she sauntered upstairs.

From above she called out, "Do it and I am yours, Allen. Anything you want." Her footsteps ceased with the slam of a door, followed by a flowing showerhead.

Allen sat alone in the dark. This was another line he wasn't ready to cross. He didn't think he could bait someone back here with the intention of murder, especially if it meant seeing another angry spirit at night.

No choice.

He stood and headed for the car. It might be hard to live with this, but it wouldn't be hard to do.

He already had somebody in mind.

Someone that might not even be missed.

●

Lucy brushed pine needles off her knees and squinted toward the sky. The sun was an orange ball collapsing on its nightly descent over Lake Wahkan.

An entire day gone. Spent trying to find this place.

She stood at the edge of the summer camp, crouching behind the aggressive width of a hemlock tree.

Nick was among the group of kids splashing around during a game of Marco Polo. There was a swell of nostalgia for her summers here. Her first kiss had been on that waterfront after one of the socials. Seth Landry's breath stunk of too many onions on his hot dog, but his hands wasted no time exploring her chest beneath a pastel blue Camp Wahkan shirt.

He hadn't been the most attractive boy, with acne pocks on his cheeks and a feminine lisp, but he wasn't afraid to let her know he was interested.

In hindsight, it hadn't been a very good night but she realized there was a stitch of fondness for it now.

An uncomplicated sliver of life.

Things were different for the Eastman kids now. Nick didn't know it yet and she had no idea how to break the news. He no longer had a mother to go back to. What he did have was a monstrous father with no interest in him and a sister cursed with something she couldn't explain.

She wouldn't let Rory do the same to him.

She also didn't know how to keep Nick safe from her. She dialed Aunt Rose's number.

"Auntie, it's Lucy."

There was no way to do this without sounding like a loon. Hopefully, Aunt Rose would take her word at face value.

"This is going to sound weird but please listen. Something's happened to Mom and I think my father is involved. He's after me now. Wants to hurt me. Please come and get Nicholas. He has nowhere else to go."

She made Rose promise she would come get him before hanging up. Then she went back through the thick forest, making her way to the main road. She didn't have her car anymore. No idea where it was. And it didn't matter.

It was time to leave Greifsfield.

No hope for greener pastures here, not when the instinct to hurt those around her was increasing with every passing moment.

Lucy jammed her hands into her pockets and started down the street. It was going to take a while to get where she needed to go, and her tight t-shirt and short shorts guaranteed she'd be able to thumb a ride to get there.

What she couldn't guarantee was whether or not she'd hurt the driver.

It would be night soon and her dark visitor was already itching to come out.

She felt it simmering just beneath her surface.

Waiting.

●

With Elisabeth's appetite quelled, she beckoned for Allen. The wolf came and nestled against her, panting.

Allen's whiskers tickled her ribs, and she wiggled uncontrollably. He knew what he was doing, wrinkling his brow before snapping a healthy portion of the dead girl into steel-trap jaws.

Each bite brought Elisabeth closer to rejuvenation and by the end of dinner her wolf was ready to return. The unsightly bullet wound was free of infection, warded off by familiar nourishment.

Their feast was now just scattered remains on the bedroom floor.

Allen had gone out and brought back one of the town's barflies. Her pup was more dutiful than she could've imagined. She almost felt guilty about it.

Almost.

She lay still for a while, watching the contented wolf ease back into Allen's form. A naked young man curled into a ball at her feet. She brushed her toes against his tired mouth, stuffing them inside and moaning as he unconsciously sucked them.

When she grew bored of the sensation she gave him a gentle kick and he lifted in her direction.

"The dreams," he said. "Sondra was just here...told me I could save myself if I went back to Greifsfield and found Jack."

"She wants you to get yourself killed."

"Why am I having these dreams?"

"They are not dreams, per se. Your victims, or what remains of their aura, come to you in your sleep because that is the only time they can reach you. You see them because guilt controls you. The only way to make it stop is to do as she says and kill yourself. That is not an option for you, my love. So just expunge these feelings of remorse."

"How?"

She planted cotton kisses on his neck in between words.

"Easy."

Peck.

"Just let them go."

Peck.

"You are a wolf now."

Peck.

"And wolves..."

Peck.

"...are very instinctual creatures."

"Figured that part out already," he said.

"We hunt to feed, yes, but sometimes we enjoy the sport, toying with our victims to heighten the experience. Terror sometimes creates a more bountiful feast. It hardly seems worthwhile to empathize with your meals, right? I already asked if you've ever left a restaurant haunted by remorse for the cow that died to become your steak."

Allen stared at the shapeless carcass in the corner of the room, wondering how they were going to clean this up and hide the body without his parents catching any blowback.

"*I'm* what you want," she said, kissing him once more. The best defense against apprehension.

"You are."

"Then promise me you will put these stupid girls out of your mind. That one served a purpose and can be forgotten."

"Is that how it happens for you?"

"Yes. I can hardly recall my parents beyond vague recollections. Fragments."

"Jesus."

"It is not a bad thing to live in the present. Many dwell in the past, pretending things were better when they were younger, desperate to keep those days alive. Remember, I plucked you from a life of monotony, allowing you to live, Allen. Live with me."

She pointed to the body.

"Do you think she was ever going to amount to anything? Or me, had I stayed a peasant girl? Or you, had you gone on to finish college and then enter the rat race."

"That never sounded bad to me. It sounds bad to you. Who are we to put our importance above others?"

"You are not *more* important, just different. Superior. We are evolved in the way that Homo Sapiens have progressed past primates."

"I never went around killing monkeys when I was human."

"You ate meat, indirectly causing the deaths of millions of cows, chickens, pigs, deer and whatever else your society deems acceptable to ingest."

"You're not making any sense. I went to high school with that girl over there. I didn't have Ancient and World History with the cow I ate at Texas Road House."

"I should not have asked you to do this in your hometown. It is my fault for being so narrow-minded. You have already been through enough. Killing an old acquaintance on top of everything isn't how I make you accept your fate."

She pushed Allen onto the floor and mounted him, taking his hands and placing them over her breasts. He squeezed them together, stiffening again. The boy's sex drive was endless and that suited her fine.

"Tell me you love me, Allen."

"You know that I do."

"Do I?" She forced her weight onto his mid-section to provoke him.

"I love you, Elisabeth," he said and slipped inside her.

"Good. Realize then what you did here was for me. I would never have been the same without it. You brought me back to life."

She rocked him while his hands grabbed.

"We must strengthen our bond by finding something we can accomplish together. Something that will provide you with enough satisfaction to embrace your wolf."

"Anything." He grunted between warm thrusts.

She patted his chest playfully. "No, no. I want you to tell *me* how we're going to do it. It has to be your idea." She lowered herself to his face.

"That bitch," he said, nearly breathless. "The one who tried to kill you."

She tried withholding a smile.

Of course it was this.

"Go on," she said.

"I'll kill her. I will track her down and kill her."

"You would not have a problem doing that?"

"I want her to pay."

"What of your friend? Her companion? I would so enjoy killing him while you avenged me."

"Him too," Allen moaned as their bodies danced. "We will kill them both. *Oh God...*"

Elisabeth bounced until a crippling orgasm seized them both, seemingly at once. They quaked and rocked and he erupted inside her. Satisfied eyes stared at satisfied eyes for what could've been hours, a world of understanding between them.

Allen was a stubborn one, but it had been easy to get him back on track. All she needed now was for his mind to click into place once the pendulum swung toward her. There was plenty of unfinished business in Greifsfield to make that happen.

They lay together for the rest of the night, bathed in moon glow.

●

Jack watched Amanda disappear into the Berlin Post Office. She hid behind a pair of aviators, keeping her bruised and, likely memorable, eyes out of sight. An oversized coat masked the flak jacket she habitually wore, and thick black Doc Marten boots added another inch to her length.

She had mocked him for saying it, but Jack thought she was nothing if not badass.

He sat in the cab of her battered truck, picking pieces of pastrami out of his teeth that had been wedged in there since breakfast.

They'd stopped at an all-night gas station and convenience store where he'd helped clean buckshot out of her ankle wound with a water bottle and some hydrogen peroxide.

The register jockey thought they'd been screwing behind the locked door, banging on it to say he was calling the police while Amanda grunted and ordered Jack to "get it." He rescinded his threat when Amanda hobbled out and bought a box of ACE bandages. Two of them now wrapped over the fresh cleaned wound.

She admitted there was pain, but nothing that restricted her movements.

Jack watched her through the large glass window as she spoke with the employee behind the counter, her hands alive with more expression than he'd ever seen her use. It couldn't be great news.

He fiddled with his toothpick, gums almost free of errant meat, although one last piece proved elusive.

"Hi, Jack."

He turned to see Lucy step up against the window and smile.

"Luce?"

It was her, just not as he remembered. That vibrant aura, so characteristic of her, was extinguished. A despondent demeanor lingered in its place. Her skin was pale as usual, but without the usual color flush. Her long, red hair was pulled tight against her scalp, tied into a fiery ponytail that hung through the strap of the baseball cap tugged over her head.

It hadn't been a week, but Lucy looked years older.

"I've been trying to find you," he said. "Calling and calling. You fell off the face of the earth once you told me you were going to nail your father to the wall."

"I never got out of there." Her voice was dead, as if she'd been up all night smoking cigarettes. He got to have me."

"Jesus, Luce..."

"Don't worry, Jack. There's nothing you can say so don't try. Know what you need to do? Listen." She gestured to the lot behind the post office.

Jack jumped from the cab without hesitation. Better Amanda didn't find her here. She'd have too many questions and Jack knew what happened if she got answers she didn't like.

Lucy led the way to a chain-linked fence that hid a row of dumpsters.

"If you're in trouble," Jack said.

"You're the one in trouble. I picked up your scent a few nights ago and tracked you to that motel. Your scent. Know what that means?"

Jack's grimace spread across his face.

"I'm a fucking monster," she said. "Like the rest of Greifsfield. From what I saw last night, you already know what's going on."

Lucy was right, there were no words. It was hard enough to find the right consolation when someone lost their job, or a loved one, but there was no cure for this. No upside. It was bad. All he could do was warn her.

"I'm with someone that you don't want to meet."

"I know. I'm not sticking around, believe me. You're my last stop."

"What about your mother and brother?"

A sideways look toward the dumpsters.

"I killed my mother. My father and I did it together. I can't get the image out of my head any more than I can bring myself to be around Nick. I don't know what I'll do. The hunger is so over-powering. Since everyone I know lives in Massachusetts, the best thing I can do is get the hell away from them."

She was right, it was the best thing for everyone. But he didn't like hearing it.

"If your friend thinks she can do some good here you need to listen. Two nights from now, there's going to be a gathering at that mansion on Adams Street. The Sarandon House. I've no idea what the purpose is, but it's big. My father is involved with one of them, some guy called Anton Fane. Seems like he's got a lot of say in what happens here."

First Allen, now Lucy. God knows what happened to Molly. Jack was the last man standing, but for how long? An emotion-ally detached supernatural assassin and a twenty-seven year old English major against a pack of wolves? How was this reality?

He told Lucy about Allen and Elisabeth. She winced at the part where Amanda put a bullet in her skull.

"I guess I shouldn't hang around. Or maybe I should, de-pending on how you look at it."

"Stop. There's gotta be help for you. I can go with. The two of us on the road to nowhere."

"Road trip to find a magical cure? Think there's a rare plant hanging atop a cliff somewhere that can reverse it?"

"Anything's possible."

"You and I aren't going anywhere. I can't spend every sec-ond wondering when I'm going to snap and kill you."

"Tell me where you're going so I can look in on you."

"I don't think I'm going to do that."

"C'mon Luce, you can't run off by yourself."

Wiping a hefty tear off her cheek, she cleared her throat.

"Remember that first class we had together?"

"Popular Theories of Science Fiction?"

"Yeah. I was a freshman and you, well, God knows what the hell you were back then. What are you, thirty now?"

"Your condition hasn't affected your sense of humor, jerk."

"The only thing it hasn't affected. Anyway, you had to sit next to me because you showed up late and it was the only seat left. I think it took you three full classes before you even looked at me."

"Come on."

"I'm serious. I would always watch you, wondering why you wouldn't turn and look at me."

"I knew I felt your eyes on me. It was completely uncomfortable."

Lucy raised her arms in defense. "Okay, I made you uncomfortable. What's new? But we talked eventually. I mean, I had to initiate it. Twice. Maybe three times. Then we settled into a routine, remember? I'll go so far as to say you tampered with my little freshman brain. I didn't go to college looking to load up on wine coolers while shitty guys begged me to kiss my roommates. And I definitely wasn't there to play beer pong in a fucking basement. I wanted to get smarter. I hoped for the opportunity to surround myself with interesting and original people. Once you started speaking up in that class, I knew you were one of those mythical beings—a student interested in an exchange of ideas and information. I liked listening to your insights on whatever book or movie we were studying. Most of those freaks were there for an easy A and certainly not because they wanted to read. The class has to be full of dead weight before Mr. Outcast, Jack Markle, is gonna start talking."

"Total dead weight."

She smiled. "Definitely. I never told you how much of an impression you made on me. And sometime during that class I realized I was in love with you. I still am. Not sure why I kept it from you, but there. I figured we'd eventually have our chance. A cheesy moment where you professed your love for me. God, how lame."

"Not at all."

"It's an awkward thing to drop in a person's lap. I'm sorry. But I had to tell you. Just once. It's not like we have a lot of time left."

"I'm not letting you run off by yourself."

"You don't have a choice. I'm a werewolf now. And I'll eat you."

That Lucy clung to her oft-kilter sense of humor proved he'd been an asshole to keep her at arm's length because of his failure to commit. He'd taken her emotions for granted and felt lower than low. He kept his mouth shut. Not to save face, but to save Lucy's.

Her admission couldn't have been easy. Telling someone how you felt was sometimes impossible and yet she'd just done it. She'd always been the gutsier of them.

"I should go," she said.

And then kissed him. More than a kiss. Her lips opened slow against his, allowing their tongues to press. Her mouth was hot, prompting his imagination to wander through sweaty and inappropriate corners of his mind.

Her hands touched either side of his face as their tongues worked out three years of repression and angst.

She broke it off all too quickly. Just as his cheeks felt flushed.

"One for the road, ya know?" Her voice was unstable. "Take care of yourself, nerd."

"Lucy."

"I have to go. And you have to let me go. If I had any guts at all, I'd march over to your friend and tell her what I am so she can put me out of my misery. But for some reason I can't do that.

Dying scares me more than whatever I've become. Please, Jack. Just let me leave."

Jack nodded. There was nothing left to say and even less to do.

He wondered how many death warrants he'd signed by allowing a wolf to go free, but it was Lucy he cared for. Faceless victims were just that. Faceless.

Lucy stepped back with reluctance, holding his eyes for a moment before turning away. Nothing more was said as she walked hurriedly around the building, disappearing from his life.

Jack walked back down the crab-grassy embankment as Amanda pushed from the building, a shoebox-sized package tucked under one arm.

"Where were you?"

He jerked a thumb over his shoulder. "Taking a piss. Everything is in that one little box?"

Amanda looked at the parcel. "Too risky to ship everything direct. This is food for the Glock, along with directions to where we can make a pick-up."

They climbed into the cab. Amanda was saying something about a meeting, but Jack wasn't listening. He thought about Lucy, about how he wasn't likely to see her again.

There wasn't time for guilt. It wasn't his fault Lucy's father had lusted for her. Jack couldn't have known he was a werewolf.

So why do I feel like all of this is my fault?

●

"You're a tasty morsel," Julianna nipped his cheek.

"Stop coddling me." Fane ignored her friskiness and tugged his tie, loosening the knot. "I don't need positive reinforcement. I simply need to get this over with."

"Don't be a tosser, it'll be over right quick. I can't wait to be curled up at the base of your throne."

Fane liked her pontifications, but shrugged them off as they crossed the Hudson River on the George Washington Bridge. Julianna was right to be enticed by daydreams of a better world. It disgusted him to consider their species' monotonous history. To realize how far they *hadn't* come in centuries.

Their evolution had plateaued. The varcolac were content in their shadow world, a myth among men. Alina didn't believe in dominating the docile genus that stretched from one corner of the globe to the next, and she would one day come to regret her spinelessness.

Fane resented the satanic majesty. She'd turned a repeated deaf ear to his pleas, content to ignore the changing world for tradition. She couldn't even be reached by conventional means. An audience with her meant a trip across the Atlantic, followed by an arduous journey by train and then foot.

That was an advantage in the old days. Now it did them a disservice, which was why he would delight in making Julianna his queen.

Truthfully, he'd wanted Elisabeth. Her beauty and abject cruelty were second-to-none. No bitch more worthy to rule beside him. The things they'd done together in centuries past dwarfed any modern headlines of publicized sadism.

He loved those memories and was willing to overlook her insubordination. There were more important things to worry about in the immediate future. Tomorrow's Turning, for example.

All that mattered was there was a Huntress at his side. Julianna fit that bill as well as anyone, even though she did very little hunting on her own. She preferred their sentries to drag bodies kicking and screaming to her feet.

Fane had once heard a business partner refer to his wife as *high maintenance*, and if he was the laughing type, he would've done it, because that didn't start to describe Julianna.

He admired her gluttony.

They were en route to his newly purchased waterfront property. Rory Eastman swore it was the perfect location for this venture. The guy might've been an insignificant blight, but his business prowess was finely honed. That made him an asset since this had to be legitimate.

A stagnating forty-minute stretch through the Bronx tried his patience. The driver took them down a series of narrow thru ways, slowing in front of a large stone gate headed off by two iron doors. They were cracked open, revealing sprawling harbor front property just beyond.

Two cars were parked near the entryway.

Rory and his Realtor waited to greet him outside.

"Anton," Rory approached with an open palm.

Fane shook it and directed his focus to the man whose name he didn't know. "You must be the Realtor?"

"That's him," Rory said. "Jeremy Green."

Green provided a greeting that couldn't mask his disinterest, though he perked up when he caught a glimpse of Julianna's bouncing bodice as she slinked from the limo.

"We just came from closing," Rory cleared his throat in an effort to redirect Green's attention.

Green gave Rory a colleague's pat on the shoulder. "We lowballed them. Global economy's nosedived so nobody wants these old places. Pretty shortsighted, I'd say."

Fane had no reason to give Green another look. "Let's look inside."

Rory followed alongside Fane. "Thank you Jeremy. You made this fast and easy for us."

"Be sure to use my number next time you're gonna scoop up some gorgeous NYC property."

Julianna paid the Realtor no attention as she swayed past, a gesture that delighted Fane to no end. He turned toward his new building, grinning.

"This will do. Congratulations, Rory, on a job well done."

Eastman shrugged. "After all you've done for me, there's no need to thank me. I, for one, am honored to be in this partnership."

Fane tried not to wince at the thought of a partnership. Let the fool believe what he wanted, but it was far from the truth.

"What a charming roost," Julianna said. "Can I claim the corner with the mound of rat droppings?"

"I didn't buy this with one shred of your approval in mind. It has nothing, *nothing*, to do with you. I don't even recall asking you to come along today. So kindly stay quiet and let me think."

Julianna crossed her arms. "Terrific sense of humor."

He ignored her and walked the perimeter. The back had two docks and the stone fence extended around all three sides. Only way in was by braving the polluted Hudson chop, and sentries would be posted here at all times.

The smell of blood overpowered his thoughts. It drifted through the air as casual as pollen on a summer afternoon. From Rory and Julianna's expressions, they were hyperaware of it as well.

"You're in the fish and meat district," Rory said. "Flanked on three sides by different packing plants. Best way to blend right in."

Fane nodded. "Let's see inside."

Rory unlocked the bay doors and they retracted, sliding to a stop on the suspended track bolted to the ceiling.

They walked into the vacant warehouse.

"Rory, do whatever you need to in order to show the Big East is supplied its beef from our little operation here. I'll touch base with my people to make sure we get a constant supply. Sufficient cover, I'd think." He pointed to the open second floor, walled on three sides by glass. The front remained wide open for the stacking and storage of pallets. "The lab goes upstairs. People will be here tonight to get the equipment set up, and our chemist is flying in from Singapore tomorrow."

"Don't you want to see the rest of it?"

"No need," Fane said.

He felt like a different person on the drive back. Victorious. He'd been planning this for ages, cultivating the idea even longer. Hard to believe all the restless, frustrated nights were almost behind him.

The drive back to Greifsfield, usually so tedious, was tolerable. He even enjoyed Julianna's banal attempts at small talk. Everything was bearable now, because there was an end in sight.

And it couldn't get here fast enough.

•

Allen watched from the hilltop as Elisabeth collided with the fast approaching car, sending it off its right wheels and back down with a crash. Exploding windows filled his eardrums with thunderous definition, rendering each crack with crystal clarity. From the very back of his wolf's mind, the human appreciated this brazen tactic, one he wouldn't have attempted on his own.

The vehicle skidded in a U-turn before Elisabeth, its tires scorching the tarmac before careening into a tree. She watched from her haunches, arms outstretched, clawed fingers wiggling with anticipation. Once the vehicle reached its destination, she trotted toward it with eager breaths.

Allen smelt the driver's mortality spilling from several orifices. The car's front end looked like an accordion. He dropped to all fours and headed to the wreck for a better view, circumventing jutting brambles and a thick tree stump on his way to cold blacktop.

Elisabeth snatched the young woman through the wreck's

busted window, hurling her to Allen's feet.

The way she toyed with her victims before the kill aroused him. Cruelty. An emotion he hadn't ever felt, and would never assume he possessed. Luring the barfly Jewel to her death might've been troubling, but it beat the alternative of losing his raven goddess.

From where he stood, she had recovered rather nicely from her assassination attempt. That's what mattered.

Elisabeth howled at the moon.

Allen howled back.

Their blue eyes met in the fading glow of dying headlights, her fur stained with blood from the twitching body at her feet.

Elisabeth offered a contented growl as he neared.

Go on, eat this, it seemed to say.

He dropped to all fours. She teased him with a few gentle nips on his ears. He tried getting her back, but she was too quick. His mouth chomped air and he growled in frustration.

Elisabeth darted off, melting into the night. Allen leapt onto the hood and followed, calling out after his lover with grunts and growls. Ahead, Elisabeth stopped long enough for him to catch up. Almost. She dashed off once more as he neared, careful to fire her playful eyes back at him every so often, ensuring he kept pace.

He did.

●

Rory Eastman returned from the city to an empty house.

He tossed the keys on the kitchen counter and snatched a bag of potato chips from the pantry. The goddamn things were so blasé on his tongue, but forty years of habit was hard to break. Dropping onto the couch with an ice-cold brew and a sack of over-salted snacks used to be one of life's simplest pleasures. After Julianna's bite, however, the fulfillment was gone.

The leather sofa was cushy and took the day's burden off his legs. Fane had been happy, which in turn made him happy. He could relax now.

Rory popped the bag and let the chips tease his nose. Even the smell underwhelmed. He was going to have to hunt tonight. Fane wanted him to practice selective feeding on the town's inhabitants since he needed the majority of them. That was fine, but Rory figured it would be okay to take a resort guest without stirring the pot.

And I still need to find Lucy.

He hadn't wanted to abandon pursuit, though it was best to let her work through the trauma. The little slut would come around once the hunger was too great to ignore.

He'd also overestimated the power of the first bite. He expected it to send her into a feeding frenzy, instead she'd balked and took off running. Just because he'd abandoned all his principles without hesitation didn't mean everyone adjusted to the wolf that way.

His daughter apparently wasn't as immoral as her old man. Good on her for that. Guess her cheating whore of a mother had done a halfway decent job of raising her.

He crunched a pile of chips from the palm of his hand as footsteps descended the carpet steps behind him.

He turned hoping for Lucy.

Her.

He didn't know her name, only that she'd been at Fane's gathering a few nights ago. He'd wanted to get up in her guts, but a beauty like her was out of his league, something Fane had been quick to remind.

She cleared the last step and brushed wet hair from her shoulders. The white bathrobe was cinched at her waistline, dangling open with a little suggestion. Her long, pale leg was naked from what he saw, slipping from the robe's slit as she strode in.

He made no attempt to hide his ogle.

Fane must've changed his mind. The son of a bitch felt guilty about how he'd treated a reliable business partner and this gorgeous slice of trim was the peace offering.

"Hello, Rory," she said, taking a seat on the couch across from him. Her legs crossed, leaving her white milky thigh completely exposed. Tastier than a drumstick.

"I'm not sure I've had the pleasure of your name," he said.

"I never gave it. I am here to ask Anton Fane's money man a question."

"Ask me anything, beautiful. Want a drink?"

"What is he doing in Greifsfield?"

Was this a test of loyalty? If Rory had learned anything throughout his career, it was that you didn't show confusion in any situation.

He wouldn't put it past Fane to try that.

"I will not ask again," she said.

He had a good thing going with Fane and wasn't about to flush it away because some twat had questions.

"Our friend operates on a need to know basis, and if you don't, you won't."

"Spare me," she said. "I'm asking *you*. You said it was the two of you who ran the town, yes?"

"Damn right."

"Then why should it matter who I get my answer from?"

"Let me pour you a drink and we can discuss."

She clapped her hands and a light brown wolf tore through the plastic sheeting that covered the busted bay window behind him. "Answer me, Rory, or he tears your heart out before you have time to spout a tail."

Rory dropped the chips into his lap and threw his hands into the air. "I assumed you were on the ins with Fane. Jesus, you don't have to threaten my life to get me to play ball. He's using this town as a haven. He's turned just about everybody over the past six months. The ones who haven't been changed yet will soon. Open season on humanity tomorrow night."

The wolf was closer now, breathing pockets of foul air against his neck.

"What else?" she said. "Why go through all the trouble to recruit so many? Why is Fane building an army?"

"He'll kill you for this."

"Not for you to worry about."

"Trust me, whore, it is."

She launched from her seat, flying forward with frustration bursting from her eyes.

"I do not fear Anton Fane any more than you feared eating your wife. You might wish to remove her corpse from your upstairs hallway before she begins to attract unwanted attention, army or not. Why do you think you were unable to detect our presence? It is easy to hide behind a wall of stagnation. Now talk, or shall I gouge your eyes from your skull? Believe me, they will not grow back."

"Everything grows back, bitch."

She lashed out at his left eye, pinching three pointed nails beneath the orb. A squeeze popped his eyesight with a plop. Her nails pushed down and scraped the inside of his skull.

Rory screamed.

"You still have another." Her voice rose to get on top of his.

Rory cupped a hand against the ocular cavity. Blood and pus mixed into orange goop.

When she least expected it, she was going to feel the intrusion of a glass bottle between her legs. And once her pussy was torn and bleeding, he'd use her blood as lubricant to fuck her to death. Losing an eye would be nothing compared to that.

He thought tough but couldn't talk it. "I'll tell you." His voice was defeated.

"Hurry then, you make a funny face when the pain is fresh. I kind of want to see it again."

"I don't know everything. What I do know is that he's making this a stronghold. It won't be open to all wolves, just those who swear allegiance to him. A new order that brushes aside your queen's stuffy rule."

"What makes him think he can pull this off?"

"He thinks lycanthropy should be branded. He wants to market our lifestyle to anyone who wants to live it. For a cost."

"Charging for bites?"

"Sort of," he said. "I'm not sure how exactly he intends to do it, but it's not a direct bite. Some kind of drink or pill, I think. He doesn't tell me much."

Her eyes bugged, looking like a wolf had pissed all over her grave. And she wanted to talk about funny faces.

"You wanted to know," he laughed. "Now you know."

Her features began to bubble and pulse. "Thank you," she said in a deep growling voice nothing like her own. She turned and hurried from the room.

Rory didn't dare move with the wolf at his back, but he heard ascending footsteps retreating to where they had come.

"Kill him," she called from above.

Rory leapt up before she'd finished giving the order, but the wolf had been faster. Clawed fingers curled around his shoulders and strong arms followed, locking him in place. Just like that, the spray of junkyard breath was even closer.

His chest exploded, every sensation falling silent as rib cage fragments scattered across the living room. The animal's paw extended through his busted chest cavity, palm-up, clutching a still-beating heart.

Rory lived long enough to see it stop beating.

●

Amanda sat on the hood of her truck beneath the NA-THAN'S FRUIT STAND sign, a roadside attraction just over the Massachusetts border boasting pesticide-free peaches and pears. It wasn't more than an extensive lean-to, overlooking farmland sprawls in each direction.

John Fontaine was late. Couldn't blame him for having trouble finding the place, though.

"Bought you a kiwi." Jack returned with a plastic bag of fruit swaying in his hand. "You can't skip supper. Sometimes I don't eat before class and all I can think about for the next seventy minutes is my empty stomach. You've actually got something important to do, so eat up."

"I hate kiwi."

"Okay, contrarian. More for me. Have this orange." He tossed the fruit into her hands.

Amanda had grown used to having him around. It was nice having someone, even an asshole, to face the uncertainty of death.

I'll remember that if I get out of this alive.

John rolled into the parking lot kicking up a gravel haze. Amanda put her collar over her mouth and walked through the dust.

"John."

"Church. *Really* nice to see you." He didn't bother masking the disdain in his voice. Same old cocksucker.

"Dex told me this was the pickup place?"

John blew his Bubble Yum. It popped against his chin and he spent the next minute pulling clingy strands off his jaw line.

"He's got the strangest connections, don't you think?" John spat his gum and threw another piece into his mouth. "Was he a fruit vendor in another life?"

The packages had been waiting when she arrived. It wasn't clear if the owner, a stocky bald man in his 50s, was the titular Nathan, but he was unconcerned with the process. Had her pull around the back of the lean-to so he could load it.

If Dexter said this was the place to go, it was good enough for her, although Amanda had checked to make sure there were more than cantaloupes in the packing crates.

"I've got everything," she said, glancing at the truck bed. An oily tarp was pulled tight over a mystery mound. "No idea how Dex is able to get this stuff together on such short notice, but there's even a brand new .50 cal back there for you."

John pumped his fist.

"We'll need everything," she said. "It's bad."

"Yeah? How many, exactly? Dex didn't feel like elaborating."

"A whole town."

"What?"

"All we have to do is sever the snake's head. Pretty big anaconda, though. They've got a mansion on the outskirts and I want to have a look inside."

John gave a doubtful smirk that undermined everything she'd said. Amanda suppressed the urge to belt him in the mouth. Fontaine was good, partly because he took the boring, repetitive jobs that no one else wanted. When the assignment called for someone to sit sedentary for the better part of a week, Johnny Fontaine went out into the field. Hitting the open road with uncertainty was more her domain and she wouldn't change it for anything—sure beat punching a clock.

Plus, she couldn't knock him too hard. He'd shown up.

Her thumb cut into the thick skin of the orange, pulling

it back to expose the flesh beneath. She popped a bite into her mouth as they spoke.

"When are we making our move?" he asked.

"Gotta recon that house. Lots of bodies coming and going, and I think it'll give us our best shot at catching a good chunk of them together in one cluster. Slice that head clean off, maybe the body dies, maybe we become heroes."

John offered a creepy smile. It was hard to say if he liked the plan or loathed it.

"Only problem," Amanda said. "No matter how many of them are bunched together, there's bound to be plenty of strays. Wherever you're sniping, I can't guarantee your safety."

"Let me worry about that. If Dexter sent everything, I should have a nice bag of tricks."

Music to her ears.

John lifted himself over Amanda's shoulder, baffled by Jack's presence. He was hard at work on his second kiwi, the fuzz a pile of brown shards at his feet.

"Boyfriend?" John asked with perverted glee.

Amanda turned and saw shredded green fruit stuck to his lips. He looked about as capable as the Gerber Baby.

"Obviously," she said.

"Well, dump him. We can't take him into a war zone."

"I've tried. He's got friends there. He'll just follow the bricks we tell him to hit."

"Great." Fontaine said, peeking beneath the tarp.

He wasn't an intimidating guy. His physical presence was probably more unassuming than hers. His skin was pasty, his eyes encrusted with white calcium deposits. There was zero muscle tone to his build and the blonde, unkempt hair rivaled the disaster currently Chia-petting out of Jack's head. He prided himself on being a professional, same as Amanda, but he looked like a plumber.

"You should both hear this." He motioned them into a huddle. "Got a call from the padre. Here's how it is, nobody thinks much of a town called Greifsfield out this way. Look at a map. You'll see Pittsfield and Springfield within driving distance. At first glance, Greifsfield fits the area like a glove, doesn't exactly roll off the tongue, though."

"Go on." Amanda tried to ignore the drowning feeling in the pit of her stomach.

"The padre accesses Vatican archives, deep stuff we'll never see. Took the better part of a week to find reference to this place. You know that Dex will send a guy to outer space if he needs a bird's eye view of the situation. So, officially, puritans founded Greifsfield in 1737. Again, normal for this area."

Amanda chomped the orange even though her stomach no longer wanted it.

Fontaine went on. "Greifsfield can be traced back to a German village in the mid 17th century. A place called Greifswald."

"I hate where this is headed," Jack said.

Amanda agreed. The church had decided to suppress a nasty piece of European history, enabling her to waltz into a den of rabid dogs in the process. It was hard enough to serve the greater good without some higher power making you feel expendable.

"Greifswald," she said. "Let's hear it."

"By some accounts the village was home to an endless scourge of wolves. You can find the story on the Internet, though I'm guessing the padre had access to the good stuff. Anyway, the things overran the town, wreaking all kinds of havoc. People barred their doors, boarded their windows, and lived in fear of the howling outside their walls for the better part of sixty years. Sixty. Years."

"A long time," Jack said.

"A lot of people turned. Friend against friend, family lines drawn...chaos, getting worse with every season. Finally, a couple of scholars figured out a way to fight back. Because trust was a dwindling commodity, they moved in secret to collect all the silver they could get their hands on. At night, they melted it down into pelts for their guns, created makeshift blades, anything that could cut down a wolf. In the hours just before dawn, they fought back, breaking from their confines armed to the teeth. Several creatures were killed and the remaining ones fled for the hills just before daybreak. It took a week to rid Greifswald of the creatures and," his voice rose with excitement. "You get one guess where they ended up. And when."

"Here?" Jack was in disbelief.

"We are a nation of immigrants," Fontaine said.

"Weren't too subtle about their name change, either," Amanda said. "Maybe they'll go someplace else once this is over."

"Leaving someone else to deal with it in a few hundred years?" Jack said.

"Hopefully it doesn't come to that," Fontaine said. "Wolves have been a part of Greifsfield for centuries without incident. Something must be causing the influx of activity."

"The Sarandon House," Jack blurted out. "That's the house you're talking about."

Amanda's brow wrinkled. Her mouth sprung open to question the legitimacy of Jack's information, but he continued without prompt.

"Anton Fane lives there," he said. "He's at the top of whatever's happening. Got a text from Lucy. I still don't know if she's in trouble, but she said Fane lives in that house and that he's planning to turn the whole town."

Amanda felt satisfied with that information.

"Sounds like someone wants you to drop by the Sarandon House." Fontaine folded his arms across his chest and shook his head. "See, they're feeding bad intel through her. I told you, we gotta cut him loose."

Fontaine was right, and Amanda hated admitting that. But Jack's loyalty might be a liability she hadn't fully considered. She wanted to believe they were past the idea of another slugfest at the mouth of a turning wolf, but if they encountered Lucy in the hairy flesh it was going to be round two and she'd take him down.

"No way," Jack said. "I've come too far."

"Way too far," Fontaine said. "Time to catch a bus."

Amanda found it hard to send Jack packing. She and Fontaine could wield every weapon in the world and, as soon as the wolves realized the assault was two strong, they'd be done. Maybe a third body extended their chances by a sliver, but that could be the difference between sinking and swimming.

Amanda knew her chances of survival were so abysmal that they couldn't even be flagged as odds. Her fate was sealed, but Jack had a choice. Saving his life might count in the next one.

"Come dawn I'll show you the target and we'll formulate a plan," Amanda said. "More importantly, we establish an escape route. And I have to talk to Dexter."

Fontaine nodded. "Told me to have you call him as soon as I was done giving you the good news."

Amanda turned to Jack. "We're dropping you at the nearest bus station. You've helped a lot and I thank you for it, but I can't keep an eye on you once the bullets start flying."

"I never asked you to look out for me," Jack said. "Tomorrow, when you're off doing your thing, I'll be off doing mine.'

Amanda was too tired to argue. They headed to the truck without looking at each other.

"Pittsfield seems like a nice place to stay," Fontaine called on his way back to his vehicle. "It's a thirty minute drive, but it doesn't feel like we've gone two hundred years back in time, either."

Amanda nodded and followed.

Eleven

The forest was thick, almost impassable. Her moccasins fell on littered pine needles as she brushed through endless strings of brambles. The sun pushed into the early morning sky, bringing streams of light hovering over endless treetops.

Elisabeth hadn't been here in years.

No way of telling how long, exactly, but it felt like a lifetime ago—had television been invented yet? That memory was foggy and irretrievable, though she remembered him pleading with her to leave and never return. It was an odd way to treat a friend and she wondered if he still considered her one.

Navigating this mess as an animal would've been easier, but the still-healing headshot had taken more energy than expected. Even the simplest of tasks exhausted her, which was the only reason she'd allowed Allen to take Rory Eastman's life. She'd needed the human-to-human face time and didn't trust the wolf to surface fast enough to put him down.

Killing Eastman brought short-lived satisfaction, one that resigned itself as soon as Allen lobbied to spend the night back at the Gleason house. Fane was most likely occupied with his Turning, but she did not like being in such close proximity knowing they were now enemies.

Allen couldn't grasp the severity of the situation, making

proclamations of strength while delivering professions of romantic love. All so irritating. The arrogance. The wolf had taken a great foothold in him, but his emotions were inconsistent and unchecked. It would take time to settle into his duplicitous skin and understand how vulnerable he truly was.

He'd even insisted on joining her this morning. For *protection*. An endearing but ridiculous gesture.

Greifsfield had descended into the palm of Anton Fane, and they were unsafe because of it. He wouldn't be expecting them to slip back into town and take shelter at her former residence, though. Which was why she was comfortable with leaving Allen while she came out here.

Things needed to be set in motion.

Elisabeth's ears pointed her east, detecting running water ahead. The thick brush yielded, giving way to a narrow trail. She treaded with caution, her hand resting upon the hilt of her bone knife. She wouldn't hesitate to use it but hopefully it wouldn't come to that. Hopefully Mason still considered her a friend.

Fur and dander pulsed inside her nostrils. She wasn't alone out here, rocking on the balls of her ankles, narrowing her eyes into guarded slits as her body braced for what might come.

The knife lifted an inch from its sheath.

What if Fane had gotten here first? It wasn't exactly Greifsfield, but fifty miles north. If the bastard wanted maximum recruitment it wasn't outside the realm he'd extend his reach this far, especially to land an old soul like Mason.

Fane's boys couldn't be out this deep, though. Not right now. They had too much to worry about. Fane was paranoid and vengeful, but Elisabeth was but a blip on his radar. That was the arrogance she'd exploit. He didn't expect the Huntress to bypass established hierarchy and betray him when she was shackled to Alina's traditions.

Traditions Elisabeth Luna had put away long ago.

A narrow snout poked from a nearby bush and bulging yellow eyes that swirled charcoal black followed. Elisabeth leapt away as the shrubbery birthed a gigantic wolf that came stalking out on its hind legs. She stared at the enormous torso and chiseled shoulders pitching forward. Mason gave no indication of recognition.

But he didn't attack, either.

He only circled, moving ever graceful on his hinds. Saliva trailed from his jagged butcher's grin. His dark mane was interlaced with bristles of gray, and his head featured a patterned swirl of jet-black fur streaked with silver.

A beautiful, distinguished creature.

"Mason."

The wolf snapped toward her and paused. He fell to all fours and growled, pushing his face against hers. There was nothing to fear, Elisabeth knew, though her heartbeat quickened and her limbs chattered. The animal gave her legs a brush as he moved in a tighter circle.

Elisabeth smiled and relaxed, glad there would be no struggle today. Her body wasn't ready, and she didn't think she'd easily best her old friend. She rustled the hair on his head and the creature panted approval.

A spasm of change surged through him and he dropped to the dirt. His height and weight shrunk before her. The thick coat of dark fur retracted into follicles, revealing deep black skin underneath.

She knelt and pressed a soft hand against his chest. "Relax, Mason. Breathe." Regressing on request wasn't easy. It required considerable willpower and was only achievable with great self-control. Even Elisabeth had trouble doing it with any consistency.

The wolf had left, leaving Mason as a shivering husk. His clenched eyes cracked open, re-adjusting to the limited vision while the boils and pustules melted into his mocha skin.

"I really hate this body," he said, taking deep breaths as his ribcage restructured between loud snaps.

She cocked a playful eyebrow and looked him over once he finally stood, using a tree to regain equilibrium. "It does not look so bad to me."

"I never understood this about you, you know. I ain't been walking two worlds nearly as long, but I've had my fill of these limitations. Changin' to and fro, that's the real bitch."

"Some might even call it a curse."

"Why I want to be a man when everything hurts so much more? Only turn back to arrange my thoughts, ya know? Too many hours as a beast and I can only think like one. Hate living in this skin, but I ain't trading in my memories, either. Only thing I got that still brings happiness."

Elisabeth wished to hell he'd lose them. Mason was one of the few memories she felt remorse over.

"You need to find the balance," she said. "Wolf and woman can exist together."

He rubbed his temples in slow rings, sighing at her words. Once his discomfort passed he looked her up and down. "Nice to see you, Huntress."

She was glad to hear it. Her heart loosened. Time healed all wounds. She was living proof of that, pressing her fingers to her necklace to remind herself. She hoped Mason felt the same. Or at least forgave Elisabeth. Deep down she resented the guilt. Never liked apologizing for what she was.

"It's not a social call, is it?" He said.

"I have no one else to turn to."

"My home is not far. Please join me in walking there so I might mask my pride and offer you what little hospitality I have."

"I'd like that," she said.

The trail edged up against a lake. Mud closed around her

shoes as they veered into thick brush, trudging until they hit a small clearing. A wood cabin surrounded by layers of green brush stood before them, looking ready to be swallowed whole by hungry flora.

This was the sort of place she should've made home: simple, quaint, and at one with its surroundings. A contrast to the temple of modernity she'd taken as residence. Until now, she considered herself in touch with her past. *Old school,* as Allen called it. Truth was that she'd grown accustomed to the modern world and its advances: fast cars, plasma televisions, and Keurig. Especially Keurig. Strong coffee was ideal for those mornings when the body refused to accept it had been another species just hours before.

She balanced this by wallowing in her outdated tradition of stone washing. She hated it, but it was the only way to retain her roots. In reality, Elisabeth knew she was punishing herself for becoming a walking contradiction. It was a way to pretend she still cared about traditions, while adhering to a select few.

Why not change with the times?

You sound like Fane.

She followed Mason inside where he hoisted a pair of ripped pants up to his waist. "I have tea." He lifted a kettle off a small wood stove.

It was served in a thick wood goblet and its flavor was something she was not accustomed to.

"From the Dark Continent," he said. "Rooibos. Naturally fermented leaf and stem scrapings."

It stung with powerful sweetness. "I would not think this is very easy to come by in North America, let alone Western Massachusetts."

"In its purest form it is not. Many tea companies offer diluted versions, but what you drink comes from directly beneath the South African sun. You have good timing, my friend. You come not long after I have returned from there. This tea is one of the few things I cared to take with me, as it jogs my earliest memories. The ones in danger of falling out the back of my head."

I know the feeling.

She wanted to catch up with Mason, but the day couldn't be spent this way. Elisabeth had hoped he would move beyond self-imposed exile, but it was clear he wasn't through punishing himself.

She tried to wipe the pity off her face before Mason took note, but her brow felt heavy and he hadn't taken his eyes off her.

"A question," she said, eager to fill the silence with something. "Have you heard the cries of our brothers and sisters at night?"

"Far too many. They are amassing here."

"I was approached by an old acquaintance. He wanted to recruit me."

"I have no interest in this," he said.

"Me either, Mason."

"I came to these woods when they were nothing but nature. I knew our kind lived in the dark, kept to ourselves and, more importantly, kept to the night. The howls are ever present now, day or night, it does not seem to matter. No good can come from such boldness."

"My old sire is raising an army," she said. "He'll overthrow the queen's rule and destroy what we have."

"What we have?"

"Expatriation. The right to our lives as we want them. If Fane succeeds..."

"What will you have me do, Elisabeth? I have known this day would come, that you would have me pay this debt."

"I never thought I would collect, Mason. All I ask is for you to journey across the sea and alert Alina to the perversion here."

"All you ask?" Mason nearly laughed in his tea. "Never

been there, nor does the queen hold my words with the weight of yours."

"You will be my envoy."

"Stirring a hornet's nest..."

"...needs to happen," she said. "I am in love. I will not lose Allen the way I lost Aetius. The difference is that I see this threat coming and am poised to stop it."

"If your queen must know, it is for your benefit and hers that *you* tell her."

"She's your queen too, Mason..."

"No. Do not pretend I have ever subscribed to your hierarchy. I serve no one, Elisabeth."

"Fane's power play is an act of boredom, the sign of a man who's lived too long, has too much. All that's left is to become a God."

"Perhaps it is for another reason altogether." Mason said.

"When his army does whatever it intends, the world will know about us. Tell me they will not hunt us to extinction."

That thought hung on Mason's face. "You say you are in love, yet go rushing off to war. You should be running in the opposite direction."

"Please do not make me ask again."

"I won't say no, I only ask you reconsider. Don't throw it all away on idealism."

Elisabeth smiled. Her case had been made and Mason would not ignore her pleas.

Long ago she'd heard his cries when he was the property of a Louisiana plantation owner. Coming off a sordid New Orleans bender she'd decided to tour the countryside, craving more death than the city had given her. She found him bloodied and beaten, left to rot beneath a mountain of chains in the summer sun.

His back had been flayed, every inch peeled clean off, left

in a pile of bloody strips beside him. Nerve ends and sweat glands exposed to the elements, eyes swollen like peeled strawberries. With his final breath, he reached up and clasped emaciated fingers around Elisabeth's thigh, mumbling pleas of vengeance.

His hatred struck a chord.

Elisabeth stripped her clothes off and dropped to all fours, invoking the change while tasting blood from his cheek on the way to plant a proposition inside his swollen cauliflower ear.

"You will become more animal than man and they will fear you like nothing else. Is that what you want?"

He'd been quick to accept her offer just as he now agreed to her forced pilgrimage.

"If we don't do this, Mason, there might not be a home to come back to."

"That's why I go," he said.

She placed a conciliatory hand on his muscular shoulder. "I'm sorry the circumstances aren't better."

After Elisabeth turned him, Mason's master had been stunned to discover he'd survived the night but tired of his inability to work. The sickness spread through his body for three days, gradually changing him inside and out. His *masters* had no patience for any of it, trying to facilitate his demise in a number of ways. But Mason proved impossible to kill.

On the final day, the owner put a musket ball in his skull and discarded the body in a shallow grave. Mason rose that night, his transformation complete. The wolf wasted no time chasing down his captor, tearing his body into pulp. Mason didn't stop there. He took the whole plantation, killing hired help and servants alike, saving his captor's family for last. Each kill whipped the wolf into greater frenzy until he'd forced bestiality upon the master's wife, tearing her insides out as her took her with ferocious glee.

It still wasn't enough. Mason's bloodlust was unquenchable, driven by animal instinct. The wolf stormed the slave shacks next, and then other plantations beyond.

Elisabeth had watched all of this from the shadows, amazed by the destruction. Living vicariously through it. Her own revenge hadn't the luxury of centralized brutality. Mason was immediately guilt-racked with sorrow, the kind that consumed.

But Mason surrendered to the guilt. She tried assuaging it, but her efforts goaded his hostility. They left the south together, spending uneasy nights prowling for victims, while Mason cursed her for stoking terrible urges.

"Cruel bitch," he'd say. "You know I wish to be left alone, and you refuse."

Once they reached the northern territories, Mason couldn't get away from her fast enough.

"Huntress," he called from the doorway.

She turned.

"What am I going to tell the queen when she asks why I have come and not you?"

"Tell her I will see her soon if I do not fail. If that does not happen, Fane has already gotten past me."

"Good luck, my friend."

"Thank you, Mason."

She hurried through the brush eager to get back to Allen and pursue that *better life*. Perhaps Mason had been right to urge her to run. What if she was getting in over her head?

What did Fane's ambition matter?

I know him. I can stop him.

If not, he would never stop coming. Maybe not soon, but the need for vengeance never left barbarians. She wouldn't be content with Allen until she confronted the demon from her past.

●

Jack stood at the edge of the familiar driveway. He walked it with caution, gun in hand, ready to unload silver rounds into the first thing that popped out.

Stillness muted the early morning, not so much as a barking dog within earshot. The house looked quiet, too. A car he didn't recognize was parked against it.

Amanda and Fontaine wouldn't understand his driving need for closure. He'd slipped out of the Pittsfield Motor Inn at the first hint of daylight and cabbed back to Greifsfield, leaving only a vague note on the night table stating he was leaving Massachusetts. Might've written something about cold feet in there as well.

Amanda wasn't stupid, but she just might buy it considering her own toes were a bit frosty.

With Lucy gone Jack had no further stake in Greifsfield. Didn't feel like sticking around to die for nothing.

Amanda's Glock felt awkward in his hand. Despite having fired a few killing shots, he was no gunslinger. Just an aging English major trapped in a shit storm. The responsibility stunk, and the thought of heading toward his ultimate fate with a handgun felt absurd, despite the possibility of truth.

Jack started at the familiar stairs. Allen would be less than thrilled to see him. Probably wouldn't give him a chance to speak.

I'll have to be quick if that's the case.

He stepped through the still-busted glass. The hum of kitchen appliances kept the place from utter silence. He proceeded through each room, pistol at the ready. Once the floor was clear he took a deep breath and headed for the staircase.

Allen stood on the landing, leaning against the rail. No trace of humor in his smile. Fangs pinched his lower lip and a legion of sores bubbled across his forehead. His eyes widened and kept widening into orbs of yellow and blue swirls.

Jack's first instinct was to plug the abomination, but this

creature's resemblance to an old friend quelled that desire. As long as he had this gun he had the upper hand. And he hadn't come to initiate violence. Instead, he stopped his ascent and lowered the weapon, searching for the right words.

Allen beat him to it. "Glad you came, Jack. It takes the fun out of the hunt, but spares me the trouble of finding you later."

Jack pretended it didn't bother him. His poker face was harder now, though the wolf could probably sense fear. He still wouldn't give him the satisfaction of showing it.

"I'm not here for that," Jack said.

An inhuman stare fell to the gun, growling with menace.

"Okay," Jack said. "I have this. But as a precaution."

Allen's laugh was a bloody gargle. His throat flexed and expanded as he spoke. "I'll take that before you can even lift it to me."

"I don't want it to come to that, man."

"You're under the impression there is still a *you and I*? After what you did?"

"I can't make it right, there's no excuse. You have to believe me, I was trying to help. The way you showed up at my motel room, scared to death..."

"You make decisions for me?"

"I didn't think of it that way. I assumed you were in trouble. I came here with Amanda thinking we could help."

Allen stretched his arms out, wiggling his killing claws. "I have never been happier."

This mockery stung. Jack's intentions were pure, thinking only of his friends and how he could help. That Allen might never have wanted or needed rescuing did not occur to him.

Allen descended the steps, bumping Jack's shoulder as he passed. From the floor, he waved for Jack to follow.

"No sense sticking around inside, bright boy," he said. "It's a beautiful day."

Jack reluctantly followed Allen, transfixed by the outpouring of hair that covered his face. He looked like a guy who hadn't shaved in a year.

"I didn't realize you were so happy."

"You wouldn't," Allen said. "You're too busy being the expert. You tell everyone how they're *supposed* to act like you've got it all figured out. Except your own life is a mess and you never see it."

"You bounce from girl to girl like a pinball," Jack said. "You've done it so many times I just assumed that's all Elisabeth was."

"And if so, what business of it is yours?"

"Just an opinion."

"Opinion? You brought a blonde Charles Bronson into my house for an opinion?"

Jack had nothing more to say. Every defense was another insult, and the tension was thicker now. No way of diffusing this.

"The whole time we've been talking," Allen said. "I've been trying to decide what to do with you."

A threat from Allen wouldn't normally resonate. He'd made plenty of idle ones in the past. Usually where women were involved. Nothing that came anywhere near fruition, however. Only now he wasn't so sure. It was safe to say the circumstances had changed.

"You do what you have to do," Jack said, remembering the pistol in his hand, wondering if Allen was as quick as he claimed. "But there's one thing you need to hear. I don't have the words to apologize for Elisabeth without patronizing you, so I won't try. But something's going to happen in Greifsfield, tonight..."

"I know."

"What?"

"It begs the question, what are you doing here if you know the town is hunting humans tonight?" Allen's metamorphosis paused as he fought to speak. A rash of hair rushed from the edge of his jaw up to his ear while he tried to wrestle control of his mouth. "That's not what you're talking about?"

"I'm talking about Amanda. She's coming back with an army and they're overturning every rock here, killing the were-wolves hiding under them." He embellished the army, hoping to send Allen scampering.

"This doesn't excuse you, or her."

Jack was defensive, but the gun brought confidence. "So what? We're going to have a final confrontation while Rome burns? I didn't come here to fight you to the goddamn death."

Allen's globular eyes were a mockery of an old friend. He had more to say, tensing his body as the wolf's changes pushed outward.

Jack threw his hands up. "I'm sorry things had to end this way. I really am."

He started around Allen when an approaching vehicle took a hard left and thundered down the long driveway, tearing through the dustbowl, directly toward them.

Allen hobbled for the tree line in the perfect mimicry of a terrified black and white monster pursued by angry villagers with torches.

"Stop!" A thick European accent called out. "Do not make us shoot."

Two men armed with rifles jumped from the van, but Allen ignored the warning. He slipped into the bush as weapons thundered. One of the bolts pegged him square in the back, forcing him to taste dirt. He reached for his back with a yelp.

Jack figured these guys for the cavalry. Amanda had been here once before and must've supplied them with directions. But his relief was short-lived once the hotel room ambush came back to his mind. These guys had the same weapons.

One approached with a triumphant smile, slinging the

shotgun over his shoulder. His teeth were capped in gold and his pupils were the most disgusting shade of yellow he'd ever seen, the color of a spent handkerchief.

"Drop the fucking gun." He said.

Jack tossed it into the grass and placed his hands over his head without being told.

One of the riflemen returned to the van with Allen propped between them.

"Take both. One is our crusader and the other is Huntress's little cub."

They were loaded in, eager weapons pointed at their chests.

The van pulled away a second later.

Jack was painfully aware of where they were going.

●

"We're going to burn everything."

Amanda liked Fontaine's proposal, even though it was risky. Those things hated fire and it was the quickest way to send a whole pack howling to hell. Fuckers went up pretty quickly, too. Like they were perpetually doused in gasoline.

"Some will escape," she said.

"Counting on that," Fontaine said, holding the .50 cal, stroking its lengthy neck, oblivious of the phallic implications. "That's what this is for."

"Silver .50 cal rounds. Amazing."

Fontaine couldn't contain the excitement in his voice. "It'll rip them to shreds and contaminate the bloodstream. No chance of regeneration."

Amanda took a deep breath. The plan was coming together better than it had any right to. The past month had been a trying one. The town of Greifsfield was a rotten onion, and each layer she pulled back revealed worse decay.

Fontaine continued strategizing. "I'll set myself a good distance away from the action in order to cover you. So you'll be going in alone. What you need to do is plant the C4 in an arching perimeter around the mansion."

John slapped the olive green satchel down between them. "The drought should work in our favor, considering the forests are drier than matchsticks. The fire will spread quickly if we start it properly. The explosives will ensure they come funneling through the front door, which I'll be covering. You'll slip inside and make a few additional placements. There are options, so you can choose a few of them later. Once you detonate, those things will fry."

They sat at the edge of Adams Road. No action on the property yet, and certainly no important guests gathered at the Sarandon House.

Tonight, Anton Fane was supposed to host a gathering for newly recruited *soldiers*. Amanda was determined to kill as many as possible. Lining the perimeter now meant she'd have less to do tonight.

There was always the risk they'd find the C4 before the festivities got underway, so it'd have to be hidden well.

"Sounds like I get the hard part," she said.

"You want to leave yourself in the open with your back to the forest, be my guest."

"Good point. What are you doing to cover your flanks?"

"That's the funny thing about these things," he said. "Not too stealthy. I'll hear them coming before any get close."

Amanda stepped from Fontaine's truck dressed head to toe in woodland camouflage fatigues: a hot weather jacket with a flak vest fastened over it. Matching pants offered reinforced knees and ass for whichever position she had to crouch. Her outfit and equipment added a good fifty pounds to her weight and if she didn't run five miles every day, she'd be fatigued before she got close enough to plant the bombs.

She slipped into the forest and was on the run, charges dangling from the satchel clutched in her hand. The MP5 was tight in her other hand, loaded up with more silver rounds than she hoped to need.

The west side of the Sarandon House was upon her. She took a brick of C4 and smothered it in dirt, planting it at the base of a tree before inserting the detonator. She kicked a smattering of pine needles over it and dabbed the area with a spray of wolf urine, hoping the bastards wouldn't think too much about their own smell.

Amanda slithered around the outskirts of the forest on her stomach, setting the rest of the explosives with as much care. She kept low and scanned the wrought iron fence for sentries.

There was going to be war in Greifsfield tonight. Tomorrow the papers would report it as a tragic fire that took the lives of several brave citizens. Martyred monsters. She almost laughed at the thought.

She stuffed the last charge against the base of a tree on the east side and disguised it appropriately beneath some broken branches. Another douse of wolf piss and she was on her way back to Fontaine.

She was nearly there when an approaching van got her on the defensive. She dove for the dirt and pulled against the base of a nearby tree. A VW van puttered toward the Sarandon House, passing Fontaine's truck without stopping.

Two familiar heads were visible through the back window.

The idiot hadn't run. He'd gone back for his friend. And got caught.

"Shit," Amanda said, returning to the truck. "Jack was in that van."

Fontaine picked himself off the cab's floor, a .44 clenched in his fist. "Come on. He got cold feet and ran just like his note said."

"Dammit," she sighed. "How could I have been so stupid?"

"He should've listened to you, Church. He's dead now."

Amanda wasn't about to be so dismissive. Her time with Jack had been short and more than a little turbulent, but only because he'd been motivated by concern for his friends. He was an idiot, sure, that guy in the horror movie who goes back into the house after his friends have been killed there. But every cliché came from somewhere. That one was Jack's.

She couldn't leave him behind.

Fontaine seemed to anticipate her thoughts. "No way, don't even think about it. If you go chasing after them you'll blow our chance to take Greifsfield's finest by surprise."

"I'm going into that place tonight anyway. Only difference is I'll be bringing somebody out."

"You're sticking your neck out for that guy?"

She nodded.

"You know what they're going to do. If they don't turn him they'll kill him."

"I'll get there before that happens."

"Maybe Dexter *is* losing faith in you. Your judgment is skewered, Church."

"I'll plant the fucking charges inside. I'm not putting anything before that. If I can get Jack out I'm doing it."

Dexter had often praised her detachment. Life wasn't that valuable to her, which is what made her an efficient killer.

Remove the human component from this line of work and it was a cakewalk when the tough decisions didn't keep you awake at night. She thought back to the little girl in the bathtub, sure she'd made the right call, but resentful there hadn't been another way.

Tonight there might be another way.

Jack spent the last few days proving human bonds and connections were important. There was no choice but to go back for him, the one guy who'd been able to remind her that human decency wasn't dead.

•

Allen could barely lift his head, let alone think straight.

Blurry eyes struggled to focus. The small of his back stung like hell from whatever they'd shot him with, and his jaw was swollen from the beating they'd given.

They wanted the Huntress and it had been a balled fist to the mouth each time the question of her location brought silence. Hard to say how long he'd been tied up in that guardhouse, but the sky was dark when they'd finally taken him out.

Armed guards dragged him up the pavement, through the front door, and into the entrance hall where they weaved him around a sea of curious onlookers. His escorts led him down a winding stone staircase illuminated by sporadic torch sconces, their descent drowning out the sounds of the commencing party.

The stairs spilled into a cold stone passageway. Rows of metal doors lined the right-hand wall like a medieval prison. It was dark down here, with intermittent torch glow to light the way.

One of the guards pulled open the nearest door with a creaking echo.

"Toss him in."

Hands seized Allen's shoulders and jostled him like a ragdoll, hurling him headfirst into darkness.

The door slammed and he crawled to the nearest wall, resting his back against it. His bullet wound trickled blood and burned beneath his gentle pokes and prods. It was an inconvenience, but not a silver one. From everything he knew about this *gift*, it should pass without any medical attention.

"Still think I'm against you?" Jack said from the opposite corner of the cell.

Allen should've seen him there, but his eyes were as effective as a dying flashlight. His head pounded from whatever tranquilizer had stopped him. And when he ignored the question Jack went to the door and tugged the vertical bars lining the small window.

In the hall, the orange glow of flickering torches cast a terrified shadow over his friend's face.

"Allen, can you move the door, pull out these bars or something?"

"Iron bars are iron bars. I'm no superhero."

"What do they want?"

It was a good question, but Allen didn't know. He kept quiet, wondering when Elisabeth would find him.

After a long stretch of silence the cell door reopened and two armed men pointed assault rifles inward.

Allen didn't flinch and Jack's fear spread like a rash.

"Please, no heroism." The voice from behind the guards was pleasant. "I sent them looking for you earlier. They did not have silver ammunition because I did not wish to risk your death." Anton Fane entered the room as his men flanked the door. "They are now packing bullets that *will* kill you."

Fane's eyes were dark brown, hinting at age and wisdom beyond Elisabeth's. He stood at Allen's feet to show this was an audience with him only, studying the young wolf with curious jealousy.

"I see your appeal, you know. She does not often allow the company of man to become so intimate. I hope you consider yourself lucky, boy."

Allen didn't know what had happened between Elisabeth and Fane, but she held no appreciation for him and he kind of wanted to let him know. There must've been a good reason for it, one he wasn't about to contradict. He continued listening but said nothing.

"I know the Huntress will come looking for you. She'll do her best to take you. That outcome, my friend, will be up to you. See, your induction comes at something of a momentous point in our history. I am bringing us into the 21st century, forcing humanity to take notice for the very first time. You can imagine this will take time and effort, yes? I will need leaders, lieutenants, visionaries. I need you and the Huntress to help me do that."

"She isn't interested. Neither am I."

Fane nodded, expecting the resistance. "You're a wolf now, like me. The only difference is you're new at this. Still adjusting. But think about it, a year from now, when you and your woman are shacked up in some tiny corner of the earth, how are you going to feel knowing your bestial side is a prisoner? You'll invoke your true form only when mankind says it's safe to do so. At night. In isolation. Your days will be spent dispelling suspicious neighbors who wonder what the two of you do for a living, and why you're such night owls. You'll keep running, afraid your nasty little secret will eventually get out. Elisabeth would have you exist on the fringes of civilization, traveling from trailer park to trailer park when things get really bad. You may even grow to believe that lifestyle suits you. And it might. For a time. But one day the wolf will tire of your human prison. I speak from experience."

Fane outstretched his bulging arms, looking at them as he spoke. If it was a welcoming gesture, it was anything but.

"In that moment you will understand what I am trying to do here. We exist in the Fallen One's image. Why should we continue to aspire to a life of exile?"

Fane's statement had merit. Elisabeth might be able to make a counterpoint to every word, but it was an enticing pitch. He wondered how much happier they would be living in a world that encouraged their existence.

Fane's smile was unexpectedly warm. "Pledge your allegiance. You are not signing up for anything beyond a mutual goal. I do not ask you or the Huntress to go about your lives any differently. All I wish is stop fledglings like yourself from enduring this misery."

Fane knelt, aware that his words were seeping through the cracks. His hand rested on Allen's shoulder, his fingers were squeezing clamps, as if physically attempting to force a *yes* from his mouth.

"When we roamed the lands the people would hide in fear, ignorant that it was their fear that led us right to them. Curfews were imposed. Crusaders took up arms. People asked God for protection. That's what it was like to rule the night. Now? We're action figures in novelty shops. Fantasies for social outcasts. We deserve better. People today believe in nothing but what they can see and prove. Technology has bred ignorance under the guise of enlightenment. I want them, those cynics, to be afraid of something again."

Allen didn't speak. It wouldn't do to entertain these thoughts beyond passing. Elisabeth would never allow the allegiance, which meant it wasn't worth considering.

Through a slight smile, Fane told him to think it over. He was past the armed guards when he turned and said, "If your cellmate is dead by the time I come back, I know you've agreed to join me. You have potential, boy. Do not disappoint."

The iron door swung, leaving dark silence once Fane left.

Allen folded his arms over his knees, resting his forehead atop them. Beneath his forearms, his eyes scuttled across the room, falling on Jack who sat baking in terrified silence.

A thin smile pierced his lips as he basked in the sweet stench.

Fane was right about one thing. People needed to be scared.

It made the kill all the more sweet.

●

Elisabeth arrived home at dusk. The satisfaction of putting Mason on track to Castle Daciana was short-lived once she realized her mistake in leaving Allen alone.

He was gone.

And the smell of gypsy filth lingered.

With less than an hour of sunlight left in the day, this was not the night to swing by Fane's mansion. But that's where she needed to go.

She tugged the red sash around her waist that held her dress against her body, but thought better of it. The wolf shouldn't be the one to go there. Fane and his guests would read it as an act of aggression.

But the killing time was upon her.

She jumped back into the Spyder and drove for Adams Road, determined to bring Allen home before the festivities got underway.

The guard at the gate halted her as she rolled up. A naked foot pummeled the brake, skidding to a stop before the thick iron bars.

"Fane is expecting me," she said.

The guard nodded. His armed partner sidled away, both dashing back to the gatehouse. In a minute, the barricade creaked open, allowing passage.

Elisabeth drove through, passing dozens of cars on either side of the drive. Once she couldn't go further she killed the engine and hopped the side.

Two more guards were positioned on the front steps, watching with heightened nerves. They made no motion against her. One gave a knowing smile and stepped aside.

Smart boys.

Massive oak doors were etched with carvings that Elisabeth might've once been able to identify. It was all just décor now and she stared at them without meaning, stealing a deep breath of air to calm heightened nerves. Once they were as tempered as possible, she pushed in, thinking how smooth this needed to go. Allen was in here, and Fane would kill him without another thought.

That Fane had used him as a bargaining chip, one last desperate move to get her back, made her shake with the kind of fury she couldn't set aside. The wolf wanted to come out, but sensed the amount of opposition and hoped the human knew what she was doing. Elisabeth wasn't certain she did, and hoped she'd get through this without the bloodshed Fane so obviously tempted.

In the main hall, heads turned and a sea of stares crashed over her. She felt growing urges in these guests. They viewed her as nothing more than an object to be ogled. A familiar set of breasts bounced through the crowd. Julianna had managed to make herself look more ridiculous since their last meeting in the South of France: bleached blondish-white hair, skin that wasn't tanned but cooked. Her dress was open in front, leaving nothing to the imagination. Her gigantic breasts looked bolted to her chest with flimsy, sparkling fabric covering a sliver of those jiggling globes.

"Elisabeta," she clapped her hands and kept them extended, drawing silence and attention to the confrontation. "Where's the action?" Her eyes focused on the pointed blade in her fist. "This is a party, luv."

"Where is Fane?"

"Right. All business now, I suppose."

"Where?"

Julianna wasn't about to be intimidated at her own party, on her property, and surrounded by acquaintances who were over-eager to please Fane.

"He asked me to take you up to him," she said, slipping a

hand around her hip and urging her through the crowd. Fingers closed over Elisabeth's ass, giving it a fruit squeeze. It was about getting a reaction, so she forced a grin and walked in-step. It took more than this to get under her skin when they had Allen prisoner.

"It has been a long time, Julianna."

"Not long enough, I'd say. If Anton didn't want you here, I'd be fine with forgetting you existed."

"Where is he?"

"Tending to last minute details." A caddy smile. "Somehow he knew you'd be gracing us with your presence."

"How about that?"

"Personally, I wouldn't have let you in here dressed like you're making brisket for Sunday dinner. I had my way, you'd be out on this little arse of yours." Another squeeze, this one longer and more degrading.

"You've yet to have your way, Julianna. Too busy hitching your wagon to the nearest payout."

They climbed the stairs side-by-side, legs lifting in time. Julianna's movements were restricted in her form-fitting dress, and she struggled to get her knees high enough to take the steps without wobbling.

Elisabeth was desperate to send the girl tumbling. It was because of Allen's life that she didn't.

Julianna led the way to an office decorated with artwork that must've been stolen over decades. Elisabeth surveyed the walls for her stuff and was disappointed to see that he didn't have any. Then she was disappointed in herself for being disappointed.

Fane was seated behind a large desk. Julianna slinked toward him, dropping into his lap and attacking his mouth, brushing his tongue with hers and guiding his hand to one of her breasts, forcing his fingers to squeeze. She moaned and pushed his head closer against her mouth, staring at Elisabeth through the affectionate exchange with a smile at the corner of her mouth.

Elisabeth crossed her arms and turned toward the paintings as Fane pushed Julianna off and slapped her ass.

"Leave," he said.

The girl did as she was told, scoffing as she passed Elisabeth on the way out, slamming the door in one final display of childish jealousy.

"Admittedly, she can be a foolish girl," Fane said.

"Where is Allen?"

"Thinking things over."

"He has nothing to think over."

"I knew you wanted a toy more than you wanted a partner."

"Give him to me and let us leave."

"I can't." Fane came around the desk and pulled his tie loose, staring at the coiled silk in his fist. "What is it about the suit and tie that implies trust? It's a convention as outdated as Alina herself, isn't it? I offer those unwashed masses down there the opportunity to evolve, and yet, I must do so according to *their* mores. It is not enough to free them from human confines. They seek a return on investment. They don't simply want the wolf, they're all equally desperate to be *someone.* They demand to be my lieutenants, my businessmen, my politicians...those are the prices of loyalty."

"Anton, I just want Allen."

"I shouldn't have expected them to care about our prosperity. How can they when the concept of lycanthropy is new? An oversight I should've expected. That I need to prove ourselves to these wretches in the meantime, well, that fills me with the kind of rage I cannot overlook."

"You feel everyone owes you loyalty just *because.* That's why you've taken Allen."

"No." Fane leaned in and their eyes held level. It was the first time his gaze wasn't contemptuous. "I need you and your pup.

Now more than ever I need you. Because you know what we are. The gift we possess. I need you to help make those fools downstairs understand. Help me find the other voices lost to history, so they can help teach too."

He fumbled his way down the row of buttons on his shirt, snapping them away one-by-one.

"I'm sorry," Elisabeth said. "What you are doing here, there is a reason I left this life."

"I've already told you how badly I need you by my side. I need you to my left and Allen can sit at yours."

His shirt slid from his shoulders.

"I want things like they were, Huntress, please. Wield this power with me. There is not another varcolac in this world I trust more than you."

"Afraid your pup army is really just rats?"

Fane was at his belt now, sliding it free from each loop on his pants.

"A little. But someone has to do this. I have decided to make a better world."

When Elisabeth said nothing more, he stepped free of his pants and pulled his boxers down next.

"I will not hesitate to slice you," she said of his nudity. "Step closer and see what happens."

He laughed and sidestepped her. "You are so arrogant, my ice princess. All those centuries of being wooed by royalty and celebrity have made you a victim of your own hype."

Fane went to the far corner of the room and poured himself a drink. He didn't offer Elisabeth one.

She felt Allen close by, tasted his musk on her tongue.

"Let me show you something." He swallowed a shot of brandy and motioned to the television monitor atop his desk. Fane refilled his glass and carried it back. "You love to pretend you're the prototypical creature, don't you? The high and mighty Huntress, whose rounded figure and flawless face have lured many men and women to untimely demises."

"If you say so."

"I was surprised to see you make a careless mistake like this, Elisabeta."

Fane flicked a button and brought the monitor to life. A full-color, high angle shot of a cabana hotel room. Elisabeth recognized it instantly as the Big East and felt her chest tighten. A young woman emerged from the bathroom wearing a white towel, pulling the front door open. After a moment, Elisabeth stepped into the shot.

Her jaw dropped as the bottom fell out of her stomach— her insides in free fall. Soon, it felt like she was sitting in a sauna.

Fane was unable to contain his smile.

"There's a lot of down time on this video." He hit the forward button. "I couldn't get Eastman to place cameras in every bedroom, so we must use our imaginations while determining what the two of you were doing in there. How fortuitous, though, that you decided to slink into the bathroom to bait the girl. Ah, here it is..."

Elisabeth reappeared, her naked body moving across the living space and slipping into the bathroom, closing the door behind her.

"I think we both know what comes next," Fane said. "But I'll leave you to see."

And she saw.

Saw the nude girl approach. Saw splinters explode in her face. Saw her own furry hand pull her against jutting wood. Saw Molly's face sliced open as she spun toward the camera, screaming. Saw the wolf burst through the door completely, attacking in a flurry of claws. Saw the quick and bloody struggle before the young woman and gigantic black wolf slipped from frame.

"How does it feel? Knowing that you, of all wolves, could

be our undoing? The Huntress might just lead to the ultimate scientific discovery of the 21st century, the existence of lycanthropy. Once this video hits the web, they'll hunt us in every country. And that will be the beginning. Just wait until humans are killing other humans out of fear and paranoia. Think of the headlines, *Man kills suspected werewolf neighbor!* They'll capture us, turn us into lab rats. All because of this. I mean, we would've taken her without you, Elisabeta. I would've had a beautiful young woman like that converted, but you, self-serving as always, wiped her away for your own selfish needs. So allow me to cut to the chase, bitch. Leave here saying anything other than *yes*, and I will make sure you are disgraced. Alina will learn precisely who heralded our destruction."

Elisabeth seethed. "You may get off on having me under your thumb, Fane, but think about this: where is your money man, Rory Eastman? I had his fucking heart torn out. But not before he told me everything. What do you think happens to all his assets when he turns up deceased, and he will. Outside of Greifsfield so you can't sweep it under the rug. Did you think that turning him was protection enough? That you did not have to tie up every legal loose end?"

Fane didn't flinch.

"I needed Eastman to get me into Greifsfield but, guess what? I'm here. You've done me a slight disservice, true. But eliminating someone as bothersome as Rory Eastman saves me the trouble of having to do it myself."

"Several of us are en route to Daciana as we speak. Alina will know everything soon."

She might have embellished the numbers, but Fane couldn't know that. Mason was fast and formidable. He could get there as quickly as anyone could. Hopefully he was boarding a ship right now.

"That was bound to happen," Fane nodded. "It changes

nothing. There are plenty of mouths speaking into Alina's ear. My offer stands, ally with me or suffer the shame of disgracing your kind."

"I say *yes*, what of it? Are you really going to trust my loyalty?"

"I'll keep this disc to insure I do."

"We are in a cynical age, Fane. People will not believe a video recording."

"That's the beauty. It doesn't matter if they believe it. But it plants a seed. Of course there will be cynics. But nobody will know for sure. Especially when the victim in the video no longer lives. This evidence is convincing enough for many and you know it."

Elisabeth gave a consolatory nod. Like that, she'd been beaten, and at such a shameless game. Fane knew no other kind.

Once more he had her obedience.

"I want to see you mingling," he said, massaging her shoulders. "This is not your first Turning. Smile, entice our young pups, and, when the time comes for me to address all those who've survived their injuries, stand beside me. I want them instructed properly, with respect for traditions. That is the cornerstone to the long term loyalty I need."

Elisabeth allowed herself to be ushered from the room. She turned back as Fane closed the door. He paused momentarily, his face in the beginning stages of transformation.

"Before you get any ideas," he said. "This file has been copied and copied. It's in the possession of many other people around the world. All I have to do is give the word."

The door slammed.

Julianna leaned against the corridor wall, her arms folded beneath her breasts. She smiled, knowing full well Elisabeth had been dealt a losing blow.

"Enjoy the party," she said as Elisabeth passed. "I'm happy to be working with you."

●

Amanda peered out from the underbrush and surveyed the mansion's back yard. The better part of the afternoon had been spent this way, lying on the forest bed with fatigues drenched in wolf piss to camouflage her scent. The precaution didn't always work, but with so many human guests converging on the spot, it was enough to keep her off their instinctual radar.

Night had come to Greifsfield and she moved around the forest's rim, keeping close to the freshly chopped grass that lined the perimeter's edges.

It was nearly eight. Thirty minutes until Fontaine blew the charges and turned this place into a barbecue pit. Time to cover a few load bearing walls with plastique and smuggle Jack out before that happened. Not much time considering she hadn't yet been inside.

She spotted a guard on the west side of the house. He walked into the back yard and stood motionless, automatic rifle cradled in his arms.

Amanda steadied the MP5 and paused her breathing. Without night vision, he couldn't see her from his position, though he was also too far away for a guaranteed kill shot. There might be more guards lurking just out of sight. No sense in them seeing their friend take a few shots to the skull when the element of surprise was all she had.

Time to get closer.

The trees covered her as she moved in silence. Overreaching shadows provided additional shelter. Black and green camouflage caked her face, creating more perspiration than she would've liked. Ditto the black wool cap tugged down over her blonde bun.

Distance to the guard dropped to twenty feet. She got on

her stomach and leveled the gun at his chest. Her finger curled around the trigger and prepared to squeeze.

The target turned east and headed for the other side of the house before she could get a clean shot. Amanda squinted to make sure they were alone. The west side was clear.

She was on her feet again, stealthing toward the target. She let go of the submachine gun as she advanced, leaving it to dangle from the strap hooked to her flak vest. Her hand reached instead for the serrated steel blade and unsheathed all ten inches.

The guard didn't have time to turn.

Amanda clamped a hard hand over his mouth and pulled him off balance. He grunted once before she plunged the saw-like blade into his throat, cutting straight down to the bone. A thick gurgle of blood coughed out of his new mouth while her hands hooked under his arms and pulled him back the way she had come.

When the body was discarded, face down in a thick patch of brush, she retrieved the knife and went running, wiping the blood from it with her gloved hand as she moved. The explosives would eradicate all evidence of her breech before anyone had a chance to be curious. As far as she had observed, the guards didn't check in at neurotic intervals—a misplaced confidence that Anton Fane shouldn't have. She headed for the second floor terrace that jutted out six feet from the house.

Amanda squatted beneath it in the shadows, studying her limited options. Second story access was restricted to the terrace, probably more than twelve feet overhead. For all her arsenal, she had nothing to help with the ascent.

The ticking clock weighed heavy, as did Jack's fate. It was still hard to believe she cared about him, as if getting him out might make up for all the bodies she'd failed to save over the years.

Wide eyes scanned the yard, desperate to find assistance with the balcony. This wasn't a normal home and, therefore, it was unlikely that the gardener had left a stray hose coiled up in the grass.

Think, dammit!

It was all for nothing if this was as far as she got. She looked down at the MP5, her fingers running along the lengthy strap that clipped onto her.

There was no time to consider it. Clicking on the safety cache, she pulled the weapon free and separated the strap from its loop, straightening it with her thumb. Once finished, she etched out from under the terrace and took a deep breath. This was going to be loud and clumsy.

Amanda tossed the gun upward. It rounded over the railing and cluttered against the vinyl surface, strap dangling between rails.

Oh shit.

She tugged it, dragging the weapon until it wedged firmly against the banister. No guarantee this would work but it was all there was. With a deep breath, she took hold of the strap and climbed.

She didn't weigh much on her own, but the extra fifty pounds of equipment—the Glock, Smith and Wesson .44, the .45 Magnum, the bombs, not to mention the silver-forged machete that Dexter had packed special—made this more difficult than it needed to be.

The MP5 clanked against the rails, scraping up and down as she pulled toward it with a series of muted grunts.

Almost there.

The strap supported a hundred and seventy pounds of weight quite admirably, though its integrity slipped away with every heft. There was even a tear after the last hoist.

Just...one...more...tug..

Her gloved hand reached out and took hold of the railing bar, hands locking around it. Amanda swung her leg over the rail.

Then the other. Back on solid ground. She took twenty seconds to catch her breath, and then threw some glances below to make sure her presence was still undetected.

Somehow, the element of surprise remained hers. She looked at the surrounding forest. When the explosives blew, it would be a mass of spreading flame so large she could almost hear the pained howling now. Then she gave the door a gentle tug and wasn't surprised to find it locked. The slim jim she jostled out of the machete hilt's spare pocket would rectify this. She slipped it into the tiny space against the jamb. Several quick tugs clicked the lock, allowing her to glide the door aside.

Amanda grabbed the MP5 from its resting place against the rail and switched the safety back off. Took a deep breath to cast aside the despair and entered the house, pulling the sliding door closed so not to arouse suspicion.

Below, the sounds of a party in full swing: pulsing, foreign music was the backdrop for an enthusiastic assortment of laughter and friendly conversation. Sounds of orgasms were peppered in through some of the rooms below.

She moved across what appeared to be a spare bedroom, the unused linen smell making it feel like a hotel. A quick sweep revealed it to be empty. The party was young and people wouldn't be sneaking up here until they'd had plenty to smoke and drink. She pressed an ear to the exit and listened. Only silence greeted her back.

Fingers on the knob, she tugged it toward her and peered through the quarter-inch crevice. A guardsman's back wasn't one foot away. He turned, tipped off by the sound of a creaking door.

Amanda didn't have time to think. She flung it aside and fired. A silent trio of *pfts* exploded into his back and side, his weapon cluttering to the carpet. He dropped to his knees, staring through the floor with dead eyes.

She grabbed him by the belt and dragged him into the

bedroom, stuffing him and his weapon beneath the master bed. She took the hallway next. Now that it was stained with blood, the time for anonymity was dwindling. The mansion was huge and Jack could be anywhere. Her heart raced at the possibility she might not find him.

Where would they store a prisoner?

The end of the hallway split off to either side, though there was nothing significant veering her attention in one direction over the other. Party noises continued rising from the floor below, and Amanda was determined to check every room up here before plotting a downward path into that lion's den. She hoped Fane had stashed Jack in one of the twenty or so unused rooms up here. The quiet was often deceiving, so it was possible.

Her sweep was quick. She moved through several stale bedrooms, a couple of bathrooms so clean that her reflection sparkled in the floor tiles, and a library—each as quiet as the first room. She found two obvious load bearing walls in the study, signified by larger support columns than normal.

She placed the bricks there and found two identical walls in the next room. It made sense, since these rooms were close to the house's center. She slapped more plastique there. When they blew, it would send shingles raining down on the party. The bastards wouldn't be running up here for sanctuary.

Her watch flashed eight sixteen. Fourteen minutes until hell hit this doorstep.

Amanda ducked into the parlor closest to the stairs, an office of sorts, complete with a desk and wet bar. A small pile of clothes was scattered across the floor. She knew what that meant and felt her fingers tighten around the gun.

From this position she'd be shielded by the blast on the far side of the house, but the plastique would cook her skin right off her bones.

Being up here when it went off wasn't an option. One of

these rooms must've had a smaller set of stairs that led to the first floor.

Her lips mouthed a silent prayer while she searched. Fontaine's move was coming.

She took a heavy breath and braced.

●

Jack didn't know how long they'd been down here but the thick and wet air took a hefty toll on his asthma. Each breath was harder to get than the last.

Allen's vow of silence wasn't making things easier.

Jack refused to play into the quiet taunt. He suspected Allen wanted him to give him a reason—any reason—to lash out. To make Fane's choice easier.

No thanks.

The cell door reopened with an echo and their host returned. This time he wasn't alone.

"I can see you haven't done your job, boy. I suppose your ineptitude will help me prove a point."

Fane had a garish red robe around his shoulders and he looked unwell. His face wore extra tufts of hair, thick eyebrows and cracked lips. His features seemed sharper, more pointed. In the hallway light, Jack saw his eyes had taken a yellow tint and his human teeth were sliding out of his mouth one at a time. He kept his palm at his chin, catching them and the bloody runoff. Animal teeth grew from his gums, slurring his speech as he tried to remain human.

It seemed like theater. Fane was suddenly a showman trying to win over an audience.

"Come in, come in. Everyone, please, I wish for all of you to see this."

A cluster of people shuffled in, different shapes and sizes

of men and women, a few teenagers filtered into the mix. Each in varying stages of undress, with many continuing to grope one another while eyes focused on Fane.

The moisture grew unbearable as the leader bumped his way through the crowd until he was face-to-face with Jack. He fished a plastic case from his pocket, flipped it open and slid from it a single tab of paper the size of his thumb. He held it overhead, tucked between two fingers.

"This little chemical is our future. For each and every one of you, it is an investment, a symbol of a future brighter than anyone could possibly imagine."

Fane stood so close that Jack smelled a mixture of sex and alcohol on his breath.

"We are going to see it in action tonight." To Jack, "Ready to make history?"

Jack wished he'd had the composure to say something witty. He could only shake his head and look away, hoping that Fane would somehow leave him be if he didn't look.

But Fane only played to the crowd more. "Because you are my newest acquaintances and have shown incredible flexibility, I want to show you how I intend to build a new and better world. For too long I, *we*, have been nothing if not the stuff of legend. Not only do I intend to show the world we exist, I intend to trademark our experience. And it starts here."

Fane flashed the paper back toward the crowd as if to remind them.

"I don't want it," Jack said, his voice buffered with cowardice.

"Why not? It will be easier for you than it was for any of them. They were taken, one-by-one, over the course of the last few months. Put on the path to greatness. Just as I have given the gift to them, I offer it to you. Take this and you will have more power than you could ever imagine."

Jack studied the tiny blue square, thinking of Lucy. Maybe he could help her if he was like her. Fane was likely to kill him if he didn't take it. Neither option jibed, but joining them beat dying down here.

"What does it do?" He knew full well what it did but he intended to stall for every last second.

Fane refused to play.

"How does it work?" That was a question from the crowd.

"Trade secret, my friend. What I can say is that my people have found a way to harness the effects of a wolf's bite. Pop this patch onto your neck, or anywhere you feel comfortable, and let it go to work. It will seep through the skin, dissolving into the bloodstream in a matter of minutes. From there, it's a synthesized wolf bite. Fever takes over, breaking after a few days leaving only the wolf. I'm offering anyone access to a world beyond imagination, for the right price."

"What is the right price?"

"We'll let the market determine that. I'll say this, it's a one-way trip. We're denied the luxury of repeat business. The price will be high. Life savings high. And with that profit, we'll build a better world for ourselves. A world with unlimited opportunity and advancement for those who want it."

Fane slapped the patch against Jack's neck and held it there beneath three fingers. "Please," he said to the crowd. "Let us enjoy the party. Many of your human neighbors have graciously volunteered to be willing participants tonight. Remember that while you're feeding. Enjoy yourselves, but not at the expense of anyone's life. There will be plenty of time for that in the future."

The group shuffled out and Fane turned to Allen.

"I had hoped you would have pledged yourself to me by now. The least you can do is make sure that stays on him for the next five minutes. If he takes it off, kill him. If he takes it off and you do nothing, I'll kill you both."

Fane slammed the door behind him.

Jack's heart bruised his ribs from how hard it beat. A numbing sensation dulled his neck while he fought the urge to tear it free. Allen's intensity smoldered from the shadows. He lunged forward, swiping at Jack's neck.

He looked at the blue tab in the palm of his hands, most of the color had drained away, and dropped it to the floor in disgust.

"They're not turning you," he said.

"Both of us have to get out of here," Jack said. "Any chance of you breaking through that door?"

"Are you expecting a different answer this time?"

"If he comes back and sees that I haven't turned, he's going to kill us."

"I'm not worried about him."

If I'm going to die, better Allen do it.

It would be quick, at least. Better the devil you know. Or knew.

"Do it, then," Jack said, sick and tired of wallowing in misery. He was in the belly of the beast. If he got beyond that door by some miracle, what then?

"What did you say?" Allen said.

"I know you heard me with that dog's hearing you got. I told you to do it, asshole. You think I'm going to sit here waiting to die on his terms? If you've got all this power, if you're such a monster, go ahead and kill me."

"I will not send Fane the wrong message. He has put me in charge of your fate, thinking it's my loyalty pledge. I'm not joining him. I'm waiting for Elisabeth."

Had Allen lost his mind at the same time his girlfriend's was blown out?

He noted Jack's confusion and smiled. "She's here. I feel her."

"Impossible. She's dead because of me, remember? Come on, take it out on me."

"She's alive, Jack. And don't think this changes anything. You didn't know she was immune to silver. She's alive because of that. And she wants *you*."

Allen took a swing, cracking Jack's jaw and dropping him to the ground. Defeated, he lay lifeless while his mouth throbbed with white fire.

Elisabeth was alive? The thought of having to face those cold blue eyes sickened him. If silver wouldn't kill her, what could?

"Best part," Allen said. "I haven't had the dreams since coming back into town. Once you're dead, I'll never see you again."

Jack didn't know what the hell that meant.

There was no reason to think about it now. He was a dead man. Why did he leave Amanda? At least with her there had been a chance. Here, he was as good as dead. Nothing left to do but lay here and wait for it to arrive in one form or another.

Then all hell broke loose.

●

Fontaine felt like a lumberjack. He was harnessed to the tallest hemlock in relation to the mansion, approximately one and a half miles away from it. The .50 cal rest comfortably atop the tree's thickest branch, and there was a clear line of sight all the way to the front door.

There was no margin of error allowed. One inch to the left or right and these special made silver rounds would wedge into one tree or another.

Be careful. Be accurate.

Amanda's insistence on trudging back into that place troubled him. There was no guarantee she would find her friend.

What she would find, though, was a nest of werewolves ready to snap their jaws over her little head.

Yikes.

And he didn't like Amanda Church all that much.

"I hope you know what you're doing," he whispered before pressing the detonator.

Fontaine lifted his eye away from the sniper scope as the perimeter of the mansion turned into a thunderous wall of dancing flame. His hemlock rumbled in protest as the explosion rocked the Greifsfield forest.

His head fell back into place, aiming for the door.

It flung open nine seconds later.

Fontaine fired twice.

The first shot exploded the skull of a woman who looked to be in mid-transformation. Her head cracked like a piñata, soaking the man behind her in chunks of gore.

The first shot also dropped him.

He fired again and again. Two more bodies slumped onto the stone stairs and collapsed.

Above the sea of leafy hemlocks, smoke wafted into the sky.

Retribution had come to town.

●

Fane ducked for cover as two windows in the banquet room cracked and exploded. Sheets of fire licked the side of the home, threatening to invade by way of busted window frames. He felt a wave of unbearable heat against his face and turned to run.

The hall was a mass of confusion as naked bodies scrambled this way and that.

Several people lay on the floor, clasping hands over recently bitten wounds.

He stepped over them without a second thought.

The greeting room was close to the fire and would be taken first. The house would fall to the flame in no time. He turned away from it, following a crowd of partygoers bumping each other toward the mansion's rear. They stopped as the entire backyard glowed orange hot. Only way out was the front.

A naked blonde woman spouting golden blonde fur darted past in a panicked snarl. She stepped through the front door and her torso blew apart, a wall of blood smacking Fane's face. He wiped the sting from his eyes in time to see her torso collapse onto severed legs.

Who was behind this? Surely not that lone crusader? She'd survived his trap at the motel but that didn't mean she could do all this.

Guests ignored the wet body parts littering the foyer. They bottlenecked in the doorway as an unseen sniper sent them to their final demise. Human shrieks became animal growls but it was too late for the masses.

Fane backed away and spotted Julianna amidst the chaos. She motioned for the cellar, pulling the door wide open. Several creatures in mid-transformation poured through.

Mestipen appeared at his back, gun in hand. "You've got to get down there, we're under attack."

Julianna went first and Fane followed without argument. Behind them, Mestipen did his best to usher survivors to safety.

Fane felt the change coming back as he reached the bottom. This assault wasn't a threat to him, only his potential empire.

"Not yet," Julianna said, forcing him against the wall. Her strength surprised him. "You've got to control yourself."

"I am controlling myself, bitch! No matter what happens, we are safer in our true forms."

Several wolves darted past and Fane screamed for them to follow the torch-lined walls all the way to the mountain pass.

Whoever these crusaders were, they couldn't know about that. The most important thing now was that his pack survived. Let them destroy this home and walk away with a false sense of victory. As long as his numbers stayed high, this terrorism meant nothing, a victory in the most superficial of senses.

His ears perked and he looked to the cold, dank steps.

Overhead, the sound of gunfire erupted.

●

Amanda had never seen so many werewolves in one place. She double-fisted her weapons—the smoking Glock caught a quick break in her right hand while the MP5 sprayed a round of silver bullets into the chest of an approaching monster.

Gray fur popped into little splotches of blood as it whelped and collapsed. Yellow eyes looked up with weakness and humility before going completely cold.

The fire was at her back and getting hotter by the second. The summer-long drought helped it spread in an immediate wave, but it was the windy mountain air sealing this mansion's fate. The power had just flickered and surged, leaving the entire place in darkness, save for the raging fire.

She moved toward the master staircase from one of the first floor wings. The main hall was littered with naked corpses from Fontaine's coverage. For a second, Amanda flirted with doing a cut and run. The exit was right there, this place was lost and countless wolves had already died.

But she halted that thought as her boots pattered through pooling blood. She'd have to be quick about sweeping these rooms, Jack didn't have much time left.

The door closest to her broke apart and a black wolf launched from the darkness. Amanda covered her face with the Glock to shield herself from spraying splinters.

The creature looked at her, forced itself up onto its hind legs and glared from behind fiery green eyes. An MP5 spray should've put it down, though it was too fast. It anticipated her move and leapt to one side, sprinting ahead of the gunfire.

It didn't stop until the automatic weapon *clicked*.

Amanda wasn't done trying to kill it. The Glock took aim and fired twice. Panic fire whizzed past the monster both times. It trotted forward, its talons clacking against the marble floor in a death charge, slashing outward as it got close, swiping at her buckshot leg.

She cried out and stepped back as the jaws snapped shut, missing her thigh by an inch. The Glock fired wildly in reflex, three shots nailing the creature in the head and dropping it to the floor in a pool of spreading blood.

She holstered the empty pistol and fed the MP5 another magazine, reloading in time to take out a naked, red-haired man with fangs and paws. He slid across the floor with still-smoking bullet wounds in his chest.

Her options on the ground floor were limited. The outer rooms were thick with smoke, and the flames spread inward.

Amanda searched the unaffected rooms with as much scrutiny as she could afford. Jack was nowhere.

She turned a quick corner and skidded to a stop, boots squeaking on the cold tile. Two wolves turned, and she hip fired, nailing the larger creature in the mouth and muzzle. It backed off, covering its bleeding face with its paws. The other creature seized the moment and lunged. One bullet nicked its arm but did little to deter the advance. Two sets of talons tore into Amanda, puncturing her flesh and drawing blood.

She screamed in shock as she went down. Her left shoulder erupted into unquenchable throbs. The claws retracted with a wet *phluck*. The other caught her on the right forearm, leaving three nasty lacerations.

Amanda wasn't pinned, but the MP5 was under her back. She'd fallen on it. Couldn't get the machete, either. It was out of reach at her waist. Her only bet was the silver blade sheathed on her vest. Her wounded arm lifted in an attempt to distract the creature. It swatted her away with a snarl that resembled laughter. She used that time to pull the knife free and jam it deep into the wolf's back, pushing in until it was buried to the hilt.

The wolf howled, releasing a saliva rain across her face. She gagged on the rotten breath and stretched for the .45 holstered on her right thigh.

The wolf's eyes widened once it noticed the barrel.

Amanda blew its eye out the back of its head.

She was up again. The throbbing slashes on her arm hurt more than her mutilated shoulder, and the combination slowed her movement while the burning house grew hotter. Pushing past the pain wouldn't be easy as each new step delivered a steady influx of it.

Jack was nowhere, and it was time to abandon the search before they both died. She snaked back through the rear hall, following it the way she came until it connected again with the Great Hall.

A blade sliced through the air.

Amanda's reflexes, thankfully, hadn't been dulled by her injuries. She dipped below the strange, grayish/white blade as it whooshed overhead.

A familiar figure stepped out from behind the doorway wearing a tight-lipped smile.

"You can't be alive."

But the dark-haired wolf woman grinned and took another stab. Amanda lunged, swinging the MP5 upward to deflect.

She grabbed it by the barrel and yanked it with a violent tug. It knocked Amanda off her feet. She collapsed onto her twice-damaged foot and leg.

"You already tried to kill me with these," the wolf woman said and hacked the weapon strap free of her vest. When it cluttered to the floor, she grunted and kicked it away.

Amanda watched helplessly as it slid across the marble, disappearing into a mass of flame.

"I saw you die," she said, rolling onto her back and staggering to her feet.

The wolf woman watched through narrow blue eyes that glowed with amusement. "I cannot die," she said, showing no fear of the collapsing environment. Didn't wince as the rear hall gave way to fast-approaching fire. Didn't flinch at the sight of a silver-loaded gun.

Fuck her.

Amanda grabbed for the .45 again, determined to empty a magazine into her chest. The wolf woman was too quick, slashing her blade down and carving a thick gash into her hand. The .45 tumbled to her feet.

Next she pulled the machete from its sheath in a desperate bid for her life, her mangled shoulder sending throngs of pain through her chest and neck. Blades clashed amidst roaring flame. Amanda locked her attention on the wolf woman's ebbing blade, her only concern was staying out of its way. She'd always passed Dexter up on those fencing classes, and marveled now what a mistake that'd been.

"You would destroy yourself rather than escape?" Amanda said as the creature backed off.

"I spent the last three nights dreaming of this moment," she shouted over the fire's rumble.

Amanda lashed forward while the wolf woman was in mid-sentence, aiming for her bladed hand. If she could damage it—

The wolf was fast, parrying and offering a counter-attack. Amanda turned mid-lunge and lowered her blade in time to ward off another swing. The cling of silver on silver rattled.

The raven-haired wolf was unrelenting, pushing and slashing again. The blade cut the air just inches from her head with an all-too-close *whoosh*.

Desperation got the better of Amanda. She had no desire to burn to death and wanted to die at the hands of this psycho bitch even less. She stepped out of yet another blade swing while a tremendous burst of heat crawled her back. The rear hall snapped and, in an instant, gave way to the upper floor. A massive crash brought a whole room into what used to be the Great Hall, raining debris behind them.

"I'd hoped for the opportunity to taste you when I killed you. Sadly, it looks as though I am about to be denied that luxury."

There remained one option that Amanda could see. She dashed through the rubble, anticipating the wolf's dodge. As predicted, she slid to her left and readied her blade. Amanda shifted her weight, lowering her shoulder and colliding with her body. Both women hit the wall and tumbled down, weapons falling from their hands. Amanda didn't have time to look, pressing her thumbs against the wolf woman's angry, open, blue eyes instead.

She wasn't having it. With a tremendous show of force, she pushed free.

Amanda's mangled shoulder smashed against the unpadded floor. She would've screamed if the wind hadn't been knocked from her.

And the bitch was up, scrambling overhead.

Amanda tried to reach for the .44, still unused. It might not kill this bitch, but the stopping power would be enough to drop her for a second. Amanda only needed that long to get through the front door. If she could, and the wolf gave chase, Fontaine's bullet would do the rest.

She never got the chance.

The blade ripped through her stomach and a bitter rush

of blood poured past her lips. An agonized cry found just enough air to escape. The cold blade retreated from its gash, allowing Amanda to feel blood spilling down her front and back—her body shutting down.

Sleep.

No. Not with Jack still missing.

Overhead, the wolf woman's footsteps stalked off. Amanda caught a glimpse of the dripping blade in hand before she was gone from sight.

She tried to push herself up but only succeeded in spitting gobs of blood. Then she fell back onto the floor and prayed the bitch would walk outside and take a .50 caliber round to the face for murdering her.

●

Elisabeth knew full the crusader wasn't dead. There hadn't been time to finish the job.

Not with Allen missing.

If he were safely outside of Greifsfield, she would've spent hours toying with the blonde. Drag her into the forest and have a ball. It had been years since she'd last faced that kind of persecution, savoring the violent tête à tête so much she wondered if she hadn't missed it some. Misguided warriors like her made it easy to resent the human race.

Elisabeth doubted she was working on her own, which meant there were others out there to punish. Life felt familiar again.

All the more reason to find Allen.

She studied the litter of bodies in the entryway with apathy. Normally, a reservoir of the dead would invoke feelings of sorrow. But these were followers of Fane, and their corpses provoked relief. Each one meant less polluted minds to clean up once this was over.

The explosions and subsequent invasion into Fane's home had been a pleasant surprise. She'd been in the middle of fending off the advances of no less than nine different men and women when the place went up in flames. A shame she couldn't have reached Fane's incriminating video. If he had as many back-up copies as he claimed, it wouldn't have mattered. There'd be time to deal with that shame later.

Allen was downstairs. It wasn't difficult to follow his scent through the mixture of smoke and mold to a concealed doorway. She gave it a stern shove and it swung open, following curling steps descending into darkness.

She gripped the blade with fury, ready for whatever was at the bottom. Hoping to find Fane there.

Come on bastard, she thought. *Let's finish this.*

She was leaving here with Allen, even if that meant killing everyone who stood in her way. In fact, she'd be happy to do just that.

●

The dank cellar muted Fane's senses as he stalked further into the dungeon. His followers had already fled past and were flooding the Greyrock mountainside by now.

Beside him, Julianna was mute, her thumping heart making more noise than her rumbling stomach. Mestipen stood behind them, his weapon trained on the winding staircase.

Fane was ready to join his pack in the forest when the familiar stink of cowardice assaulted him.

He stepped in front of the iron door and peered through the narrow alignment of bars.

Both men were still alive. He sensed no change in the human.

What had possessed the Huntress to fall for someone so weak and spineless?

He pictured her reaction to tonight's setback and was furious at the thought of her validation.

"Kill them both," he told the gypsy.

Mestipen nodded, fumbling with the ring of keys on his jailor's belt.

"I want to watch." Julianna piped up with a wicked smile. "I'll tell Huntress her bloody boy toy died like the filthy mongrel he is."

"No time," he said, taking her by the shoulder and forcing her along. "Whoever did this is only just getting started. I've got to get you to safety."

In all honesty, Fane didn't care whether she lived or died. But she possessed affection for him and clung to his ideals. Now was not the time to discard willing followers. After tonight, much of his work would have to begin anew.

They followed the wall of torches.

Behind them, Fane heard gunfire and smiled.

●

Elisabeth bounded down the last few steps in time to see Mestipen tear open the thick iron door.

She realized what was about to happen and charged forward, knocking him to the ground and entombing her teeth inside his Adam's apple, rendering him a mess of twitches and gurgles.

She recalled his intrusive appearance at her home days ago, fighting a smile as his blood filled her mouth. The arrogance of his stride made sweet by the swell of plasma on her tongue. Another death she would've prolonged if possible. Elisabeth spat the chunk of throat on the ground and continued feeding.

Allen was first out of the doorway. He dropped to his

knees and joined his lover, grunting and growling in between bites.

It was a welcome sight for Elisabeth. She took a deep breath and sighed. All the terrible scenarios she'd considered could now be discarded.

She'd been certain the fates wouldn't allow her to find happiness, as if she'd unwillingly traded it for eternal life. But here was Allen, looking her over like a sight for sore eyes.

They stood, leaving the twitching gypsy to his last seconds. Elisabeth thought she could control her emotions and got as far as his hand brushing her forearm before losing it. She grabbed him, forcing a violent kiss, passion spilling from her like the gypsy's blood.

He responded by licking the gore around her lips. "What took you?"

"Don't ask."

"I'm ready to get the hell out of here."

"Yes. But there is one thing left to do," she said. "Avenge me."

Her pup pulled away, wearing hesitation on his face. Their heads turned in unison, looking to Jack who only now stepped from the cell.

Elisabeth smiled as killing teeth filled her mouth. "Don't you think we can make time for that?"

"I believe we can," Allen said.

Jack sprinted toward the stairs, racing for the fire.

She was proud of her little pup as Allen, snarling, gave chase.

●

Jack ran, praying the tab of chemical saliva hadn't had time to reach his bloodstream. He felt no different. At least, he didn't think so.

Determined to avoid the vengeance of reunited lovers, he hurried up the winding stairs and collided with Amanda.

"Christ," he said, reaching out to give her the balance she needed.

It was impossible to know how she was still moving. Her dark combat gear was stained red. Flesh and pieces of broken bone visible at the top of her left shoulder, while three severe gashes trailed across her right arm. She gripped a large pistol in her right hand while steadying herself against Jack. Camouflage make-up was smeared and her chin was coated in dark blood. Her eyes glazed, looking at him with the tiniest hint of recognition.

The gun wobbled upward as she took notice of Allen coming for them over Jack's shoulder, Elisabeth appearing behind her lover. Her contorting features looked even more nightmarish in the dancing torchlight.

"I can't kill you," Amanda's voice was a slur without conviction. Heavy eyes dotted from Elisabeth to Allen, and the barrel of her gun followed. "But I can kill *him*. Before you have a chance to open your mouth I will kill him."

"Let them go," Jack said. It was true this duo wanted revenge, but he couldn't watch Amanda pull the trigger, self-defense or not. Following Allen's declaration of their non-existent friendship, Jack still didn't want him dead.

"He's a monster," Amanda said. "Do you want his victim's lives on your head?"

I've already got Lucy's victims there.

"If you kill him," Jack said. "She will kill you. Then me."

Elisabeth started to take a position alongside Allen when Amanda cocked the .44's hammer, locking the dark haired woman in place.

"Please," Jack said. "You can't kill every last one of them."

"Maybe not." Amanda's gun hovered over to Elisabeth. "But she has already killed me."

"Then we are even." Elisabeth's body tremored amidst transformation.

"Reconsider this," Jack said. His pleas directed entirely toward Amanda. "Why do we all have to lose something tonight? For what?"

The women stared each other down.

Amanda held the gun on the wolves for an eternity before lowering it in silence.

Allen took Elisabeth by the arm and yanked her away from the Mexican standoff. He glanced back once, eyes warped, changing shape and color in the firelight. For a second, Jack saw the familiar face of an old friend, then gone in a flash.

"Don't try to follow us, Jack."

Don't worry, he thought.

They used to talk about moving to Boston after college, sharing an apartment in the Back Bay until the inevitable long-term relationship crept into one of their lives and separated them, a parting of ways that wouldn't be permanent. Because they'd eventually wind up living in the same suburb where their kids met for play dates while they smoked cigars and endlessly debated the merits of the Beatles versus The Rolling Stones.

An old dream, part of another life now.

Allen Taylor, as Jack had known him, was gone. He caught one last flash of him before the creature dropped onto all fours and trotted off, leaving the sound of clattering nails on stone to echo in his absence.

Jack turned to Amanda who slumped against him, groaning.

"Let's get you out of here." He pried the gun from her hand, fitting it into his own palm. It was heavy and he doubted he'd be able to fire it with any accuracy. Then again, he'd handled himself amiably the other night, though he was hardly eager to go through that again.

"We can't go up," Amanda said. "Everything's burning."

Apparently she and Fontaine had accomplished exactly what they'd intended. Had she come back for him? Now wasn't the time to ask.

"Straight on, then," he said. "I heard Fane shouting for everyone to follow the torches. If we deviate from the path ahead, we might be able to avoid them."

She mouthed *okay* and pressed her good arm against the runny wound on her stomach. Her hand was thick with syrupy blood.

So they took baby steps, moving through the sparsely lit dungeon with caution. Jack kept his weapon trained on the skittering shadows, having trouble discerning the flickering gloom from a creature lying in wait.

What if Allen and Elisabeth changed their minds?

They kept moving because there was no other choice. Jack offered Amanda continued assurances as her green eyes rolled back in their sockets. A low-level groan was constant in her throat.

"We're getting out," he said and forked left, moving down a tunnel without torches. "You didn't come all this way to give up now. What a waste that would be."

Amanda didn't acknowledge his levity. Possible she hadn't heard it.

They pressed on, quickening as her body went limp and her feet dragged behind them on the stone floor.

●

Fontaine watched the entryway until flames swallowed the mansion. There wasn't a werewolf left in there, of that he was certain. The continued gust of wind lapping his face was a concern, however.

It had brought the flames further than they should've

gone, spreading across the street on the tops of trees, igniting the ever-stretching sea of hemlocks.

If Church was still in there she was a goner. If she'd made it out, she was sticking to the whole radio silence thing.

Either way the job was complete, two in three days. This payday was going to be huge.

He lifted the .50 cal and loosened his harness until he was on the slide back down to the forest floor. The fire was spreading faster than he thought possible. His cheeks felt like they were dangling over hot coals.

Time to boogie.

Fontaine tugged the rifle along as he ran for his truck. It was on the road parallel to Adams St., about six hundred feet through the thicket.

A demented chorus of snarls and growls commenced. Townspeople aware they were under attack and pissed off about it.

He kept running.

His truck was there, just beyond the last few rows of trees. He pounded the pine-laden ground as nearby brambles rustled and an upright shape appeared.

Fontaine didn't look. He dropped the sniper rifle and wrestled the automatic Uzi from his belt holster.

The familiar, dark blue paint job of his vehicle glinted in the moonbeams ahead.

He cleared the trees and swung open the cab door, pushing onto the cushion. His hand pulled the door closed just in time to miss the snapping jaws of a small beast.

Adrenaline pumped as he fumbled for his keys. The truck roared to life as the miniature creature scratched and clawed at the vehicle from outside.

He threw the truck in drive and hit the gas.

A pack of wolves charged in from all directions.

Fontaine screamed out.

The monsters converged, slamming his truck, lifting it every which way. He bounced against the steering wheel and then slammed back against the seat, his head smashing the glass window, cracking it.

Growls penetrated his cab.

Wolves hopped the hood, climbing into the flat bed and breaking cab windows on either side.

Fontaine flailed, trying to keep their talons from slicing him.

Where'd that Uzi go?

Across from him, the little wolf forced its way inside through the broken window. It stood on torn upholstery and flashed a mouth of angry teeth.

He slid his feet up onto the truck bench, kicking the little creature. It dodged his foot, snarling in a high-pitched rumble.

Two adult arms crashed through the windshield, obliterating it on impact. The talons swiped across Fontaine's neck with awesome force that severed his head from his neck.

Through strained consciousness, like an electrical device on its final seconds of charge, he was aware of his head cluttering around on the cab floor, wedged between the wall and brake pedal.

Outside the creatures howled in triumph, avenging the horde of loved ones that had fallen beneath this assassin's bullets.

●

Elisabeth dropped to all fours and the stone corridor was painful on her paws.

Ahead, a cool whiff of mountain air promised escape.

She and Allen would not be welcome amongst the survivors of this massacre. They'd hit the mountain pass and keep moving, putting distance between them and Greifsfield.

The stagnant air thinned, dissipating in the wake of the clean forest smell. Up ahead, a patch of light brought with it the promise of nature.

The mountain pass.

Behind her, Allen growled his approval.

They'd made it. She wanted to kill that blonde crusader so very badly, but hadn't she already done it? The pleasure of ramming her through with Aetius' blade, the look on her face as she realized her mortal failure. Elisabeth would not forget these things and the pathetic wretch she'd left standing on the stairwell would not live much longer.

A wolf lumbered into view ahead, blotting the view of the mountain pass beyond it.

Elisabeth skidded to a halt, snapping her neck toward Allen and barking, a command to hold his place behind her.

The obstructing wolf started to approach, slumping over as it charged. Two familiar eyes grew out of the darkness. They glowed yellow in the gloom and were fastened to Elisabeth with the glower of unfinished business.

Fane.

Elisabeth hurtled toward him, knowing full well it was Allen he wanted. A consolation prize. Fane could hurt her, but he lacked the means to finish the job. She wouldn't let her enemy intimidate her, nor would he trump her in battle. And he wasn't touching Allen.

Not after all the things he'd taken from her, then and now.

Fane's massive body allowed for zero maneuverability in this corridor. He should've allowed them get out into the open air, a tactical mistake on his part.

Elisabeth leapt to her hinds and lashed out.

Fane whimpered in surprise but didn't withdraw, launching off the lumpy stone floor.

The blow connected with Elisabeth, tearing through the

skin and fur atop her head. Her scalp itched with trickling blood, though she wouldn't stop. She went on the offense, locking her body against his, their talons flurrying against each other's pelts.

Flesh tore loose, blood splattered, and both creatures snarled with centuries of simmering anger.

Elisabeth lowered her muzzle to Fane's throat, going for the bite.

The older, larger wolf sank his head and blocked his neck as he butted forward, knocking into her.

Momentarily dazed, she shook free from the fuzzy whites and sent her claws flailing, tearing through Fane's thick gray fur, slashing into the flesh below. The older wolf whimpered. He snapped and clawed back, unable to land. His abilities had dulled from forcing others to fight his battles.

Allen joined in, scraping flesh off Fane's back with a battle cry.

Elisabeth was smaller, but every slash into her old sire brought satisfaction. He'd made her for no other reason than piggish lust. The first time he took her, she hadn't been willing, terrified by the wolf planted inside her. Her tears only seemed to excite him more. That he expected her to maintain a constant air of respect afterwards gnawed at her.

This was cathartic.

Fane had always been stronger. He landed a blow on the side of her face, tearing strips of flesh from her snout.

She didn't whimper. She wouldn't give him that. Instead, she flashed her teeth and snatched a juicy hunk from his chest. Without chewing she bit again, using the open wound as her point of contact.

This gave Fane an obvious surge. He roared and took Allen by the neck, flinging him overhead.

Elisabeth scrambled to her paws, sniffing a pool of blood suddenly expanding on the ground beside Allen. Her heart lurched as she thought for a second his injury might've been fatal.

No, please.

The fear placed her back on the mountaintop with Aetius, where she was wounded and helpless, watching as crusaders hacked him to pieces with hungry silver broadswords.

These fears were overlaid, forcing Elisabeth to suffer two losses at once.

But Allen scampered toward the safety of Greyrock Mountain, hurt and vulnerable. Smart enough to run.

She attacked Fane again, springing to her hinds and thrusting her front paws forward with a howl. They sank into the large wolf with a squish.

He whimpered and then batted her away with a punch to the head.

She smashed the bricks and then crawled forward, determined to keep her consciousness intact.

The house overhead exploded.

The earth rumbled and shook, raining debris around them. The fire most likely reaching whatever heat source powered the house. Another explosion followed, judgment thundering all around them.

Elisabeth was on her legs and running when the fireball swept through the confined stone thru way, engulfing Fane in blinding light, every bloody wound evident for a moment, before the march of incinerating flame took him away forever.

The fire nipped her tail, singeing it. She pushed forward, almost to safety.

She hit the mountainside running, cutting her paws into the earth and forcing herself to take a hard right turn, leaping free of the gusting flame.

From the woods, Allen whimpered.

Elisabeth ran to him, dodging the remnants of Fane's followers who littered the mountainside.

From beyond the first row of trees she found him pinned beneath the paws of a steely white-haired wolf. Julianna's talons invaded him, her tongue dangling, panting in triumph.

Elisabeth's tattered lips curled back, flashing her white fangs. It was the closest thing to a smile a wolf could achieve, and this was long overdue. It was even going to be fun.

She ran forward.

Julianna turned.

Elisabeth struck first. Her arm rocketed straight through, a glove of claws that pierced the back of her neck, shattering bones and slicing sinew. Julianna shrieked and choked on Elisabeth's arm as it pushed rows of teeth free from their gums, slicking her beautiful black mane with stringy gore as it continued its incursion with a slurping, sucking sound. Her talons wiggled past the white wolf's snout as her free paw took hold of her muzzle, cracking it upward with a hate-filled snarl.

Elisabeth tore the wolf's head free from its neck and kicked the lifeless body aside without another thought. Her aural senses flared in the moment. Three wolves peered through the cracks in the forest green, hissing disapproval over the reunited lovers.

She stood on her hind legs, her face twisted into a hostile scowl. She inched toward the cowardly creatures in a conqueror's pose, urging them to face her. Wasn't yet within striking distance when they hauled off, scampering through the night.

Allen was slow to his feet. His wounds were plenty, but superficial.

Elisabeth pressed against him in a show of affection that lasted a few seconds. Then a reignited sense of urgency took them. The longer they stayed here the faster they'd find themselves in another fight.

He nipped her neck and she allowed him to catch her just this once. They trotted off through the forest together.

Behind them, the mansion on the hill was nothing more

than a smoldering pile of ruin.

●

All Amanda could do was hope. Her clothes were wet and plastered to her body. How did she even have this much blood inside of her? It seemed to be coming from every orifice, running with endless momentum.

It couldn't be much longer before she bled out.

"It's here," Jack said. "I'm going to put you down for a second." His voice drifted in and out of her ears.

Jack brought her up against a wall and she shifted her weight to it, leaving him to tear at the padlocked, circular plate that prevented further advancement.

It wouldn't budge so he pointed the pistol and fired. Two shots. Three. With the padlocks gone, he thrust his shoulder and the plate fell away, revealing a small, black tunnel.

"This is our ticket out."

Amanda couldn't. It hurt just thinking about navigating the tiny space, let alone doing it. Lying down right here and going to sleep was a far more preferable option.

Jack wasn't having it. "Let's go, dammit," he said, slinging her flimsy arm over his shoulder. They sauntered to the hole and Jack eased Amanda into it. A sheet of blood spilled from her, padding his hands as she climbed. "I'll be right behind you," he said.

Amanda crawled like a worm. This was easier than walking, but every bit as painful. Every shuffle was incentive to give up and close her eyes.

But she pushed through the pain, astounded by the thoughts running unfiltered through her head. Things she hadn't thought about in years—not since taking this job. It was amazing how life became precious and important the second it was threatened. She'd spent the last year daring Dexter to send her on the wildest job in the pipeline. Now when the finality of death seemed like it might just bring her some peace...

How stupid.

The cramped crawlspace shot them out into a small groundswell on the mountainside. They smacked muddy water and Jack was up in a second, easing Amanda to her feet. "You're okay, right? Let's go."

They continued down the hill, disappearing into the trees. Behind them, an explosion rocked the mountainside.

"Holy shit," Jack said, pointing through the darkness. "Do you see that?"

Amanda muttered that she couldn't see anything through her steadily worsening vision.

"I wonder if we can drive it?"

A truck wearing a familiar blue paint job fell into focus as they neared.

A wolf leapt from the passenger's seat, straight through the shattered windshield. Jack took aim with his free hand and squeezed the trigger, dropping it dead at their feet.

"One shot left," he said. "Where do you think your friend is?" They crossed the front of the truck, surprised to find the vehicle idling. Jack tugged at the passenger door. It opened and they gasped.

Fontaine's mutilated carcass lay sprawled across the floor.

Amanda climbed up regardless, reaching across the way to open the driver's door. Jack came around and pulled the headless corpse from the seat. He jumped in, booted the severed head with his foot, and threw the truck into drive.

They were off.

The scene of carnage wasn't relegated to Fane's mansion, just as Allen had said. Bodies littered the streets of Greifsfield in the wake of tonight's mass turning. Abandoned cars transformed the main roads into one perverse obstacle course.

A wolf pounced from the top of a nearby wreck, landing squarely on the hood of the truck. Jack swung the pistol up and fired through the open windshield. The creature shrieked, then fell beneath the tires. The truck rumbled over it with a gratifying crunch.

"We've got to get you to a doctor," Jack said, swerving around another charging wolf.

A doctor sounded good. There'd be no explaining her injuries or apparel, though. Not that it mattered. She wanted to live. She'd worry about the rest later. Dexter had connections all over the place. He could go the distance to ensure one of his own got patched up without suspicion.

"You came back for me. You didn't have to do that."

"Funny way of showing gratitude."

"So you have to be severely injured before you lighten up?"

"Nothing's funnier than losing a swordfight to a werewolf bitch, right?"

"Nothing."

She was tired. Her eyes weren't the only things heavy. Every limb hung limp, burdened by unseen weights. Could barely tilt her head back to take the load off. At least the pain was distant now, her body lapsing into shock.

Being tired was a hell of a lot better than suffering.

She didn't regret going back for him. If Jack could cling to the will to live, then she could do it too. Hadn't done much living over the past few years, but it was never too late to start.

As long as Jack proved his worth and found a hospital out this way. Might've been one the next town over but there was no way of remembering where that was. Her brain powered down and even recalling her name felt like too much effort now.

"Stay with me," Jack said, his voice louder than normal.

She couldn't see him. Wasn't sure if her eyes were open

or not.

"Amanda, talk to me."

"I'm talking."

"Tell me why you came back for me. For real. I would've been one of them by now if you hadn't."

"Maybe you'd have your friend back if I'd let that happen."

"Three's a crowd. I wouldn't have been welcome in that circle. Allen was always about biding his time until the right one came along. I never realized it until now."

"I had a friend like that too." Her thoughts fell from her lips with sluggishness. "In high school, wanted to be married the second she graduated."

"She go through with it?"

"Didn't make it to graduation, none of us did."

Amanda felt the car come to a screeching halt while Jack screamed.

The truck skidded along the tarmac, its rear swinging across the highway.

Amanda opened her eyes.

A tractor-trailer had jackknifed, lying on its side, spread across both lanes. Smoke bellowed from beneath the hood and a body lay sprawled across the opened passenger door.

"I think you'd better check to see if you've got any more bullets for this." Jack tapped the pistol sitting beside him.

"I'm cleaned out."

"This is bad."

It was. No getting around that truck. The forest sat to the left, its dark presence lording over them, taunting them to go ahead and try to make passage through it. To the right, a cliffside drop into a rock formation below.

"Turn around," she said. "Take us back through Greifsfield."

"Every one of those things is going to be after us. Already took the whole town from the looks of it. We're going to be pretty easy to spot trying to sneak through undetected."

"Our only other option is to sit here and wait for them to catch us. Turn us around, Jack. Take us back."

Reversing directions, Jack mumbled "shit" and pressed a foot to the gas. The truck amped up and they tore back over the town limit.

The werewolves were waiting.

A pack of them, no less than a dozen, lined the streets, growling in unison.

Jack didn't stop. Amanda felt the truck speed up, weaving around the same mounds of twisted metal. The wolves converged on them and pounced.

Jack cleared the mess with a heavy foot on the accelerator. Any mistake and they'd be dead. Any slower and the wolves would catch them. And they'd be dead.

They roared through the downtown strip, a grim apocalyptic scene of smashed storefronts, burning cars, and scattered corpses. The carnage raced past at what must've been a buck ten. In the rearview, more wolves were in hot pursuit.

The truck took a sharp corner, barreling down Route 8 past a sign promising the town of Adams in sixteen miles.

Hopefully, enough space to get clear of these things.

She wheezed and felt the sting of bitter plasma at the back of her throat.

Jack continued talking to her, but his voice was hollow and distant, like he was calling from a far-flung hallway.

The truck sped up again as her head fell against the passenger frame. A view of the constant forest whipped past through fluttering eyes.

They'd find a hospital soon. She'd get fixed up, all nice and good. And she'd look upon this job, and life, with some newfound respect.

I might even take a vacation, been years since I've worn a bikini, had a real tan instead of that spray-on shit...

All she had to do was rest. It was all she *could* do. She closed her eyes and drifted off.

The town of Greifsfield was behind them, but the bone-white moon shining overhead in a cloudless sky was a grim re-minder that the horror was still out there.

Waiting.

About the Author

Matt Serafini is the author of *Under the Blade*, *Island Red*, and *Feral's* prequel novel *Devil's Row*. He also co-authored a collection of short stories with Adam Cesare called *All-Night Terror*.

He has written extensively on the subjects of film and literature for numerous websites including *Dread Central* and *Shock Till You Drop*. His nonfiction also appeared in *Fangoria* magazine. He spends a significant portion of his free time tracking down obscure slasher films, and hopes one day to parlay that knowledge into a definitive history book on the subject.

His novels are available in ebook and paperback from Amazon, Barnes & Noble, and all other fine retailers.

Matt lives in Massachusetts with his wife and children.

Please visit mattserafini.com to learn more.

Made in the USA
Las Vegas, NV
15 January 2022